TWO
EMPRESSES

Books by Brandy Purdy

THE BOLEYN WIFE

THE TUDOR THRONE

THE QUEEN'S PLEASURE

THE QUEEN'S RIVALS

THE BOLEYN BRIDE

THE RIPPER'S WIFE

THE SECRETS OF LIZZIE BORDEN

TWO EMPRESSES

Published by Kensington Publishing Corporation

TWO
EMPRESSES

BRANDY PURDY

KENSINGTON BOOKS
www.kensingtonbooks.com

To the extent that the image or images on the cover of this book depict a person or persons, such person or persons are merely models, and are not intended to portray any character or characters featured in the book.

This book is a work of fiction. Names, characters, places, and incidents either are products of the author's imagination or are used fictitiously. Any resemblance to actual persons, living or dead, events, or locales is entirely coincidental.

KENSINGTON BOOKS are published by

Kensington Publishing Corp.
119 West 40th Street
New York, NY 10018

Copyright © 2017 by Brandy Purdy

All Kensington titles, imprints, and distributed lines are available at special quantity discounts for bulk purchases for sales promotion, premiums, fund-raising, educational, or institutional use.

Special book excerpts or customized printings can also be created to fit specific needs. For details, write or phone the office of the Kensington Sales Manager: Kensington Publishing Corp., 119 West 40th Street, New York, NY 10018. Attn. Sales Department. Phone: 1-800-221-2647.

Kensington and the K logo Reg. U.S. Pat. & TM Off.

eISBN-13: 978-0-7582-8894-3
eISBN-10: 7582-8894-8
First Kensington Electronic Edition: February 2017

ISBN-13: 978-0-7582-8893-6
ISBN-10: 0-7582-8893-X
First Kensington Trade Paperback Printing: February 2017

10 9 8 7 6 5 4 3 2 1

Printed in the United States of America

AUTHOR'S NOTE

This is a work of fiction based on the lives and legends of Napoleon's Empress Josephine and her cousin Aimee Dubucq de Rivery. Creative liberties have been taken throughout with both characters and chronology.

Fortune sides with him who dares.
—Virgil

It is more honorable to be raised to a throne
than to be born to one. Fortune bestows
the one, merit obtains the other.
—Petrarch

So freely wooed, so dearly bought,
So soon a queen, so soon low brought,
Hath not been seen, could not be thought.
O! What is Fortune?

As slippery as ice, as fleeting as snow,
Like unto dice that a man doth throw,
Until it arises he shall not know
What shall be his fortune!

They did her conduct to a tower of stone,
Wherein she would wail and lament alone,
And condemned be, for help there was none.
Lo! Such was her fortune.
—Sir Thomas Wyatt

PROLOGUE

◀◉▶

1777
The Island of Martinique

The drums pulse like a hundred heartbeats, rhythmically, seductively, hypnotically. They lull the listener like a baby at its mother's breast and cast a spell that few have it in their power to resist. There is no nay-saying them; they creep under the skin and sneak into the soul and take control, willing or no. They excite and ignite the passions. To some they even bring madness and thrashing, tongue-swallowing fits—a divine gift from the trickster gods who are known for possessing a strange sense of humor.

Caressing, coaxing, at once indolent and lusty, the tempo of the heathen drums is urgent, yet gently urging, like a serpent's hiss the rhythm whispers a slithery silken kiss against the open ear: *Come! Come here! Come! Now!* An imperial summons disguised as an invitation that cannot be ignored or defied. Only fools gamble with their souls. Even those who scoff at the voodoos—their all-powerful queen, the divine serpent they worship, spells, sacrifices, spirits, curses, and the walking-dead zombies—in the depths of their hearts still secretly fear them and shut their windows tight on the nights when the drums beat and the hellish flicker of bonfires peeps through the trees like glowing demon red eyes. That rhythmic enticement arouses and makes the flesh crawl at the same time; it issues a challenge to a sensuous, ominous dance, gliding between Heaven and Hell, a duel between excitement and dread.

While a precious few sleep peacefully, undisturbed through the night, and many only suffer a mild annoyance or fits of nerves, for some there is no rest. For those, no pillow hugged, no matter how tight, over frightened, anxious ears can deafen the call when it speaks to the soul. Every islander knows the drums of the voodoos could rouse a deaf man; they have even been known to wake the dead, to make them rise and walk again. The voodoos have the power. *Everyone* knows . . . even those who don't believe.

The hot, heavy, sultry, sluggish air of Martinique always smells like sugar, but tonight something has set it on fire. It simmers and shimmers with a power that cannot be named, an intense, relentless thrumming passion that the *Grands Blancs,* the wealthy whites in their sprawling white plantation houses, tucked up tight in their four-poster beds, shrouded in mosquito netting like bridal veils, with the covers pulled up over their heads, can *never* understand.

But the drums speak to some regardless of color, and tonight they are calling to a girl named Rose who is standing, breathless and exuberant, on the threshold of womanhood. The rhythm passes, like a ghost, though the glass panes of her bedroom window in the big white plantation house called Trois-Ilets, Three Islands. The drums find their way into the hot blood pulsing its own sensual rhythm through her veins and beating heart, snap her green-speckled amber eyes open wide, and pull the sleepy sweat-dampened head of heavy dark hair from her pillow. They compel her to turn and shake the flaxen-haired child slumbering peacefully beside her, as fair and beautiful as an angel in her white cotton nightgown, utterly untroubled by the thrumming hedonistic beats.

"Aimee! Come! Get up! It's time!"

In this child's head, groggy and befuddled by sleep, understanding slowly rises, like a fat bubble from the black bottom of a swamp, and Aimee's little white feet are already padding reluctantly across the paving stones of the moonlit courtyard. Leafy ferns and palm fronds, mango, tamarind, frangipani, breadfruit and banana trees, big red, pink, and orange hibiscus flowers, and white lilies the size of dinner plates cast sinister shadows as Rose tugs her cousin insistently along. There is no need to ask *why* or *where;* Aimee already knows, because she knows Rose. They are going to seek the voodoo queen, the all-powerful, all-knowing Euphemia David, to have their fortunes told.

It is *always* like this with Rose; though she is the elder at fourteen, a ripening woman ready to do more than just contemplate marriage, Aimee's innocent seven years trump her in common sense every time. Rose has never been able to spell *practicality,* let alone practice it. *Sense,* another word she cannot spell, falls by the wayside every time and has neither a hope nor a prayer of ever governing her life.

Rose is *all* raw, naked impulse, running wild, defying all restraints, including corsets and shoes, forever rushing and, more often than not, falling, tumbling heart over head, right into the open and waiting arms of Disaster, the one lover who will never forsake her, at least not for long. Rose *never* stops to think, to consider the situation, to weigh the dangers, ponder the possibilities, the risks and liabilities, the potential profits and losses; she just hurls herself heedlessly ahead and leaves everything in the hands of Fate, in which she believes implicitly. She is forever the reckless, greedy diver who plunges in for pearls without first testing the waters, never thinking they might be too deep or even too shallow, or harbor sharks or stinging jellies.

Desire is the ruling passion that takes precedence over peril every time. Even the precious pearl of her reputation loses its luster when desire beckons like the Devil and leads Rose to succumb to the ballroom blandishments of handsome plantation gallants and dashing officers from Fort Royal and let them lead her out into jasmine-scented moonlit gardens and surrender to their stirring kisses and hot caresses. She has even been caught, more times than her mother likes to count, swimming—with *boys* and, even worse, young *men!*—in the clear, warm turquoise waters that turn her muslin shift transparent and reveal quite plainly that she is no longer a child. When her mother complained of the indecency Rose rebelliously shucked off her shift the next time she went swimming by moonlight, brazenly revealing all to her swain. Telling Rose that she is old enough to know better or asking her to stop and consider what her future husband would think were he to hear of such escapades wastes words and accomplishes nothing; far easier to bridle and harness the wind than rein Rose in.

Perhaps this is what comes of being born in a hurricane? Her despairing relatives always shake their heads and sigh over their rash, wild Rose, remembering the day the whole family and their house servants frantically fled to take shelter in the stone sugar mill with Rose's mother already in the first pangs of labor. The child came into the world as the hurricane laid waste to the plantation house and everything for miles around. Not a stick was left standing. When it was safe to come out all that remained where the great white house had been was a dead pig lying in the middle of a crater of mud with a lady's pink brocade high-heeled shoe perched daintily atop its head. It would take *years* to rebuild it all and some of the losses could never be recouped.

Who else but Rose would dare venture out, unprotected, without a chaperone, past the midnight hour, barefoot, naked but for a thin white nightgown, with her hair streaming down her back like a horde of tangled black snakes, without pausing to at least put on some shoes or throw a shawl around her shoulders, and drag her little cousin out of a sound slumber to share her folly, with only the moon to light their way? Who else but Rose would dare to blindly brave the treacherous jungle and the manifold dangers lurking there— the poisonous scorpions, spiders, ants, toads, foot-long centipedes, bats that suck the blood of man or beast, and risk setting a bare foot down upon the lance-shaped head of that most venomous of vipers, the fer-de-lance, whose bite is certain death, or, if legends be true, encountering the wide-eyed walking dead, the damned and soulless zombies? Would any sensible soul dare venture out to beg a favor of the voodoo queen, on the night of one of their hellish rituals no less, where Euphemia David is presiding in maleficent majesty, with her lips perhaps even still wet with the warm blood of the sacrificial black cock or goat? No one but Rose.

Aimee is too young to understand, Rose insists, stone deaf to every attempt at common sense. At fourteen, Rose's future is very much upon her mind; it presses, pains, and throbs like sugar on a rotten tooth and gives her no rest. Who will her husband be? Will he be tall or short, dark or fair, rich of course, but will he treat her like dirt beneath his feet or worship her like a queen? Will she be ignored or adored?

The drums have told her that tonight is *the* night and it will *never* come again. Euphemia David will rip the veil away and reveal *all* if Rose only dares ask her to. But it is now or never. If Rose stays home, safe in bed, she will have to bumble her way through the future led by blind and dumb luck with no guiding star to light the path. But Aimee cannot, or will not, understand, and Rose is too excited to stop, stand still for a moment, and even *try* to explain in any comprehensible fashion; her words come in sporadic, nonsensical bursts about the Queen, the night—this is *the* night!—her *only* chance, and the drums calling her, a summons from the Queen.

Still, Aimee keeps trying to be the voice of reason; that is her way. Her doting parents always say this daughter who came to them many years after they had resigned themselves to barrenness was born with an old soul and a mind like a machete cutting through sugarcane.

"Surely this is an errand better suited to the safer light of day?" Aimee insists, reminding Rose that the Queen is not at all capricious about telling fortunes or receiving visitors. The door of the bloodred cottage where Her Majesty sits in sinister splendor upon a throne made of grinning skulls and gleaming bleached bones, with her great snake draped about her shoulders like a living shawl, is open every day to those who can pay or proffer a worthwhile favor in return for the Queen's aid. No one with money, or something useful to barter, is ever turned away from Euphemia David's door. Some even come in the evening after their work is done or if they require the discretion of darkness and still they are welcomed, as long as they can pay, in one way or another. Rose and Aimee are planters' daughters; they *can* pay. So why not wait until tomorrow? What good will the brilliant future the Queen is sure to foresee for Rose be if it is snatched away tonight by a fer-de-lance's fangs?

But Rose is deaf to reason; all she can hear is the drums calling her onward, drawing her deeper into the jungle. Rose's mother is right; rather than a comely young man, smiling blithely, with his head in the clouds, striding blindly off the edge of a cliff, Rose's likeness should adorn the tarot card for The Fool.

Can blood freeze and burn at the same time? Can the heart gallop like a wild stallion at the same time as terror strikes it corpse cold still? The scene in the clearing provokes such questions but gives no answers.

Huddling together and hiding amongst the bushes, fear making them forget the dangers that might be lurking there, the cousins feel like they are mere steps away from walking right into the heart of Hell and surrendering their souls the way one hands cloak and hat to a servant at the door.

Gleaming black bodies, dark as ebony, and a few red as the fearsome ants that can strip a body down to bones in moments, yellow as bananas, or lightened by the white blood of their masters, like milk poured into coffee, they are gathered in the clearing, lit by a full moon and the flames of Hell. A hundred or more, slick with sweat, loins swathed in scarlet cloth, gold rings in their ears, and tiny tinkling bells tied around their ankles, they caper like demons, leaping, twirling, whirling, and writhing, silhouetted against the bonfires, emitting the most unholy shrieks, rhythmic chants, or gibbering like the mad in unknown tongues. The spirits, the loas, have taken control of their willing bodies; they are possessed, touched by the divine. Just for tonight, the slaves and poor, free blacks are the darlings of the gods; the powerless have the power. Hips sway and pelvises swivel and thrust to the rhythm of the drums and rattle of the gourds. Breasts swing unabashedly free. Bodies buck, jerk, and tremble, every inch aquiver. They put their bodies through the most grotesque contortions; heads roll and loll on their necks at seemingly impossible angles as though they are broken; joints seem to slip their sockets; limbs jerk like puppets controlled by a satanic master. Some fall to the ground, alone, in pairs and trios, in the throes of passion or fits; sometimes it is hard to tell which. They paw and claw and bite one another until the blood flows freely. Some rut and grunt like animals mating or tear at the earth and chew the grass like famished cattle. Some women squat or lie flat on their backs with their knees drawn up and go through motions mimicking childbirth. They are all together, yet alone, in their own little world.

In a ring of fire, upon an altar made of bleached skulls and gleaming bones, the Queen of the Voodoos, Euphemia David, stands in regal, terrifying splendor. Taller than many men, she towers well above six feet; an ageless beauty, she is said to be 177 years old, the seventh daughter born of a seventh daughter born of a seventh daughter going back till mankind began. She wears a gown made of fifty Madras handkerchiefs of bloodred and turquoise, royal purple, emerald green, and banana yellow all stitched together with golden thread, each one a gift from a grateful customer whose life, love, fortune, family, property, health, or sanity the Queen saved. The points on her crimson *tignon,* the turban-like kerchief that hides her hair traditionally worn by all colored island women, angle up toward Heaven like red devil horns. Great golden hoops sway in the lobes of her ears, bangles clank on her wrists and ankles, and a necklace of gilded snake vertebras and fangs surrounds her throat. A pendant hangs between her breasts, a gilded skull the size of a man's clenched fist. Some say it belonged to a monkey, a cherished pet given to her by a pirate king who was once her lover; others claim it was a small child whose soul she saved from the Devil at the cost of its life.

Euphemia David holds her snake, a muscular brown and gold python as long as she is tall, Li Grande Zombi, the serpent god incarnate, high above her head, while her body undulates from shoulders to feet, writhing just like a snake. When the python dips its powerful head down and its tongue flickers against Euphemia David's cheek her followers fall to their knees in an ecstasy of devotion, screaming praise and adoration; their queen has just been kissed by the divine; proof of her power has been given right before their eyes. She is *invincible!*

Her all-seeing eyes are big, gold, and wild as a feral cat's. Her skin is smooth as silk and the rich golden tawny color of caramel. She doesn't look a day over thirty, but the oldest slaves on the island are in their eighties and remember her from their childhood and swear she hasn't aged a day and that their own grandmothers told tales of her. One toothless old man, wizened as a raisin, with sightless eyes like cloudy white marbles and withered limbs, claims that he was, for one brief season, her king. In his prime, the handsomest and nimblest dancer of them all, he served her faithfully each day and shared her bed every night, basking in her reflected glory, dancing in a loincloth of sky-blue silk dripping with blood-red fringe, light as a feather beneath the fortune in gold chains she hung about his throat. But the notion seems laughable. One has only to look at the Queen in all her terrifying beauty to know that it is only an old fool talking.

Those who have seen her hair unbound say it hangs all the way down to her heels in thick waves the blackish-red color of berry juice. Some say, like Samson, the source of her power reposes in those splendid tresses. No wonder every lover and devotee vies for a lock of her hair; surely there can be no more powerful talisman on earth?

Euphemia David can walk on water; dance through fire; ride a hurricane like a lover or a bucking, mad stallion; raise the dead; heal the sick; make the deaf hear, the blind see, and the lame not only walk but also dance; glimpse the future plain as yesterday; make grown men fall down on their knees and bark like dogs or cry like little girls. She can make her enemies perish in agonizing pain vomiting up snakes and snails, or even bent, rusty nails, or simply by causing their heart to shrivel up. She can sway lawsuits and contrary minds like a pendulum; lift and lay curses; blind, maim, or kill with tiny coffins left on the damned one's doorstep or balls of black wax covered with the feathers of a black cock sewn inside their pillow, or by blowing the dust of a dead fer-de-lance directly into their face. She can make or break a love affair or marriage; keep a beloved spouse or paramour from straying, an unwanted child from being born, a crotchety uncle or unforgiving father from disinheriting you. She can make a gambler's fortune with just one night in a graveyard and a powerful charm of grave dust and bones from a black cat's tail, or cause a person of inconvenience to waste away to ashes. There is no end to her power. That is why there is tattooed onto the small of her back a snake, curled into a perfect circle, swallowing its own tail, no end and no beginning. Euphemia David goes on forever. Whether they believe in voodoo or not, every living soul on Martinique respects her power. Only fools do not fear Euphemia David.

One by one the worshippers approach, fall reverently upon their knees, swearing their devotion, presenting their mostly humble offerings—hard-earned or stolen coins, a bouquet of flowers or herbs, a bell, a bottle of rum, a Madras handkerchief, a string of beads, or one perfect pearl. As each man or woman kneels before her Euphemia David fills her mouth with rum from a bottle on the altar and spews it out upon their faces in a blessing that parodies a priest sprinkling his congregation with holy water.

"Adam and Eve were blind until the Serpent gave them sight! Let the blind *SEE!*" Euphemia David takes the snake from around her shoulders and holds it out, to let its tongue flicker over the sightless egg-white orbs of an old woman whose children have brought her to kneel before the Queen and beg that the gift of sight be restored to her.

The ancient one starts up and screams like a person set on fire as the scales fall from her eyes, like the filmy white skin of eggs; then she drops back down on her knees to kiss the hem of the Queen's gown and bathe her bare feet with thankful tears. She pledges eternal devotion and promises pineapples and bananas, just as many as she can pick, and she will bake the Queen a rum cake. Euphemia David just smiles and graciously waves her away.

The King, the latest in a long line of handsome young men to catch the Queen's fancy, springs into the clearing with a great leap, his legs slicing through the air like scissors. He dances wildly, spinning like a top. Naked but for a loincloth of turquoise silk trimmed with scarlet fringe like rivulets of blood running down his black thighs, a weighty, magnificent chain of gold-dipped snake vertebras and the tailbones of black cats about his neck, gold hoops in his ears, and tiny, tinkling gold bells tied to scarlet ribbons about his ankles. His hard body, rippling with muscles, dripping with sweat, executes a series of nimble leaps and twirls in the air before he lands, kneeling reverently, at the Queen's feet for her blessing. It is given in a shower of rum and a quick caress to her lover's cheek.

The King rises and approaches the altar and, from a cage sitting in the shadows beside it, seizes a black cock that flaps his wings wildly and loudly complains. The man grasps the cock by his feet and holds him up high, in offering, to the woman the King adores. At her nod, with one quick motion, he rips open the cock's feathery black breast with his teeth and quickly reaches in to tear out the bird's heart and, even as it still beats, extends it, like a living ruby jewel on his palm, as a gift for his queen.

Euphemia David accepts the heart as her due. She holds it up high, like a woman scrutinizing a large ruby against the sky, watching it pulse. Calmly, like an idle plantation wife dipping into a box of bonbons, she puts it in her mouth. But Euphemia David doesn't chew and savor the flavor; she swallows it whole, feeling the heart's dying beats as it slithers down her throat.

Bones beat and palms pound the cowhide drums and peas rattle and shake inside gourds as the rhythm grows faster and more frantic. Spirits have possessed the drums; if the loas will it, the musicians will play until they fall down dead, powerless to stop, palms bloody, split or worn down to the white bones within.

The voodoos go wild, their screams seem to ricochet off the full moon, and the dancing takes on a new insane frenzy. Some leap, others fall, in ecstasy. They spin until they fall down dizzy; then their friends pull them up and they are off again, twisting and twirling, gyrating like mad. A black goat is led to the altar and the King slits its throat. Hot blood gushes out into a big bowl of beaten gold. The Queen drinks first, followed by the King; then it is passed around from hand to hand. Everyone takes a sip, hurrying to pass it on to the next before the blood cools.

The dancers join hands, and a convulsion ripples down the line, like a jolt of power leaping from hand to hand. Their bodies spasm and jerk and their eyes roll up until they look as blind as the old woman they saw their queen heal. The line breaks and everyone goes their own way. They dance; they spin; they leap. They shriek and speak in tongues, caress and claw and paw and sink their teeth into one another; drawing yet more blood, they fall upon the ground, in passionate congress, convulsions, or as senseless as the dead. Some are trampled, bones crack trying to outshout the drums, but no one seems to care. A few compassionate souls think to drag the prone and senseless from the clearing into the quiet darkness of the woods to recover, but most stay where they fall, coupling, convulsing, or unconscious, to take their chances beneath the dancing feet.

When the first cock crows it is instantly over. All left standing fall down to sleep or else crawl away to find their beds or the sheltering shade of a tree. Only the Queen remains.

Rose seizes the moment and, without hesitation, rushes into the clearing and drops an eager curtsy before Her Majesty. Aimee cautiously follows and makes her own curtsy; after all, it is the polite thing to do whether one believes in voodoo or not.

A twitch of amusement tugs at Euphemia David's crimson mouth.

"I *know* what you have come for. Follow me," she says.

The King starts to follow, walking respectfully several steps behind his queen. Without turning around, Euphemia David dispassionately pronounces sentence.

"Your reign is over. You have served me well, and I thank you for it, but now you are done. I have no further need of you. Find a sweet young girl and marry her, but be kind to her; if you are not, I *will* know." The threat is subtle but felt as though it were spoken openly in excruciatingly painful detail. The Queen is known for showing no mercy to men who misuse their women.

The dethroned King looks sick and shivers as a cold sweat covers his brow. For a moment there seems to be a lump, as large as a rooster's heart, in his throat that he cannot swallow down. But then it passes.

"Yes, my queen." He takes the heavy golden chain from his neck and lets the blue and red silk slip from his hips and passes them, reverently yet regretfully, into the steady sovereign hand stretched out to reclaim the royal regalia that will adorn her next consort.

Euphemia David accepts them, without thanks, never looking back.

The erstwhile king, now just a common man, stripped of his power, seems suddenly so young and vulnerable; he might be as young as seventeen but no more than twenty. Naked but for the gold hoops in his ears and the bells on his ankles, trinkets that any worshipper can wear, he falls to his knees and kisses the trailing hem of his beloved's gown. "It shall be as you wish, my queen. Thank you for letting me serve you."

The Queen takes his deference as her due and walks away, head held high, never looking back. The hem of her gown whispers fleetingly against his palm in one last caress, but he doesn't try to hold on. It is better this way. He is many things perhaps, but not a fool.

Rose, more avid now than at any etiquette lesson taught by her mother or the well-meaning nuns at the convent school in Fort Royal where she was an occasional, and most reluctant, day pupil, takes note—*this* is the way to leave a lover!

Aimee glances back, her blue eyes lingering pityingly on the young man kneeling naked in the dust, his forehead resting reverently where his queen's feet so recently walked, as though he can still feel their warm caress. His tears, silently shed, Aimee thinks, will soon turn the dust to mud. How much it must hurt to be dismissed so coldly and without warning! Life really can change in a single instant. Life, love, power, passion, and glory are such fleeting and ephemeral things. He must feel just like the cockerel whose heart he so recently ripped out; only he, this erstwhile king, must go on living, waiting for the pain to die.

The Queen's house is exactly as everyone has described it. The ramshackle little house, painted bloodred, sitting ensconced like a vulgar jewel in a setting of scarlet flamboyant trees, peculiar purple-pink orchids that are somehow lewdly suggestive, a tenacious tangle of honeysuckle vines, jasmine and night-blooming white lilies. Inside are the accoutrements of the Queen's trade: candles of many colors, some crafted into male and female form, hearts, or the engorged masculine organ, jars filled with mysterious oils and powders, wax figures and balls, tufts of feathers, bits of bone, and the tiny black coffins everyone fears finding on their doorstep or front lawn. Bouquets of dried herbs, swags of bones, and the dried ball-round fat bodies of prickly puffer fish hang from the rafters, swimming in air instead of water, like macabre desiccated wedding decorations. Dried lizards, toads, and cow hearts are nailed to every wall.

The Queen sinks down wearily into a throne of gleaming bones, situated like any other favorite hearth-side armchair, and the serpent hugs her shoulders as its flickering tongue darts out to kiss her cheek, Li Grand Zombi, the one lover she will never forsake.

Imperiously, she extends her hand. Rose eagerly offers her palm. The Queen's eyebrow arches high in a silent question.

Rose gasps. "P-P-Pardon!" she stammers, and fishes clumsily inside her nightgown for the little velvet bag hanging from a cord around her neck. Sweat has glued the velvet between her young breasts and she fumbles to draw it out. At last her anxious fingers manage to withdraw two coins; she passes one to Aimee, nearly dropping it in her nervous haste, and offers the other to the Queen.

Euphemia David nods her approval and holds out her hand again. "Your palm, mademoiselle."

Her face is a blank slate as she studies Rose's palm.

"Now yours, mademoiselle." She turns to Aimee, ignoring Rose's puzzled frown.

Aimee extends her palm with the coin resting on it, earning a twitch of a smile from the Queen.

"Yours again, mademoiselle," she says to Rose, who eagerly thrusts out her hand as the Queen's fingers close tightly around Aimee's wrist to stay its withdrawal.

For what seems an eternity, Euphemia David sits, bent forward, thoughtfully glancing from palm to palm, sometimes tilting her head, narrowing her golden eyes, nibbling her lower lip, or furrowing her brow. Finally she releases Aimee's wrist and waves Rose's eagerly outstretched palm away.

"Destiny has bound you together in a loose knot. Your fates shall be the same, but entirely different. Each of you shall live in a magnificent palace and wear a crown, greater than any queen—an empress you each shall be. But there your paths diverge. You"—she fixes a hard, unwavering golden gaze upon Rose—"will be celebrated and adored as a great man's lady. Your husband will cover the world with glory and your body with ardent kisses and diamonds. He will put a crown on your head. His ambition will burn like a wildfire that threatens to consume the whole world. Nations shall kneel down before you and sing your praises. Every garment you wear, every word you speak, every move you make, will be discussed for good or ill. You will smile at the world but in private shed many tears. You will find yourself a prisoner in a way you never dreamed possible; your grand palace will seem like its walls are made of glass. Fame will be your jailer, your crown a heavy burden when in your dreams it sat on your head light as a feather, and your wedding band the golden shackle that binds you to the life you spent your youth dreaming of. At the very hour you think your happiness is won it will in truth be lost forever. Like the most fickle of lovers, happiness *will* abandon you, and you will die alone, knowing just how little fortune and fame truly matter, and regretting more than anything the lazy, simple life you left behind when you sailed away from Martinique.

"As for you, little one"—Euphemia David turned to Aimee—"not for you the glory and fame of those who strut like pretty peacocks so proud and vain across the stage of the world's theater for all to see. The world will forget your name. Before you are twenty, everyone who ever knew you will have forgotten your face; only portraits, lifeless and flat, will remain to remind them *if* they think to glance." Her eyes shifted to the side like arrows of accusation aimed at Rose. "Only when you are dead will you begin to live. Like the serpent that swallows its own tail, your end shall also be your beginning. Your face will be hidden from the world, but do not mistake a veil for a living death, or a window you can see but hazily through. Veils not only hide; they also reveal, like the caul that covers the face of a child born with second sight. To the unknowing eye, you will be dismissed as a powerful man's plaything, a pretty toy he can break or discard as he will, but *that* will be the grand illusion, for *all* the power shall reside here in the palm of your hand." She reached again for Aimee's hand and stabbed a long, sharp fingernail down into the heart of it. "Like a sculptor with a lump of clay, you will mold and shape, and create greatness seemingly from nothing, but you will never be celebrated for it, and the steps leading to the throne will be red with blood and wet with tears. You will do things you cannot in your innocence even imagine now, unthinkable things that will make you fear for your soul and God's judgment. But on the day Death closes your eyes, should someone come to your bedside and ask, *Was it worth it?* you will know without a doubt that *yes,* it was, because of what you leave behind."

Rose sat and stared at her palm with a dissatisfied frown while Aimee studied hers in thoughtful silence, wondering if the Queen was just spinning a tale, telling two little girls what she thought they would most like to hear. Everyone, even charlatans, knew that all little girls play at being princesses; pauper or aristocrat, they all dream of growing up to wear a crown.

Rose seems poised to ask another question, but Euphemia David silences her with a gesture and stands up.

"And now you must go. I am weary and wish to rest, and there is still time for you to return to your beds before you are missed."

Aimee curtsies and thanks the Queen for the time she has given them and Rose quickly does the same, but as she starts to turn away Euphemia David suddenly reaches out and draws her back.

"Poor little thing." She stares down into Rose's face and caresses her cheek with an unexpected tenderness. "You are like a songbird in a cage who yearns to fly out into the great unknown world called *Freedom* she has heard so many tantalizing whispers about, never dreaming of the dangers that sit on the lap of Liberty waiting to *bite* and *scar* innocent little girls like you. Remember—both of you—innocence lost can never be regained; consider carefully what you do and who, and for what, you sacrifice it to."

Rose is so struck by the great sorrow in the Queen's golden eyes that she can only nod dumbly, murmur her thanks, dip an absent-minded curtsy, and follow Aimee out into the pale yellow-gray dawn. But as Rose allows her little cousin to take the lead, tugging her hand, hurrying her back to their bed at Trois-Ilets, hoping they can indeed slip back in before they are missed, that niggling feeling of melancholy falls from her like a snake's old skin.

"*Adored!* I shall be *adored* and covered in *diamonds!* Just think of it, Aimee! I shall live in a palace, wear a crown, and be *adored* and *covered* with *diamonds!*"

"I think I would rather forget," Aimee says softly without looking back. "Aren't you at all worried that Euphemia David saw so much unhappiness in your hand, Rose?"

Rose just smiles. "Forewarned is forearmed. When unhappiness comes I shall *challenge* it." She playfully assumes a dueling posture with a phantom sword extended. "*En garde,* Sorrow, *en garde.* I am *not* afraid of you!"

Aimee just shakes her head and sighs. One only wastes words and breath arguing with Rose. One moment she believes her fate is preordained; the next she is confident that she has the power to change it.

"Come on, Rose!" Aimee grabs her cousin's hand again and gives it a sharp tug. "We'd best get back to Trois-Ilets before they notice we are not in your bed and have the slaves out scouring the jungle in search of us. If we keep them from the cane fields we're likely to *feel* a cane on our backs!"

When at last their bare feet pad soundlessly across the courtyard and they slip between the cotton sheets of Rose's bed again, Aimee reaches out and catches hold of her cousin's hand.

"Promise me, Rose," she pleads with quiet urgency, "that you will say nothing of the Queen's prophecies...."

"I promise." Rose smiles and gives Aimee's hand a reassuring squeeze. "They would only laugh at us if they knew, and I've no desire to be called 'Your Majesty' in mockery. But once the prophecy is fulfilled I will tell *everyone;* it will make a *grand* tale!"

"It will indeed," Aimee agrees as she pulls the covers up to her chin and snuggles deep into her pillow, whispering silently into the gray shadows that still fill the room, "*if* it ever is fulfilled."

Life could never be that fantastic and absurd! Two empresses indeed! Aimee scoffs silently into her pillow before sleep closes her eyes.

PART I

---◈---

ROSE

CHAPTER I

My life truly began when a letter arrived from my aunt Edmée in Paris. Before that I had just been treading water for fifteen years, biding my time, sleeping till noon, lazing the days away in loose cotton dresses, unfettered by stays, walking barefoot, living on and breathing in sugar, avoiding lessons like the plague, and occasionally donning white satin, like all the other unmarried girls, to attend balls at the Governor's mansion in Fort Royal where I aimlessly flirted with handsome, diverting boys my heart truly cared nothing for.

I remember it vividly, my *true* birthday. At first, it seemed just like any other ordinary, ho-hum humid lazy day on the tropical, sugar-scented island of Martinique. I, Marie Josèphe Rose Tascher de la Pagerie, was sitting, petulant and idle, on a window seat, my detested embroidery cast impatiently aside in a tangle of hopeless purple silk knots only a miracle could hope to untie. I was watching one of the sudden summer rains wash the veranda clean and pouting over an unfortunate raspberry jam stain marring the frothy white flounces of my new muslin gown with the double row of heart-shaped mother-of-pearl buttons marching down the bodice neat as soldiers. I had been careless at breakfast. My maid Rosette, always honest even in the face of my tears, said she didn't think the

stain would ever come out. Money was dear and I had ruined the
new dress I had spent weeks weeping and wheedling Father for the
very first time I had worn it.

There was a little green lizard climbing the window glass, so close
I could see his tiny scales and beady black eyes and even count his
long, spindly toes if I had a mind to. But I wasn't interested in
lizards; I was dreaming of Paris and handsome young men who
thought I was the most beautiful and fascinating creature alive,
men who would fight duels to be the one to lay the moon at my feet
and hang the stars around my neck like a diamond necklace until
one special man, a man above all other men, placed an empress's
crown on my head.

My mother, the still-beautiful Marie-Rose Claire Tascher de la
Pagerie, was reclining wretchedly on the sofa, still wearing her ball
gown, a shimmering mulberry silk festooned with black lace, now
badly wilted and sodden with sweat beneath the armpits. She had
been wearing it for three days. She had put it on to attend a party at
a neighboring plantation.

Papa had insisted it was just the thing to chase her woes away.
Besides, her presence would ensure he didn't drink too much rum
punch and make an ass of himself in front of our neighbors again.
Papa was quick to remind her that the last time he had attended a
ball without her he had picked up the punch bowl, guzzling like a
parched fieldhand until he had drained it to the dregs, then run
giddily about giggling and squeezing the breasts of every woman he
could catch and comparing them to passion fruits and mangoes
until the Governor had finally ordered the footmen to dunk Papa's
head in a basin of cold water and throw him out into the street. So
Mama had reluctantly agreed, put on her best gown and a brave
smile, and gone to the ball to ensure her husband's good behavior.

When they returned, a slave had met them at the door with the
sad news that my sister Catherine was much worse. She was deliri-
ous, burning with fever and coughing up blood. Mama had rushed
straight upstairs to her and hadn't left her side until this morning.
Her high-piled pompadour of powdered hair was listing badly to
the left and the silk roses and black lace garnishing it hung slovenly
and slack, but Mama was too weary and worried to care. She hadn't
even thought to loosen her stays. She was lying back on the hard,

torturously uncomfortable ancient green brocade sofa. Its badly frayed gold embroidery, as prickly as a porcupine's needles, had been known to draw blood upon occasion, but today Mama didn't seem to even feel it. She had a cold compress pressed tight over her tired, swollen eyes and a tear-soaked handkerchief and her black onyx rosary beads clutched tight in her other hand. She hadn't even touched the cup of steaming black coffee her maid had brought her. She was just too tired to do anything.

My sweet, fun-loving ne'er-do-well papa, Joseph Gaspard Tascher de la Pagerie, was at his desk stealing fast, furtive sips of rum from his silver flask when he thought no one was looking and brooding over a stack of bills he had no hope of paying. He was longing, no doubt, to escape to Fort Royal and the comforting arms and bountiful bosoms and hips of his dusky-skinned mistresses, and the eternally springing hope that he might *finally* turn a lucky card or bet on the winning cock. Papa was a dreamer, not a doer, and one of the few plantation holders who had actually failed to make a profit from the sugar everyone called "white gold." He loved to put on his white frock coat with the big gold buttons and his buff nankeen breeches and tan-topped butter-soft black leather riding boots and stride around the plantation like he was the supreme lord and master of all he surveyed, but everyone knew he didn't know the first thing about running a plantation.

Thus were we arranged in the faded, threadbare grandeur of the best parlor at Trois-Ilets when Le Grande Jacques, our giant black footman, came in bearing the letter on a little silver tray.

I clamped a hand over my mouth, trying to hold back my laughter. Though Jacques had readily acquiesced to the stifling splendor of a gilt-buttoned and braid-trimmed burgundy velvet frock coat with tails that hung down to his knees and a matching waistcoat, a white shirt drowning in ruffles, ice-blue satin knee breeches so tight they might have been painted on, and even a white powdered wig, his big plank-flat feet just could not *bear* the prison of the sturdy black leather shoes with big shiny buckles and white cotton stockings. I think he would have gone barefoot even at Versailles in the presence of royalty. Jacques just could not *abide* shoes and stockings and always managed to "lose" every pair he was given. "'Dem is fo' the white folks that has been bred to such things, but nobody never tried to put 'dem on me till I was already a man growed, an' by den it was long too late fo' my feet to take to 'dem," he always said.

When Papa opened the letter and began to read I felt the world tremble beneath my feet. Here was my destiny come to meet me at last and I must let *nothing* stop me from rushing out to embrace it. I was ready to fly into the arms of the husband who would "cover the world with glory" and me with diamonds and ardent kisses. I felt my heart and heels grow wings. I *knew* that this letter was the first step along the path to the palace and crown Euphemia David had seen in my palm.

The letter was from Aunt Edmée. I had grown up relishing tales of Papa's scandalous sister who had astonished everyone when one day, right after a most civilized and unremarkable breakfast, she just up and left her husband to go and live openly with her lover, our former governor the Marquis de Beauharnais, and his most amicable and obliging wife. The three of them had left Martinique and sailed back to Paris and set up house together and remained a happy trio until the Marquise's death. Aunt Edmée was now seeking a bride, an island-born beauty, for her paramour's son, Alexandre, the handsome young Vicomte de Beauharnais.

Since her own brother was blessed, or cursed to hear him tell it, with three daughters she had naturally thought of us first. They were even willing to overlook the fact that not a one of us had even a pittance for a dowry. Of course it was not an act of benevolence but calculated shrewdness on Aunt Edmée's part. Hers was hardly an altruistic soul; her sharp eyes saw clearly the sense of keeping things in the family. Her lover was sixty-two and sickly, doughy fleshed and gouty by all accounts, and she was no spring chicken herself, hardly alluring enough to attract a new love when the old one was in his coffin. Aristocratic only in his titles and pretensions, not in his bank balances, the Marquis would leave her nothing but the debts they had acquired together. As a mistress rather than a wife, she could not rely upon his pension, that reliable though meager source of funds would die when he did, and her estranged husband was unlikely to welcome her back or offer to support her, all things considered. But if Alexandre and his bride were indebted to Edmée for bringing them together, gratitude would surely endure and they would provide her with a home and all the necessary comforts for the rest of her life.

"Let me go, Papa! *Please!* Let me go!" I cried, interrupting Papa midsentence and clinging to his arm, staring up at him with my most heartrending expression as I bounced excitedly on my toes. "Let me go to Paris and marry Alexandre!"

Paris was the dream of all dreams. By rights, my sisters and I should have been sent there to be educated long ago, but years of bad harvests, the devastation wreaked by hurricanes, and Papa's gambling debts, combined with a blockade by the British that had prevented us from exporting our sugar, had made this impossible. Thus we had all had to make do with what little the nuns at the convent in Fort Royal could teach us, though I for one found dancing with the soldiers at the Governor's balls and sneaking out into the garden or to walk on moonlit beaches, sometimes even daring to strip for a midnight swim with them, much more educational than anything the nuns ever taught me. The Sisters were for the most part sweet, but clearly they knew nothing of life and even less about love.

"Rose, I have not even finished reading your aunt's letter...." Papa shook me off, and from the sofa, over the rustle of wilting mulberry silk, Mama sighed, "Have patience, Rose...." Sometimes it seemed that was the only thing she ever said to me. "Have patience, Rose; have patience...."

Well, I was tired of having patience or pretending that I did! I didn't want to have patience! As a virtue I thought it was vastly overrated and I didn't give a fig what the nuns or Mama thought about it! I wanted to dance, and have fun, and live and love while I was young enough to enjoy it all. How could they expect me to act like an old woman and bide my time and sit by the fire embroidering flowers or placid platitudes when I was so full of vitality and passion? I was *bursting* at the seams; why couldn't they see that?

As Papa continued to read, my heart plummeted. Alexandre wanted Catherine. Of course he did; she was the youngest and prettiest of the three Tascher de la Pagerie sisters. I was the eldest and the least likely a man so exacting as Alexandre de Beauharnais would choose to marry.

My teeth were already rotting, full of cavities and stained an ugly yellow-brown. My wet nurse had weaned me from her breast with sugared milk and I had been in love with sugar ever since. I ate it raw and put it in everything I ate or drank; I simply could not go a day without it. Although I spent hours at my mirror perfecting a charming closemouthed smile, to lure and pleasure a man I must open my mouth sometime, and I couldn't hide behind my fan *all* the time. And things like that really mattered to a man like Alexandre.

"But Catherine *can't* go; she's dying!" I blurted without stopping first to think. I clamped a hand over my mouth, too late to stop the cruel, if honest, words from flying out, and glanced worriedly over at Mama. She just could not admit, poor dear, that all hope was gone and Catherine would die long before she ever had a chance to live. But Mama had already turned her face away and was fingering her rosary, still praying for a miracle that we all knew would never come; Euphemia David said so.

"I'll just go and check on Catherine," Mama murmured as she hurried out before we could see the first tear fall.

Catherine had the wasting sickness. Her golden hair was as dry and brittle as straw and her skin yellow as bananas and there was a persistent rattling in her chest like peas inside a gourd. The nuns had sent her home to die. The doctors could do nothing for her except bleed her, which only made her weaker, and she could rarely keep down the bread and milk and mushed bananas Mama diligently spooned into her mouth. No tonics, prayers, voodoo charms, or magic spells could save Catherine.

Though Mama was a staunch Catholic and unwilling to risk her daughter's soul, or her own, by consorting with witches, Papa had sent for the voodoo queen in secret one morning while Mama was at Mass. He had *tremendous* faith in her and knew if anyone could save Catherine, Euphemia David could.

She had once given him a bone from a mean old black cat's tail and a single precious hair from her head and told him to go to the cemetery and sit all night on the grave of the richest person buried there—a widow woman who had been just as ornery as that old black cat had been. She told him to put that bone in a little green velvet bag filled with dirt from the freshest and oldest graves in the cemetery, and his last gold coin polished till it shone like the sun, and sew it shut tight using a new needle threaded with her hair. But just before he made the last three stitches he was to stab his finger deep as he could bear with the needle and stick it inside the bag, right up against the bone, and leave it there until the bleeding stopped and the sun rose full in the sky. The next night with the little green bag nestled right over his heart, he walked backward all the way from Trois-Ilets to Fort Royal and into the gaming den with a slice of pepper hot enough to make his eyes stream tucked under his tongue, kept his back to the pit the whole time, placed his bet sight unseen on the red cock with the blue-black tail feathers, and won enough to prevent the plantation from being seized by creditors.

Of course, he did catch a terrible cold sitting up all night in that graveyard, the doctors came and bled him and put mustard plasters on his back and chest, and he was at death's door for nearly six weeks, but Papa said it was worth it. Mama said he got just what he deserved for dabbling with such deviltry. She had the priest in every day to pray for his tarnished soul and said if he ever had dealings with voodoo and Euphemia David again she would leave him so he would just have to choose between his own bad luck and her and that black voodoo witch and Satan-sent riches. Of course, Papa chose the former, but he was always sniffing and sneaking around the latter like a poor dog outside a locked door behind which a bitch in heat is kept.

But Euphemia David could do nothing for Catherine. She came and laid her snake on Catherine's chest and it stared my poor, frightened sister right in the face and flicked out its tongue to lick her chin, then slithered back to Euphemia David, right up onto her shoulder, and whispered in her ear that the loas had seen Catherine and decided that she was too beautiful for this world; they wanted her for themselves. She was doomed; there was nothing anyone could do. Death already rattled in her lungs and her heart was withering away fast, growing more sluggish with every hard-won beat, and soon it would stop altogether.

Papa flashed me a warning look, took another sip from his flask, and pointedly turned his back on me as he finished reading Aunt Edmée's letter in silence so loud it screamed. When he finally turned back around he shook his head. "I'm sorry, Rose, your Aunt Edmée says if for some reason we cannot send Catherine,

your little sister, Manette, will do. . . . I'm sorry, Rose, she says nothing of you."

"*No!*" I wailed. "It *must* be me; it simply *must!*" I stamped my
foot, though I instantly regretted it when I felt the worn, paper-thin
sole of my slipper split. I flung myself weeping onto the sofa, crying
all the harder when the gilt threads stabbed through my gown,
making me feel as though I had thrown myself down in a cactus
patch. "I'll *die* if I can't go to Paris! I'll simply *die!* I'll wither away
to nothing just like Catherine, then you'll all be sorry, and it'll be
doubly worse for *you,* Papa, because you'll know that *you* are to
blame for not letting me go to Paris and marry Alexandre! You'll
be so brokenhearted you'll *never* be able to turn a lucky card again,
you'll lose the plantation, and all your women will leave you because you have no money to give them, and all because *you* denied
me this chance!"

"*Really,* Rose?" Papa rolled his eyes and took another sip of rum.
"My, my, I had no idea you were so passionately fond of Alexandre!
When he visited the island you put a black wax conjure ball one of
the slaves made for you in his bed and said he was a thoroughly
nasty little boy and you hoped someone chopped off his head just
like a chicken's."

"Oh, Papa!" I cried, and rolled my eyes. "That was *only* because he kept putting on airs, grand as a little English lord, and
calling me *stupid* and *provincial* and pulling my hair hard enough to
bring tears to my eyes! And I was only *five* at the time! But now . . .
everything's different! Papa, I would endure *anything,* even hateful
Alexandre, and having my hair pulled, to get to Paris!"

"Are you so eager to leave us then?" Papa teased.

"Oh no, Papa, not you," I protested, rushing to throw my arms
around him, "but I *belong* in Paris! Paris is the most beautiful,
wonderful, and exciting place in the world! And I am *fifteen!* If I
don't get to Paris soon I'll be too old to enjoy it!"

Papa sputtered with laughter as he put me from him and turned
back to his desk. "Your time will come, Rose, and before your hair
turns white and you succumb to rheumatism, I promise you. Now I
must answer your aunt's letter. . . ."

But I didn't give up. "Papa, *please . . .*" I wheedled, rushing to
stand behind his chair and rub his shoulders, "couldn't you just

mention me to Aunt Edmée? Couldn't you just remind her that I exist and that Manette has her heart set on entering the convent and becoming a nun? Why, it will simply *kill* her if she can't give herself to God, she would rather be torn apart by lions than accept any other bridegroom but Christ, but I . . . I am eager to embrace the world, and Alexandre too, if I must; Paris is worth *any* sacrifice. Couldn't you just write something like that, Papa? And maybe you could also tell her that I am pleasingly plump, tall without being too tall, not at all sun browned, I have kept my complexion fair as snow despite the sun that beats down on us like a slave driver, and that I have eyes as fascinating as amber that is thousands of years old flecked with emeralds—a soldier I danced with at the Governor's ball in Fort Royal told me that, though maybe you shouldn't mention the soldier to Aunt Edmée, she might not understand . . . or, given her reputation, she might understand *too* well. . . ."

I nibbled indecisively at my bottom lip. "But you could tell her that I have hair as dark as midnight, wavy and long enough to ensnare and enslave a man—well, maybe you should leave that last part out too, though it was a different soldier who told me that at a different ball, a naval officer, actually . . . I think—and I am endowed with *all* the charms of youth, a nice bosom, hips that promise my future husband a family of his own someday, and I am a graceful and tireless dancer, with a lively disposition and a great zest for living, and I can also read and write and sew, a little, if I *have* to, but don't tell her that my spelling is atrocious and that I can't sew a straight seam to save my life. Alexandre is just the sort of fussy, nitpicky person to care about silly little things like that!"

Papa put down his pen and turned to stare at me. "This *is* news to me, Rose. I mean about Manette's vocation, not your spelling, or the Circean effect you have upon military men; your mother has lost more sleep over that than she has about poor Catherine's illness. Manette has been sent home from the convent *three* times for putting spiders in the nuns' veils and lizards in their beds and if it happens again they will not have her back, not even as a day pupil. Are you quite *sure* she wants to be a nun? Last time I asked her about her future plans, she said she wanted to cut off her hair, put on breeches, and go to sea and fight pirates, or perhaps become one; she wasn't quite sure which."

"Well, tell Aunt Edmée that then!" I brightened. "Oh, Papa"—
I hugged his neck and kissed the top of his head even though it
meant getting musk-scented powder in my mouth—"that's even
better! Alexandre is far too fastidious to want such a tomboy for
his bride! Just tell Aunt Edmée *something,* tell her *anything,* as long
as it reminds her that I exist and makes her choose me! If you do,
and Alexandre agrees to have me, I promise I will send you half of
whatever allowance he gives me every month for the rest of your
life. Your luck is certain to change *some*time. . . . You could get another charm from Euphemia David, maybe one that doesn't in-
volve your sitting up all night in the graveyard and catching cold,"
I added hopefully.

"Hmmm . . ." Papa tapped his chin thoughtfully. "That is an interesting proposition, Rose. Very well, if I promise to put in a good
word for you, will you go away and let me write my letter in peace?"

I hugged Papa's neck tight and kissed his face a dozen times.
"I'm already gone!" I said as I danced out onto the veranda, laughing and twirling as the wind blew the rain sideways, beneath the
roof, and over the railing, to slap-kiss me lightly like a naughty
child. I caught the little green lizard and cupped him in my hands
gently and blew him a kiss and danced him up and down the veranda before putting him safely back on the window. "Little lizard,
I am *so* happy!" I cried in pure delight. "I am going to Paris to be
married! My life begins today!"

It never occurred to me that Alexandre might say *no;* Fate had
already written *yes* in the stars and on my palm at the instant of my
birth. It was my destiny!

CHAPTER 2

———◆◇◆———

Two months later a second letter arrived. By then Catherine was already in her grave and Manette had wept so much at the mere suggestion of leaving our island paradise that the doctor feared forcibly uprooting her would be the ruination of her health. Mama, in turn, still reeling from the loss of Catherine, put her foot down. She clung desperately to Manette and insisted that at only eleven she was far too young to even be thinking of marriage. "If Alexandre de Beauharnais wants one of my daughters to be his wife," she said, "it will have to be Rose!"

I had never been so happy in my life. I won by default, but that didn't matter at all; I won. I was going to Paris, to answer Destiny's call; *that* was the important thing.

Despite some rather strong misgivings about my suitability, Alexandre was willing to accept me since he really had no choice. He had heard that I was a featherhead—he actually wrote *that!*—frivolous and flighty and prone to putting my heart before my head, provincial and uncultured with no education to speak of and no love of books.

If, as I fear, our marriage turns out badly you will have no one to blame but yourself, he wrote to me.

And, he thought that I, at *barely* sixteen, was too *old* for him!

He was firmly convinced that a wife should be not even a day less than five years her husband's junior. Since there were only two years between us he suspected this vital discrepancy did not bode well for our union.

But time was pressing. Alexandre could not afford to wait another year in the hope that Manette's nerves would settle; indeed he would not have a wife of a nervous, and very likely hysterical, disposition, he said. And he wasn't inclined to prolong the search and look elsewhere for a bride, like a fairy-tale prince trying to find the girl whose foot fit the glass slipper.

It seemed that money, not the prospect of love and domestic bliss, was at the heart of Alexandre's eagerness to marry. He could not lay hands on the inheritance his mother had left him until he acquired a wife, as the late marquise believed that marriage would have a good, steadying influence on her son and smooth some of his sharp edges.

If I was the readily available key that could unlock the vault to 40,000 livres per annum, Alexandre was willing to overlook at least a few of my shortcomings, like my age, which I could do nothing about. But he sincerely hoped that I would make it my life's work to better myself and constantly endeavor to be worthy of him in exchange for the honor he was about to bestow upon me by taking me, albeit reluctantly, as his bride and giving me the title of Vicomtesse de Beauharnais. He was already hard at work, his letter informed me, drawing up a rigorous program of self-improvement to give me as a wedding present along with a forty-volume set of the works of Voltaire and Rousseau, plus supplemental volumes on history, science, and etiquette.

Whoever would have thought that an eighteen-year-old boy could be so stodgy? If I didn't know better I would have asked Papa if he was certain Alexandre wasn't eighty. I wanted a husband, not a schoolmaster! I doubted he would be any fun at all! But Alexandre de Beauharnais was the golden gate that led to Paris, so I was willing to be generous and overlook *all* of *his* shortcomings.

Aunt Edmée wrote that there was not a moment to lose. Never mind about my trousseau; she would outfit me in Paris. I would be her living doll and she would dress me; it would be her wedding gift to me. *Do not delay; just get on a ship and come,* she wrote, her words as urgent as voodoo drums in the night.

So I packed everything I possessed and bid everyone farewell and drew in one last long whiff of the sugar-scented air. I was certain I would never come back. When my little cousin Aimee, whose destiny, Euphemia David said, was entwined with mine, wept and clung to me, I reminded her that very soon she too would be boarding a ship bound for Paris. Her father, unlike mine, was a shrewd businessman who could afford to send his daughters abroad to be educated at one of the finest convent schools. I promised faithfully that I would visit her in the convent and take her out for days of fun spent shopping and sipping chocolate at sidewalk cafés, and, when she was older, there would be balls and evenings at the theater. I would even seek a rich and handsome husband for her amongst Alexandre's friends.

As I stood upon the deck of the *Ile de France,* with my mulatto maid Rosette, one of Papa's Fort Royal by-blows, at my side, all our slave women and several free women of color, including many of Father's mistresses I'm sure, assembled on the wharf to wave good-bye.

All of them were wearing their best clothes: their brightest, gaudiest, most colorful dresses, patterned in vivid checks, bold stripes, or floral prints that looked from a distance like splashes of bright paint; *tignons*—madras handkerchiefs tied around their heads, the points arranged in intricate up-pointing fashion—and foulards, gay handkerchiefs in colors clashing or contrasting with their gowns, knotted around their shoulders, the unmarried girls seeking a husband leaving the ends of theirs untucked to wordlessly convey their desire to find a mate.

I had grown up watching these women walking the dusty island roads in their bare feet with baskets of fruits and vegetables, crabs and fish, fresh-baked bread and sweet pastries, or laundry balanced on their heads, sashaying and swaying their hips, vying with one another to have the gaudiest, most eye-catching attire and sell the most of their wares by the day's end. *La costume est une lutte*—the art of dress is a contest, they always said, words I would cherish and never forget. I would carry them across the sea to France with me and think of them every time I put on my clothes.

As the ship drew out to sea they sang to me "Adieu Madras, Adieu Foulards!," the age-old island song of farewell that Creole women have been singing for all of human memory to loved ones being borne away by the savage sea, most likely never to return again.

> *"Adieu Madras, adieu Foulards!*
> *My darling is leaving,*
> *Alas, alas it is forever!"*

Just for a moment, I thought I glimpsed Euphemia David with her snake around her shoulders, standing in the midst of the swaying, singing crowd, smiling and serenely nodding at me, giving me her regal blessing. In that moment a peculiar light appeared in the sky, like a wreath of flames, or a crown, above the ship. The passengers were awed and frightened, but the sailors were quick to reassure them that it was only St. Elmo's fire, but I knew better—it was a crown sent from Heaven and it was meant for *me!*

The voyage was *dreadful!* For *three* relentless months the waves pitched, rolled, tossed, and hurled the ship about like a child's plaything. We spun in circles and completely lost our bearings. Never before had I felt so helpless and small, so entirely at God's mercy. More than once everyone on board sank to their knees, praying fervently, certain we were about to plunge down to a watery grave. At least the storms would keep us safe from pirates and the British, I thought, but one of the sailors said no, the storms might instead fatally cripple us so that once they subsided we would be even more vulnerable to capture.

Green algae infested our clean water supply, turning it to vile green slime, but we drank it anyway, until it ran out, and, for that reason alone, we were grateful for the pounding rains; at least we would not die of thirst. Our cabin was so tiny we were hemmed in by my trunks and we had to leave off layering our petticoats in order to move about. The emerald-colored algae bloomed in thick, tenacious patches on the perpetually damp walls of our cabin and mold crusted my trunk and leather shoes. Everything we touched was damp; there was no escaping the clammy feel of wet cloth against our skin, not even in bed, where mold and algae soon blossomed upon the sheets. I was afraid I would never be warm and dry again.

Our food fast became inedible, infested with weevils and worms, the fruits and vegetables rotted and the meat turned rancid, but in our desperation we ate it anyway, praying that we would reach some safe harbor soon, before everything was gone. The idea of having nothing at all was worse than eating fare not fit for dogs. The sailors grudgingly shared their meager rations of salt meat and biscuits so hard I thought they would break my teeth; not even the rain would soften them. Every time I tried to eat one I felt my teeth wobble warningly in my jaw, making me fearful of facing my fiancé with conspicuous gaps in my mouth.

The day after we had exhausted every morsel on board, and I was starting to fear for the ship's cat, the *Ile de France,* listing badly, its sails hanging in limp, bedraggled shreds like the hair of a sea hag, lurched into the harbor at Brest. Every soul on board sank to their knees and offered up prayers of thanks.

In the pouring rain, Rosette and I trudged to the inn where rooms had been reserved for us. As luck would have it, Aunt Edmée and Alexandre were already there, waiting impatiently, impeccably dressed, with not a hair out of place, dry and warm as toast, sipping spiced wine by the fire in the big common room. My bridegroom glared at me as though he held me personally responsible for the tempestuous weather and the ship's laggardly arrival.

"Well, little savage, you certainly took your time," he sneered. "You might have at least *tried* to look worth waiting for. Disappointment at first sight—that hardly bodes well for our impending nuptials; don't you agree? If I believed in omens, I would be tempted to call the whole thing off and send you right back to Martinique; I don't think you're fit for civilized company."

He *yawned* right in my face! It felt worse than a slap!

I had been feeling *wretched* for weeks, and I hadn't bothered to change my dress, reasoning that I would be drenched as soon as I set foot off the ship, so why bother and ruin a fresh dress. I thought there would be time to prepare myself for this meeting. I wanted to make a good impression; I certainly didn't want Alexandre to see me like *this!*

I had lost flesh from lack of nourishment and nausea, so my blue linen dress hung slackly from my shoulders, straight down, almost like a sack with a hole cut out for my head and sleeves sewn on as an afterthought, hiding all trace of my womanly bosom, waist, and hips. My cheeks were gaunt and deathly pale, my eyes deep sunken and dark circled, and my nose runny and red as Papa's rum nose. I was still green tinged from seasickness and my skin was slightly windburned from all those hours I had spent on deck seeking some respite from the close confines of my algae-and-mold-festooned cabin, and raw and red from the constant damp. My dark hair had lost all of its luster and hung down lank and lifeless, plastered to my shoulders and back by the pelting rain and sprays of salty seawater. I hadn't had a proper bath since leaving Martinique and I'm sure Alexandre's fastidious nose was aware of that. I hadn't even thought to perfume myself prior to leaving the ship, I was so eager to be off it and on solid land and somewhere safe and warm again.

I was admittedly a sorry sight, hardly a morsel to tempt any bridegroom, much less one as exacting as Alexandre de Beauharnais, but he didn't have to be so *mean* about it. Surely my ordeal entitled me to at least *some* consideration? Even one tiny ounce of kindness would have meant so much!

While Alexandre was not at all impressed with me, I was so awestruck by the sight of him I almost drooled and melted in a lust-quivering puddle at his feet. He was like the god of masculine beauty, a marble statue come to life! The rude, imperious little boy I remembered had grown up into a regal prince from the kingdom of frost and ice. Tall and slender, with skin fair as fresh-fallen snow, eyes of icy blue, and hair so blond it could be mistaken for white, worn long in the fashion of the day and tied back with a black velvet ribbon, with two perfect curls arranged at either temple, he stood before me haughty and resplendent in the silver-buttoned and -braided white uniform of the Sarre Regiment with a dashing silver-tasseled cape draped over his shoulder, and tall black leather

boots so shiny I could see my hopelessly bedraggled reflection staring up at me whenever I looked down at them. He stood by the
fireplace with a goblet of wine in his hand, as perfect as though he
were posing for his portrait. He was unnervingly still; only the occasional disdainful flicker of his eyes or mouth betrayed any sign of
life. He was a perfect and unfeeling mannequin. I think I must have
known from the start that he had no heart.

I had never in all my sixteen years felt so small and unworthy as
when Alexandre de Beauharnais's ice-blue eyes looked at me. In
my island paradise men had always admired me, sought my kisses,
vied to embrace me; every single one of them told me how beautiful and desirable I was. But here was my husband-to-be staring
down at me as though I were a nasty worm that had just crawled out
of a perfect apple. His eyes were *so* cold, so *cruel!* He *hated* me! I
knew it, but I didn't know *why*. What had I done? Was looking
wretched and wan after a perilous and overlong ocean voyage and
suffering constant seasickness so unforgivable? I knew I was ignorant and had a lot to learn about Parisian ways, but I could, and I
would. I wanted to! I had left Martinique far behind me; I was
ready to be in the world and of the world!

"We leave for Paris at first light. Do not keep us waiting, little
savage. Good night," Alexandre said, and, with a crisp, militarily
precise nod, turned on his heel and headed for the stairs.

Little savage! As though I were some crazed, wild-eyed cannibal
wench who had never even *heard* of table manners! He was *so cold!*
No warmth, no feeling, no kindness at all! He didn't even say *hello*
or *welcome*. The *good* prefacing *night* was just a formality; it had no
meaning at all.

"He is . . . *striking!*" I breathed to Aunt Edmée in spite of my
wounded pride as I watched his haughty white-clad soldier's physique
ascend the stairs without a backward glance.

Aunt Edmée, a shapely and well-preserved woman in a butter-
yellow brocade traveling suit trimmed with sable, and a matching
tricorn hat sitting jauntily askew atop her pompadour of silver-
veined blond hair, turned to me with her blue-violet eyes full of
pity. She sighed and shook her head, though whether it was at my
unworthiness or Alexandre's rudeness I couldn't tell.

"*Striking!*" she hissed witheringly. "So is an egg thrown against the pavement, my dear!"

She was on *my* side! I was *so* grateful to her that I burst into tears and flung myself into her arms. It felt *so good* to have an ally! At that moment, I had never been so grateful for anything in my life.

CHAPTER 3

———◄○►———

Paris in her winter clothes was dismal, dingy, and gray, a world where ermine and sable-swathed luxury vied with shabby, shivering naked want. Even the trees were naked; their ugly gnarled and twisted branches made me miss the swaying palms and heavily laden banana and mango trees of Martinique more than I ever imagined possible. Snow, shit, and dirt sullied the white snow and the air stank of sewage, rubbish tossed without a care into any convenient corner, alley, and courtyard, or even out into the street.

I, who had been born to the smell of sugar in the air, had to hold a perfume-soaked handkerchief tight to my nose every time I went out to keep from gagging at the stench. In Paris, even the rich stank; they merely masked their odors with expensive perfumes as though a bath was to be avoided at all costs, something that I, who had grown up swimming in warm turquoise waters, could never understand. I *loved* the warm caress of water on my naked skin and could not imagine my life without it. Their cloying musk and attar of roses made me weep at the memory of the hibiscus, honeysuckle, and jasmine and giant white lilies growing wild and free on the island paradise I had left behind. Even my beloved roses, my favorite of all flowers, turned overpoweringly rank on the aristocratic Parisian bodies I encountered.

It was *nothing* like I imagined it would be! Though the city seemed enormous, I felt stifled in a new and terrifying way, like the walls were closing in on me. In Paris the streets were close and cramped and all the buildings, despite their stately, elegant façades, were crowded close together like lovers, blocking out the light and air, and every single one of them was dingy and soot stained. Everything was so *gray!* Where was all the color and life I had imagined?

I was accustomed to a world of color, light, and sugar-scented air. A land of warmth, birdsong, and tropical flowers, all washed in sun, sprawling white plantation houses, verandas and balconies, terraces, gardens, and open-air courtyards where rainbow-hued parrots chattered and lizards lounged sunning themselves on walls, and even the beggars, with their outstretched hands, wore colorful rags and a smile and would cheerfully proffer a song, a story, a joke, or even a dance in exchange for food or coins. The street-sellers of Martinique smiled and sang as though work were a joy, the women in their bold warring rainbow array of checks, stripes, and flowers balancing their wares in straw baskets atop their heads and the men displaying theirs in pushcarts or on trays hung around their necks, but in Paris those who hawked cheap goods were surly and unfriendly even if one deigned to buy. It was a world of gray ice and misery where everyone seemed to have forgotten how to smile, even this wretched little bride.

We were married a fortnight later in the small, chilly, dark church of Noisy-le-Grand, just outside of Paris. Alexandre wanted it that way; he was embarrassed to be seen with me, bitterly remarking how his elegant and sophisticated friends would laugh to see him yoked to such a crude provincial creature. The date was December 13, 1779, a Friday, and a bad omen I was certain, but Alexandre only laughed at me. He had an appointment with his banker and wasn't inclined to change it on account of his heathen bride's superstitions.

Every time he spoke to me, every time he looked at me, Alexandre always found some way to remind this "little savage" that she wasn't good enough for him. When a regimen of hearty meals rapidly restored, and enhanced, my natural tendency to plumpness and womanly curves, Alexandre added "fat" to his never-ending, ever expanding litany of my faults.

My one consolation was that my father-in-law was as kind as his son was cruel. The morning of my wedding, Papa de Beauharnais kissed my cheek and fastened a necklace of dainty rose-colored diamonds arranged in clusters, like little flowers, around my neck and presented me with a lovely hand-painted fan trimmed with gold lace and pink ribbons, and a bouquet of blush pink roses, grown in a hothouse, defying the frigid December weather to bloom just in time for my wedding day, all to match my gown.

It was the most beautiful dress I had ever seen—baby-blush pink and antiqued-gold brocade, with panniers so wide jutting out from the hips that I had to walk through every door sideways and despaired of making it down the aisle without hurting someone or hopelessly embarrassing myself. I imagined myself treading on toes and knocking hats off right and left, tearing my dress by snagging the wide, unwieldy skirt on the ornately carved pews, or knocking over the candles and setting myself, and maybe even the whole church, on fire. Swags of blush and champagne satin and bouquets of pink satin rosebuds framed in gold and silver lace adorned every inch of the full skirt. Billowing layers of pale pink lace ruffles flowed from the tight elbow-length sleeves, and there was a ladder of gilt-edged pink satin bows marching down the bodice, the largest at the top, the smallest just above my tightly cinched waist. It was cut lower than any gown I had ever owned; only a delicate ruffle of pink lace prevented the areolas of my breasts from showing. Aunt Edmée assured me that that was the fashion and offered to have her maid rouge them for me, but I blushingly declined. A chaplet of blush-pink satin rosebuds crowned my dark hair, flowing down my back in a torrent of curls, and I wore a veil of gold-veined pink lace embroidered with crystals and tiny gold and silver beads to form yet more roses. Even my pink silk stockings were embroidered with bouquets of gold and silver roses at the ankles. My pink satin slippers, with roses twinkling with crystal dewdrops blooming on the toes, had heels so high I teetered about like a fool on stilts, clownishly, clumsily lurching and grasping at any person or piece of furniture within reach whenever I felt myself falling.

My mirror, Aunt Edmée, Papa de Beauharnais, and my maid, Rosette, all said I was beautiful; only Alexandre had no praise for me. He saw only a pathetic, untutored little Creole savage staggering about on unaccustomedly high heels, a free and easy island child utterly lacking the brilliant, diamond-hard, sophisticated Parisian polish he was accustomed to. He said I looked like exactly what I was—a poor little ignorant island-born fool playing at dress-up, pretending to be a great lady, but utterly lacking the talent, grace, and refinement to carry the illusion off. He urged me to resist the temptation to ever take part in amateur theatricals; my ineptness would spoil every performance. He made me feel as lowborn as a milkmaid. The fact that my father had been a page at Versailles in his childhood didn't matter a jot to Alexandre.

After the wedding there were no celebrations, not even a champagne toast, a cup of rum punch, or even a piece of cake. I barely had the chance to throw my bouquet as Alexandre yanked my hand and rushed me impatiently out of the church. I aimed badly and it landed in the holy water font, from which it was fastidiously fished by a frowning priest. Alexandre just rolled his eyes and sighed, "Can you do *nothing* right?"

As Alexandre was shoving me into the waiting carriage, I glanced back. A tall blonde gowned in glacial green and an emerald velvet cloak edged in white fur was standing outside the church, staring at me with eyes as hard and cold as the emeralds around her neck. She looked like she wanted to stab me through the heart. But *why?*

I wondered who she was. A mistress Alexandre had callously cast aside? Someone whose heart he had broken? She was so haughty and disdainful when she looked at me, it *had* to be some matter of the heart. Surely she had no other reason to hate me? I didn't even know who she was.

I wanted to ask Alexandre, but the moment I opened my mouth, before the first syllable was even out, he rolled his eyes and snapped at me to "*shut up!*" and yanked the leather window screen down as though he was ashamed to even be seen riding in the same coach with me. I cowered back like a dog that sees a whip in its master's hand and hated myself for it. Where was my spirit? How, in this city of cold, cold ice, had my backbone melted like butter left out in the sun?

* * *

Back at the house on the rue Thévenot, I was left alone to await my husband in an ice-cold room amongst towering stacks of books—Alexandre's wedding gift to me—the complete works of Voltaire and Rousseau accompanied by assorted texts on etiquette, mathematics, history, science, and politics. There must have been at least a hundred volumes. I warily kept my distance. I feared they might all fall down and crush me. I had no desire to read any of them. I was so cold I was tempted to throw some on the fire.

The house that was to be my new home was high ceilinged and drafty; it was the gloomiest house I had ever seen, full of heavy old furniture and musty tapestries darkened by age, dust, and soot; I doubted they had ever been properly cleaned. It was never warm or bright enough to suit any of us even with a fire in every room and all the candles lit. The chandeliers tinkled constantly, the dangling dusty crystal prisms stirred by the ceaseless draft. It was as cold as a tomb; no wonder Papa de Beauharnais and Aunt Edmée were both self-professed martyrs to rheumatism.

When the door opened I smiled hopefully, I was so *desperate* to please Alexandre. His disdain only made me doubt myself. If it continued, soon I would have no confidence left. But alone, in our bedroom, with clothes and elegant manners cast aside, perhaps I could please him? As it was, there were moments now when I wondered if my admirers had only been making do with the best they could find on Martinique when they had praised and favored me so much.

I sighed with relief, like a condemned prisoner granted a last-minute reprieve, when I saw that it was only Aunt Edmée. She had another gift for me, one she felt certain could not fail to delight even the most exacting of husbands—a sheer pink lace nightgown held up by slender pink satin straps that she tied over my shoulders in pretty, flirtatious bows that seemed to beckon a man's fingers to reach out and untie. I was completely naked underneath. Somehow that thin layer of lace veiling my body made me feel even more naked. The cold puckered my nipples and made them poke prominently through the delicate lace. I blushed hotly, fearing what Alexandre would say when he saw me. Would he denounce me as lewd and call me a harlot? I was unbearably cold; my knees knocked and I hugged myself and huddled near the fire.

"Rose!" Aunt Edmée sighed and threw up her hands. "Poor girl, you have *so* much to learn!" She grasped my shoulders firmly and pulled them back. "Stand erect! Bosom out, girl! Don't be afraid to show off your charms! Have confidence, Rose!" she urged, forcing my arms down at my sides. "Be the proud and beautiful girl you are! You are the Vicomtesse de Beauharnais now, so act like it! Present yourself as the woman you want Alexandre to see you as. You don't want him to see a bashful little girl ashamed to show her husband her figure; do you? Be proud of the beauty God has given you! It won't last forever, you know!"

"Yes, Aunt Edmée," I answered obediently, fighting back my tears, and forcing myself to keep my arms down at my sides when all I wanted to do was hug myself and run away and hide somewhere—*anywhere!* I was wretchedly unhappy. I wanted to go home! I was afraid I had made a *terrible* mistake. So far, the Paris I had seen was *not* worth this, or any, sacrifice.

After Aunt Edmée left me, I went to sit on the foot of the bed, idly resting my cold bare feet on a stack of formidably thick books. I didn't have long to wait. A few moments later, Alexandre strode in, already dressed for bed in a burgundy velvet dressing gown and matching slippers. I leapt up, smiling hopefully, to welcome him.

I couldn't help but flinch as he approached me. His eyes looked *so* cold and angry. His arms reached out, but instead of embracing me, he shoved me down hard, flat onto the bed.

"Well, little savage, let's get this over with!" was all he said.

Then he was upon me, tearing the flimsy lace and raking my bare, vulnerable flesh with his nails as he gathered the skirt up around my hips. Without a single kiss or caress as a tender preamble, he thrust inside me. The pain was unbearable. He clamped his hand over my mouth to stifle my screams.

"Be quiet, you little fool; you'll wake the servants!" Alexandre hissed. "Be still and let's be done with this!"

Not one kind word, not one tender caress. Not *one*.

I think I fainted. As he finished, I dimly remember him tremulously whispering a name in my ear as he shuddered on top of me. But it wasn't mine. It sounded like "Laura."

The next thing I remember Alexandre was standing beside the bed, knotting the sash of his dressing gown, commenting dryly, "Well, my fat little savage, life is not entirely without surprises, it seems—I didn't expect to find *you* a virgin."

Then he was gone. And I was alone again, alone on my wedding night, surrounded by ominous towers of imperious books, appearing as arrogant and superior as my husband. I lay alone in our marriage bed soaking the pillows with my tears, crying because the act of love was supposed to be beautiful, but Alexandre had made it ugly. At that moment, I wished with all my heart that I had never left Martinique. All I had found in Paris was disappointment. I wanted to go home, but I was too proud to admit I had been mistaken . . . and a fool.

CHAPTER 4

————◇————

In the four years that followed I saw little of Alexandre: he was often away with his regiment or enjoying the company of people of greater interest and importance than me, like the mysterious "Laura" no doubt, leaving me alone in that cold and gloomy house with a pair of sickly elders and nothing much to do since I wasn't inclined to sew or read. I wrote him letters, which he returned to me covered in red ink corrections, more schoolmaster than spouse, crowding his comments—all criticism, no compliments—into the margins. When he was at home, in Paris, Alexandre refused to take me out. He was afraid that I would embarrass him. "Ignorant little Creole, let us be frank," he said. "You have *nothing* to contribute to a conversation."

I gorged myself on sweets—candied violets were my favorite—and sat at the front window and watched the world pass by, such as it was, the rue Thévenot being neither a particularly busy nor a fashionable street. Mostly I saw servants and tradespeople hurrying about their business, and the occasional elder out for an afternoon stroll, often accompanied by a man- or maidservant or a pet dog.

Since marrying me secured Alexandre's inheritance for him, one might be tempted to think that he would have shown me a modicum of gratitude, but he didn't. The only time he showed a trace of pride in me was when he trotted me out before the bank president, beaming as though I were a prize thoroughbred, pointed to the gold ring on my finger, and introduced me as his wife.

When he was at home, we coupled but rarely, yet these loveless encounters still bore fruit. I gave him a child—Eugène—the son every man wants. But even my fertility was not enough to make Alexandre proud of me. Alexandre said it was unseemly how swiftly and seemingly easily I gave birth, like a peasant woman squatting in a field, then hurrying back to her work. I didn't think the birthing was swift or easy—it *hurt!* I felt like I was being torn apart. I thought I was going to *die!*—but Alexandre didn't care what I thought.

I loved my golden-haired little boy; I called him "my sweet-faced cherub" and spent as much time as I could cuddling and playing with him. I did not want him to grow up to be a cold and mean man like his father. I wanted Eugène to imbibe love, warmth, and kindness and, when he was a man grown, to *never* raise his voice, or his hand, to a woman. On his wedding night, I wanted his bride to know only tenderness, not the pain and horror I had experienced. I lived in perpetual dread of the day when Eugène would be old enough for Alexandre to take an interest in him. I feared that the day my husband took my son under his wing, the next time I saw Eugène I would be looking at a little stranger with eyes as cold as ice who had learned to parrot his father and call me "worthless," "common," "ignorant," "provincial," "savage," and "fat." Candied violets had conspired with pregnancy to make my curves more generous than ever and Alexandre found this intolerable as well as unforgivable. He suggested I subsist solely on soup, but I just couldn't bear it; my life was sad and dreary enough.

I had no friends, apart from my father-in-law and Aunt Edmée, and, truth be told, I didn't exert myself to make any; I rarely went out. By then my little cousin Aimee was enrolled at a fashionable convent school on the outskirts of Paris, but I couldn't bring myself to face her.

I kept postponing visiting her, making excuses and filling my letters with lies about how busy and happy and in love with my husband and my adorable baby I was and how our life together was a constant merry whirl of parties and balls and friends. I even invented a story about being presented to the King and Queen at Versailles with my hair piled as high as it could be stretched, powdered like a pastry, and crowned with white ostrich plumes three feet tall, in a gold-spangled white satin gown with panniers wider than I was tall and a train ten feet long. I lied to her because I knew that all it would take was just one look and Aimee would know the truth—my life was a lie, my marriage a sham; I was a failure in every way that mattered. I was too proud; I didn't want her to see me like that.

I lolled late in bed or lay all day prostrated upon a couch, eating candied violets until I felt sick and suffering excruciating migraines and nausea because we were one street away from an avenue of butchers and a thriving tannery. Even with every window locked the piteous screams of animals dying to be rendered into fine leather goods pierced my ears and made me weep, my sorrow for their suffering cloaking my self-pity, like rain hiding tears. The stench was *unbearable!* The butchers threw the waste meat right out into the middle of the street and left it there to rot amidst swarms of blackflies and stray dogs. Papa de Beauharnais would pat my hand sympathetically even as Aunt Edmée admonished me for being too softhearted for my own good.

Recognizing that the aged and ailing were poor company for a "pretty young thing" like myself and sensing that Aunt Edmée's persistent attempts to help me improve myself only made me feel worse, Papa de Beauharnais urged me to attend the Friday night salons of Alexandre's cousin, Fanny de Beauharnais, where I was sure to meet many interesting people and make friends. "Fanny and her crowd are not as exacting as Alexandre," he assured me. "By all accounts they are a fun and lively lot."

Fanny was a lady novelist, subsisting extravagantly on inherited wealth, not the fruits of her pen. Her latest novel was called *Blinded by Love*. Its entire plot was literally condensed and contained in its title—the hero was blinded by the heroine in a riding accident, but, as is always the way in such books, love conquers all. Fanny was a tall, gregarious woman possessed of a gargantuan appetite for novelty and change in constant motion. Her hair color, her décor, her passions, and her lovers seemed to change every five minutes; it was maddeningly difficult to keep up with any of them.

I never knew when the butler opened the door whether I would walk into faux medieval splendor or the imagined tomb of a long-dead Egyptian king. Another Friday I might find a funereal black room in which all the guests wore shrouds and lay in coffins contemplating death, or a stark white room devoid of furniture where everyone was barefoot and draped in diaphanous white sheets, sitting on the floor in a circle hand in hand communing with the spirits of ancient Greek philosophers or standing up and striking poses, pretending to be statues. After that fad had run its course each guest would be greeted at the door and presented with a palette of paints and urged to choose a blank patch of wall and make it their own immortal masterpiece, which would be papered over with gold-striped champagne silk before the week was out when Fanny had a yen for regal splendor again.

One simply never knew with Fanny; that was the fun of her. Palmistry, pirates, pagans, pottery, painting, confectionary, fairy tales, farm animals, dragons, midwifery, nature foods, astrology, knitting, mesmerism, music, murder, demonology, the mysticism of the ancients, wild Indians, Americans, medieval history, the mysteries of Catholicism, tropical birds, botany, Shakespeare's plays, and mythology all consumed her soul, devoured her hours, dictated her décor, and filled the pages of her novels before she was on to something new.

One Friday all she wanted to do was dress as a shepherdess and dance on the dew-dampened grass in her bare feet, so she had the lawn uprooted and rolled up like a carpet and carried into the ballroom where white-wigged footmen stood by to drench it regularly with gilded pails filled with rosewater, to keep it delightfully damp and sweet for the guests' dancing feet.

All her guests were said to be brilliant, and at every salon they would rise and regale us with readings from their novels and essays, recitations of their poems, or performances of music they had composed, or unveil their artwork, and everyone would stand and applaud and shower them with extravagant praise; even the man who presented a stark, blank white canvas framed in gilt was pronounced an "immortal genius whose art would be adored through the ages." Most of their "brilliance" sailed hopelessly over my head. I understood none of their prose, poetry and philosophy, and though I always smiled and clapped politely along with the rest, I was often bored to tears and happy to plead an unfeigned headache and go home to my bed.

I found only acquaintances in Fanny's drawing room, never friends, and I knew in my heart I didn't really belong there. I went only to please Papa de Beauharnais, to prove I was making an effort to ease my lonely plight.

To escape the tedium and ennui of my life, I began going for a daily walk or carriage ride. Like a fairy-tale princess emerging from a hundred-year slumber, I was slowly awakening to the charms of Paris. Spring seemed to bring out its best. The trees were in full fragrant flower, festooned with blossoms of white and delicate pink, and people strolled leisurely beneath them arm-in-arm and smiled like they were in love. I saw beauty now wherever I looked.

One day I saw a turquoise silk gown in the window of a dressmaker's shop. The color sent my heart sailing right back to Martinique and the clear warm blue waters I had so often swum in. Impulsively I went in and inquired the price, knowing full well it would be too dear for my purse. Alexandre begrudgingly allotted me only a pittance of pocket money each month; it was barely enough to keep me in candied violets. But the modiste was ambitious and new; she said the "Vicomtesse de Beauharnais"—it still thrilled my heart to be called that, it made me feel so important and grown-up!—had only to select whatever she wished, the goods would be delivered to me, and a bill would be sent to my husband.

It seemed such a sensible and simple thing to do; I marveled that I had not thought of it before. So I bought the turquoise gown, and another of sunset-orange satin, and a third of gold lace. And of course I must have hats and gloves, stockings and shoes, fans, shawls, and parasols to match, and pretty things to wear underneath my new dresses, the modiste said, and I happily agreed. The next day I went back for a softly flowing rose satin negligee to accent my womanly curves and the day after that I fancied a frock the color of wet violets.

I soon found the milliners, corset-makers, perfumers, fan-makers, and jewelers of Paris were all equally obliging to the Vicomtesse de Beauharnais. No one expected me to have ready cash; it didn't matter at all that I didn't have enough money. I could still have whatever I wished! I felt like I had just discovered a new world!

Alexandre was irate when he saw the bills, but his indifference and his absorption with the mysterious Laura had helped me grow a backbone, and I calmly reminded him that without me he would have no money at all and surely that entitled me to a few trinkets and trifles. Henceforth, he paid my bills with ill will, but in blessed silence.

And there were many more bills to come. I had discovered that spending money was a balm to my hurt feelings and pride. It relieved my boredom, provided thrills, and, at least for a time, all my feelings of inadequacy melted away beneath the modiste's or the milliner's praise and cunning fingers and the meaty caress of the stay-maker's pink palm against my tightly corseted torso as he stared at me with smitten eyes.

My promise to send half my allowance back to Martinique for Papa each month crumbled away like piecrust and I guiltily swept the crumbs underneath the carpet. I dreaded his letters so much, and the angry or wounded words of reproach they would surely contain. Whenever one arrived I always delayed opening it for several days.

And so life went on. Overall, it wasn't all that different from my life in Martinique, except the Paris winters were beastly cold, but I had my furs now—cloaks, coats, and muffs of sable, fox, and ermine—and could endure it while looking ravishing at the same time.

Every time I passed a window and saw something I liked I went in and bought it. I never bothered to ask the price; that was Alexandre's problem, not mine.

I slept until noon, played with my little son, lounged about eating candied violets, and went out to promenade beneath my parasol or ride in my carriage or, in snowy winter, my bell-spangled sleigh. If I felt fatigued, I could always stop at a café for a cup of chocolate. And there was always more shopping to do. At night there were private balls and supper parties, the opera and plays, or a public ballroom to go to where I could be seen and admired, drink until I was giddy and giggly, and dance till dawn. I still had a weakness for soldiers and Paris was full of them, and they all, with the notable exception of my husband, seemed to find me irresistible. Everyone it seemed, except Alexandre, wanted to make love to me.

In Paris I found that being married was never a hindrance. Half the husbands and wives I discovered despised or were indifferent to each other; rare indeed was the marriage founded on actual love or even fleeting passion. But I never did much more than kiss and flirt. In my own stubborn way, I was still besotted with Alexandre, waiting for, and dreaming of, the day when he would turn to look at me with desire instead of contempt in his eyes.

All in all, it wasn't a bad life. It was a way to pass the time while waiting for the crown Euphemia David had seen in my palm.

CHAPTER 5

O ne morning, in the fourth year of our marriage, I awoke to the hard, stinging slap of a sheaf of papers in my face and Alexandre's voice bellowing, "I'm done with you and paying your bills!"

By the time I could rouse myself, blot the blood blossoming from the paper cut on my nose, and get my window open the hooves of Alexandre's horse were clattering loudly across the courtyard and the back of his cloak was waving good-bye to me.

The next news I had of him was that he had sailed away to Martinique with his true love, his mistress, Laure de Girardin—at last I knew the haughty blonde's name—and the infant son she had recently borne him. The ship they sailed upon was ironically called *Venus*.

This sudden callous abandonment left me reeling and made me so sick I took to my bed. For weeks I could not lift my head. I felt like such a failure. Every time I tried to eat I felt like I was vomiting my heart out.

I had tried so hard to please Alexandre. I had given him a son almost right away instead of making him wait and hope for years like many men had to do. I thought with my new clothes I was acquiring the elegance and sophistication he considered essential. And I had hoped that if he saw how much other men admired me he would begin to see me with new, and more appreciative, and in-terested, eyes, the way little boys always saw other boys' toys as in-finitely more desirable. But it wasn't enough. All my efforts were in vain; my husband still left me.

Soon all Paris would know if they didn't already. And time would soon reveal that it was more than Alexandre's betrayal that had sick-ened me. One of our rare, dispassionate, cold couplings had left me with child again. I impetuously sent a messenger racing after Alexandre, chartering a fast ship to catch the *Venus*. Foolishly I imagined that if Alexandre knew about the child he would come back to me.

Stone-cold silence was his only answer. I heard *nothing* for *months*. I was still in bed recovering from the birth of our daughter, Hortense, when a letter finally arrived. In a torrent of fierce, ugly words overflowing with hate Alexandre disowned our newborn child, claiming the seed that had sown it was not his own. I was *horrified!* One had only to look at my lovely flaxen-haired little girl to know that she was Alexandre's daughter.

Alexandre branded me a whore, "the vilest creature I know," and "beneath all the sluts of the world." He said he could barely hold his head up in Martinique because everyone was calling him a cuckold and a fool and laughing at him. He had heard so many sto-ries about my wild, wanton ways as a young girl on the island—midnight rendezvous, naked swims, and frenzied couplings on the warm white sands in the silver moonlight. I had played him for a fool, he said; I was not a virgin on our wedding night. I had doubtlessly re-sorted to some harlot's tricks in order to deceive him, a bladder filled with pig's blood surreptitiously inserted inside of me or something of the kind.

He informed me that he was in the process of collecting a series of notarized statements to prove my depravity to the lawcourts so he could divorce me and marry his true love—Laure de Girardin—and acknowledge their son as his rightful heir. As for me, I could take my pair of bastards and my whorish self and go straight to Hell for all Alexandre cared.

Gossip would soon inform me that they had been in love for years, but Laure had been married to a much older man who doted upon her and gave her everything she desired; she was beautiful, rich, and adored. Alexandre, desperate to come into his inheritance so he could compete with Monsieur de Girardin's bounty in wooing the fair Laure, had finally given up on waiting for his elderly rival to die and had married me instead. Then, mere months after our marriage, Laure had become a widow. It made Alexandre hate me all the more; he believed that I had ruined everything for him.

But it was not *my* fault! I had married Alexandre in good faith. I knew *nothing* of Laure; *he* was the faithless one! And while it was all too true that I had flirted and dallied in my lazy, carefree island youth and many times I had been reckless and imprudent, I had *never* bestowed the ultimate favor on any of my beaus; I had preserved my virginity for my future husband. Nor had I, since the day I said, "I do," to Alexandre, taken any other man into my body or bed. I had been flirtatious, but I had been faithful.

In his wrath, Alexandre sold the house on the rue Thévenot right out from under us and withdrew all financial support, even the allowance he had given his father, because Papa de Beauharnais loved me and took my side. Alexandre ordered me to a convent since he lacked the authority to send me to prison, where he thought I truly belonged.

Aunt Edmée and Papa de Beauharnais, with only his meager pension to fall back on, withdrew to a small rented house in Fontainebleau. His pension was barely enough to support two ailing gentlefolk and I could not bear to burden them with myself and the children, so I had no choice but to do as my husband said and seek shelter with the nuns.

I feared I would be shamed and judged, but, to my surprise, I found a safe haven. Instead of a dour, bleak, gray prison, I found a place of loveliness and light, embraced by ivy and beautiful gardens, and a world filled with welcoming arms, understanding hearts, and clever heads all ready and willing to help me.

The convent of Panthémont was full of kind, worldly wise, and sympathetic women: steel-willed dowagers, widows not inclined to remarry, spurned wives, dowerless daughters and sisters, inconvenient spinsters, plain, disfigured, independent-minded, or abhorring the male sex, women who could not or would not marry. The nuns, far from being sour and strict, were kindly and lax. Their only rule was that we must attend Mass once a day; otherwise we were left to do as we pleased. We weren't even required to stay inside the convent walls; we could come and go as we wished and even receive visitors. Some ladies even snuck lovers into their beds or crept out to spend the night in theirs.

The ladies of Panthémont took a special interest in us. They doted upon my two precious, sweet golden-haired tots, and, like sophisticated mother hens, they took me under their wing. For the first time in my life I was inclined to study and learn. I became their most apt pupil, more industrious and attentive than I had ever been at the convent school in Fort Royal. I daresay if they had wanted me to I could even have learned to spell under their tutelage.

They taught me how to dress and to apply cosmetics like a *real* lady. The changes in fashion favored me as though they had been made for me. The heavy brocades, yards of embroidered ribbons and laces, billowing hoops, and cumbersome, jutting panniers, tight lacing, and steep mountains of ornately bedecked and powdered hair garnished with gauze poufs, flowers, feathers, tassels, and pompoms, and even model ships were just not for me. Fortunately, Queen Marie Antoinette had begun to feel the same way. Now gowns had more graceful, flowing lines and light and airy muslins and silks replaced the hot and heavy velvets and gilt-encrusted satins and brocades. Pure white and delicate, sweet pastels comprised fashion's palette, complemented by straw hats and shawls, and women let their hair fall down loose in cascades of curls, eschewing powder except on the most formal occasions.

My new friends urged me to work on my voice, noting, as I often had, how it tended to grow louder when I was nervous and ill at ease. They suggested I slow and lower it to a husky, sultry drawl and keep just enough of my Creole charm to fascinate and lend me an exotic air. I remembered the way the colored women on Martinique had walked with baskets balanced atop their heads, hips swaying and sashaying languidly to a sensual rhythm only they seemed to hear, and made it my own, practicing for hours alone in my room at night.

These clever ladies taught me how to flatter and flirt like a true Parisian, to recognize the *right* people to wile and beguile, to seduce or to let seduce me. "You can either use men or be used by them." They advised me to live my life with those words always in mind.

Amongst my new friends there were the wives and widows, sisters and daughters of lawyers and judges who gave me legal advice so I could best Alexandre at his own game. I discovered that I was not unique or alone in my humiliating plight. I was not the first, nor would I be the last, wife to be cast aside with evil aspersions hurled like stones against her reputation. I found it both comforting and reassuring that several of the ladies who lived at Panthémont had stood before judges on trumped-up charges, falsehoods concocted by fickle husbands not content with the casual adulteries so common in aristocratic circles but desiring instead a legal severance of the marital bond, and with it all financial responsibilities to their spouse.

My aristocratic patronesses introduced me to powerful and influential men who could help me, and soon I had a lawyer, and the means, to fight Alexandre.

I sent letters back to Martinique soliciting testimonials to my good character and contradicting the charges made against me. When my lawyer discovered that many of Alexandre's informants were illiterate slaves, I wrote to plantation owners and Creoles residing in Paris who could affirm that slaves were like children and words easily put into their mouths, that they would unquestioningly sign their mark, a crude X in lieu of an actual signature, on any document if a *Grand Blanc* told them to. And many of Alexandre's informants had been mere children, five years old and even younger, when I left the island, hardly of age to produce such damning evidence against me; one, Petit Sebastian, had barely been out of his cradle when I sailed away. Men who were named as participants in my youthful dalliances gallantly denounced the tales as spiteful gossip, lies spun out of playful and innocent ballroom banter and harmless strolls in gardens or on beaches. Not a one of them admitted to ever having carnal knowledge of me or to ever having been alone with me without a chaperone.

In the end, Alexandre's case against me fell down like a house of cards the moment I breathed on it. The judge took my side; he could find no fault with me. I had clearly been a true and faithful wife to Alexandre and tried at every turn to please him. The children were undoubtedly his. *He* was the one who had abandoned me and sailed away to Martinique with his mistress and their newborn bastard. The "evidence" against me had clearly been concocted by a man avid to be rid of one wife so that he might take another.

But since Alexandre was hell-bent on a separation the judge agreed to give him one; however, all the terms were distinctly in *my* favor. The children would stay with me—Hortense until she married and Eugène until he was old enough to start military school, after which he would return to me every summer—and I was free to leave the convent and live wherever I pleased. Alexandre must pay me an allowance of 5,000 livres per annum with an additional 1,500 livres for Hortense until her wedding day.

Alexandre went white as a ghost and fainted when he heard the judge's decree.

I had to keep telling myself it really was a victory. In my heart I felt a keen sense of defeat, an aching hollow filled only by sorrow. I had failed, and the crown Euphemia David had prophesied for me seemed further away than ever.

CHAPTER 6

———◄○►———

I needed a change, a fresh start. I was twenty, the mother of two small children, not a wife, yet not a widow, but I no longer had a husband to try to please. By the law, I could not remarry as long as Alexandre lived; separation and divorce were not the same thing. I decided to go to Fontainebleau, to visit Aunt Edmée and Papa de Beauharnais, who swore I would always be his daughter, come what may, Alexandre be damned.

A charming village surrounded by lush green forests, Fontainebleau was the traditional hunting seat of French kings. During hunting season, everyone who was anyone congregated there for three weeks, jockeying for royal favor and to be seen and meet the right people. It was the perfect place and time to form lucrative alliances, for business and pleasure, so I decided to join the crowd and see if I could make myself stand out.

It was time to put the lessons the ladies of Panthémont had taught me to good use. Five thousand livres a year would not go far, and I wasn't even certain Alexandre would pay it. I had a feeling that he would part with his money as readily as a vain coquette did her teeth. If the payments came at all, they would not be prompt.

One of the ladies at Panthémont had given me a letter of introduction to Denis de Rougemont, a banker with an eye for the ladies.

He was still handsome, vigorous, and virile, despite his advancing years, with a charming crooked smile, and his curly dark hair was still thick and barely touched by silver. I liked him, and he liked me. He was generous and kind. We made each other laugh. It was far easier than I feared it would be. "You were made for this!" he breathed rapturously as he caressed me. A part of me had to agree. I found his company, and his caresses, most agreeable. I didn't *feel* like a whore when I took his money and gifts and welcomed him into my bed to thank him for his generosity.

Soon I was living in a lovely little ivy-covered cottage with a wardrobe full of new dresses, and all the other accoutrements of an elegant and well-groomed lady. I even saw the best dentist in Paris, who did what he could for my unsightly teeth, filling yet again the deep cavity island sugar had dug into my left incisor. The children had a governess, toys, and a lovely garden to play in, and I was able to spend several bliss-filled, worry-free hours with them every day. Our bellies never rumbled with hunger; the table was always well laden. I had a beautiful rose garden with a fountain at its center; a pug dog named Fortune; a rope of pearls nearly as long as I was tall in my highest-heeled shoes; a black-lacquered carriage driven by a handsome liveried coachman; and lean, high-stepping horses to ride, and a crimson velvet riding habit to wear, when I followed the King's hunt.

Monsieur de Rougemont took me to supper parties, sophisticated salons, balls, concerts, the theater and opera, and for long leisurely strolls and picnics beneath the trees or a full, silver-coin moon. We had champagne and breakfast in bed every morning when he stayed the night with me. He was fond of the children, and always had a ready smile and gifts for them. They called him Uncle Denis. We were almost like a little family. And when business in Paris kept him from me, I need never be alone if I did not want to be.

My time was valuable and men were willing to pay for it. My bed was rarely cold or empty. I had by that time made the acquaintance of other kindhearted aging gentlemen. Between Monsieur de Rougemont, the Comte de Crenay, and the Chevalier de Coigny I never lacked for comforts or company. Money flowed through my fingers like water, and I could never have enough of it. One bene-factor simply wasn't enough; I needed three or four, or even more.

Now when I looked in the mirror I knew who I was—"*la belle Creole,*" a woman who depended on the kindness of men. They petted me, praised me, gave me presents, took me out and showed me off, and paid my bills. They asked little of me in return except that I be pretty, charming, and obliging, in bed and out, and wear as little as possible when we were alone together. But they paid to keep the fires roaring when I entertained them wearing only a sheer peignoir with my legs bare and my breasts spilling out. They were not jealous, exacting, possessive, controlling, or demanding as a younger lover might have been. They bought my body, not my soul.

Though I would sometimes catch myself staring wistfully after the handsome young men I passed in parks and public ballrooms, especially those in uniform, who reminded me of the gallant, sen-sual playmates of my island youth and how handsome and regal my husband had been in his silver-braided white uniform, I remained steadfast in my resolve, even when they smiled and looked at me in a way that made my whole body throb. I resisted the temptation. I would not have another Alexandre in my life. I had myself and two children to support and I could not promise fidelity. I would have no jealous scenes, wrecked nerves, or guilty conscience. Such men could be of little help to me; they were as prone to living beyond their means as I was. In the world I lived in youth, beauty, and debt seemed to go hand in hand. I had to be practical. So I looked and sighed, and sometimes fantasized, but I said *no* to the handsome ne'er-do-wells who would demand my exclusive devotion.

I had become accustomed to doing as I liked. My life was much calmer and easier now than it had been when I lived each day des-perate to please Alexandre, agonizing over where my husband was and who he was with. It was liberating in a way to finally be able to please someone and to hear only sweet words and compliments in-stead of constant criticisms.

Alexandre, as I had feared, was tightfisted and constantly late with my allowance; I had to threaten him with the lawcourts just to pry a few precious livres out of him. He was completely unreasonable—he wanted me to account, precisely down to the very last sou, exactly how the money was spent! He hated me more than ever now that Laure had left him. In Martinique, where he took her, she'd become reacquainted with her childhood sweetheart. They had fallen in love all over again and, acting on a sweet, spontaneous impulse, married; the deed was already done before Alexandre found out. I had to bite my tongue not to tell him it served him right for the way he had treated me.

I had grown up. I was mature, sophisticated, and seasoned, no longer the crude provincial island export Alexandre had seen every time he looked at me. I was a woman of the world who haunted public ballrooms, theater boxes, salons, sidewalk cafés, and parks, like a beautiful spider smiling come hither and hoping to ensnare flies who could provide me with sustenance and luxuries in my web. I had many acquaintances but no real friends and none of my lovers truly loved me. And every time I stood before my mirror arrayed in my new jewels and gowns, practicing my close-lipped smile, I tried very hard to pretend I liked myself as much as my benefactors did. I was glad I had stopped writing to Aimee, spinning tales and making promises brittle as piecrust that I knew I would never keep; I didn't want her to see me like this. Though it now seemed to have shrunk to the size of a seed pearl, I still had my pride after all.

CHAPTER 7

W hen my son was five, Alexandre came to take him away, to
start military school. My sweet Eugène was excited; he
dreamed of growing up to be a brave soldier just like his father.
After I kissed Eugène good-bye, I took to my bed and cried myself
blind. I was so afraid that when summer rolled around a cold, icy-
hearted little stranger, a miniature Alexandre de Beauharnais, would
come back to me, prod my hips and thighs with a toy sword and call
me fat, and flaunt his book learning against my ignorance. I had
nightmares about the vilest and cruelest insults coming out of that
sweet little mouth. *Nothing* could cheer me.

Red, swollen eyes and sorrow were hardly alluring attributes,
and my lovers began making excuses and I saw the easy, comfortable life I had made for myself in Fontainebleau slipping away from
me, like water through my fingers, just like all the money I had frit-
tered away on frivolities that didn't really matter. It was time for another change; it was time to return to Paris.

I found the city alive with a constant thrum of nervous excitement. The King and Queen were greatly despised. Louis XVI was
regarded as a great fat oaf who slept in bed like a log every night

while his wife danced till dawn at the Opera Ball and lost fortunes at faro. Marie Antoinette's lavish spending on clothes, diamonds, her mansion in miniature, the Petit Trianon, her faux rustic farm where the sheep were bathed and wore blue satin ribbons before they were permitted in the royal presence, and the manifold luxuries she lavished upon her special friends—some called them "Sapphic amours"—the Princesse de Lamballe and the Duchesse de Polignac, as well as her rumored affairs with her brother-in-law, the Comte de Artois, and the dashing Swedish Count Fersen, had made her the nation's scapegoat for everything that went wrong. If there were shortages of bread or the cost of meat was too dear the finger of blame was pointed squarely at the Queen. When she put aside her ornate court gowns and had her portrait painted in a simple ruffled white muslin frock and straw hat like the ones I had worn in Martinique people said she was trying to ruin the French silk industry. How awful it must have been for her, poor woman; no matter what she did, it was *always* wrong.

There was much talk of America's victorious war to free itself from "the yoke of British tyranny." I must have heard the words *freedom, liberty, revolution, equality,* and *democracy* a hundred times a day. But I didn't pay too much attention. Politics bored me. A casual glance at a newspaper was enough to lull me to sleep. It all seemed to me a vile and potent witches' brew that stank worse the more it was stirred. I wanted nothing to do with it. I was only interested in myself and my children's welfare; France, its people and sovereigns alike, must fend for itself.

Alexandre was laggardly paying my allowance again, so I sold some of my jewelry to get by. I rented a house and bought new dresses more suitable for Paris. I began to go out, to public ballrooms, salons, cafés, and theaters, showing myself off, and soon not only did Denis de Rougemont come back to me and start paying my bills again, but I had four more wealthy and distinguished lovers who adored me.

But experience had taught me that I could not depend on them; they would be good to me as long as I was pretty, amusing, and good to them, but in times of illness or sorrow when I was not looking or feeling my best they would forsake me like rats fleeing a burning house. And who could blame them? No man wants a maudlin mistress. If they wanted melancholy, tears, coldness, and boredom they would stay at home with their wives.

Time too was my enemy along with my free-spending ways, my inability to resist any pleasing trinket or trifle that caught my eye. My teeth were terrible, decaying and dingy, and already there were fine lines around my eyes. I was already dyeing my hair with dark coffee because I couldn't abide the fear of seeing the first strand of silver there. I had put nothing by for the future, to support me in my old age or to help my daughter attract a husband.

I was supposed to be saving for Hortense's dowry, for which Alexandre, when I could pry the money out of him, was supposed to pay an additional 1,500 livres a year. But I had borrowed from that fund *so* many times, always with the best of intentions, promising each time to pay it back as soon as I could, with interest like any other loan, but never quite managing to do it until, I'm sorry to say, Hortense's dowry had dwindled away to nothing. Thank heaven, my daughter was comely and had the sweetest, most docile disposition; she would surely be able to catch a husband on her own merits.

To make matters worse, Alexandre had heard about my new mode of living and was threatening to drag me before a judge, to denounce me as a prostitute, a professional courtesan, to seek the court's permission to withdraw his support altogether. Why did I need his money, he demanded, when I was enjoying the largesse of so many other men? And *why,* I could not help but wonder, did it sound so much worse when *he* said it? He made me sound *vile,* little better than one of those women who paraded the streets in the Palais Royal baring their breasts to entice custom. I was not so far gone as that!

I was in the midst of my twenties and my looks would not last forever, and there would always be younger and prettier girls to woo my lovers away from me. I *had* to do better; I just *had* to! The future and old age were creeping closer every day. No matter how fast I danced I could not evade them forever; they were waiting to tap me on the shoulder sooner or later.

I tried to forget my fears in the merry whirl of the ballroom, champagne, and my lovers' arms. Shopping alternately eased my nerves, then shattered them when I was confronted with the bills and my own guilt and worries about whether I could persuade my lovers to pay them. Tomorrow, always tomorrow, I promised my-self I would start to save, but every day some new temptation beck-oned. I could not resist the balm of beautiful things. I had to keep up with the fashions; I had to keep up with the other women who relied on the generosity of men. If I was dowdy and passé my lovers would desert me.

The scalding witches' brew of politics soon boiled over and flowed through the streets of Paris. A furious mob marched upon the ancient prison known as the Bastille, determined to tear it down brick by brick and liberate the prisoners inside from regal tyranny. The mob killed the guards and beheaded the prison governor, mounted his head upon a pike, and marched it through the streets. People cheered and sang like it was a victory parade. Soon the King and Queen were prisoners of their own people and everyone was talking endlessly of "liberty, equality, and fraternity" and sporting tricolor ribbons and rosettes of red, white, and blue.

Almost overnight everyone was leaving their hair unpowdered and wearing clothes with smart, simple lines borrowing heavily from dapper, tailored British riding habiliments—redingotes, greatcoats often with double or even triple shoulder capes, double-breasted frock coats, neat square-cut waistcoats, and black leather riding boots with tan tops. Tall beaver hats took the place of tricorns, steel buckles replaced silver and gold, and linen neck cloths, often tied in front with a simple knot or bow, ousted the frothy lace frills of yesteryear. Tricolor sashes and steel buttons embossed with patri-otic sentiments or symbols were all the rage, and polished pieces of charred stones from the ruins of the Bastille were preferred over precious gems. And no one dared be seen in public without the red, white, and blue revolutionary rosette blooming on their lapel or hat.

Gentlemen renounced their aristocratic pastel satin knee breeches and replaced them with thigh- and calf-hugging pantaloons of soft, skin-tight cashmere, doeskin, or nankeen, often in buff or sulfur colors. Panniers and the sweet simplicity of shepherdess frocks in pastel colors fell by the wayside as women rushed to adopt the new patriotic fashions, donning tailored, mannish jackets and waist-coats worn with naturally flowing skirts, sometimes with a slight

bustle at the back, and tall black beaver hats over long curls as towering tresses fell down all over Paris. Ladies who were accustomed
to waiting upon the Queen donned white muslin "mobcaps" like
their housemaids wore and wrapped muslin fichus about their
shoulders, crossing them in front over their breasts.

The poor proudly hailed themselves as *sans coulottes* (without
breeches, the emblem of the aristocracy) and covered their limbs in
loose striped trousers with ragged hems reminiscent of those that
sailors wore and put on red carmagnole jackets, tricolor sashes, and
red felt Phrygian "liberty caps," always with a tricolor cockade
pinned to the side, and thrust their feet into clunky clogs or striped
stockings and English-style riding boots.

All Paris was awash in red, white, and blue to the point of drowning, and I was right there in the thick of it, swimming along as best I
could. I was a follower, not a leader, going along, as I always did,
with every new fad and fancy, singing and dancing to the song of
freedom in the streets and trying to ignore how ugly and dangerous
my world had suddenly become with all the ominous rumblings
about hanging all aristocrats from lampposts, lifting up and exalt-
ing the lowborn, punishing all those born to wealth and privilege,
and killing the worst offenders of all—the King and Queen.

I soon had more cause for sorrow. My little cousin Aimee—
funny how I always thought of her as the little girl of eight she had
been when I left Martinique, though she was by now a woman of
eighteen—had been summoned home by her anxious parents.
They were frightened by the revolutionary fervor sweeping Paris,
and when it only grew stronger, rather than passing away like many
another fad, they booked her passage on the very next ship.

She never reached Martinique. Months passed with no word of
her, and then reports came suggesting the worst possible fate,
worse even than a watery grave; the ship she had been traveling on,
Lazarus, had been attacked by pirates. No ransom demands were
ever made as was customary with wealthy captives; Aimee's parents
would have beggared themselves to buy her freedom and bring her
back home. Murder, most likely preceded by violent rape, had surely
been poor Aimee's fate.

Whenever I was alone, in moments of quiet, when no lover came to share my bed, I wept long into the night, lamenting my cruel selfishness. What must she have thought of me and the way I had abandoned our friendship? I never visited her, not once. I kept making excuses, and then I simply stopped writing at all when I ran out of them. Surely gossip must have reached her even in the convent, and I was too ashamed to face her, too afraid to see the condemnation, or even worse the pity, in her eyes. She must have thought I didn't care.

Euphemia David had been *so wrong* about *everything!* Neither of us would wear a crown except the glory of tresses that God had grown upon our heads. Visions of Aimee's violated and bloody corpse sinking down into the depths of the sea, her long golden hair tangling in green seaweed, haunted my dreams. I wanted to pretend that she had not died at all but sailed away to some exotic distant land where she would indeed wear an empress's jeweled crown, but I knew I was only trying to salve my guilt with childish dreams. Pirates were merciless brutes; once they laid their hands on her pure white flesh Aimee was doomed. Sometimes I had visions, both waking and sleeping, of Aimee, at turns proud and defiant with her head held high, regal as a queen, or cowering with fright, like a child, the back of her skirt soaked with the piss of sheer terror, walking the plank, then, falling, falling, into the deep blue sea from which there was no coming back, no rescue, no mercy, only death, by drowning or sharks' teeth.

In the end, my own fears of the unrest in the city, and grief over my lost and neglected Aimee, drove me to book my own passage on a ship bound for Martinique. I packed my clothes and jewels, sold the furniture, my gilt-edged Sèvres porcelain painted with yellow roses, silver plate, and Venetian glasses, charmed 6,000 livres out of Denis de Rougemont, wrote my darling Eugène a tender farewell, picked up Fortune, and took Hortense's hand, and, with my maid, Rosette, in tow, we boarded a vessel with the grandiose name of *Sultan*.

CHAPTER 8

———◄○►———

I was going home, sadder and wiser, and far worse than I had left it, the empress of nothing, a wife without a husband, a woman whose dreams had died, who bartered her charms to put baubles on her body and bread on the table for her children and was seemingly incapable of saving a sou for tomorrow. What would everyone think of me?

The voyage passed thankfully without incident. The seas were utterly calm in comparison to my first tempestuous crossing, but my mind was in constant turmoil. Every time I lay down to sleep I was tormented by dreams of Aimee besieged by pirates wielding cutlasses and phalluses like battering rams. So many times I shattered the peace of the night with my screams; I'm sure the crew was tempted to throw me overboard so they could get a decent night's rest. Every time we sighted another ship I was consumed by fear until the sailors reassured me that it was not the pirate vessel I dreaded coming to punish me for my cruel neglect of Aimee.

I told my daughter tales of my carefree youth, painting her beautiful word pictures of sunshine, white sandy beaches, warm turquoise water, a plentitude of fruit and flowers and birds with plumage every color of the rainbow, and air that always smelt of sugar. Soon I was as excited as she was; Martinique was already working its magic on me. I told her about Aimee and how we had once dared hold out our palms for the voodoo queen's scrutiny. Hortense particularly relished the old tale I had been brought up with about how the fer-de-lance always knew before any human when our volcano, Mount Pelée, was about to erupt. It was then that these serpents, who always kept to the bushes and brambles, and preferred night to day, came down from the mountain and slithered through the streets of Fort Royal in broad daylight, seeking a place of greater safety, terrifying everyone not just with their poisonous presence but also with the dire warning it carried.

When we sailed into the harbor all my excitement perished. Hortense clutched at my hand and stared doubtfully up at me. She had been expecting paradise, and so had I, but the world of my youth had vanished like ashes on the wind. The air no longer smelled of sugar, but of carnage, charred wood, gunpowder, and dead and rotting flesh. The dangerous fever called revolution that was afflicting Paris had spread to my native land and infected the slaves. They were now seeking revenge for years of enforced servitude and torture, all the beatings, brandings, blindings, mutilations, drownings, hangings, and rapes. I still shuddered at the memory of slaves found guilty of some terrible transgression being bound, slathered head to toe with honey, and left to perish in the utmost agony atop anthills.

A hundred bonfires turned night to day and the voodoo drums never stilled; some of the *Grands Blancs* had been driven mad by the constant rhythm. They were afraid to close their eyes at night for fear their nightmares would become waking reality. Some had even taken poison rather than die at the hands of their vengeful slaves.

The heads of white men, stumps bloody and buzzing with flies, eyes stone gray and blind, adorned pikes planted at every crossroads and field of neglected sugarcane. And there were the bodies of infants, the charges of seemingly devoted black nursemaids, who had been spirited away into the jungle, then brought back speared upon swords, their little dead limbs dangling grotesquely like broken dolls.

Some wives and daughters had also been taken away, deep into the jungle where their menfolk dared not follow, and forced into naked servitude to the black men who used to wait upon them hand and foot in their plantation houses. Sometimes their captors, like cruel plantation overseers, dressed in leather waistcoats and breeches, with gold hoops in their ears, menacingly toting machetes and whips, brought them back and tauntingly paraded them before their menfolk, who were powerless to do anything against "that vast army of black devils." These once proud women were forced to show themselves, stark naked, covered in bruises, their heads hung low with shame, their hair cropped short so they could not cover themselves with their long tresses. Many had their pale lily-white bellies swollen great with black babies conceived in the course of rape. Their captors groped, fingered, and fondled them openly, knowing each touch wounded and disgusted their menfolk to the core. Even if they somehow got their women back they would always regard them as tainted; no one would ever be able to forget.

I was *terrified*. I couldn't rest. I felt like I had blithely led my little girl by the hand straight into a viper's nest and urged her to take up and stroke a fer-de-lance like a pet. I wanted to run away, but there was nowhere to run to; no place on the island was safe. All we could do was wait and hope and pray for a ship to come carry us away, and that we would be amongst the lucky exodus to make it aboard. No vessel could hold all those anxious to flee this island of terror.

Life had become a tense and terrible waiting game—waiting for the attack we all knew was coming, waiting for a ship, for rescue, for armed or divine intervention, hoping that it would arrive in time, praying that death, if it came, would be mercifully swift, not long, drawn out, torture. I was not the only one tormented by memories of seething anthills and screams.

At Trois-Ilets, Papa, in a posture of weary defeat, sprawled in an armchair and drank rum all day; he just couldn't bear to face reality. Mama, ravaged by illness herself, tirelessly nursed Manette. My poor little sister had lost most of her hair and several of her teeth had fallen out. The fever had left her wizened and frail, like a little old yellow lady, instead of the pretty tomboy I remembered. The girl who had dreamed of disguising herself as a boy and going to sea to fight pirates or perhaps become one despaired of ever getting a husband now that her looks were gone at only twenty-one. The incessant drumming and fear of being murdered by their own slaves had sapped their strength and will to live. They were so listless, so empty eyed; it was almost as if the voodoo drums had cast a spell turning them all into zombies, the living, walking dead.

No one said anything about the failure of my marriage. It turned out that Alexandre had behaved *so* badly—like "the most pompous ass in creation," Papa said—flaunting his mistress and bastard son all over Fort Royal, brazenly trying to buy ill reports of my youthful follies, bedding any willing woman white, yellow, or black, running up debts left and right with any merchant who would extend him credit, handing out copies of Choderlos de Laclos's scandalous novel *Les Liaisons Dangereuses* and proudly proclaiming that he was the model for the profligate rake, the Vicomte de Valmont, and moaning like the world was about to end when he was laid low with a tropical fever, that practically the whole island had cheered, and there was even dancing in the streets, when he finally sailed back to France.

When I asked about Aimee, Mama merely sighed and shook her head. She crossed herself, murmuring phrases such as "better off dead" and "a fate worse than death." Aimee's parents had lately died of grief; they had been buried while I was still at sea. Their hearts were so broken and battered by sorrow they could not force themselves to be strong and stay alive for the one little girl they still had left.

Fifteen and still dressed in deepest mourning, for her parents as well as her lost sister, Marthe had gone weeping to the altar to marry the ancient Guillaume Marlet, the proud owner of Anse d'Arlet, the most prosperous coffee plantation in Martinique. Poor little girl, she didn't know what else to do with herself. Unsophisticated and almost painfully shy, Marthe had never been alone; she'd clung to her parents and familiar home rather than follow Aimee to France. The big, wide world had seemed so frightening to Marthe; tales of the unrest in Paris terrified her and she begged her parents never to send her there. She was far too young and naïve to be burdened with managing a plantation that required a shrewd head and constant care to thrive. The day after she buried her mother and father, with a blue marble memorial stone for Aimee between them, that gnarled and age-spotted old man, burning with desire for Marthe's tender, innocent young flesh, had come along and told her *exactly* what she needed to hear—that he would always be kind and loving and take care of her so that she need never want or worry about a single thing as long as she lived; even after he was gone his fortune, combined with hers, would continue to provide for her. In her position, I would have said *yes* too.

When I called on her, Marthe seemed as wan, vacant eyed, and lifeless as my parents. She looked like a tiny stick-limbed doll half-reclining on her husband's opulent gold brocade sofa in her black mourning gown; she barely seemed to have the strength to sit up. She had little to say and tears streamed from her eyes the whole awkward time. When I rose to take my leave, she pressed a miniature portrait of Aimee into my hand. It was set in a golden oval frame with a bail at the top that a ribbon or chain could be threaded through. The likeness was said to be an excellent one. There had originally been three; her parents had gone to their graves wearing theirs.

"I thought you might like to have it since you knew her better than I," Marthe croaked in a hoarse whisper as yet more tears seeped from her swollen red eyes.

The portrait had been painted in Paris the year before Aimee boarded that doomed homeward-bound ship ironically named *Lazarus*. Golden-haired and sapphire-eyed, gowned in blue silk and white muslin and lace ruffles, with blue ribbons and white flowers in her hair, she was even more beautiful than the ghost girl who haunted my dreams. "What a waste!" I whispered every time I looked at that sweetly smiling face. Such beauty and grace lost forever! She deserved so much better than rape and a watery grave. I put the miniature portrait on a ribbon and wore it around my neck as a penance, to remind me to never again neglect anyone I loved or who was kind enough to love me.

I was afraid the drums and constant state of terror would drive me mad. As the days, then weeks, and months, dragged sluggishly past, the only thing that kept me strong and fighting to resist the strength-sapping languor was Hortense. I constantly reproached myself. I had thought I was doing the right thing, bringing her out of the hotbed of revolutionary fervor France had become to a world I remembered as safe and sugar sweet, only to discover that it was on fire with the same ferocious fever.

On the humid, still night when the slaves finally attacked, I thought only of my daughter. I leapt from my bed, barefoot, clad only in my sheer muslin shift, and snatched Hortense from the cot where she was sleeping at the foot of my bed. I thought of nothing but our survival—not money, jewels, clothes, or even family.

With Fortune barking at my heels, I ran down the stairs and out of the house, plunging boldly into the black night. I never looked back—I was afraid that fear would freeze me—not even when I heard the bloodcurdling screams and saw the hellish flicker of the scarlet flames casting dancing shadows upon the white sands of the beach and reflected in the dark sea. Shells sliced like knives through my bare feet. More than once the soft, shifting sands caused me to stumble and fall, but each time I picked up Hortense and kept going, running toward the sea where, in the distance, I could see the silhouettes of tall ships etched against the midnight sky. Warships! They were coming to save us!

Suddenly there was a deafening crash that shook the earth beneath my feet. I fell hard as a shower of white sand and shrapnel rained down on us. A high-pitched ringing filled my ears, blotting out every other sound. I feared I had been struck deaf, but it only lasted a few moments. I sat there stunned and bleeding from a myriad of tiny, fine cuts, feeling as though my skin had been rubbed with sandpaper, cradled in a crater of sand, with Hortense wailing beside me as she tried to rub the gritty sand from her eyes and Fortune whining and nudging me, begging me to take him in my arms. A cannonball had landed not even three feet from us.

Only then did I look back. A legion of what looked like fierce black devils, clutching cutlasses, machetes, and flaming torches, was running across the beach, only the shifting sands, sucking at their feet and throwing them off balance, slowing them down. The night was alive with drumbeats and gunshots and a thousand voices— I could hear them now—chanting, shouting, wailing, and screaming. Another cannonball roared through the air and exploded nearby, raining scorching sand down on us again.

Behind the demon army, Trois-Ilets, my childhood home, went up in flames. But I didn't have time for tears. *I'll weep tomorrow,* I told myself, as I snatched up my daughter and ran. At the water's edge, gasping as the salt stung my torn and bloody feet, I hoisted Hortense onto my back and plunged blindly into the sea and began swimming toward the ships. Fortune paddled beside me. I feared his tiny pug legs would not be able to keep up and that I would have to watch, helplessly, as my little dog drowned. But I couldn't stop, not even for my beloved Fortune; I couldn't carry him and swim too.

I heard shouting and splashing behind me. Hortense, my sweet, chubby girl, clinging to my back, was weighing me down, but I would rather drown than die at the hands of those black devils. Every inch of me was aching and weary, pain shot arrows through my limbs and back, and I longed to stop and rest . . . to catch my breath . . . just for a moment . . . but I couldn't. I *had* to keep going; if I didn't I feared I would sink like a stone and those behind us were getting closer, always closer, every moment. I *had* to keep going.

A cannonball streaked through the air, high above our heads, and landed on the beach behind me. I heard the screams of dying men. Severed arms and legs landed in the water all around us. I wanted to tell Hortense to close her eyes, but it was too late; she had already seen. The ships were awake and alive, firing on the rampaging slaves. I was near enough to see men swarming like ants across their decks. Then—miracle of miracles! I knew then that there truly *is* a God!—a rowboat was coming toward us. Strong arms fished us from the sea. Even Fortune.

Safe in the little boat, wrapped in a seaman's cloak, I looked back and watched the bonfire that had once been my beautiful home. I thought of Mama, Papa, Manette, and Rosette, my secret half sister who had grown up alongside me, schooled to serve me as my maid. Had they been murdered in their beds? Or, by some miracle, had they also been saved? My ears began to ring again; then everything went dark and I felt my head slump against a strong shoulder.

When I awakened I was on board the battleship called *Sensible*. I was in an officer's cabin, lying on his bed, wrapped in a wool blanket, with Fortune curled up, snoring, beside me, his fur stiff with salt just like the wild, tangled mess of my hair. Beneath the blanket, I suddenly realized, I was naked save for Aimee's sweet, serene face resting in the hollow of my throat. My face flamed as I wondered who had taken my shift from me. The door opened and I quickly sat up, hugging the blanket close around me, as a man in uniform came in and gently pressed a steaming cup of black coffee into my hands. Was he the one who had undressed me?

"You're safe now, Rose," he addressed me familiarly in a voice from the past.

Memory came flooding back—a naval uniform and a white satin ball gown lying crumpled on the beach; discarded stockings entwined like amorous snakes; warm water splashing against my naked skin as a pair of strong arms enfolded me and a pair of lips grazed my ear, whispering words of love. Below the water's surface, his limbs entwined with mine. I felt his manly hardness against my feminine softness. I had never been so tempted to surrender to the passion.

Lieutenant Scipion du Roure, tall, lean, and ginger haired, with skin bronzed by the sun and what was surely one of the world's whitest and most dazzling smiles, towered over me like a sun god.

Then I remembered the most important thing. "Hortense!" I cried, my bleary, sand-grazed eyes darting frantically about me.

"She's safe, with the ship's cook," Scipion hastened to reassure me, reaching out just in time to keep me from spilling the cup of hot coffee on my lap. "He's a proud papa with a daughter her age, so they're getting along just fine; he's telling her stories and letting her help him make biscuits."

Relieved, I slumped weakly back against the wall, surrendering to the exhaustion that was fast overwhelming me; even with the ache still pulsing through my limbs and back, I wasn't sure how long I could keep my eyes open. It felt like the ship was my cradle and the waves were trying to rock me to sleep.

Scipion understood and took the cup of coffee from me. "You need sleep more than you need this," he said as he set it aside.

"But first, let me tend to your wounds," he said. "I'm afraid those cuts will fester if I don't."

As he moved about the cabin, fetching a basin of water, a jar of ointment, and a roll of linen bandages, I touched my face and then looked down at my bare arms, legs, and feet. I was covered in a multitude of little red, stinging cuts, most of them thankfully so fine they would not leave scars. My feet had suffered the worst— long red, jagged cuts along the sides and on the soles. They looked like some madman had attempted to shred them with knives.

Scipion drew up a small three-legged stool and carefully washed my face, arms, and legs, gently daubing ointment onto each cut; then he took my feet onto his lap, into the basin, and bathed and bandaged them. When he was done, he helped me to lie down, drew the blanket up to my chin, and kissed my brow.

"Go to sleep, Rose," he whispered. "Tomorrow will be a new and brighter day."

And it was! Each of the next fifty-two days we spent at sea was brighter than the one before. The sky might have been cloudy and gray, but inside Scipion's cabin I felt the sun shining radiantly down upon me. And oh, how I basked and gloried in it! I cursed the voyage for being so swift.

One of the officers had been bringing home a bolt of gay yellow cotton covered with tiny blue flowers as a gift for his daughter, but since Hortense's need was clearly the greater—like me she had nothing to wear but a thin muslin shift—he gave it to her. A sailor, who had been apprenticed to a tailor before he went to sea, stitched a neat little frock for her. And another officer presented her with the red satin dancing slippers intended for his own little girl's birthday. Every evening the sailors sat in a circle and made music with Hortense right in the middle, dancing and singing for them. They adored her one and all.

As for myself, I found I didn't mind my conspicuous lack of garments; I was more than content to stay in Scipion's bed even after my shift had been cleansed with rainwater and dried out and the aforementioned sailor who was skilled with a needle had fashioned me a dress out of odds and ends of spare cloth that he found about the ship or were offered up by the crew.

I broke my rule and took a young man as my lover and, for the first time in my life, I fell in love, *truly* in love.

Caught up in passion's thrall, I ignored reality. Martinique was Scipion's world, but it was no longer mine. I had no desire ever to go back; the slaves' rebellion had spoiled it for me. But he would be going back, just as soon as the *Sensible* took on fresh supplies and men. He was determined to douse the hellish fires of revolution, to rebuild the gentle, languid world he had always known and loved, and to start anew. He was ready to give up the sea for a plantation and a family.

A family! How could I have been so foolish and reckless? Without the special herbal teas Rosette brewed for me there was nothing to keep my womb from quickening, but I could no more have insisted that Scipion withdraw at the crucial moment than I could have cut off my own hand with a butter knife. Our passion was too intense to be interrupted! Yet I was quite certain that I didn't want another child and Scipion said he wanted a dozen; for his future wife's sake I hoped he was joking. I loved the two children I had like a lioness loves her cubs, I would fight for them and I would die for them, but I was rather inept at providing for them. Being pregnant would keep me out of the social whirl for *months,* my lovers would leave me, and then how would we live? I was going back to Paris with far less than I had left with! I hadn't a coin to my name, I was barefoot, and I didn't have one decent dress to stand up in.

Wisely, I didn't tell Scipion of my suspicions. I let him think that the horrors of my ordeal—that army of black devils chasing after me; the cannonball landing so close to me; seeing my childhood home consumed by flames; my uncertainty about my family's fate—had temporarily stopped my monthly flow. I assured him I would be all right again once I was back in Paris. It was not *exactly* a lie—I knew a woman who could help me.

We knew as we stood on deck, watching the silhouette of Brest—the same seaport that had given me my first dismal welcome to France—appear upon the horizon, that we could never agree. We two could never be one; it was foolhardy even to think so.

Martinique—that was the true sticking point. Even if peace was restored and the plantations rebuilt and the smell of sugar hovered in the air again, and there were fields of sugarcane, coffee, and cocoa waiting to be harvested as far as the eye could see, and the drums only sounded on the nights of voodoo rituals, I still wouldn't want to go back.

I was selfish; I wanted Scipion to stay in Paris with me. But Scipion despised the shallow, artificial life, constantly changing fads, and fickle morals of Parisian society. He disdained the so-called march of progress the Revolution with all its talk of liberty, equality, and fraternity was ushering in. He questioned its principles and intentions; he said its ideology was as full of holes as a moth-eaten coat. He wanted the grand old, placid, peaceful life of his childhood in Martinique back: evenings spent taking his ease on the veranda after a day riding out to inspect the fields; visits to friends and family at neighboring plantations; monthly trips to Fort Royal to purchase supplies and dance with girls in white satin at the Governor's ball; nights of love with a devoted wife; and a big white house filled with happy, laughing, carefree children.

But that was not the life for me. I found the pace of Martinique, even at its best, far too slow after Paris. Now when I remembered the years I had spent on the island everything seemed sluggish and dull in a maddening way instead of lovely and languid. Paris had become my home and I *longed* for its fast pace and pleasures. I was ready to throw myself back into its mad, giddy whirl. I would try to stop my ears to all the boring and danger-tinged talk of politics and revolution and dance away from anyone who seemed too serious. I just wanted to be happy, have money to spend, beautiful dresses to wear, and, most of all, to have fun and try not to think about tomorrow.

CHAPTER 9

———◇———

The moment I set foot off the *Sensible* a crowd surrounded me. "Citizeness Beauharnais?" asked those who did not know me. "Citizeness Beauharnais!" cried those who recognized me, their eyes lighting up at the sight of me despite my bedraggled, woebegone appearance with my crude patchwork gown, straggling, unwashed hair, and bare feet.

Suddenly I found myself being hefted up high onto the shoulders of strong men and carried in triumph to the inn. All around me people waved and cheered and blew kisses and threw flowers at me. For the life of me, I couldn't understand why, unless it had something to do with my escape from Martinique. But how could they have known about that? Still, I smiled and waved back; I didn't want to appear standoffish or rude.

Scipion trailed along behind us, the lone frowning face in the jubilant crowd, with Hortense clutched protectively against his chest and Fortune scampering along beside him, barking and nipping at the ankles of anyone who threatened to tread on him.

At the inn I was given the best room. The first thing I asked for was a bath. A tub was brought without delay and placed by the fire along with perfumed soap and towels, and a hearty meal and strengthening red wine were laid out on a table nearby.

An assortment of dresses, shoes, hats, and all the other garments necessary to equip the wife of the Revolution's brightest shining star—Alexandre Beauharnais (he had doffed the aristocratic "de" along with his title)—lay spread out upon the bed, most in the requisite revolutionary red, white, and blue.

There was also a bound copy of Alexandre's speeches, which I found so boring I regretted in years to come that I had not saved it to use as a sort of literary sleeping potion on all the long, restless nights that lay before me.

Alexandre was now the darling of Paris. With his blond hair tied back with a black ribbon, natural and unpowdered, in his austere black suit and plain white neck cloth, with a tricolor rosette blooming from his lapel, and steel instead of silver buckles on his black shoes, he shunned and distanced himself from his aristocratic birthright. Every time he stood up in the National Assembly, which now ruled the nation while the King and Queen languished in prison, people poured in, crushing and falling over one another, and spilling out of every door and window, to hear Alexandre's rousing speeches. They hung on his every word as though their very lives depended on what he would say.

I attended one of his speeches once—once was enough. I was given a seat of honor away from the crush of worshipful humanity screaming his name. I must admit I was not impressed. I hid my yawns behind my fan and had to jab myself with a pin to stay awake. It seemed to me that he talked a great deal but never really said anything. But every time he uttered one of the magic words— *liberty, fraternity, equality*—the crowd stood up and cheered and threw their hats in the air. In the speech I heard, Alexandre must have used those words at least fifty times.

Afterward, crude, dirty men in the clothes of the common man— loose, ragged striped trousers, red carmagnole jackets, liberty caps, and clogs—carried him from the Assembly on their shoulders into the nearest tavern. Women followed, pelting him with flowers. While he sat inside and drank his beer and ate sausages, *hundreds* of people gathered in the street outside, swaying and holding hands, singing songs about liberty and brotherhood, hymns of freedom and equality.

I thought the whole spectacle was absurd, but I forced myself to keep smiling. I pretended that I was proud and adored my husband just as much as those people in the street did.

Even though we were estranged and parted, I, rather than whatever woman was his mistress of the moment—and apparently there were many mistresses and many moments, but who was I to judge?—was the one the public had chosen to adore alongside Alexandre.

I had left Paris deeply in debt and dependent on the generosity of aged gentlemen, but I had come back to find myself famous, celebrated, and adored, without my having done a *single* thing to deserve it. Everyone knew my name and wanted to know me. Everyone wanted to hear about my daring escape from the slave uprising in Martinique and to see my scars. My picture was sold on every street corner, often framed alongside Alexandre's as though we still cared for each other; our estrangement never penetrated the public's imagination. Women were avid to know, and then imitate, what I was wearing, and more men than I could count wanted to be nice to me and pay my bills. I was able to pay for a dancing master and music lessons for Hortense and a lovely white-haired spinster with steel-framed spectacles came twice a week to teach her to paint roses on teacups—her future husband would be so pleased! When I took up residence in an elegant white house on the rue Saint Dominique everyone wanted to be invited to dine at my table and dance in my ballroom. People climbed the fences just to pluck roses from my garden, to take home and press to have a souvenir of me. They fought just to touch my hand or the hem of my gown and to hear my soft, husky voice addressing them; men told me they could die happy now that they had heard me speak their name. If I dropped my handkerchief, rather than gallantly returning it someone would run away with it, calling back over their shoulder that they would cherish it like a holy relic until their dying day. When I rode out in my carriage handsome young men would unhitch the horses and put themselves into harness and pull me through the city streets, even out into the country for a picnic if that was where

I wished to go. I *loved* being famous! And to think I owed it all to Alexandre!

Maybe Euphemia David had not been wrong after all? Alexandre was so popular perhaps the Parisians, even though they said they were done with kings and queens, would elect him their emperor and we would reconcile and he would cover me with diamonds and ardent kisses and set upon my head the crown of empress. I was certain I could see my future unfolding before me like the regal purple velvet carpet I would walk upon on the day of my coronation, leading right up to the altar where I would be, at long last, crowned. Every night, before sleep closed my eyes, I lay awake planning my coronation gown. It would have to be red, white, and blue of course, to pay homage to the revolution that had paved the way to my throne.

I was so caught up in my newfound fame that I forgot all about Scipion. I didn't even have a chance to thank him and say good-bye before he sailed back to Martinique.

"Safe voyage and happy life, my love," I whispered when I realized that he had gone.

I tried to be stoic, but I couldn't quite manage it.

"Why didn't he come to see me one last time?" I wailed to Fortune, and flung myself weeping onto my bed, supremely conscious of the fact that the *one* man I truly wanted was not there to share it with me.

For the first time, I had a tiny niggling feeling that perhaps fame wasn't everything. I had the sudden sad realization that even if I pulled myself together, dried my tears, painted my face, and put on my prettiest gown and went out to dance and let the masses adore me, no matter how many people surrounded me I would still be lonely. I found such thoughts so disturbing that I quickly banished them from my mind.

I roused myself from my bed of sorrow and hastily scrawled a note to the midwife I knew who could void my womb of its mistake.

She was prompt in coming to my aid the next day. She had a sure and steady hand with her long bone knitting needle. I trusted her and was certain I would soon recover. After she had left me and I lay in bed, atop an old quilt to spare the fine linen sheets, with my womb racked by cramps and still seeping blood, I read the letter that had come that morning from Martinique.

Mama was alive, thank God, but Papa and Manette were dead, of disease and no will to live, not, thankfully, murdered in their beds or tortured by the slaves. There was nothing left but ashes, debts, and graves. Papa could leave nothing to me. What little he hadn't squandered had gone up in flames. Mama was determined to rebuild Trois-Ilets, to manage it herself, and make it into the fine plantation it should have been all along. But it would take years before all the debts and loans were repaid and Trois-Ilets began to yield a *true* profit. I wished her luck, but that was all I could give her. I felt like I had suddenly become an orphan; the place I had always thought of as home wasn't home anymore. There was no going back anymore, only forward. I had become a true daughter of Paris.

CHAPTER 10

———◄○►———

Every star that rises must also fall. Adored today, reviled tomorrow. And so it was with Alexandre. He became so caught up in his speechifying that he neglected his military duties. Something he was responsible for went terribly wrong, I'm not sure exactly what—perhaps a battle was lost, or too many men were killed, or some aim was not accomplished—and his star plummeted down to earth. Those who had once cheered and kissed him cursed and spat at him. Instead of throwing flowers, they pelted him with horse dung scooped up out of the streets.

He was taken to Les Carmes, the former Carmelite convent that was now the most abysmal prison in Paris. *Abandon hope all who enter here* should have been engraved in the stone above the door. It was rare indeed for anyone who went in to ever walk out again except to go bow before the Revolution's killing machine, Madame Guillotine.

When I heard the news, I decided to leave Paris and go to the country. I was dancing too close to the edge of the precipice. I must think of my children.

Eugène, my dear little man, was back with me. Alexandre and military school had not spoiled Eugène's sweet nature at all; he was just as loving as ever. He was determined to be the man of the house and protect his little sister and me. Most likely they would soon lose their father, and I didn't want them to lose me too; the world is not kind to orphans. So I made up my mind to live as quietly and inconspicuously as possible until the danger had passed.

Paris was now a *very* dangerous place. Robespierre, with his mad delusions that made him see an enemy around every corner, was the man of the hour. Everyone was suspect. Anyone nobly born or with any aristocratic associations, even the most tenuous, was suspect and liable to be arrested. Envy and revenge, the pettiest of grudges, were enough to get rid of a rival, enemy, erstwhile lover or friend, or inconvenient relation; in those days many a detested mother-in-law ended her life upon the scaffold. All one had to do was whisper their name in the right ear or write it on a slip of paper and drop it in a box. The guillotine was venerated and worshipped like a saint; it became the most popular form of entertainment for the common people. Women took their knitting and sat and watched the heads fall.

The King had his neck shaved by the National Razor, one of the many pet names for the killing machine, and his wife, Marie Antoinette, soon followed.

Before I left Paris, I watched from a window, for one last sight of her, as the crude wooden tumbril rolled slowly past, its wheels bumping clumsily over the cobblestones. There were no cushions, no grand gilt-trimmed carriages, at the end for Marie Antoinette. How sad and weary she looked in her loose white gown and mobcap, adorned by nothing but her dignity. A pale, pathetic figure, old beyond her thirty-eight years, with her hair, blanched white by sorrow, crudely hacked off, she stumbled and stepped on the executioner's toes as she struggled to mount the thirteen steps of the scaffold with her hands bound behind her back.

"Pardon, monsieur, I did not mean to do it," were her last words. One had the sense that she was apologizing for so much more than treading on one man's toes. I also think she was ready to be done with it all. She had learned by then that she could never win. I heard it said later that when she left her prison cell and someone tried to speak some comforting words, about the swiftness of this method of death, she declared that dying is easy, it takes far more courage to live.

*   *   *

I took a house in Croissy, but it wasn't far enough.

They came for me on Easter Sunday, not an hour after I had tucked the children into their beds. The sun had barely set on what had been a pleasant day with a picnic in the rose garden behind our house. We were a patriotic family and had made our own Tree of Liberty, decorating it with tricolor rosettes and red, white and blue streamers. We danced around it until we fell down dizzy and then we had some more lemonade and cake. Then I had sat in the grass, leaning back on my hands, with my children's golden heads resting in my lap, and gazed at the château of Malmaison, glimmering in the distance, through the trees, across a wide green park, and dreamed that it was mine.

It was glowing a delicate buttery-yellow gold in the afternoon sun, its gray slate roof touched with the blue of the sky, and I thought it was the most beautiful house in the world. I knew it would give joy to anyone who lived there. I imagined writing to Mama in Martinique and asking her to send me seeds and cuttings of the tropical plants that grew there. I would hire a skilled gardener to play nursemaid and nurture them along in the hothouse I would erect for this purpose. My guests would be amazed to see them. I would become famous again, for my graciousness and hospitality, my rare plants, and my beautiful home, and everyone would wheedle and vie for invitations.

I was *terrified,* but I can't honestly say that I was surprised. I, as Alexandre's wife, was guilty by association, though I had never socialized or reconciled with him. A legal separation and emotional estrangement were not enough to save me; I had basked in the sun of his fame. Alexandre had been a vicomte and I his vicomtesse, his father was a marquis, and my father had, in his childhood, served as a page to Louis XV at Versailles. It meant nothing that we had cast our titles aside and now called ourselves "Citizen" and "Citizeness."

No one cared now that Alexandre had served his country well, in both army and Assembly, or that I, abiding by revolutionary law, which ordained that each child must be instructed in a useful trade, had apprenticed my son to a carpenter and my daughter to a dressmaker and none of us was ever seen without the tricolor prominently displayed upon our person. My pug even wore a tricolor collar. I sent my daughter to her lessons with tricolor ribbons in her hair, and my son wore a sash. I even bathed with red, white, and blue ribbons in my hair and a tricolor rosette always bloomed between my breasts on my sheer white muslin nightgowns. I can truthfully say I was never naked; I always had the tricolor on me. No one could ever take me by surprise and catch me without it. But none of that mattered.

We were damned by our past pretensions. There would be no mercy for us. It was only a matter of time, of playing that waiting game I had learned so well in Martinique where the drums beat incessantly and the slaves congregated outside with the evilest intentions. I was to join Alexandre at Les Carmes and wait to be called to make my curtsy before Madame Guillotine. In the meantime, I could only hope and pray for a miracle.

Careful not to wake them, I kissed my children good-bye and left them to the care of their governess, Mademoiselle Lannoy. As I embraced her, I whispered in her ear where my money box was hidden. She wept and pleaded with me to let her wake Hortense and Eugène, so that they might have the consolation of seeing me one last time. I refused, telling her, "I could not bear to see them cry. It would deprive me of all strength."

I took Aimee's portrait from about my neck and pressed it into Mademoiselle Lannoy's hand as a gift for Hortense, who always delighted in my tales of the two little girls sneaking out to see the voodoo queen who foretold a royal future for each. Time and again Hortense had begged me to tell her that story. She always refused to believe that Aimee was dead, her golden beauty lost to the deep, dark sea, insisting that she was alive and following her own road to a crown just like me. I wished that I could believe that too.

Fortune whimpered and tried to follow me. I picked him up tenderly, petted him and kissed his little pug nose, then entrusted him too to the safekeeping of Mademoiselle Lannoy.

As I followed the guards out the front door I hurriedly threw a cloak over my white muslin gown. The bold tricolor sash I wore cinched tightly about my waist and the red, white, and blue rosettes floating in the waves of my free-flowing black hair failed to persuade them that I was a good daughter of the Revolution, loyal and true. I had been foolish to think that dressing the part would save me.

That night I entered Hell, the dwelling place of the desperate and the damned, and became one of them. Three hundred lost souls were crammed into what had once been the abode of Christ's earthly brides. Rats darted across my path and I shied back and instinctively turned to run, but my stone-faced guards pushed me onward. I gagged repeatedly at the stench of unwashed bodies and human waste. It was so strong and foul that my eyes began to stream. The gray stone walls and the floor beneath my feet were thick with a foul-smelling slime, and in the dim light of the flickering torches—mounted high so no prisoner's hand could touch them—I bumped into a pail overflowing with piss. The white ruffled hem of my dress was stained yellow and brown before I even entered the prison proper.

There they were, the aristocratic enemies of France, damned because of who they were or who they knew, sitting on piles of straw, weak and wretched, in filthy flea-ridden, stinking dishabille but determined to die with their dignity intact. Every eye turned to look at me, acknowledging and accepting me with almost imperceptible nods as one of them. Rats and black beetles scuttled amongst them, burrowing into the straw or the folds of the women's skirts, but they had become accustomed and, for the most part, ignored them; precious few, I saw, had the spirit to resent and squash or slap away such vermin.

Some of the women were fully dressed; they sat with their backs as straight as though an iron rod had been inserted down their spines, hands folded primly in their laps, eyes staring straight ahead. Others wore only soiled and grimy shifts or flimsy nightgowns, feet bare or in stained satin mules, some trimmed with fur or wisps of feathers. Some wore their hair high and proudly pinned; others let it fall down in snarls and greasy hanks. Some, surrendering to the inevitable, had cropped their hair to save themselves the indignity of submitting to the executioner's shears and to make the lice easier to manage. There were men in full military dress who retained their proud, erect carriage, white-wigged courtiers in satin breeches who had remained steadfast in their devotion to their sovereigns, and others less formal in their shirtsleeves. Some lounged hopeless and empty eyed with their backs slumped against the slime-seeping walls, feet bare, clad only in breeches with their shirts open and untucked, faces unshaven, and their heads wrapped in handkerchiefs to try to keep out the lice. Amongst this last pathetic lot, I found Alexandre.

Wordlessly, he held out his hand to me. It was the first time we had touched since our bodies merged to make Hortense. I was surprisingly grateful and sank down next to him, forgetting for one foolish moment the slime-slick wall behind me, wincing as my back instantly absorbed its cold, rank wetness. Before I had lived one full day in prison my white dress would be dark with filth. I shivered, the guards had taken my cloak, and Alexandre put his arm around me. Neither of us spoke a single word. It was funny, in a peculiar, sad way, I thought. Words had always been so important to Alexandre; he had used them to display his superiority and to criticize, scorn, admonish, belittle me and blacken my name, and his stirring speeches had made him the darling of the Revolution, but now there were no words between us. We had no need of them.

I leaned into him, more grateful for a man's touch than I had ever been. I needed him, and he apparently, at long last, needed, or at least wanted, me. In the darkest hours of the night, when the lights had burned down low, I felt his body roll onto mine. All around me, others did the same. Life was slipping fast through our fingers and we were all desperate and determined to grasp and wring each drop of passion and pleasure remaining out of it.

We coupled with the frenzy of animals, grunting shamelessly and clawing at each other's hair and backs as we rutted, not caring if our nakedness was exposed or who saw us. It was the best way we knew to remind ourselves that we were still alive and were still capable of feeling more than desolation and fear. And there was always a chance that as a result of these loveless acts of love a few ladies, maybe even me, might obtain a precious reprieve—pregnancy guaranteed a stay of execution, though women had been known to go directly from childbed to guillotine with their wombs still open and bleeding. But a whole life could change overnight, so think what might happen in *nine months*—the Revolution might end and our world be set right again. We were all playing, and praying, for time.

Though I let Alexandre spend his seed into my body every chance he could, I was past my girlish infatuation with him. I had grown up and knew he was not the man for me, though I had been happy to catch a ride on his coattails when it led to fame and adoration for me. Our reconciliation, though it seemed like a sweet dream that had finally come true, and provided some consolations in the dark days we spent in Les Carmes, would never have survived the harsh sunlight of real life. If we had been set free to walk out of that prison hand in hand Alexandre would be criticizing me and I would be crying before we even made it home to our children.

One of the jailers, Roblatre, a crude, stubble-headed, vulgar man who was constantly scratching and fondling his crotch, singled me out as a special favorite of his. He led me out into the corridor one day, backed me up against the cold, oozing wall, making me shiver with cold and loathing, leaving grimy handprints on my once white skirt as he hoisted it to my hips. As rats and beetles swarmed around our feet, he told me that a privileged few were given cells with mattresses to sleep upon. He could get me into one if I was nice to him. It would be less crowded, with only two other ladies to share it with me. I knew a good bargain when I heard one, so I smiled and reached down and caressed his cock and guided it between my thighs, gasping with feigned delight as he thrust deep inside of me. Afterward, we shared a bottle of red wine that hadn't yet gone sour and a loaf of nearly decent black bread. It was a definite improvement over the usual prison rations—half a bottle of sour red wine and a hunk of black bread hard as stone once a day.

If Roblatre's lust could keep me alive, I would encourage it every chance I got and give him every proof of just how grateful I was. *Anything* to stay alive!

My new accommodations were indeed much nicer. The barred window actually overlooked a garden where roses bloomed. "Fertilized by the blood of those massacred last September," one of my new cellmates, the proud Duchesse d'Aiguillon, informed me, pointing past the roses to a wall still stained with blood.

The Duchesse had been a good friend of Marie Antoinette's cherished favorite, the gentle Princesse de Lamballe, who had suffered great indignities at the hands of an angry mob that ghastly September day. Mercifully, she was half-dead, after being stripped naked and brutally raped by at least a dozen men, "peasants eager for the chance to despoil a princess," when her head had been stricken off, to be paraded on a pike through the streets to the Tuileries, it being their intent to hold it up to the window for the imprisoned queen to kiss. But first, they had stopped along the way at a hairdresser's establishment and ordered the terrified man to dress the dead woman's long golden hair, so Marie Antoinette would be sure to recognize the woman long wrongly regarded as her Sapphic lover.

My other cellmate would both change and save my life, though I didn't know it at the time. Theresa Cabarrus was the most beautiful, fascinating woman I ever saw. A Spanish girl, only twenty years old, the widow of an elderly marquis, which accounted for her being in prison, she was guilty by association, just like me. Her satin-sleek black hair hung down her back like a cloak, grazing the backs of her knees, and her eyes were the color of fine brandy wine. She had the face of an angel, the lush, voluptuous body of a grand courtesan, and the morals of a common alley cat. She was the mistress of Jean Tallien, a journalist raised to power by the Revolution, a clever man who always managed to be on the winning side. She was still wearing the sheer red peignoir, and nothing else, from their last tryst. She had been seized in the night, just like me. They waited to take her until after her lover was gone.

We were two of a kind and became fast friends. Whenever I despaired, Theresa urged me not to.

"Tallien will save us. He will not lose this body to the grave," she would say, flinging the diaphanous red folds open wide and shamelessly revealing the object of his desire. Thanks to the attentions of Roblatre and several other guards, she was still voluptuous, despite the near-starvation diet of prison rations.

Theresa took great delight in her body and loved to show it and share it with everyone; she would gladly give herself to any man, or woman, who desired her, and if there was no one she would pleasure herself. Many nights when we all gathered, huddling fearfully in the common room to hear the dreaded list read out, the names of those destined to die on the morrow, everyone wondering if this night would be their last, Theresa would throw off her peignoir as soon as the jailer finished reading and dance in the nude, performing the gypsy and Spanish dances she had learned in her youth.

"This is all I have, and I will give it gladly, if it can bring even a moment's joy back into their lives and make them forget the fear of death hovering always over our heads," she said.

Her spirit was unbreakable. Even when the rats gnawed at her toes one night while she was sleeping, Theresa didn't shed a tear as I tore strips from my petticoat to bind the bleeding wounds. She just shrugged. "I shall cover the scars with jeweled rings and start a new fashion. A day will come when everyone will know me by the rings on my toes."

In Theresa and through Theresa I found love. She introduced me to a handsome young soldier who kept to his own solitary cell. He was rich and important enough to be able to procure fresh linens and fine wines and meals that, though truly only simple fare, seemed sumptuous to my famished eyes and rumbling belly.

His name was Lazare Hoche; he was a disgraced general, guilty of some offense against the Revolution that he seemed not to be overly concerned about. He stayed in his cell, biding his time, reading books, sipping wine, and writing letters to his little child bride, Adelaide, whose portrait, worn in a golden locket around his neck, he cherished. Theirs was one of those rare marriages based truly on love and I *hated* her every time he spoke her name or something in his cell reminded me of her existence.

He reminded me of a much younger and more dashing incarnation of my first benefactor, the banker Denis de Rougemont. Lazare was handsome beyond words with a head of the waviest dark hair I had ever seen, blue eyes that seemed at times tinged with gray or jade green, and a dazzling, slightly crooked, smile that made my heart melt.

I fell in love the first time I saw him. And he was bored, and perhaps smitten, enough to take me into his bed, filthy and bedraggled as I was. He seemed happy to share himself, and his cell, with me, and even his bathwater and dressing gown. He made me feel strong. I felt safe in his arms. He made me believe that even in the shadow of the guillotine love and life were still possible. I began to dream that perhaps someday, if we were still alive when the Revolution was over, we might be together. My mind conveniently glossed over Adelaide. She was just a child after all and could hardly hold his attention for long. She wouldn't know how; she didn't have the talents of a woman like me, adept in the arts of pleasure. Besides, they had only been married a week before Lazare was arrested, hardly long enough to form a lasting connection. I was certain he was just being sentimental. But then he was taken away from me, after only twenty-six blissful days. His name was on the list one night and I thought I would surely die of grief. But I did not.

Not too long after that Alexandre's name appeared on the list of the damned. I was holding tight to his hand, both of us quaking with fear and holding our breaths, as his name was read out. His face went deathly white beneath his prison beard. He staggered like a man who had just been shot. I took his hand and led him, like a bewildered child, back to my cell. The Duchesse and Theresa understood and left us to ourselves and found somewhere else to sleep that night. Neither of us spoke a single word.

For the first, and last, time in our marriage we touched each other with tenderness and he cared enough to want to please me. The time for the crazed wild animal ruttings had passed; now it was all about comfort and peace and saying good-bye. We made love all night.

Afterward, as the dawn and the scent of roses were softly stealing through the iron-barred window, I took the Duchesse's scissors from their hiding place and cut Alexandre's greasy blond hair to the nape of his neck. Better I, who might have loved him if he had been kind to the little Creole savage I used to be, than the executioner. When I was done, I silently handed the scissors to Alexandre. I turned my back and tried not to cry as he cut off my long black hair. We knew that time had run out for both of us. Once a husband's name was read his wife's would inevitably soon follow. It might be a day, or a week, a fortnight at most, but soon I too would be mounting the thirteen steps of the scaffold to bow before Madame Guillotine.

Alexandre's head was resting on my breast when they came for him. It was time for him to join the other condemned in the cart. He stood and dressed and then, for the first time, spoke to me.

> *"'Base Fortune, now I see that in thy wheel*
> *There is a point, to which when men aspire,*
> *They tumble headlong down; that point I touch'd,*
> *And seeing there was no place to mount up higher,*
> *Why should I grieve at my declining fall?*
> *Farewell, fair queen, weep not for Mortimer,*
> *That scorns the world, and as a traveler*
> *Goes to discover countries yet unknown.'"*

It was obviously a literary quotation, though I knew not the source. I forced a smile, tears raining from my eyes, as Alexandre bowed over my hand and kissed it, gallant as a courtier bidding his queen adieu. I reached out, one last time, with a trembling hand to touch his hair and stroke his neck where, all too soon, the blade would fall.

I watched him walk away from me, biting my lip, *yearning* to run after him, to catch hold of his hand and beg him to stay and tell me who this Mortimer was, to play the schoolmaster and educate this ignorant little Creole. Caught up in the moment, I imagined that I still loved him. When he turned the corner and was lost forever to my eyes, I ran back into my cell and flung myself down on my straw-stuffed pallet. I cried until the stars came out and the jailer returned to read his abominable list of names. Mine was on it. A wife always meekly follows her husband.

I became wildly hysterical, spinning round in circles, grasping out at anyone who came near, screaming, begging, and pleading for my life. "No! I don't want to die! I cannot! I have children! I *have* to live! I have so much life inside of me yet! I *can't* die!"

Some of my fellow prisoners turned uncomfortably away. Others glared hard at me with eyes scornful and withering. *They may take our lives, but they will never take our dignity,* was the code they lived and died by and I was breaking it right in front of their eyes, and in the most shameful way.

Theresa and the Duchesse led me sobbing back to our cell. My knees buckled and they had to drape my arms about their shoulders to support me, my bare toes—my fragile white slippers were long gone—dragging in the slime and grime. They tried to calm and comfort me as best they could, but I would not be soothed. I kept on wailing and weeping.

"Poor soul," the Duchesse said, "I fear she has gone mad."

When Roblatre and another jailer came in I threw myself at them, grasping at their shirts, easily tearing the filthy, cheap cloth, then clawing at their bare, hairy chests with my nails.

"I *can't* die! I *have* to live! I am going to be an empress someday, greater than a queen, Euphemia David said!"

In my frenzied state, I somehow imagined that this revelation would make all the difference in the world, but they just laughed at me.

"*Now* I've heard everything!" Roblatre said.

"No, no, I tell you it is true! It is! I *will* be an empress, greater than any queen, so I *cannot* die! You will see! Euphemia David said so and she is never wrong!"

"Well, when you appoint your household, my dear, pray remember me," the Duchesse d'Aiguillon quipped, "... if I am still living."

Her mockery angered me; she was one of those born aristocrats who, though she might pity me, also looked down upon me. She just couldn't understand how fear could get the better of dignity.

"Laugh if you like, but it is true!" I shouted at her. "Euphemia David said so!"

"I know of no such person," the Duchesse yawned.

By then I was spinning in circles, constantly pleading for my life, denying the sentence, and clinging desperately to Euphemia David's prophecy as though it was the only thing that could save me. The laughing faces of the jailers, the scowling scornful countenance of the Duchesse, and Theresa's worried face and concerned arms reaching out for me, all kept passing me by in a whirl. And then I saw another face! One it seemed I had last seen a lifetime ago—Euphemia David was right there in my cell! I *saw* her! Bloodred *tignon* on her head, the points sticking up like devil horns stabbing the heavens, gold hoops in her ears, bangles on her wrists, a necklace of gilded snake vertebras and fangs around her throat, a fist-sized skull dipped in gold hanging between her breasts, clad in her regal gown made of fifty madras handkerchiefs in all the colors of the rainbow stitched together with golden thread. Her snake, Li Grande Zombi, draped around her shoulders like a living shawl, reared its great head up to kiss the caramel skin of her still-smooth, eternally ageless cheek. Euphemia David smiled at me. "Fear not!" she said, and reached out and touched my brow.

My whole body began to quake then, jerking and spinning just like one of the voodoos when the loas entered their bodies, possessing them at their ritual dances. Head to toe, tremors raced and rippled through me, and in my ears I thought I could hear my blood humming. My eyes rolled up, showing their whites, and my bladder shamelessly voided itself onto the already filthy floor. I heard a scream, as though from far away. I think it was Theresa. Maybe it was me? Then everything went black.

When I opened my eyes again several days had passed. Theresa was sitting, sobbing, beside my mattress, pressing a wet cloth to my burning brow. A doctor had come and gone. He had given me up for dead and advised my jailers not to bother sending me to the guillotine. The fever would soon finish me off, he said. I had at most a week, maybe two, to live.

"Don't cry for me, dear friend," I whispered through my parched and cracked lips. "I shall not die. You will see. . . . I shall live to be an empress. Euphemia David said . . ."

Theresa leapt up, determined to act now. Tears pouring from her eyes, she fumbled the loose stone from the wall and took the bejeweled Spanish dagger, a family heirloom, from the hiding place she had fashioned. Wiping away her tears, she made her way across the little room to the table where our meager supply of paper—another favor from Roblatre—was kept. She dipped our only quill into the last of our ink and scribbled one bold sentence addressed to her lover Tallien: *I die in despair at ever having belonged to a coward like you!*

From over her shoulder, she drew the whip-long black braid of her hair and began sawing at the top of it with the dagger, ignoring me when I begged her to please stop. Theresa had the most beautiful hair, raven black glinting with deep wine-red lights. There was no reason for her to sacrifice it; her name had yet to appear on the list of the damned and she had sworn not to let the lice get the better of her no matter how much they made her scalp itch. She wrapped the note around the dagger and twisted her braid around it. With the last gold piece in her possession and the promise of her body "later tonight," she persuaded Roblatre to deliver her message.

It had the desired effect. When Robespierre stood up to address the National Convention, which had replaced the Assembly as the governing body of France, Tallien shot up like an arrow, waving Theresa's long whip-like black braid in one hand and her jeweled dagger in the other, and roared: "*Down with the dictator!*"

It was the signal everyone had been waiting for. The deputies turned upon Robespierre en masse. Like mad dogs hungry for blood, they chased him through the streets, to the Hôtel de Ville. When they stormed the building, the terrified tyrant tried to kill himself, but his hand was shaking so badly he managed only to shatter his jaw. He only had one shot in his pistol, so he could not try again. He was dragged away to prison in agonizing pain with a bandage tied around his head to keep his jaw from detaching completely. The next morning he kept a fatal rendezvous with Madame Guillotine. The Revolution was over.

CHAPTER II

---◄O►---

Tallien was the hero of the hour and Theresa the heroine. When the prison doors were thrown wide he was there waiting for her, eyes filled with love and arms open, but she didn't run into them. She left him waiting where he stood; it was as though she didn't even see him.

"It's good to be free, to walk in the sun again!" she sighed, ruffling her short-cropped hair and tilting her face up to the sun like a woman welcoming a kiss from her lover.

"Do you love him?" I asked her, discreetly tilting my head toward Tallien.

It occurred to me then that I had never heard her speak of him in terms of affection, let alone passion, except that which he felt for her. When she talked of Tallien, it was always of his usefulness, as though he were a human coatrack or umbrella stand, not a virile flesh-and-blood man.

"He serves a purpose . . . for now." Theresa shrugged, smiling as she was suddenly lifted up high onto the shoulders of two strong men and the people surged around her, offering flowers and praising her as "our Lady of Liberty," the one who had brought about Robespierre's downfall. "She slew the dragon with love! Her love caused her knight to spring into action and save her!"

Laughing, blowing kisses, and waving, she was carried through the streets of Paris, with her legs bare and her breasts spilling out of her tattered and grimy bloodred peignoir. She was the one who was famous now.

But Theresa didn't forget about me. She welcomed me into her world. And what a world it was! Though the killings had stopped, Paris was still the same city of desperate want, where the prices of the bare necessities were constantly rising and people fought tooth and nail over a loaf of bread. But there were still men with money. Paris was full of bankers, profiteers, moneylenders, black-market speculators, army suppliers, contractors, and the rising stars of the new government, and they were willing to pay a charming woman's way.

Those of us who had lived beneath the shadow of the guillotine threw ourselves into a bacchanalian celebration of life. Life was motion, death was stillness, so the party never seemed to stop. As long as we could find a way to have fine clothes to wear, a decent roof over our heads, and a bed to sleep and make love in, we didn't care if we still had to eat stale bread. Life was so precious to us now we could hardly bear to waste even a few precious hours of it sleeping.

Once I had been joyously reunited with Eugène, Hortense, and Fortune and we were all settled comfortably in our new little house, I began to go out every night with Theresa and her friends.

The *Bals des Victimes* were all the rage. Men and women with shorn hair, and thin red satin ribbons tied around their necks in remembrance of those who had died, and as a reminder of how close they had themselves come to death, danced and made love all night. Former prisons, including Les Carmes, were cleaned up and turned into macabre public ballrooms with bloodred walls, decorated with red glass globes on the lamps, crystal skulls, tables patterned like tombstones, and chair backs shaped like coffins and guillotines. Dances were even held in the cemetery of Saint-Sulpice, where people danced and brazenly made love on top of the tombstones, and an open-air dance floor had been erected amidst the ruins of the Bastille. The guillotine was immortalized in jewelry and dances with jerky, bobbing motions mimicking severed heads falling, and chemise and prison smock–style dresses in the pure white of innocence or garish bloodred were the height of fashion. Loose clothing and dim lighting made it so easy for us to spontaneously surrender to our great lust for life. The Revolution had taught us that life could change forever in an instant. We took that lesson to heart and vowed that we would live only in and for that instant and not think, or plan, for the future.

Theresa was the one who set the fashions now and I, having always found it easier to be a follower rather than a leader, went along with her. She found her inspiration in ancient Greece and Rome and began draping her splendid body in clinging, diaphanous gowns gathered by a ribbon or belt just beneath her breasts and flowing down, following every line and curve of her figure, to sweep the floor behind her in the slightest train. They were easy to whip off at the slightest provocation. Gone were the days of needing a maid to both don and doff one's garments; one could be stark naked in seconds. Stays and petticoats were abolished, we wore nothing beneath our clothes, and Roman sandals with long ribbon straps winding about the ankles, sometimes all the way up to the knees, replaced shoes and stockings. Sometimes the dresses had no sleeves, just little straps clasped together with cameos; other times they had tiny puffed or caped sleeves. Flesh was no longer concealed but celebrated, dresses had to be sheer, and sometimes the boldest ladies wore their *décolleté* so low their breasts were left entirely bare, or gowns inspired by Roman togas fastened over a single shoulder, leaving one breast completely exposed. Skirts were sometimes split all the way up to the thigh.

We wore so little now that Theresa once won a bet that every stitch she had on, including her jewelry and sandals, did not weigh more than two gold pieces. She ordered servants to fetch the scales and then she stripped and won the wager. I had to laugh now every time I recalled my face-flaming shame when Aunt Edmée had dressed me in a pink lace negligee on my wedding night. Now I thought nothing of going out in a white gown so transparent that my nipples glowed through like embers—rouging them was second nature to me now—and the "little black forest" was fully on show. I shamelessly advertised everything I had to offer every time I went out my front door.

True to her word, Theresa hid the rat bites on her toes under jeweled rings; she became known as the lady with rings on her toes. We layered our bodies with bracelets, necklaces, and brooches inspired by ancient treasures. Sometimes we wore no jewels at all, only flowers. Rather than let it grow out again, we kept our hair short cropped in the popular coiffure *à la Victime*. Sometimes, just for the fun of it, we wore wigs, usually in wild, vibrant shades of orange, blue, purple, pink, yellow, or green, as well as more natural hues of blond, brunette, black, silver, and red. Between us, Theresa and I owned a collection of sixty, which we happily shared.

We had such fun seeing how outlandish we could be. One day we went out wearing big, curly powder-blue wigs to match the short spencer jackets we wore over our white muslin dresses that were slit up to the thigh to reveal our blue-and-white-striped stockings and black leather high-heeled shoes with huge silver buckles. Another day we went out sporting green wigs to match the green coins embroidered all over our yellow dresses and stockings. We adopted every fad and fancy from long nut-colored gloves to spraying our already sheer gowns with rosewater to make them even more clinging and transparent.

We often went out with our mutual friend Fortunée Hamelin and were collectively known as "The Three Graces." Fortunée was a Creole like me. She had survived the Revolution with her long black curls still down to the small of her back and often crowned them with a bloodred, banana-yellow, or turquoise *tignon* with little black kiss curls framing her face and gold hoops in her ears. It called to mind the old island saying "*La costume est une lutte*"—the art of dress is a contest. We had such fun seeing who could best the other.

I became reacquainted with General Hoche at one of the Victims' Balls. He hadn't died after all; the Revolution deemed him too valuable, so he had merely to bide his time in another prison until it ended. Upon seeing each other, we were so overcome by passion that we fell into each other's arms and made love leaning against the bloodred wall as the dancers swirled past us. But it was only the one time; he was adamant that he still loved his wife and would never leave her, even when I wept and told him that the new government was godless and a divorce was now very easy to obtain and it was a true, complete, and entire separation of the marital bond, leaving both partners free to remarry, unlike the years stuck in limbo I had endured with Alexandre. Theresa had in fact married Tallien because "the lock in wedlock is now so easy to pick; I'll divorce him when I get bored or someone better comes along." But Lazare didn't care, he didn't want a divorce, and he wasn't interested in maintaining me as his mistress.

I tried so hard, but I couldn't make him understand. All I wanted was for someone to take care of me, to keep me safe and never let harm touch me again. I wanted to laugh at fear from the safety of my lover's arms. Why couldn't Lazare Hoche be that man?

CHAPTER 12

I drifted with the tide, taking lovers for pleasure and profit, to supply my needs, and feed my children. But, in moments of quiet, when I was being completely honest with myself, I often lamented that there was no real love in my life except that which my children gave me. The faces of the men were always shifting, blurring, changing, as they came and went in and out my bedroom door; there was never one steady, solid masculine presence in my life. As much as I embraced my freedom, I sometimes found myself longing for a husband—someone rich, good, and kind, who would truly love me and keep me safe, someone I could still be myself with and not lose myself in. Truth be known, I think it was security as represented by a husband that I was truly longing for, more than any actual man.

Though I readily embraced the new philosophy of living only for the moment, there were times when I could not help but think of the future. The lines I saw on my face when I sat down at my dressing table with it scrubbed clean, ready for a fresh application of powder and paint, *made* me think about it.

I was now running with a pack of girls nearer my daughter's age than my own. I was thirty, a full ten years older than Theresa, and some of the reigning beauties of the day were as young as seventeen. I was living my life at an exhausting pace, a dizzying whirl that stilled only in slumber, falling into bed at dawn and rolling out of it at noon to breakfast and a stinging douche calculated to keep my womb empty, spending the afternoon shopping and socializing in sidewalk cafés over cups of coffee or chocolate, and getting ready to start all over again, to dance and love through another reckless night. This way of life, I knew, could not go on forever; there is only so much candlelight, cosmetics, charm, and bedchamber talents can do. Time was running out for me and it was foolish to deny it.

I thought my worries were over when Theresa introduced me to Paul Barras, the new man in power, the most formidable of the five directors of France's latest form of government—The Directory. He was forty, tall, dark, and handsome, and *very* rich, but he was also dishonest, debauched, and diabolical. I soon found out not only was I playing with fire; I was also sleeping with the Devil on his black satin bed in a chamber of mirrors, the better to show him my every weakness, failing, and flaw.

But when one makes a bargain with the Devil one had best keep it. Both my children were completing their educations in the finest schools. Eugène was intent upon a military career and Hortense was the darling of Madame Campan's school, delighting all with her sweet temperament and talent for music and painting. I had a house of my own on the rue Chantereine and was regarded as the lady of Barras's own town and country abodes where I reigned as hostess over every gathering. I had clothes and jewels, the most exquisite décor and rosewood furniture upholstered in sky-blue and rose silk, Etruscan urns filled with fresh flowers every day, crystal chandeliers, silver plate and crystal goblets for my table, servants, a personal maid, a carriage and coachman, and finely bred horses, everything I could possibly want. All my bills were paid without a murmur or even a lift of an eyebrow. Barras never called me a spendthrift or accused me of being lavish; he merely paid my bills without comment. It was *heavenly!*

I should have been happy, but I wasn't. Barras often expected more of me than I wished to give. He was not above sharing me with other men, to cement a business deal, or just for the pleasure of watching. He liked to watch and he liked to have me watch when he bedded other women, and sometimes even other men or young boys. My stomach would turn sickly somersaults whenever I was called into his bedchamber to be his audience, surrounded by mirrors so I would not miss anything, always *dreading* the moment when he would beckon for me to take his place or come and join them on the black satin bed. I tried to pretend to be sophisticated and blasé, to feign enjoyment, but I *hated* every moment of it. I couldn't bear what the mirrors were showing me; I never hated my reflection more. Such evenings could never end soon enough to suit me, but they always seemed to go on forever.

Whenever I tried to decline or showed even a sign of hesitation, Barras's anger would flare. He would show me the Devil hiding inside the man and remind me just how much I owed to him. He was *determined* to break down every single one of my inhibitions, to make me just like him. He would see me with women, dwarves, giants, or even Negroes if such was his pleasure, and it was.

He even ruled my wardrobe. Clothes, he said, did not exist for me unless he said so; I would wear them *only* when he allowed it. Even my transparent white muslin gowns were judged too modest by Barras and he would have me parade around nude before his guests, wearing nothing but a smile, the jewels he bought me, or a chaplet of roses in my hair.

There were days when Theresa, Fortunée, and I would all pile into a carriage, naked save for sandals, shady broad-brimmed hats, and parasols to protect our skin from the sun, and drive out into the country to picnic with Barras and his guests. There would be gauzy tents and canopies set up to further protect our complexions, but nothing to preserve our dignity; that was already lost. We would play blindman's buff and whichever man caught us won our body as his prize; we would never know who was on top of us, inside us, until the blindfold was ripped off at the climactic moment. Other afternoons there were Barras's famous naked hunts with the gentlemen in dapper riding vestments mounted on horses pursuing us as we ran naked through the trees. When they caught us, we were theirs to do with as they pleased. Some nights we dressed as Vestal Virgins and told bawdy fortunes for Barras's guests and promptly dropped our veils and white robes to make them come true. Other nights we painted our bodies white and powdered our hair and posed like living statues. When Barras snapped his fingers we would come to life, writhing lewdly, shedding our scanty sheer white draperies as we danced. Then the orgy would begin.

I was not as uninhibited as Theresa and Fortunée, who would happily walk down the street naked, but I tried. I drank champagne to give me courage because it went straight to my head, quicker than wine. Drunk, I could be free of my inhibitions, free of my conscience, free of me; I could become the woman Barras wanted me to be.

There were mornings when I would wake up to the warm feel of sunlight on my face and the dew on my back. For one sweet moment I would think I was back in Martinique. Then I would sit up and look around me and find myself naked in Barras's garden, surrounded by wine bottles and other slumbering bodies, my clothes nowhere in sight. I would fight back the bile that rose in my throat as I remembered the night before when, to please my all-powerful protector, Theresa, Fortunée, and I had come in to supper nude. It had become something of a ritual. We would go around the table, which seemed a mile long, bending over and dipping a breast into each guest's champagne glass, then offering it to him, or her, to suckle, letting them draw us onto their laps if they wished to fondle, or enjoy like attentions from us. I *despised* myself and how far I had fallen! I was never lewd before I met Barras!

While society might have celebrated Barras's mistress, I *loathed* and *despised* her. I was all for fun and free and easy love, but this was a sort of servitude that had *nothing* to do with love and it certainly was *not* fun, though everyone else seemed to think it was. I often wondered if I was the only one who was pretending. I had become someone I had never meant to be. But I didn't know how to break the chains. I would be *ruined* without Barras. He ruled the republic and society, king in all but name, and I was his uncrowned queen.

Maybe this was what Euphemia David had meant all along? I wasn't married to Barras, at least not yet, but he *did* cover my body with diamonds and ardent kisses. I was his consort—famous, celebrated, talked about, admired, and imitated. When he claimed me as his own I thought all my worries were past, but that happiness, hard won, fast paled when I found out the price I had to pay for it—the degradation and humiliation of being passed around and partnered with those I would never have chosen of my own free will. In private I did shed many, many tears, and yes, I *never* thought I would say it, but I did miss Martinique. Sometimes I revisited it in my dreams. But there was no going back. That life was gone forever.

I kept Aimee's miniature in a drawer now, facedown. I didn't want her to see what I had become. She would be so ashamed of me.

CHAPTER 13

In 1795 Fortune again favored me. I saw a way out. I thought at first it was a step down, but I was very much mistaken.

Fortune's answer came in the improbable form of a skinny little Corsican general with the impossible name of Nabuleone Buonaparte. *Everyone* laughed at him; because of this I felt sorry for him and tried always to be kind to him. I too knew what it was like to be a foreigner—we were both island bred; we had *that* much in common—and considered too savage and uncouth for sophisticated Paris. He was poor, awkward, crude, and rude, with a total disregard for tact; I'm not certain he even knew what it was. He would tell a woman fishing for compliments that her dress did not make her look fat, she was in fact fat. His brown hair hung down around his gaunt face in long, lank greasy strings, his uniform was shabby and ill fitting, and his boots were badly scuffed. Since he could not, or would not, buy gloves, his fingernails were always dirty. At twenty-six he had clearly never known the touch of a woman of elegance and refinement; no wife worth her salt would ever have let him out of the house looking like that.

But despite his boorish manners, he was also capable of great kindness. When private citizens were ordered to surrender their arms and Eugène, most reluctantly, turned over his father's sword,

General Buonaparte intervened. He saw how much it meant to my son and graciously allowed him to keep it as a cherished family heirloom. When I thanked him, the General seemed barely capable of speech; he just stood there, staring at me, drinking me in with his eyes, like he had never seen a woman before. It completely unnerved me.

He had the most intense gray eyes I had ever seen. Those eyes . . . they seemed to be always hungry. They followed me everywhere; they seemed to stare right through my skin and scorch my very soul. It made me uncomfortable just to have him look at me, for the harder he looked, the more I burned. There were times when I found myself blushing and growing flustered like a convent virgin, lowering my eyes and finding some excuse to leave the room, so I could have time to calm and collect myself. That penetrating stare . . . it seemed more intimate than the carnal act itself. Barras seemed to know that the little Corsican was at heart a prude who would not approve of our more bacchanalian gatherings and always invited him on nights when our clothes would stay on and we would behave with some pretense of propriety.

When Barras first introduced the idea, I told him emphatically *no*—"I can do better!" But the ardent young Corsican had scored a great victory over a royalist uprising aiming to put the exiled Comte de Provence on the throne where his unfortunate brother Louis XVI had so lately sat. Barras thought this Buonaparte could be useful, but it was *essential* to ensure his enduring gratitude, so, first came full command of the French army; then came the greatest gift of all—me.

"Take her and marry her," Barras magnanimously told the hot-blooded little Corsican. Barras didn't really care about me at all, only how he could use me to further his own interests.

Buonaparte *burned* with passion, which he poured out to me in letters that seemed written in fire, *blazing* across the countless pages he devoted to me. He was so impatient to get the words out that the pen punched through the paper and there were blots everywhere, like a dog shaking water from its coat after a bath. It made me exhausted and my eyes ache just to read them. He had never been in love before. Love, he believed, weakened a man. I was his Delilah and he was Samson shorn at my feet, but still adoring me, entirely in my power, and he didn't mind at all; he was exactly where he wanted to be. Every time he looked at, or thought of, me he felt "a mad desire to get married." He was a great believer in Destiny, and with me beside him he was certain he would achieve untold greatness. Something about me told him that I was his lucky charm come to life, in human form, so he must always keep me near. Luck would be his as long as I was.

Barras ultimately told me that I might as well take General Bonaparte—he had by then, thank goodness, adopted the French style of his name, Napoleon Bonaparte, making it a more manageable mouthful—for if I didn't, he was done with me. There would be no more favors, no more money. Barras would single-handedly turn society against me. I would be a pariah, shunned and snubbed every time I dared show my face in public. He had raised me and he could also knock me down and ruin me. If Barras turned against me, I knew I could never survive, so I did what I must.

That cold December night, as the snow fell outside my window, I let Bonaparte in to warm me. In the candlelight that is the kindest friend of all to an aging woman, I waited for him in a soft pink negligee made so it would look as though my body were covered entirely in rose petals. Pink, besides being pretty and sweet, is also a kind color; it generously lends its rosy hue to a woman's skin. I had also dressed my bed in it and filled the room with crystal vases of hothouse pink roses.

He was so impatient he didn't even take off his boots. They sullied the pink satin quilt as he fell on top of me and ripped handfuls of faux pink petals off my body in his haste to bare it. There was no time to waste fumbling with vexing ribbons and frustrating fastenings. The act itself was over in five minutes. He was entirely without finesse, like a starving dog attacking a roast chicken. He spent his lust and then he slept, like a child, with his head upon my breast.

He was like no other man I had ever experienced before. Though his eyes and his kisses burned and devoured me and his hands groped and explored all of me, he made me feel like a cold marble goddess, not a flesh-and-blood woman.

He said he loved me, so many times, as though repetition would teach me to believe, but it was *not* true. Bonaparte never *loved* me; he *worshipped* me. When he looked at me he saw only his *ideal* of me, not the flawed, flesh-and-blood woman I really was. The bed where I lay, or the chair where I sat, was like a venerated altar to him before which he must kneel. He told me he wanted to kiss the hem of my gown, my feet, my hands, my lips, my breasts, and "much, much lower down."

Each time I would smile, soft, gentle, and aloof. I humored and indulged him and let him do as he liked. But when he touched me, I had to look down to reassure myself that I had not actually turned to marble; it always surprised me to see my skin yield softly to his touch. And when I caressed him, I was only going through the motions, repeating by rote what experience had taught me about giving pleasure to a man, trading favors for favors. Alexandre was wrong; I wasn't a complete failure at amateur theatricals. My audience was never disappointed; in the theater of the bedchamber I could hold my own against any professional.

When Bonaparte awoke with the dawn, he caressed my sleeping face and kissed me awake. First my brow, each of my eyelids in turn, the tip of my nose, and last, most lingeringly, my lips, turning my waking yawn into a passionate, soul-devouring kiss.

"*Rose,*" he said, then repeated it with a distinct air of disdain, wrinkling his nose as though it stank like a sewer. "*Rose* is far too *common* a name for a woman like you! From this moment on you shall be Josephine—*my Josephine!*"

PART 2

———◆◇◆———

AIMEE

CHAPTER 14

I felt like my life was ending when I was sent away to the convent far across the sea in France. I never wanted to leave Martinique, it was my home and I loved it, and I had never known, or wanted to know, anything else. I was never one of those little girls who dreamed of going to France and being a lady-in-waiting to the Queen or marrying a prince amidst the gilded splendor of Versailles. But I was only nine years old, too young to know what was truly best for me, or to have earned a say in my future.

The day before my ship sailed was a Sunday. I sat on Papa's knee, the full skirts of the white satin and lace dress I had worn to Mass overflowing his lap, and Mama caressed my golden hair as I wept. They reminded me that I was their "precious girl" and they had given me my name—Aimee—because it described me best, I was their "dearly loved" daughter. I had come to them late in life, when their hair was already turning gray, and though God had seen fit to send me a little sister three years later, that did not mitigate the miraculous blessing my birth had been in any way.

"You are our precious pearl," Papa said as Mama fastened a delicate cross of white pearls set in gold filigree about my throat, "and we only want the best for you, even if it means you must leave us."

No one sets such a jewel in base metal or trusts it to the hands of an untried or inferior craftsman, Papa explained, so I must go to Paris for the finishing touch, to the Convent of the Dames de la Visitation.

Papa was known as "a man of iron with a heart of gold," and there was no saying *no* to him. So I stopped wasting precious time weeping and went out to say good-bye to my island home.

I drew the sugar that infused the very air deep into my lungs, trying to hold on to it, determined to carry it away with me, to Paris. My fingers lovingly caressed the bright pink, orange, and yellow hibiscus blossoms and the peculiar orchids that were at once purple and pink, which I had often heard people say had "a lascivious shape," whatever that meant. My hands lingered long over the dear familiar palm fronds that had provided me with shade my whole life long. Marianne, my *da,* as we called our Negro nurses, had taught me to weave fans from dried palms when I was three years old. I had heard the only palm trees they had in Paris grew in silver tubs and were kept in hothouses until they were required to decorate a ballroom. And what of breadfruit, bananas, mangoes, frangipani, passion fruits, papayas, and pineapple? Would I *ever* taste the fruits of my childhood again?

A noisy flock of red, blue, green, and gold parrots exploded like fireworks from the trees. As I watched them fly away tears ran down my face and I turned and gazed back at my home, La Trinité, the three-story plantation house so glaring white in the tropical sun it hurt my eyes just to look at it. I was certain its image would be seared upon my eyes forever, a memory I would always carry with me wherever I went.

My grandfather Pierre Dubucq de Rivery was a hotheaded young man exiled from France after he killed a nobleman, the Chevalier de Piancourt, in a duel over a fickle and faithless mistress who could not decide between the two of them. With the King's men hot on Pierre's heels and his horse layered in sweat and foaming at the mouth, close to falling down dead beneath him, he made a mad dash for the harbor. A ship was just pulling away, the gap between dock and deck ever widening. He had no idea where it was going, but he urged his mount to make one last valiant effort and leap across the dark water onto that deck. A purse of gold persuaded the Captain to look the other way.

The ship was bound for Martinique. Since it was prison or the West Indies for Pierre Dubucq de Rivery he wisely chose the latter. He built a grand white plantation house, La Trinité, overlooking the turquoise waters of the Harbor Robert and erected the first sugar mill. White gold—sugar—made him a very wealthy man. But not content with one fortune, he soon made another by cultivating cocoa from the trees that grew wild upon the island. It was made into a popular drink called "chocolate" that first the French, then the whole world, fell in love with.

I never knew my grandfather, he died long before I was born, but he left a message for me. "Tell your daughter," he used to say to Papa, "that every time someone drinks a cup of chocolate they are adding a coin to her dower chest."

I was known as "the black and white heiress"; chocolate and sugar would ensure my future. "Good times or bad," Papa said, "people always crave sweets."

As I prepared for bed that night, I lingered by my window for a long time gazing out at the papayas and purple bougainvillea, breathing in the jasmine, roses, and honeysuckle. I had the most terrible, frightening feeling that I would never see this place again.

Mama came in and waved aside my *da,* to braid my hair herself for what might be the last time. It would be *years* before I returned to Martinique and she was no longer a young woman; neither disease nor accidents respect youth or age, so it was quite possible we might never meet in this world again. I was to stay at the convent until I was eighteen, though privately I couldn't imagine what the nuns had to teach me that would take me *nine* years to learn. Surely the social graces were not so complex? I was to be given a *lady's* education, not a soldier's or a statesman's; philosophy and mathematics would occupy little, if any, of my time.

Mama tried to comfort me by talking of Rose. She was married now, in Paris, the wife of the Vicomte de Beauharnais, a man so handsome he was rumored to have inspired the hero of a scandalous novel that I was far too young to read, which made me want to read it all the more. *Les Liaisons Dangereuses*—the title alone sounded *fascinating!*

I had wept and clung fiercely to Rose when she came to say

good-bye, but she had promised that she would come to visit me at the convent every chance she could. We would have lots of fun, she said, and being a married lady, a vicomtesse no less, and my kin, she could command the Mother Superior to let me out for the day. Rose and I would go shopping, she would help me out of my dreary convent habiliment, dress me up in elegant clothes, and we would ride around Paris in a fine carriage. We would sit and sip cups of chocolate at a sidewalk café and watch the fashionable world pass by, and gentlemen would stop to bow to us and admire our pretty hats and say that we had roses in our cheeks. She would have me to stay with her every Christmas and, when I was old enough, she would take me to balls and the theater. I might even find a beau, a man of fortune and fine figure and features, amongst her husband's friends.

Mama reminded me of all this, urging me to see that I had so much to look forward to instead of mourning what I was leaving behind in Martinique.

That night I dreamed I saw Euphemia David standing over my bed in her scarlet *tignon* and gown of madras handkerchiefs with big gold hoops in her ears and her snake draped and slithering about her shoulders. She bent to kiss my cheek and whispered in my ear: "In my end is my beginning." When I awakened I found a charm, a gilded serpent with ruby glass eyes swallowing its own tail, lying upon my pillow.

I still wasn't sure that the Queen of the Voodoos wasn't just a clever charlatan, adept at reading people and probabilities, more physician and mathematician than prophetess, but something made me thread a cord through the golden *O* of the snake's body and wear it around my neck alongside the pearl cross my parents had given me.

I never dreamed an ocean voyage could be so dreary. When our ship, the *Godspeed,* rocked it was more like a cradle lulling a baby to sleep than Neptune's fury. The waters were so calm and the winds so well behaved that we stayed on course and made the voyage in a swift seven weeks instead of the usual two months or a baneful storm-tossed three. I stood on the deck for hours each day, staring at the placid blue sea, hoping to spy something of interest like a shark's fin or a school of dolphins cavorting. Sometimes the sailors sought to relieve my boredom with wondrous tales of mermaids and sea serpents and exotic lands they had visited, but when one tried to scare me with stories of pirates and what they would do to a pretty little golden-haired girl like me, Marianne, like a fierce chocolate-skinned giantess, seized him by the throat and threatened to throw him overboard if he ever came near me again.

I had thought my boredom would surely end when my feet touched French soil at last, but I was woefully mistaken. I soon found there was something else that could be even more tedious and dull than seven maddeningly tranquil weeks spent at sea—*nine years* in a convent school.

The Mother Superior had sent the mustachioed Sister Claude to act as my jailer and convey me to prison. She had such a deep, gruff voice and broad shoulders I wondered if it wasn't really a man hiding beneath that wimple, black veil, and shapeless chin-to-toes black robe. I saw nothing of Paris since Sister Claude insisted that the leather blinds be put down and *stay* down before the wheels of the carriage even started to turn; the one time she caught me trying to peep she gave my knee such a vicious thump with her fingers it raised a livid bruise that would be aching for weeks afterward.

I passed the time inventing all sorts of lurid tales about Sister Claude and her mustache. My favorite was that she was a convict who had escaped from prison and met a kindly nun along the road, robbed the Good Samaritan of her habit, and then sought sanctuary in the nearest convent to elude capture. But his greatest vanity was his fine black mustache, so he refused to shave it off; luckily the Mother Superior was so shortsighted she thought it was a rather unfortunately placed birthmark.

Mother Angélique was *nothing* like an angel. If I had been charged with naming her I would have chosen something more fitting like Diabolique. I was certain she had a pair of devil horns on the bald head hidden underneath her wimple and veil. We butted heads at once like two goats who couldn't peacefully occupy the same pen or pasture.

Her rules were stifling and nonsensical. Whoever heard of taking a bath with your clothes on? And by the light of a single candle positioned far on the opposite side of the room! If God made our bodies why was it a sin to touch or look upon them in the pursuit of cleanliness and good health? Besides, my eyes were no strangers to the human form. In Martinique, the slaves wore very little when they labored in the cane fields and even less when they danced in their voodoo ceremonies and I, and other white plantation children, often swam naked, or nearly so, in the sea. But Mother Angélique said we must mortify, *never* glorify, the flesh, and I must cleanse my soul of sin.

I felt like a fool stepping into the tub in the long unbleached linen bathing robe that had been given to me. It tied at my throat and had long, wide sleeves so I could reach in to wash my arms, and ties all down the front that I might open, but only one at a time, to reach in and swiftly bathe the flesh within reach. If we took too long, we were accused of sinful explorations. The nun who sat sentry beside the single candle minded the time we spent over our ablutions and reported any dawdlers to the Mother Superior. These absurd rituals and expectations removed all trace of relaxation from bathing and turned it into a race, to be done as soon as we could to avoid unjust punishment. When the time came to quit the tub, the robe was so weighed down with water I was afraid it would pull me back down to drown, since lifting it to wring it out was also not permitted as that would expose the limbs.

My classmates were quick to tell me that the Queen of France always bathed in such a garment. But I was not impressed. The Queen was also known to sail through ballrooms with a model of a fully manned battleship on top of her powdered hair straining at its roots to stand three feet off her scalp and to wear skirts with panniers so wide she could not walk through a door without turning sideways. During my time in France I heard Marie Antoinette called many things, but never the quintessence of common sense.

If one of us fell ill and the doctor was summoned we were not even permitted to disrobe for him. And when we slept we must keep our hands above the covers at *all* times. One of the sisters sat and watched us in the dormitory all night, and those who disobeyed risked having their wrists bound and spending a sleepless night being prayed over. A natural urge to scratch an itchy calf or thigh was instantly suspect. That was how strict Mother Angélique was about safeguarding our sinful skin.

I was already beginning to wonder why nuns, who so vigorously despised the body and its natural functions, were chosen to mold young girls into perfect wives. To my mind, it was like hiring a man blind from birth to paint your house both inside and out and giving him free choice of color. I once asked Mother Angélique what we were to do when we became wives, subject to our husbands' amorous demands and the expectation of procreation. She said we should shut our eyes and pray throughout the ordeal, or think of the blessed fruit that might come of our union nine months later if God willed it. I then asked her what of the midwife. Surely it would be necessary to expose ourselves to her gaze. I doubted whether a baby could be safely delivered in pitch-dark or by the light of a single candle set far across the room. I had my palm split open with a cane and was sent to spend the night in chapel fasting and praying for that impertinence. Mother Angélique said I dwelled overmuch on sinful, and bodily, things and should look to my soul more. But when Marie Antoinette defied convention and scorned a midwife and had a *male accoucheur* attend her in childbed, the brother of her own chaplain no less, Mother Angélique was scandalized. Her face turned red as flames and she momentarily lost the power of speech. I laughed until I cried. It left me with a new respect for Marie Antoinette; apparently she was not as cowed by etiquette as I at first thought. A fashion-mad flibbertigibbet she might be, but she was also a rule breaker just like me.

Our daily lessons were such that I feared my mind would be both numb and dumb by the time nine years had passed. We had to learn to curtsy perfectly to personages of various ranks. And to glide as gracefully as an angel across a sea of smooth glass with her head held high while wearing wide, jutting whalebone panniers sticking from our hips on either side, our torsos laced to near rib-cracking tightness in corsets, with a heavy court train trailing six feet behind us, and our hair piled and pinned as high as it could be stretched off our heads.

Even dancing lessons, which I expected to bring at least a small degree of fun to our otherwise dreary days, were just as trying. Sometimes we spent an entire *hour* learning to point our toes just so without causing a single ripple in our satin skirts; the fabric must stay as straight and smooth as if it had just been ironed. It was a pointless exercise in futility, I thought. Why should anyone care? Why shouldn't our clothes move with us as we danced?

Our poor brains were constantly bombarded with such thorny quandaries as: If the Pope and all the ruling families of France, England, Russia, Germany, and Italy did us the honor of dining at our table on the same night how should they be seated so as to avoid giving offense to any of our august guests? When I asked Mother Angélique why she did not also include the Emperor of China and the Sultan of Turkey, she said they were heathens and not deserving of a seat at a Christian table, and I was exiled to chapel with a smarting palm to reflect upon, and, it was hoped, repent, my impertinence again. The same question was endlessly reshuffled with various dukes and duchesses, comtes and comtesses, princes and princesses, vicomtes and vicomtesses, marquis and marquises, and visiting ambassadors and assorted dignitaries and churchmen thrown into the mix. Another variation ran: If the princess of such and such was about to hand Her Majesty her gloves and the princess of so and so walked in should the first princess step aside in favor of the second?

I honestly could not have cared less. I just wanted to go home and forget all the ceremonial garnish and pointless fussiness that attended life in France. It was not to my liking; I preferred a more commonsensical approach to living. When I thought of my future, I saw myself as a happy and contented plantation wife, concerned only with my husband, our children, and running my household, socializing with our neighbors and relatives, not handing the Queen of France her gloves or the Pope a finger bowl filled with rosewater. In Martinique we took our clothes off when we bathed, and when we danced it was for fun, and a wrinkle in her satin skirt as she pointed her toe was the last thing on a woman's mind.

Honesty behooves me to admit there were some lessons I enjoyed, like the intricate embroidery and practical sewing that allowed me to create beautiful things with my own hands. To ease as well as express my homesickness, I embroidered the flora and fauna of my homeland: bunches of yellow bananas and gilt-thread pineapples on an apple-green skirt; flocks of tropical birds spreading their wings and flying across a turquoise gown; vines of honeysuckle twisting and twining all over a dress of virgin's-blush pink. I even embroidered the dreaded fer-de-lance coiled around the hem of a nut-brown gown. I enjoyed music as well; I learned to play the harpsichord and to sing. And I liked to read, though I preferred to choose my own books rather than the endless tomes of etiquette and saints' lives and bland but pretty poetry that the nuns assigned. I liked to lose myself in tales of romance, adventure, history, and fabulous journeys to far-off, exotic lands.

I thought often of Rose and looked forward to her letters even though they were full of excuses about why she could not come to see me and grew fewer and briefer as the years passed until they stopped altogether. I longed to see her, but I was not one to beg, and I feared an outright request, or a forthright reminder of all the promises she had made, would stop her letters completely.

Girls who had family to go home to on holidays, or for special occasions, told me that the true story of the Vicomte and Vicomtesse de Beauharnais was far from the happy romance Rose recounted in her letters. Their union was sorely troubled, Alexandre was certainly untrue, and perhaps Rose was too. They eventually separated and rumors of immorality continued to dog Rose. Some of the bolder girls said she had become a courtesan, selling her favors to any man who was willing to support her.

It made me very sad. I remembered with what happiness and high hopes Rose had set sail for France. She had been so eager and excited and had left Martinique with the spirit of a conqueror, determined that within a year she would be the toast of Paris. Now it seemed, if gossip could be believed, that all her dreams had turned to ashes. I prayed that she would rise, like a phoenix, from them. I didn't like to think of Rose defeated, knocked and beaten down by life and her own perfidious husband.

I wish she hadn't stopped writing, and even more that she had come to see me and let me be her friend again. Though I had often tried to fetter it with common sense, she had the freest spirit I had ever known, and a part of me always secretly admired her and wished I could be more like her. Perhaps she felt the seven years between us more in sophisticated Paris than she did in Martinique? And if we met it would be awkward, she would be a grown woman with children, and I a little girl still, and we would have nothing to say to each other. But in my heart I think Rose feared most that I would judge her, or the image of herself she would see reflected back at her when she looked in my eyes.

Whatever you have become, whatever you have done, I still love you and remember you fondly, I wanted to write to her. It is one of the great regrets of my life that I never did. But with only gossip to guide me, and no actual knowledge, I feared my words would seem like a presumption of her guilt. I didn't want to make Rose cry, I loved her too much, so I let the silence between us remain unbroken.

CHAPTER 15

A s I approached eighteen I was more eager than ever to go
home. I sat for a portrait painter, Monsieur Frobisuer, and had
miniatures painted for Papa and Mama and my little sister Marthe,
to show them how grown-up I was. The artist made me look like a
porcelain doll but somchow also managed to convey maturity; a
certain frankness, and just a hint of mischief, in my blue eyes.

As he plied his brushes and applied his paints, he shamelessly
flirted with and flattered me. He said my skin was like the finest
Sèvres porcelain painted with pink roses, my mouth was a pink
rosebud, my eyes perfectly matched sapphires, neither too pallid
nor too dark, and my hair like spun gold.

I wore a sapphire-blue silk gown to complement my eyes, and
my golden hair caught up loosely with a band of matching blue silk
and white flowers, with long curls cascading down my back, and
one over my shoulder, like a finger pointing down, indicating my
now womanly bosom framed by deep ruffles of white lace. I was so
eager for them to see that I was not a little girl anymore. I wanted to
go home!

Paris conspired with me to make my dreams come true. There
was so much unrest in the city. The King and especially the Queen

were more unpopular than ever. All those with aristocratic blood were reviled, and as the days passed the poor seemed to hunger for blood as well as bread. There was much talk of the war the Americans had fought to free themselves from "the yoke of British tyranny," and the word *revolution* was heard with increasing frequency in Paris. These men who made speeches on street corners and in coffee-houses wanted to pull the King and Queen down from their thrones and erect a democracy in place of the monarchy. They wanted to create a new world where liberty, equality, and freedom held sway and no man was better than his neighbor.

The situation seemed to me to be like a coin, with two sides, one idealistic romance, the other violent bloodbath. It was an exciting time to be alive and in Paris, to see a new world being born, but it was also very dangerous and frightening. I could not help but feel sorry for King Louis. He seemed like such a gentle soul, a shy fat man, lost without his spectacles, who would far rather have been a locksmith or a clock-maker than a king, but Fate had decreed that he play that role. And I thought his giddy butterfly wife more sinned against than sinner; she reminded me in some ways of Rose. I hoped neither the King nor the Queen would be harmed. If they must step down from their thrones, I hoped they would be allowed to live out the rest of their lives peacefully in comfort and unmolested.

Mama and Papa heard the news from France and were frightened too. They had always tried to shelter me from the evil of the world; now I was right in the middle of this maelstrom. They were afraid something terrible might happen to me. The convent was filled with girls from the best aristocratic families in France and Mama began to suffer blood-drenched dreams of an angry mob making us the target of their vengeance. She saw such *terrible* things in her sleep she could not bear to put them down on paper for fear it might make them come true.

A passage was swiftly booked for me on the next ship bound for Martinique, a sturdy but swift little vessel named *Lazarus*.

I all but danced through my last remaining days at the convent. I was going home! I sang the old island song of farewell, "Adieu Madras, Adieu Foulards!" as I helped my old *da,* Marianne, pack my things. I kept stopping to smile and reach out and squeeze her hand. "We are going home, Marianne, *home!*"

I could not wait to see Papa and Mama and my home, La Trinité, again. I could see it shining white in the sun; I wanted to run to it and fling open the doors and throw myself into my parents' loving arms. I wondered if little Marthe would even remember me. And Euphemia David. I clutched the serpent charm I wore alongside my pearl cross; I wondered if she was still alive, as feared and powerful as ever.

At last everything was ready. My trunks were already aboard the *Lazarus.* I was leaving with so many beautiful things. I had a gold-tasseled pink taffeta ball gown, with yards of billowing skirts and panniers to support them, packed safely in its own trunk with sachets of lavender and rose petals. I would wear it to the ball Papa and Mama would give to welcome me home and introduce me to the sons of the neighboring plantations amongst whom I was sure to find a beau and, eventually, a husband. I had three more trunks filled with beautiful satins, silk, velvets, and laces that would, in time, form my trousseau, and all the things I had made, embroidered with my memories of Martinique, including gifts for all my family. I could not wait to show them to Mama; I was certain she would be proud of me and see my love for my island home in every stitch and make sure I never had to leave it again. And I had a big box full of books to occupy me on the journey, including *Les Liaisons Dangereuses,* which I had by then read several times.

I stood in the austere whitewashed dormitory that had been my home for the past nine years bidding a happy farewell to my hard cot and my classmates, all of whom had suddenly grown weepy and sentimental at my impending departure. They stood around me, admiring my elegant traveling dress of bottle-green satin and terra cotta–colored velvet trimmed with gold braid and black lace, and the elegant little tricorn hat with a spray of speckled feathers perched at a jaunty tilt atop my golden hair. It had a black lace veil that matched my gloves. I had never felt so grown-up. They crowded close to press kisses onto my cheeks and bouquets of flowers and boxes of candy, books of poetry and romantic novels, and handkerchiefs they had embroidered with my initials into my arms.

At the very last moment, Mother Angélique came forward, put her hands on my shoulders, looked hard into my eyes, as though she was trying for the last time to drill some discipline into me, then leaned forward and kissed my cheek. I instinctively recoiled at her sour smell. She frowned and handed me a dictionary as a parting gift. I promised I would treasure it always, though I planned to drop it into the sea at the first opportunity.

As I was just about to step into my carriage, Sister Claude came forward to embrace me and present me with a book of saints' lives. Her dragoon's mustache, still as magnificent and dark as ever, tickled my face and I giggled.

After I was seated in the coach, I leaned from the open window and begged sweetly to ask Sister Claude a question.

"Tell me, please, I have been wondering for nine years, and I do so want to know, were you really a dragoon who was so madly in love with his sweetheart that when she chose to be a Bride of Christ rather than yours you could not bear to part with her and so disguised yourself as a nun and joined her in the cloister?"

"*Mademoiselle Aimee!*" Sister Claude gasped incredulously. Her face turned bright red and she kept opening and closing her mouth, though no words came out. She looked like she was going to drop down dead of apoplexy.

My classmates stood back, mouths agape, amazed and appalled at my audacity, and Mother Angélique looked like she wanted to flay my back open, not just my palm.

I couldn't help myself; I had been languishing in want of fun for *nine years* and I couldn't hold myself back any longer.

"Were you Sister Claude's sweetheart, Mother?" I smiled and asked sweetly.

"*Go!*" Marianne glanced at me with worried eyes and pounded the carriage roof and ordered the driver, "*Now!*"

As the carriage wheels began to turn, carrying me away, at long last, from the Convent of the Dames de la Visitation, I collapsed against the cushions, shaking with laughter.

Beside me, Marianne just sighed and shook her head. "Nine years wasted trying to make a lady of you, you little hoyden!"

CHAPTER 16

The first part of our journey was tranquil and uneventful; it reminded me of the first time I had crossed the sea as *Lazarus* glided serenely across the glass-smooth waves. This time, I kept mostly to my cabin, lying on my bed and reading or sitting by the window, when the light was good, and embroidering the bright hibiscus blossoms I remembered on a white satin bed jacket I had made for Mama. But sometimes I grew restless and just had to go up on deck to stretch my legs and breathe the clean sea air, though my *da* always looked upon these outings with dismay and urged caution. I was now a beautiful young woman, Marianne said, and must be careful; I must not consort with the crew and encourage undue familiarity. Men, long at sea and longing for a woman's company, might presume to take liberties.

Halfway through our voyage, in the Bay of Biscay, the *Lazarus* was caught up in a fearsome gale. We were tossed and thrown about as though Neptune and the Devil were playing catch with our poor little ship. The waves smashed into us, at times knocking the *Lazarus* almost onto its side. Each time I feared it would be the end and the force of the waves would drive us down into the depths of the sea, never to rise again. But *Lazarus* would not go down without a fight, it was true to its name, and each time it managed to resurrect itself. But fatal blows do not always kill instantly. The seams, so badly battered by the brutal waves, had begun to open up, and we were taking on water. By dusk it seemed certain that we would not see another dawn.

Then a miracle happened. A large Spanish ship appeared upon the horizon. Prayers of despair turned to jubilation; some even danced upon the slanting deck. We were saved! To compound the miracle, our rescue ship was improbably named *El Salvador*—The Savior.

As *Lazarus* sank into the sea, never to rise again, I stood on the deck of *El Salvador,* surrounded by my trunks, with Marianne's arms hugging fiercely tight around me, and gave thanks for our survival. I would be late getting home, as this ship was bound for Majorca and I would have to find another Martinique-bound vessel there, but that was far better than going down to a watery grave.

The sea was calm again, the sun shining like a big golden coin in the bright blue sky above, and the pink spires of Majorca were already looming in the distance. Our ocean ordeal was almost over. I had hardly slept in days with the stomach-tossing torment of the waves that had battered the valiant little *Lazarus,* so I lingered lazily in bed. I was dozing when I heard a disturbance up on deck. Men were shouting and I heard the clang of metal.

I was still in my nightgown and could not think of going up on deck until I was dressed. I turned questioning eyes to Marianne, sitting up on the floor beside my bed where she had been sleeping, but before I could ask or make a move to rise and dress the door was kicked open and the most fearsome man I had ever seen stood before me, leering down at me and brandishing a bloodstained cutlass, with more like him crowding in behind, peering over his shoulders at me.

Coarse and swarthy, with dark eyes and long straggling black mustaches and greasy hair beneath their red felt caps, their garments a motley mixture of rags and riches, they gathered around my bed. *Pirates!* These were the dreaded Barbary Corsairs, the scourge and terror of the Mediterranean, who menaced the seas under the protection of the Turks, preying on any vulnerable vessel that had the misfortune to cross their wicked path.

Slavery, ransom, rape, murder were the words that tumbled wildly like dice through my mind. Which would it be? I waited in frozen fear for the answer. *Ransom,* I prayed silently, *please God, let it be ransom!* That was my only hope of going home and seeing Papa and Mama again.

The pirates' captain spoke some words in a language I could not understand and pointed at Marianne whereupon his men seized hold of her and dragged her out, kicking and screaming, fighting tooth and nail.

Fear forgotten, I leapt up from my bed and faced the Captain boldly. "Let go of her!" I shouted. "Don't you *dare* hurt her!"

The pirate captain looked me up and down. There was laughter and also lust in his eyes. He reached out a hand to touch my hair. I slapped it down. He laughed and grabbed hold of the lace collar of my nightdress and tore it open, down the front, all the way to the hem, exposing my naked body to the eyes of all those evil men. They laughed and leered at me and some of them boldly fondled their crotches. As I tried to cover myself, the Captain pushed me back onto the bed and used the tip of his cutlass to part the tattered folds of my nightgown again, baring my nakedness to every eye.

"Touch her and you die!" he said to his men, speaking these words in their barbaric tongue, then repeating them in French for my benefit.

He bent over the bed and trailed his fingers slowly down my body, dawdling over my breasts, plucking at my pink nipples, then letting his greasy palm glide across the smooth flat of my belly. I couldn't move. I was terrified of what he might do to me. Was he going to rape me? He had warned his men away from me; did that mean he had chosen me for himself? His fingertips combed leisurely through the golden curls between my legs, gently brushing the pink folds of forbidden flesh underneath. My face flamed with shame and fury. I raised my hand, intending to slap his away, but he just laughed and waggled that dangerous, sharp cutlass at me like a scolding steel finger.

I lay back on the bed defeated, praying that death would be merciful and swift. Suddenly his roving fingers stilled and he savagely plucked out a single golden hair. I was surprised and jumped and cried out at the unexpected pain, but he only laughed at me.

"Every hair worth a piece of gold," he said. Did that mean he was going to *sell* me? Like a slave in the marketplace? Would I be stood naked on a block and men come to poke and prod me and examine my teeth?

He made a sign for his men to withdraw and, to my relief, he went too. I heard the door lock behind them.

I trembled and wept and wondered what would become of me.

CHAPTER 17

———◄◦►———

Draped in a big orange-and-brown-striped shawl smelling of to-bacco, dust, and dung that one of the pirates had flung at me, I was led in chains through the twists and turns of the filthy and narrow cobblestone streets of Algiers. A butcher threw some bloody entrails from the back door of his shop and several rats ran boldly across my path to feast on them. I screamed and leapt back when one of them dashed across the top of my foot. I felt its tiny claws graze my skin. But the pirates had no sympathy or patience and shoved me onward.

They had taken almost everything from me. I had nothing ex-cept for the pearl cross and snake charm I wore about my neck, the tattered remnants of my nightgown that I had managed to crudely tie together, and my fragile, thin-soled satin chamber slippers. The corsairs had taken away my trunks and all my belongings that had been scattered about the cabin, reasoning that I might strangle my-self with a stocking or swallow a needle or pierce the veins in my wrist with it. They were not about to let Death deprive them of such a valuable prize, the pirate captain had said when I protested their removal.

Tears rolled down my face when I saw palm trees and smelled spices. As we passed the marketplace, I saw parrots, like the ones that flew free on my island home, crammed into cages for sale, prisoners just like me. Everywhere in Algiers, this notorious den of thieves, it seemed there were bittersweet reminders of home. Even the people's clothes reminded me of Martinique. They loved their bright colors, bangles, and beads and some wore turbans on their heads, reminiscent of the *tignons* of the island women, and many carried baskets or jars atop their heads. Just like home!

Tears poured from my eyes. I wanted to go home! An old woman, her hair and the bottom of her face hidden by a veil—that seemed to be the custom here, I noted—looked at me with sad eyes. She seemed to sense my sorrow and forced her way past the pirates and embraced me, just like a mother. She handed me a sprig of jasmine, the same fragrant flower that grew outside my window at La Trinité and all over Martinique, before the corsairs shoved her away so violently that she fell.

As I passed, everyone stared back at me with curious eyes, and many approached, crowding around us, clamoring for a closer look at me. Fingers reached out, trying to touch my golden hair and white skin, and they stared in unabashed wonder at my blue eyes, but the corsairs spoke sharply to them and warned them away with their cutlasses.

I began to understand then; they stared at me because *I* was different. Every person I saw had skin much darker than mine, whether it was bronzed by the sun or tinted so by God's hand, not porcelain pale like mine. In my world, pallor was prized; every woman aspired to have skin white as fresh-fallen snow and guarded her complexion accordingly with parasols, shady hats, and veils. Every pair of eyes that looked my way were likewise dark; I saw no blues, grays, or greens, only varying shades of brown, most so dark they seemed nearer black. It was the same with their hair, though I saw an occasional hint of red, purple, or blue when the sun shone down on an uncovered head, I didn't spy a single lock of hair lighter than black coffee except for a few gray elders. I was a curiosity here, a freak of nature; they had never seen anyone like me before. It only made me more frightened. What were they going to do with me?

I was taken to what must have been a palace. It glowed like a pearl in the setting sun. The courtyard I was led into was paved with turquoise-blue tiles. There were fig trees and a beautiful white fountain gently splashing clear water in the center of it. I wanted to run to it, dip my hands in, and let the cool stream caress my arms, drink my fill, and wash all the dirt and dust away. But of course I didn't dare. I couldn't, with all these men watching me.

A corpulent old man with a diamond-paved patch covering one eye, in robes of white silk embroidered with gold and red, wearing heavy gold chains about his neck, came out to inspect me. I know now that he was the Dey of Algiers, Baba Mohammed ben Osman, master of the Barbary Corsairs, answerable to no man save the Sultan of Turkey.

He caressed me with his one good eye. I shrank back in horror as his hands rose and reached out eagerly to touch me, but with a sigh, as though he had suddenly remembered something important, he forced them back down again. I could not understand his language, but his tone conveyed regret as he wistfully fingered a long lock of my golden hair, caressing it lingeringly from root to tip.

He turned away from me and spoke brusquely to my captors, apparently issuing orders. The end result was that I was taken away again, back through the filthy, maze-like city, and put on board another ship.

I was locked inside a cabin. A woman with bronze skin, dark hair, and burning hostile black eyes came and went, bringing me food and water, but never speaking a word to me. She was rough and rude. When I tried to talk to her, she ignored me. If I touched her she slapped my hand away.

I do not know how many days and nights passed. I was so downhearted I lacked the will to count them. What did it matter? Every day took me farther and farther away from Martinique. I think my heart already knew that I would never see home again. Would Mama and Papa ever know what had happened to me? Would they even know to look for me? Would they make inquiries and try to buy my freedom, to ransom me? Or would they think I was dead, my body thrown, food for fishes, into the deep blue sea? It would break their hearts! They would put on black and mourn me; sorrow might even hasten them to their graves! When I thought of that I cried as never before; I couldn't bear it. My birth had made them so happy, and my presumed death would surely kill them, and Marthe would be an orphan. I *had* to find a way to let them know I was still alive!

I sought refuge in sleep; it was the only way I could escape. In my dreams I ran toward La Trinité, where Mama and Papa stood on the veranda, smiling, so happy to see me, their arms open, outstretched, ready to enfold me. But the moment my foot touched the first step it all disappeared and I awoke in agonized tears.

Sometimes I sat and stared out the barred window, watching the red earth and crumbling white ruins, and distant, mist-shrouded outlines of blue mountains passing by, and then nothing . . . seemingly endless sea as far as the eye could see.

One morning I awakened to a marvelous sight between the bars—a city of a thousand golden domes glittering in the sun. Towers, spires, minarets, and cupolas, great domes shaped like onions swirled with stripes of ruby, emerald, and sapphire, as though a master jeweler had crafted this spectacular city. Even the window glass twinkled like diamonds flashing in the sun. Everywhere I looked there was the glitter of gold dazzling my eyes. I never dreamed such a place could exist. It took my breath away. I had never seen anything so splendid in all my life. Even the boats gathered in the port were gilded; some even seemed to be set with jewels.

When night fell, dimming the glorious golden world outside my window, the servant woman returned. She pulled me roughly to my feet and threw a thick, musty black veil over my head. There was only a narrow slit for my eyes to peep out and it was so long it trailed behind me and I had to gather whole handfuls of it up in order to walk.

There were no chains this time. Where would I run to even if I managed to break free except to throw myself in the sea? I couldn't possibly save myself by swimming; I would only tire myself out and drown if my captors didn't fish me out. And I didn't want to die; I wanted to live. I wanted to go home. So, for now . . . there was nowhere else to go but to the city of gold. Maybe there I would find a friend, someone sympathetic to my plight who could understand my language and would be willing to help me.

I was forced into a little boat. The servant woman was right behind me shoving me along, grudgingly helping me with the folds of my veil. I noticed that she was veiled now too. Once I was seated, the men began to row. None of them said a word, and even if they had I wouldn't have understood it. The sea looked like liquid silver in the moonlight and I reached down to trail my hand in it; it was so deliciously cool I wished I could dive right in, but the servant woman caught hold of my wrist, slapped my hand like a stern mother reprimanding her child, and shoved it back onto my lap, under my veil.

As soon as my feet, shod in the crude, overly large black leather sandals the servant had given me, touched solid ground again I was swept up in powerful arms and lifted into a litter with a heavy dark curtain that was tied shut from the outside. I could see nothing; I was alone in pitch-darkness. All I could do was sit and wait alone and wonder what would be my fate.

I felt the litter sway and tilt. I braced myself, for a moment fearing I was going to fall. We were going uphill. I felt whole eternities pass in every moment. I just wanted it to be over. Not knowing seemed somehow worse. At last, the litter stopped. I heard shouting and a creaking noise, like a gate being swung open. The litter was set down and the curtains opened and a hand reached in to pull me out.

I saw the light of torches and imposing walls of stone, bricks of various colors arranged in intricate patterns, then my eyes lighted upon the most horrible sight of all—a pyramid formed of several severed heads, eyes sightless, like gray marbles, stumps still weeping, sitting in a wide, shimmering pool of dark blood; I could see the light of the torches reflected in it. They must have only just been killed. Were they going to kill me too? I staggered. I thought someone struck me a fierce blow, but it was only my face hitting the paving stones as I fainted. I was dimly conscious of people shouting and swarming around me, hands lifting me, but I was already drifting far, far away, to a place where no one could touch me.

When I opened my eyes, I saw the moon, like a perfect opal set high in the midnight sky above me, through a dome of glass. As I slowly lowered my gaze I saw walls of deep orange, shimmering gold, and black patterned damask. For a moment I thought I had shrunk to the size of a pearl and someone had laid me in their jewelry box on a cushion of black satin. I looked around and saw windows with gold lattice-shaped bars, sconces shaped like golden fists clutching thick ivory candles, ornately carved and gilded chests, mirrors, tasseled and embroidered cushions on low-slung couches or tossed upon the carpeted floor in artful abandon, and delicate gilded tables. I was lying in the middle of it all on a soft mattress covered in black satin, my aching head resting on a pillow with long gold tassels that mingled with my hair. There was a strong scent of incense that made me think of Mass and a slightly acrid aroma that I was certain was strong black coffee. Though I had always preferred chocolate, I suddenly wanted a sip very badly. Papa and Mama had both loved coffee, the stronger and blacker the better.

Suddenly a face appeared leaning over mine—a stern, unsmiling black man wearing a tall yellow turban shaped like a tulip sprouting tall peacock feathers clasped in a giant ruby brooch. I gasped and shrank back in fright.

I heard a babble of voices, all foreign and incomprehensible, and turned to see the gilded arch of the doorway filled with dark, dusky, bronze and gold-skinned women in the strangest costumes I had ever seen: a rainbow of billowing satin caftans and robes, all embroidered in silver and gold; full, baggy-legged trousers cinched around their ankles; strange headdresses, some akin to *tignons,* others peculiar hybrids, trailing long gilt- or pearl-edged gauze veils; rich necklaces and weighty, clanking bangles; jeweled girdles; golden slippers with pointy upturned toes; and long dark hair, either flowing free or arranged in braids. They were all crowding and craning their necks to get a better look at me.

The strange black man was still hovering over me. I looked him up and down. There was a curious soft quality to his face I noticed that made him appear almost feminine. He was quite tall, but round and soft bodied, rolls of fat jiggled on his chest whenever he moved, giving the appearance of breasts, and he had a great paunchy belly that almost made him look pregnant. He was resplendent in flowing robes of rich butter-yellow silk covered with a golden garden of embroidered tulips. His thick waist was girded in pearls and a long mantle layered in peacock feathers was tossed over his shoulders. He held out his hand to me. I shrank farther back and didn't take it. He frowned and leaned down and seized hold of my hand

and jerked me to my feet. I was wearing only a thin, grimy chemise that the servant woman on the ship had given me and I tried to cover myself, but he would not let me. His fingers bit hard into my wrist as he spoke to me. I couldn't understand the words but the meaning was clear: *I rule here and you will do as I say.*

How curious, I thought, to see a Negro so opulently clad and in a position of such obvious power. In Martinique, the only person of color I ever knew to hold any degree of power was the voodoo queen, Euphemia David; everyone, black and white, was afraid of her. All the other blacks I knew were poor and free or slaves working the fields and mills of the *Grand Blancs'* plantations. But this man was clearly no one's slave; he was treating *me* like one!

He turned and motioned a woman to come forward. He called her a name that sounded like *Kiya.* She was short and fat with a face and figure as round as the moon, youthful still, but not young. She was dressed in the same curious fashion as the other women. A long robe lavishly embroidered in silver hung open to reveal satin trousers and a pearl-spangled bodice, all in a pale, milky-blue hue. Her heavy black hair hung down almost to her knees in a pair of fat braids plaited with ropes of seed pearls. Her headdress resembled a satin *tignon* entwined with a long veil edged in silver braid dripping pearl and crystal tears that fell down her back almost to her heels. Her eyes were lined thickly with black paint and the lids smeared with silver, and her lips and cheeks were rouged a deep cherry red. Strange designs, almost like lace, were painted in dark red ink upon her caramel-colored hands and the tops of her feet above golden slippers with toes that curled up and in upon themselves.

She smiled reassuringly at me—here at last was some sign of kindness!—as she reached out and took both my hands. She began to speak, the tone of her voice was gentle and very kind, but I felt so frustrated that I could not understand a single word that tears began to pour from my eyes. Desperately, I tried to speak to her in French, but she just shook her head apologetically and tugged gently at my hands. She began moving slowly backward, toward the door, her voice and hands coaxing me to follow her, treating me like a frightened animal she was trying to gentle. There was nothing else for me to do, so I gave in and let her lead me from the room.

The other women followed, chattering amongst themselves and pointing at me, some even presuming to reach out and poke or stroke me.

As we continued down a long corridor I noticed that there were other black men in silken robes and turbans with womanish faces and soft, round figures. They seemed to act as guards, or guardians, of the women. Some of them spoke together, quite amicably, like dear old friends, in their, to me, unintelligible babble, whilst others were like stern schoolmasters scolding their pupils. I saw one take off his curly-toed red slipper and strike a woman on the face with the thin sole of it in what I would later learn was a common act of punishment. Discipline was meted out carefully here; where beauty was so highly prized it would not do to cause unsightly marks or, even worse, scars.

I was taken to a vast bathing chamber that was like nothing I had ever seen before. The walls were covered in beautiful tiles of every shade of blue and green. Lining the walls, white marble columns supported a series of arches, creating alcoves in which couches, cushions, and tables were set. Women, all unabashedly naked, lounged within, gossiping over gilded cups and trays of confections, combing and braiding each other's long dark hair, or applying cosmetics, while others lay upon their stomachs having their bodies massaged with perfumed oils, or reclined on their backs smoking long ornately jeweled and gilded pipes. Each alcove had a fountain set into the wall where water flowed in a constant stream from out of a gilded spout into a deep blue marble basin and there were shelves cluttered with various vials, bottles, jars, and stacks of embroidered linen towels.

At the center of the room was a large, round, shallow pool, paved in blue tiles, with a white marble fountain rising out of its midst, and high above was a domed glass ceiling to let in the light of sun or moon. Yet more women sat around, or in, the pool, laughing and splashing one another, talking, or just going about the business of bathing, alone or with assistance that was sometimes given in a *very* affectionate manner. It was rather unnerving to see how they openly kissed, caressed, and fondled each other. I had never seen so many naked women in my life, and all of them completely at ease in their own skin, utterly unconcerned about who might gaze upon them. It was certainly a far cry from baths in the convent! It almost made me wish Mother Angélique were standing beside me just so I could see the look on her face.

There were several women clad in red loincloths with red *tignons* over their hair. They must be the bath's attendants. They were everywhere, helping wherever they were needed, scrubbing backs and washing or braiding long hair, serving refreshments, applying perfumes and lotions, wielding pumice stones over rough heels or elbows, or giving massages.

As I passed through a swirl of sulfurous vapors I started at the unexpected heat beneath my feet. The blue marble floor was so hot I wanted to turn back, but my escort smiled reassuringly and put out her hands to stop me. One of the bath attendants hurried forward and knelt and quickly eased my feet into a pair of wooden shoes beautifully inlaid with mother-of-pearl that had high, raised soles, so I could no longer feel the heat beneath my feet. She then reached for the hem of my filthy chemise and started to draw it up over my hips. My first instinct was to fight, to shove her hands away, but I suppressed it; I knew that it would do no good. I was helpless and woefully outnumbered. Any resistance would be futile and only make things worse for me, so I stood still and let her undress me.

The moon-faced woman in blue watched me intently, studying my figure in a manner that made me very uncomfortable. When she saw the pearl cross and snake charm I wore about my neck she pointed adamantly and spoke rather sharply. The attendant hurried to obey, stepping behind me and lifting the heavy, greasy unwashed weight of my hair over my shoulder so she could get at the fastenings. Vainly, I cried out in protest and cupped my hand tight around these treasures, trying to hold on to them, but they were taken from me just the same. Now I truly had nothing but my memories to remind me of home.

Blinded by tears, I let the bath attendant lead me into the pool. She gestured for me to kneel and began ladling hot water over my shoulders. My skin instantly turned pink from the heat of it. She then began scrubbing me vigorously with a large, rough sponge. She treated me like a child, pushing my hands away and shaking her head when I tried to take the sponge from her. I tried desperately to find some way to tell her that I was quite capable of bathing myself, but she wouldn't let me and continued diligently scrubbing until every part of me was so pink I felt raw. When she gave her full attention to washing the most intimate part of me, between my legs, her fingers provoked strange stirrings of not quite pleasure that bubbled up through my embarrassment. I tried to make her stop, but she would not surrender the sponge to me. I averted my eyes and stared down at the blue tiles shimmering beneath the water, trying to will my soul away, to rise above this terrible indignity, but their color only reminded me of the turquoise sea of home and brought fresh tears to my eyes.

While I was being bathed, several women gathered around to watch. As the grime was washed away they gasped as the bright gold of my hair was fully revealed and reached out to touch it. Another, rather impertinent, dark hand painfully tweaked one of my nipples, its owner babbling in her strange, guttural tongue presumably about its rosy color, so different from their dark and tawny teats. Another hand tilted up my chin so that dark eyes could gaze amazed into my blue ones. Others pointed and jabbed and plucked at the golden down growing on my arms and legs and frowned and made little sounds of disgust. I noticed then that their bodies were entirely smooth and hairless.

My attendant guided me from the pool and gestured for me to sit down upon a slab of blue marble; then she knelt before me and began to spread a thick layer of a peculiar burning paste all over my arms and legs. She raised my arms so she could get at the hair underneath and even pushed my legs wide apart to reach the thicket of golden curls growing there, carefully dabbing at the paste with a linen napkin when it threatened the tender pink skin underneath.

Tears of pain and humiliation overflowed my eyes. I was afraid that awful stinging paste was going to burn my skin off. It made me wonder which was worse, this paste or the poisonous, ravenous ants on Martinique that could strip a man or beast down to bare bones in a matter of moments. Some of the women made sympathetic noises and patted my shoulders and stroked my hair, but that only made me feel worse. I *hated* being on display like this! A person should be allowed to bathe in private! The Catholic schoolgirl in me wondered if this was some kind of punishment in reverse for my rebellious attitude against the excessive, obsessive modesty of the convent.

Several minutes passed; then the attendant began carefully scraping the paste away with what looked like a small, blunt sickle. Every hair came away with it, and my skin, though raw pink-red and smarting terribly, was now smooth as silk. I was led back to the pool again for rinsing and another vigorous scrubbing. Just when I thought it was over, she produced a pumice stone and went to work on me with that. It felt like she was trying to scrub all my skin off and wouldn't be satisfied until I was reduced to my skeleton, and even then I feared she would start polishing my bones until they shone like perfect white pearls.

After what seemed like hours of steaming and scrubbing, my hip-length hair was twisted up loosely in a towel of embroidered white muslin and I was taken from the pool again and led into an alcove. The attendant gestured for me to sit upon the couch. I was tired and overcome and courage, at last, deserted me and I began to weep piteously. *Everything* was so strange here and even though I was surrounded by dozens of naked women I felt all alone. There was no one I could trust or call friend here. No one could understand my language, and I *hated* being stared at like some poor naked freak in a fair and being touched and handled in such an intimate fashion, and by strangers.

Several women came and clustered about me, trying their best to comfort and soothe me. They stroked my head and shoulders, patted my thighs and knees, and held and caressed and kissed my hands. They pressed strange little jellied cubes coated in powdery white sugar into my hands and gestured for me to eat them. I was starving and gobbled down four, one right after the other. They were like no sweets I had ever had before. The first one tasted oddly of rosewater, and the others were flavored with lemon, cinnamon, and honey, and all had nuts chopped very finely within.

I was handed a gilded cup filled with a cool, sweet, delicious drink that had an odd perfumey flavor, a medley of fruit and flowers, an intricate, sophisticated blend that my weary head could not decipher. "Sherbet," the woman said, pointing at the cup from which I had just drunk. She smiled broadly and nodded encouragingly when I repeated the unfamiliar word back to her. She then took one of the sweets I had just sampled and identified it as *rahat lokum*.

The round-as-the-moon woman in blue returned again and spoke in an urgent tone and clapped her hands sharply. The other women quickly withdrew, to resume their own couches and diversions, as my attendant unwound the wet towel from my hair and began combing the tangles out with an ivory comb while I sat and nervously sipped the sweet sherbet.

There was a rustle of heavy fabric and feathers and an almost overpowering odor of attar of roses as the black man in yellow and peacock feathers, with the enormous tulip-shaped turban balanced atop his head, swept into the alcove and came to stand before my couch. I thrust the cup of sherbet from me and pulled my hair over my shoulders trying to shield my nakedness with its golden length.

I saw annoyance flit across his face as he reached out and jerked me to my feet again. He began to slowly circle me, my downcast eyes watching the sweep of gold-embroidered yellow silk and peacock feathers going round and round, like exotic ingredients in a mixing bowl, as I stood there helplessly, wishing vainly that I could just disappear. He then began to touch me in a way that, though I had never experienced it, I had seen many times, when female slaves mounted the auction block in Martinique. He forced my chin up and my jaw down so he could examine my teeth. He lifted the wet, golden weight of my hair and searched beneath to make sure it hid no moles, birthmarks, or scars. His fingertips trailed over the curves of my shoulders down to the tips of my own fingers. I flinched and snapped, "Don't do that!" when he felt my breasts, squeezing them like little melons, but he ignored me, exchanging comments, back and forth, with the woman in blue. His hands traveled down over the curves of my waist and hips and he circled me again, traced the length of my spine, and poked, prodded, and squeezed my buttocks.

Tears of shame seeped from my eyes. For the first time in my life I truly understood what it meant to be a slave, to have no rights, and for no one to care about me or how I felt. My being a *Grand Blanc* meant nothing in this strange land ruled by this regally robed Negro.

He pointed to the couch, and the bath attendant, anticipating his orders, grasped my shoulders and pulled me back to sit and then, at a motion of his hand, to lie down. The woman in blue moved to stand behind the black man, to get a better look, as he examined each of my legs in turn; even my toes and the soles of my feet were subjected to the same exacting scrutiny. It was excruciatingly frustrating not to be able to understand a word that they were saying. Was he planning to buy me? Or had he already bought me? He paused, deliberating over my big toe, noticing that the nail had grown unevenly, and the bath attendant, her tone conveying an apology, hastened forward with a file. When she was done he smiled and nodded his approval and the woman in blue did the same.

When he started to part my legs, I could stand no more of this demeaning inspection. I lashed out and fought to pull free, but the woman in blue and the bath attendant restrained me. I felt his fingers intrude where no man had ever touched before, where even my own fingers had never gone, right into the secret depths of me. I gasped at the unexpected pain. Then it was over; his fingers withdrew. A smile lit up his face and he began conversing excitedly with the woman in blue. They were both smiling, their voices happy and eager as they began to walk away, without giving another glance to me.

The bath attendant began to slather me with a slick pink rosescented lotion, but I defiantly pushed her away. I ran to the nearest group of women, reclining on couches and cushions resting upon the floor, eating sweets, gossiping, and doing each other's hair.

"*Please,*" I implored, "does not at least *one* of you understand French?"

They stared back at me blankly, shaking their heads, as the bath attendant came and led me back to the couch where I had no choice but to submit to her ministrations.

After the whole of me was rose scented and sleek as silk, another servant came in to help me dress. I was given a pair of baggy white satin trousers that ballooned gracefully around my limbs and cinched in about my ankles, and a black satin caftan embroidered all over with silver flowers embellished with seed pearls and tiny crystals. I stepped obediently into silver slippers with those funny turned-back toes. A circlet of braided black and white veiling entwined with pearls was set upon my head and twin black and white veils flowed down my back past my knees. The tiring woman showed me how to draw the veil forward, to fasten it on the opposite side, to hide my face entirely below my eyes. I knew she was giving me instructions of some kind, but I couldn't understand.

She gave up with a sigh and left my veil to fall naturally down my back and motioned for me to follow her. I was taken to a long, narrow room lined with gilded divans, all covered in sumptuous, jewel-hued satins, with quilts and plump pillows. This was nothing like the dormitory at the convent, yet that was exactly what it was. Many of the divans were already occupied, but enough women were awake to come crowd around me and stare at my white skin and golden hair.

But I only wished to sleep; exhaustion had driven all the fight out of me. I sank down gratefully onto the plum-colored divan that the servant had indicated was mine, laid my head down on the pillow, pulled up the covers, and closed my eyes. Sleep was my only refuge, my only escape. As I drifted off I prayed that when I woke up I would be back in my bed at La Trinité and that all this would prove to have been only a bad dream.

CHAPTER 18

I was left to sleep as long as I liked. When I awakened I was alone in the dormitory except for a servant who had been left to watch over me. As soon as she saw me stir she scurried out and came back with a big golden tray laden with strong bitter black tea, a strange kind of bread that was flat and firm with tiny oval seeds baked on top of it, honey and a variety of jams and preserves, crumbly white cheese, olives, melon slices, a flaky layered pastry baked with honey and nuts, and a creamy white custard. She wasn't sure which I liked, so she had brought me many things to tempt my appetite.

I looked around for a spoon, but there wasn't one. The servant mimed using her fingers to raise phantom food to her mouth. It seemed like the sort of thing a person entirely without refinement would do, but I was hungry and that white custard looked so inviting.

I eagerly scooped some up on two fingertips, expecting it to be sweet, but it had a strange sour taste, both bitter and bland, there wasn't the slightest sweetness to it, and it burned my throat instead of cooling it on the way down. The servant girl pointed to the preserves and honey, miming that I should stir these into the deceptive custard. When I did it improved the taste considerably. I tried to ask her what it was called, but she didn't understand. So I pointed to it and asked, "Sherbet?" and then *"Rahat lokum?"*—the only words for food I knew, though I knew very well it was neither of these. But she understood and shook her head. "*Yoğurt,*" she pronounced.

After I finished eating and had bathed my hands and face, I was astonished to see two black men in long white robes and turbans carrying a trunk in. I recognized it at once; it was the special one that had held the beautiful pink ball gown, and everything that went with it, that I had intended to wear at my homecoming ball. I ran and knelt before the trunk. Someone had pried open the lock and the lid lifted easily. I reached inside and lovingly caressed the pink taffeta. How proud Papa and Mama would have been to see me in it, all grown-up, gowned and gracious as a proper French lady. I would have surely found a beau that night, maybe even my future husband.

The black man from the night before swept in, wearing robes of crimson brocade this time, with a mantle of white peacock feathers studded with a rainbow of gemstone brilliants and a spray of white feathers on a mammoth sugarloaf turban so tall they almost grazed the ceiling. He was followed by two servant girls. He pointed to the trunk full of pink finery and they began carefully laying out each piece. He lingered in the doorway a moment, watching, then nodded, apparently satisfied, and left me to their care.

They stared at each garment in wonder. The panniers that supported the voluminous skirt were completely foreign to them, as were the whalebone stays that cinched my waist in tight and pushed my bosom up high, and the heels like little stilts on the pink satin shoes.

They undressed me and washed me with rosewater and looked me over carefully, making sure not a single hair had defied that dreadful, caustic paste. Then, in a lengthy process punctuated by much pantomiming and frustration, the three of us managed to get me dressed and to put up my hair in the French fashion, crowned with a lavish garnishment of pink ribbons, a wreath of pink silk roses, and a bevy of frothy ostrich plumes from palest to deepest pink, with a pair of long golden ringlets falling over my right shoulder.

The women in this strange land seemed to have a heavy hand when it came to applying their face paint, but I would not let them go so far with me. I preferred to appear as I was, fresh and young, with just a light dusting of powder, a darkening of my far-too-fair brows, and a touch of rouge on my cheeks and mouth to enhance their natural rosiness. As I fastened the delicate gold filigree and pearl drops in my ears I lamented again the loss of the cross my parents had given me. Not only would it have matched the earrings, but it also would have served as a constant reminder of their love and given me the strength and courage to bear whatever I must, and to never stop hoping that I would find a way to get back home.

I stood before the long mirror and stared at a me I had never seen before. The skirt was *enormous,* all pink flounces, rosettes, bows, and swaying gold tassels, jutting about three feet from my hips at either side and belling out over numerous taffeta petticoats. I fancied my silk-stockinged limbs beneath it were like the clapper of a huge bell. As I turned slowly before the mirror, I thought I looked like the most decadent pink birthday cake ever created.

The black man returned. This time he smiled at me. He rubbed his hands together and his face and eyes radiated pure delight. He came to stand behind me at the mirror and took from inside his robe the pearl cross I thought I would never see again. I almost wept in gratitude as he fastened it around my neck. I met his eyes in the mirror. "Thank you," I whispered, and hoped he understood even though we did not speak the same language.

I did not know how to ask for it, but I wanted my talisman, the serpent charm Euphemia David had given me. I pointed to the cross at my throat and made a circling motion. Fortunately, he understood and produced it from within his robe. I could not wear it, the cord was missing, and it would not have complemented my gown, it was after all just a crude little thing, its only value springing from pure sentiment, so I wrapped it in my lace handkerchief and clutched it tightly in my hand.

"Thank you," I said again. He bowed his head in acknowledgment and then held out his hand to me and this time, after only the slightest hesitation, I took it as best I could with my panniered skirt standing between us.

He led me out into a vast courtyard where several cages with gold bars were mounted on wheels to be pulled along by teams of strong, sturdy-footed white horses. Each cage contained a wild animal, captive and denied its natural God-given right to freedom, just like me. My escort walked me leisurely alongside them, pausing to inspect each, sometimes speaking a few words to the animals' attendants, who were all clad in red shirts, bright yellow breeches, black leather boots, and round red felt hats with flat tops and a long, dangling black tassel. Each man had a jeweled dagger and a whip tucked in his black leather belt. Everyone bowed and treated the regal Negro with the utmost obedience and respect. He was clearly someone of great importance. I wondered if he might be a Nubian prince.

There was a lion, a tiger, a zebra, a leopard, a gazelle, a crocodile, a hippopotamus, a great bear standing up on its hind legs, a mighty black ape, and a smaller shaggy-haired orange one that stuck its tongue out at me and tried to grasp the feathers in my hair through the golden bars. I laughed and stuck my own tongue out as I dodged its grasping hand. In the next cage was an enormous brown and gold snake, its long body twisted into powerful bone-crushing coils, just like the one Euphemia David used to wear around her neck like a living, slithering shawl, only this one was much larger. I doubted she would have even been able to lift this great snake; it was the largest one I had ever seen.

"Li Grande Zombi!" I cried—here was something familiar at last!—and impulsively reached through the bars to touch it, but I was quickly pulled back and delivered a stern admonishment.

"It isn't poisonous," I pouted, but of course no one understood me.

The cage at the end of the line was empty; the door at the back stood open wide and there were steps leading up to it. I understood then what was expected of me. Like victorious Romans' conquered captives taken back to Rome, paraded in chains through the streets behind their chariots, I was to be put on display.

I looked at the man standing next to me. Was he the king of this land of golden domes and veiled women? Was I, his lone pearl-skinned slave, the ultimate tribute to his power and vanity? He urged me toward the steps, gesturing for me to mount them and enter the gilded cage.

Reluctantly, I obeyed. I had no other choice. Disobedience might mean death, and that was not the escape I was looking for; if I was ever to go home again I had to stay alive and endure whatever I must.

My skirt was so wide I had to squeeze in sideways. The door instantly swung shut behind me and I heard the rattle of chains and a large lock snap shut. I turned around to look. They were all gold, just like the bars of the cage, brightly polished and shining like the sun, but a gilt cage is still a cage; precious metals do not make it any less a prison.

I watched my red-and-yellow-clad keeper adjusting the chains and locks; I understood this was all part of the show. The whip and dagger in his belt suddenly angered me, as though he thought I might need taming like a tiger or a lion.

"What are you going to do if I don't obey, beat me or stab me?" I demanded, though he just shook his head and shrugged his shoulders as a puzzled frown furrowed his brow.

I caught an amused smile flitting across the face of the richly robed Negro as he stood studying me through the golden bars. I had the strongest suspicion then that he had understood me, my actual words, not just my indignation.

"You *do* understand French!" I rounded on him accusingly.

"I never said I did not, mademoiselle," he answered me in fluent, though oddly accented, French.

"Who are you, and where am I, and what am I doing here? What do you want with me?" I stamped my foot and demanded furiously. "I want to go home *now!* I am Aimee Dubucq de Rivery; my father owns a plantation in Martinique; sugar and cocoa have made him very rich; he will pay you well if . . ."

My words trailed off and tears pricked at my eyes. He was already shaking his head.

"This is the first, and last, conversation we shall have in your language, mademoiselle," he said in a firm voice that brooked no argument. "You must forget it and learn ours. Your father's money is of no interest to us; we are only interested in you. . . ."

I gasped and stepped back, instinctively wrapping my arms around my breasts. Though I was fully dressed and he had already seen me naked and probed my most intimate parts with his fingers, the way he spoke those words and looked at me made me feel very vulnerable and bare indeed.

"You asked who I am and where you are," he continued. "You are in Constantinople, within the walls of Topkapi Palace, in the harem of the Sultan of the Ottoman Empire. I am the Kizlar Aga, the Chief Black Eunuch of God's Shadow on Earth, Sultan Abdul Hamid I. I walk but one step behind him, after him I am the most powerful man in this palace, and *I* rule here; in the harem *my* word is law. My name is Lâle. Your new name is yet to be decided, but you are no longer Aimee. If you please the Sultan tonight your education begins tomorrow."

He started to walk away from me, but I was not ready to end the conversation.

"And if I *don't?*" I challenged his bejeweled back. "If I *don't* please your sultan, what then?"

"You will be sewn in a sack with rocks at your feet and thrown into the Bosphorus to drown," Lâle answered matter-of-factly without turning around. "The Sultan would *never* give such a rare and splendid jewel to another man. A woman with skin like a pearl, eyes the color of perfect sapphires, and hair like gold, you are worth more than all the sugar and cocoa your father could grow even if he lived one hundred years; there has *never* been anyone like you here. I have no doubt that Abdul Hamid will drop his handkerchief for you." At my puzzled look he explained, "When the Sultan drops his handkerchief for a woman that is the signal that he has chosen her for the night. Please him or die, mademoiselle; that is the *one* choice you *do* have. When you are presented to the Sultan I suggest you bow and kiss the hem of his robe."

He left me then, alone in my gilded cage, to contemplate my fate and whether or not I had a future.

Before long, the wheels beneath my feet began to turn. As the procession of cages lurched slowly along, I curled my hands around the gilded bars and willed myself not to cry. I wouldn't give them the satisfaction of seeing my tears. I listened to the cries of the animals in the cages before me; they were angry and frightened, just like me.

They were prisoners too, destined to die, for sport or their skins, or to spend the rest of their lives behind bars being stared at; it all depended on the Sultan's pleasure. I already hated him.

We were taken into another courtyard where a large dais had been erected. Hundreds of jewel-colored cushions had been arranged around it where richly appareled and bejeweled beauties with lavish veiled headdresses and heavily painted faces lolled. Upon the dais sat three thrones, occupied by three men in opulent embroidered robes and jeweled turbans. The first was quite old, the second but a few years older than myself, and the third a beardless boy of about twelve or so. The Sultan and his heirs, I assumed.

As my cage was rolled in I was struck by how bored everyone seemed. None of the women rose from their indolent poses to take a closer look at this zoo on wheels; they seemed more interested in their long jeweled pipes and the trays of sweetmeats and gilded cups of coffee and sherbet servants were passing amongst them. The men upon their thrones seemed equally indifferent.

When I first sighted the Sultan he was yawning. The hand that rose to cover his mouth wore great glittering rings on every finger and there was an emerald the size of my fist holding a spray of white feathers on his tall gold-and-silver-striped turban. His silken robe was so densely embroidered in silver and gold I could not tell the color beneath it.

After a lengthy pause the gilded wheels began to turn again, all the animals exited, but my cage, the last in line, was driven to a more prominent position, directly opposite the Sultan's throne.

Perhaps it will seem vain of me to say it, but I woke them all up. The Sultan sat up straight on his throne and his eyes opened wide. He sat forward, rubbing his hands against his thighs, smiling and drinking me in with his eyes. Beside him, the elder prince fumbled in the folds of his lavender and silver robes and withdrew a pair of gold-framed spectacles and put them on, craning his neck forward to get a better look at me. The younger prince's mouth hung open in a perfect O of astonishment; I saw him gesture to one of his attendants and mime the shape of my panniers, sticking out from my hips, presumably asking if I was shaped like that underneath. All the ladies sat upright on their cushions and took note, of me and the Sultan's reaction; even the ones who had seen me before were seeing me now with new eyes, tinted, I feared, by the malicious green cast of jealousy.

Rubbing his hands and smiling broadly, showing a set of perfect ivory teeth, Lâle came around to the back of my cage. He ordered the attendant to unlock the door and let down the steps. He beckoned to me and held out his hand to help me descend. My panniers were so wide he could barely grasp my fingertips as he walked me around to stand in front of the cage.

The ladies were now pointing and whispering about me and my—to them—peculiar mode of dress, and the way I wore my hair in a mound of fussily bedecked and befeathered curls. Some of them made gestures about their hips, and I knew they were talking about the panniers that made my skirt stand out. They had never seen such a thing before.

"Proceed!" Lâle whispered to me in French, and I felt the slight pressure of his hand on my back, urging me forward.

Nervously, I bobbed a hurried little curtsy that was far from worthy of Versailles or any sovereign; if Mother Angélique had seen me she would have laid my palm open even though I was standing before a heathen potentate. My curtsy was instinctive; it seemed the proper and polite thing to do. I was after all in the presence of royalty. But even as I did it a little voice in the back of my head was *raging,* how *dare* I even *think* about being courteous to this barbarian who was holding me captive, *enslaved,* against my will.

The Sultan's hand rose, beckoning me forward. I took a few steps, then faltered uncertainly. The Sultan smiled encouragingly and his fingers moved again, urging me onward. He was smiling and his eyes were shining, and that made me *very, very* frightened. I had a feeling that if he had been frowning my fear would have been lesser. Lâle was at my back again, giving me another little push. "*Go!*" he hissed.

When I was only a few feet away from the Sultan he reached inside his gilt-encrusted robe and drew out a white silk handkerchief edged in gold. I watched with mounting dread as he held it up high, for all to see, and then he let it fall. I felt only horror as I watched it flutter to the floor.

"Bow! Kiss the hem of his robe!" Lâle whispered urgently behind my back. "Show your appreciation, you stupid girl! He likes
you; he has chosen you!"

"*No!*" I shook my head adamantly. "*No! I will not!*" I whirled
around defiantly and ran from the courtyard as fast as my feet could
carry me, bolting through the nearest door, though I had no idea
where it led, taffeta skirts rustling like a flock of frightened birds
and my pink satin high heels clacking a loud, desperate rhythm on
the polished floors.

I raced frantically through the twists and turns of the maze-like
palace. Soon I was hopelessly lost. When I met a man in one of the
corridors he flung up his arm to shield his eyes and turned his back
and hurried away from me. I didn't understand why, and I didn't
know the words to ask him for help.

"Sir, *please!*" I ran after him, but that only made him quicken
his steps. "Harem!" I kept desperately repeating, hoping he would
understand that I was lost and trying to find my way back there. I
didn't know where else to go; even if I were able to find my way out
of the palace into the city proper my coloring marked me out as so
unusual I feared the attentions of any man I might encounter.

I don't know how long I wandered through that great, magnificent maze, more luxurious than anything I had ever seen, before a
pair of black eunuchs came and shepherded me gently back to the
harem and my divan in the dormitory. I was so relieved to see it that
I flung myself down upon it and wept.

Lâle came to me a little while later.

I sat up and hastily dried my tears. Euphemia David's snake
charm fell from my handkerchief, onto my lap. I caught it up and
clutched it tight in my hand, praying that it would give me courage.

"Have you brought the sack?" I asked Lâle.

"No," he answered, "I have come to take you to the Sultan."

"*No!*" I stood and stamped my foot. "I will *not* go! I will not be
that old man's concubine!"

"You *will* go to him," Lâle said calmly. "Dry your tears and fix
your face. If he sends you from him in disgrace before this night is
over, I will have the sack ready, waiting for you when you come
back. If the morning light finds you still in his favor, you will begin
learning our ways, and our language."

He took a step toward me and clasped my face hard between his hands and stared deep into my eyes.

"Do not be a fool, girl; your future will be as golden as your hair if you but let it! You will *never* go home again, whether you please the Sultan or not. The life you knew is *over;* consider it dead and buried! Your family has probably already given you up for dead. Even if you could get word to them, to reassure them that you are still alive, do you think it would make them feel better to know where you are, and what you are now—a concubine in the Sultan's harem? Most Christians would account it a fate worse than death; some would rather see their daughters dead. . . ."

My breath caught in my throat and almost choked me. I had never thought of that! My poor parents, how they would weep; they would be inconsolable if they knew I was living but lost to them in this most shameful and dreadful manner. Their torment would be constant; they would never be at peace. From convent girl to concubine, it would surely kill them. They must *never* know. I would rather keep my silence and let them mourn me as dead than torture them with the truth. The Aimee they had known and loved had been lost at sea, so it was not *exactly* a lie. I was about to be reborn as someone new; soon I would even be given a new name, and a new tongue to speak. *Mama, Papa, keep that girl alive in your hearts,* I prayed. *Think of her fondly, once in a while gaze upon her picture, and always remember how much she loved you.*

Lâle gave my shoulders a shake, to get my attention. "Think about that later, when you have time! Meanwhile . . . your new life begins tonight! Or . . . you can resist the Sultan and die for it. Even if he should choose to be merciful and spare your life, yours would be a living death and this place your tomb until misery drives you to take your own life or else you waste away grieving the opportunity you scorned. For I tell you now, once lost it will *never* come again; there are no second chances in the harem. Or you can be sensible and wise, please the Sultan, and prosper; if you do, you will reign here, and you might someday rule. Just because you are a slave does not mean you have to be powerless. You might find someday that you hold the reins of power right here in your hand." He tapped my palm.

When he touched my hand and spoke those words I gasped and

stepped back as though he had struck me. Though he did not know it, Lâle was echoing words spoken by a voodoo sorceress long ago. I sank down onto the bed and uncurled my fist and regarded the golden serpent with ruby glass eyes swallowing its own tail. I remembered the words Euphemia David had whispered to me the night before I sailed away to France when she had given me this talisman.

"In my end is my beginning," I whispered tremulously.

I took a deep breath, willing myself to be strong, and then I stood and went to the mirror to straighten my hair and repair the damage my tears had caused to my maquillage. Impulsively I knelt, said a quick prayer, and crossed myself. *God give me courage and forgive me for what I am about to do!*

I squared my shoulders and held my head up high, like I was about to enter the grand ballroom at Versailles, not that terrible Turk's bedroom, and imperiously held out my hand to Lâle.

"I am ready now."

"Yes, you are!" He smiled and took my hand and triumphantly led me down the Golden Path. That was what they called the long corridor of gleaming gold-flecked stone, lit by ivory candles clasped in golden fists, that led the way to the Sultan's bedchamber. Every woman in the harem dreamed of walking it . . . except me. I felt like a condemned prisoner walking the last mile leading to the scaffold. I both wanted and never wanted it to end.

CHAPTER 19

The Sultan's bed was the biggest I had ever seen; I doubted any French king ever had one finer. It occupied fully half the room. It was set low as beds and couches were in this country, but unlike the backless, armless divans the women slept on in the odalisques' dormitory, it had a framework and canopy just like a four-poster bed, though more opulent than any I'm sure that had ever existed. The posts were carved like braided, entwined vines gilded silver and gold from which rubies, emeralds, and sapphires the size of hens' eggs and carved like tulips bloomed. It was hung with stiff gold brocade curtains encrusted with diamonds and pearls, ruby, emerald, and sapphire brilliants all set within whirls and swirls of silver embroidery. The curtains were open in the center, to reveal the Sultan sitting cross-legged on his mattress, waiting for me.

He was still wearing the same rich robe, turban, and jewels as when I was presented to him and I wondered if I was expected to undress him. I had assumed he would have already changed to his sleeping attire or else be nude in his bed, waiting for me to join him. Lâle had said nothing of this when, outside the door, he had given me my instructions. I was to kneel before the Sultan, kiss his feet, and then advance upwards, all the way up his body, until my lips met his.

"Even in Paradise," Lâle explained over my appalled and out-
raged protestations, "Muslims believe that a woman's place is beneath the soles of a man's feet. In token of this belief, to show your
humility and respect, you start at the Sultan's feet."

"You'd best go see about that sack!" I said tartly as I flounced
past Lâle in an indignant rustle of pink taffeta and irately swinging
gold tassels. I just wanted to be done with all this. I didn't want to
die, but they were probably going to kill me anyway, so I might as
well get it over with while trying to preserve some degree of dignity.

Instead of entering gracefully, like a lady, I flounced in like a
sulky, pouting child. The lamps were burning golden and low and
the incense formed a dense blue-gray cloud. I heard the music of
lutes and harps and was startled to see a pair of musicians sitting in
the shadows.

"Don't worry; they cannot see you. They are blind," said a kind
voice in the same oddly accented French that Lâle spoke. I was so
grateful that the Sultan spoke my language I almost wept. At least
this awkward seduction would not have to be conducted in pan-
tomime!

That was when I whirled around and had my first sight of the
weary Sultan sitting cross-legged on his magnificent bed. Abdul
Hamid was sixty-four, jaded and weary. He had the eyes of a man
who thinks he has lived too long and seen too much. His beard and
hair were dyed a startling black, but this only served to emphasize
his age and the deep lines hewn into his face rather than encourag-
ing the illusion of youth. His hands, the skin thin and crinkled like
crêpe, bearing the dark spots of age, rested in the lap of his regal
robe, seemingly exhausted by the weight of the enormous rings,
great slabs of gemstones set in heavy gold, that he wore on every
finger. There was a general air of weariness about him, like he carried the weight of the world upon his shoulders and was only waiting for the day when he could at last lay this burden down.

I stood and stared and then recollected myself and bobbed a
quick curtsy.

The Sultan chuckled. "Come here," he said.

I took a tentative step forward as the musicians finished one
song and began another. I paused and glanced back at them.

"Did *you* blind them? Or order it done?" I asked. I was sud-

denly overcome with curiosity. I had heard that some of the songbird sellers in Paris believed that blind birds made better singers,
so they carefully stuck pins in their eyes. I thought it was terribly
cruel and hated to think that there were men in this world who
would do that to another and that I might have the misfortune to
be standing before one of them.

"No, they were born that way," the Sultan said patiently.

There was an amused smile on his lips as he held out his hand
to me.

I knew what must be done, so I might as well do it and get it
over with; brooding about it only made it worse. But I certainly
wasn't going to go groveling on the floor to him. Pride aside, my
stays were laced so tight they would never allow it.

As my hand landed lightly as a hummingbird in his the Sultan's
smile broadened. "Ah, how *beautiful* you are!" he sighed. "A living
woman of gold and alabaster with sapphires for eyes!"

In that moment I realized that unlike any other concubine who
had ever come to him before, he was looking up at me instead of
down. In all the years that women had been coming to Abdul
Hamid's bed, first as a prince, and then as a sultan, *I* was the only
one who had approached him on her feet instead of crawling on
her knees.

"Thank you," I whispered, and curtsied again so he would not
think me insolent, if he didn't already, since we both knew I really
should be kneeling.

"Lâle told you what to do?" he asked.

Now the subject was out in the open. I almost felt relieved.

"He did." I nodded.

"So why do you not do it?" Abdul Hamid asked in such a way
that I wasn't sure if he was curious or cross.

"Well . . ." I nibbled my lower lip thoughtfully, then decided to
throw all caution to the wind. Boldness, I decided, would be either
my destruction or my salvation. "It could be that I would rather die
on my feet than live on my knees, or my stays are too tight to allow
me to grovel about on the floor like a pig after truffles." As I spoke
I touched my torso, tracing the lines of the whalebone beneath the
taut taffeta bodice in case the Sultan, like his ladies, was unfamiliar
with corsets. "Then again"—I smiled—"it *might* be both; a woman

mustn't give away *all* her secrets upon first acquaintance, Your Majesty." This time I made the *perfect* slow and graceful curtsy; after the nine years they had spent drilling me in this routine day after tedious day, the nuns would have been *so* proud of me.

Abdul Hamid threw back his head and laughed until tears ran from his dark almond eyes. "How marvelous!" he cried, and gleefully clapped his hands. In that moment, the years seemed to fall from him, and I glimpsed the boy that still lived deep inside the old man.

"Lâle said I should endeavor to please the Sultan," I said. "I hope in this small way I have succeeded by giving him the gift of laughter."

"And fearlessness," Abdul Hamid added. "You are not afraid of me."

I didn't dare disappoint him by telling him that I was, so I just smiled. *Brazen it out,* I kept telling myself.

"Come, sit with me"—he patted the mattress beside him—"if you can manage it," he added, smiling as I struggled with my unwieldy skirts. "Tell me of yourself, and this"—he flourished his hand to take in my attire—"*thing* you are wearing. And do not speak of dying; you are so very young and have so much life yet ahead of you; for you the end of the road is not even in sight."

"Ah, but what sort of life, Sire?" I sighed, glancing around at this dimly lit damask-lined room with the subdued glimmer of gold everywhere my eyes lighted upon—in the weave of the carpets and the wall hangings, in every fixture and ornament, the lamps swaying overhead and the incense burners. It was like being trapped inside a perfumed jewel box.

"That remains to be seen," the Sultan said. "As does what is beneath all this." He batted playfully at my pink flounces. "Generous hips are believed to be a sign that a woman will be fertile and give her husband many sons, but surely your hips are not quite so generous as this." He indicated my panniers.

Now it was my turn to laugh. "Not even by half, Sire. It is the fashion in Paris. The Queen wears them even wider than this; they have had to have all the doorways widened and raised at Versailles to accommodate her skirts and hair." I touched my rose-and-plume-festooned pompadour and raised my hand to show that Marie Antoinette wore hers even higher.

Abdul Hamid shook with laughter. "That is the most preposterous thing I have ever heard! A beautiful woman has no need of such foolish adornments."

I was surprised by how easy it was to talk to him, and by how much I enjoyed it. He asked many questions and wanted to know everything about me. My life in Martinique and at the convent school in France—my battle of wills with Mother Angélique particularly amused him—the voodoo and black magic that existed side by side with the Catholic faith on my native isle, and Parisian society and its customs and ever-evolving fashions.

He was keenly interested in King Louis XVI and Queen Marie Antoinette, and that beautiful lady's flamboyant foibles and fashions. King Louis was said to be bookish and almost painfully shy and to prefer clock and lock making to royal pageantry and affairs of state, and to be lost without his spectacles. These descriptions of him reminded Abdul Hamid of his nephew, and heir, Prince Selim. I learned then that in Turkey the throne does not pass from father to son in a direct line but is instead inherited by the eldest surviving male. Abdul Hamid did have a son, Mustafa, the young boy I had seen seated with him on the dais, but the throne would only be his when death claimed his cousin Selim.

Abdul Hamid was kind and wise, with a wry sense of humor. He put me at ease and made me laugh too. I found it impossible to hate him or think of him as a cruel barbarian, a Terrible Turk, holding me captive. And it made me feel good to know that I had lifted the mantle of weariness from his shoulders and brought a light back to his eyes. As we sat and talked, sipped sherbets and nibbled sweetmeats, that jaded and world-weary air that had been almost the first thing I noticed about him disappeared entirely.

"You replenish me," he said, and I accounted it a very great compliment. "You peel the years away from this old husk"—he touched his chest—"and make me feel almost young again."

"Sixty-four seems not so old to me, Sire," I said. "Euphemia David, the Queen of the Voodoos on our island, is said to be over one hundred years old, some say she is nearer to two hundred, that she was still a young woman when their own grandparents danced to the drumbeats, and I have known slaves well into their eighth decade, many of them still quite spry."

He smiled into my eyes and reached out to caress my cheek. I did not avert my eyes or flinch, not even when his fingers strayed down to toy with the golden ringlets falling over my shoulder, onto my breasts. He touched me gently, respectfully, almost reverently. I did not feel sullied or cheapened at all, nor any of the self-hatred I had always been led to believe a woman of easy virtue and low morals must feel. I didn't feel wrong at all, only right.

At last, the Sultan asked, "Will you stay the night with me?"

I knew what he was asking and what was expected of me. I wondered what would happen to me if I said *no*. Was there *any* chance he would take pity on me and send me home to Martinique? Or would all his good humor vanish and a vengeful barbarian rise up before my eyes, ready to cut me down or entomb me alive? I thought of the weighted sack and wondered if Lâle already had it ready, waiting for me. But what surprised me most was that I didn't really want to see what the bitter fruits of refusal would be; it was only idle curiosity with no serious intent behind it. Of my own free will, I wanted to stay and find out what would happen if I said *yes*.

I struggled to my feet, hampered by my heavy skirts, almost knocking over a gilt pitcher of sherbet with my panniers, and turned my back to the Sultan, leaving him wondering, just for a moment, if I was about to walk away. I glanced back over my shoulder and smiled as I drew his attention to the pink laces crisscrossing the back of my bodice. "I cannot manage this on my own."

"I shall be happy to help you." Abdul Hamid smiled as he came to me. "Tell me what to do; I have never before played tiring woman."

He put his arms around me and kissed the curve of my shoulder. "As novel as this costume is"—his hands glided over my tightly cinched waist, then followed the lines of my panniers, taffeta trembling and rustling with every touch—"I think you shall look even more alluring in Turkish clothes; and they are much more easily shed. And you will be more comfortable, and less clumsy too. Your hips will not be putting pitchers in peril every time you turn around."

Layer by layer, with an abundance of shared laughter, we managed to divest me of my French finery. As each garment was laid aside I told him the name of it. And when it was my turn, with nervous, trembling hands, to help him disrobe, he told me the name of each garment in Turkish.

When we were naked as Adam and Eve in the Garden of Eden, kneeling on the bed, he was patient with me, and so very kind. I kept my eyes wide open all the time. Mother Angélique would have been *appalled!*

As I lay beneath him, a maiden no more, but a woman who had just experienced the most exquisite pleasure—he had taken such care with me!—Abdul Hamid smiled down into my eyes and kissed my brow. "*Nakshidil,*" he whispered tenderly. "Do you know what that means?"

I shook my head. His tone told me that it was an endearment, but I had no idea of its exact meaning.

"That is your new name. It means 'embroidered upon the heart.' " He kissed my hand and laid it over his heart as he spoke my name again: "*Nakshidil!*"

PART 3

—◆—

JOSEPHINE

CHAPTER 20

From the moment Bonaparte changed my name, my life would never again be the same; *I* would never be the same. The moment I let him touch me, I felt my *true* self, Rose, fading away. *Josephine*—in truth, I *hated* the name! Only one thing good could be said about it: It provided a means by which I could always divine and divide my true friends from the flatterers and favor-seekers; the latter always called me Josephine, but to the former I would always be Rose.

When Bonaparte left my bed that chilly dawn, still in muddy boots and rumpled uniform, he uncorked the champagne that had sat all night, untouched in a silver bucket filled with ice. He insisted that we must drink a toast—"To Destiny!"

Without giving me a chance to take even one sip from my glass, he drained his, flung it into the fire, and fell on me again, spilling champagne all over the pink coverlet as the glass tumbled from my hand.

"You, Josephine, are my destiny!" he cried as he ravenously took possession of me again.

I didn't say anything. I was too overwhelmed to speak or even clearly think. My body instinctively did what was required of it while my thoughts were racing about, lost and afraid in an indecisive fog. I didn't want this, Bonaparte wasn't the man for me, but the alternative was too terrible to consider. My instinct was to run away as fast as I could, but where to? Where could I be safe? Was there anywhere far enough away to escape Barras's campaign of slander or Bonaparte's mad, obsessive passion? They would pursue me to the ends of the earth, I was sure. And what hope had I, at my age, of starting over again? I was thirty-two, though I lied and told everyone I was twenty-nine. I was certain I could never make a success of it even if I tried. I would surely die a pauper.

I was a coward and I took the coward's way out. I decided that it was better to marry Bonaparte and make the best of it than risk Barras's wrath and spending the rest of my life a poor outcast. Security was like a drug I craved and Bonaparte could give me a lifetime supply of it. He would "love" me in his way and always take care of me, even if his embraces and kisses stifled me to the point where I wanted to scream.

I woke to his letter lying on the pillow beside mine with a pink rose, wilting from the cold, on top of it.

> *I wake up filled with thoughts of you. Your image and the intoxicating pleasure of your touch allow my senses no respite. Sweet and thrilling Josephine, what strange power you have over my heart! My happiness depends on you. Are you annoyed with me? Are you unhappy? Are you upset? My soul is broken with grief and my love for you denies me repose. But how can I rest when I submit to the feeling that overwhelms my very self, when I drink from your lips and from your heart a soothing flame? Yes! One night has taught me how short your portraits fall of reality! You start at noon; in three hours I shall see you again! Till then, a thousand kisses, mio dolce amore, but give me none back for they set my soul on fire!*

I glanced at the clock, groaned, and pulled the covers up over my head. God save me, he would be at my door again in half an hour! It was all *too* much! I wanted to bury my head under the pillows and pretend I wasn't home, but I didn't dare.

I know that I should have been both grateful and flattered to be the object of so great a love. Here was a man who would lay down his life to keep me safe, my tears melted his heart, my smile warmed it, and just the touch of my hand drove him wild, yet I felt suffocated by his attentions; he was *always* there. As soon as I woke up, he was the first person I saw except for my maid, and the last when I went to sleep at night. He would not give me air; he would not let me breathe! I felt like an animal in a trap—*his* trap—I wanted him to just let go. The truth is I think I saw too much of myself, and my foolish girlish young dreams, which had been so coldly and cruelly shattered by Alexandre de Beauharnais, in Bonaparte's passionate adoration of me. He was so besotted, and I was so indifferent, and he was so oblivious and blindly confident that he could win me and I equally certain that he could not. I don't think either of us really knew what love was. I had been selling my body for too long, to buy security or just to escape unpleasant realities, I had forgotten, if I ever really knew, what love felt like. I was afraid I already knew how this story would end, but I didn't want to think about it. Facts are brutal; lies soften and sometimes evade or delay the blows. Was it any wonder that I far preferred the latter?

Every time Bonaparte looked at me and called me his Josephine, Rose was *screaming* inside, pounding on the door, trying to get out. I had never been good enough for Alexandre either. Josephine was *his* ideal, *his* creation. It was *not* only a name! Shakespeare was wrong: Names *do* matter; a rose *must* be called a rose. My name was only the beginning. I was already losing myself in Bonaparte's love, and it frightened me, because I thought it meant that he didn't really love *me;* he had to make me into someone else he could love. From that first dawn after I let him into my bed there was anger and resentment, and fear, *always* fear, lurking behind my sweet smile.

When I tried to talk to them about it, Theresa and Barras laughed at the vision of Bonaparte at my feet worshipping me like a goddess. They knew the real me; to them I was all too earthy and flawed. They didn't understand; they thought such adoration should please me.

Everyone said I was doing the right thing; marrying Bonaparte would give me security. It was "the perfect tonic to an aging woman," as Barras rather bluntly put it.

If Bonaparte continued on his self-ordained path to greatness, I, as his wife, would share his glory. His victory over the recent royalist uprising had already brought him a measure of fame. The boorish little Corsican general was no longer a nobody. People cheered him in the streets. *Shades of Alexandre again,* I thought, and shuddered, remembering how my estranged husband's fame had brought me almost to the guillotine.

My children and I would be protected and provided for, Barras continued persuasively, and it was hoped that I could rub some of the rough edges off Bonaparte. We would be *so* good for each other! He would lend me strength; I would give him gentleness in return. My softness would pillow his hardness; my elegance would be an antidote to his crassness. We would each supply what the other lacked.

Barras told me not to fret; after the wedding Bonaparte would soon be on his way, chasing glory, off to conquer Italy, and I would be left in Paris, in peace, to do as I pleased. The Directory thought my presence would prove too distracting; they wanted a victory. Bonaparte must give his full attention to military matters, not bedchamber idylls, so there was no question of my accompanying him.

And after that . . . Barras was quick to remind me that ardor is always most intense in the first flush of passion, but after that it fades so quickly; a man soon discovers that one woman's kisses are very like the rest. There is no such thing as undying love. Bonaparte's ardor would be only a minor, and fleeting, annoyance; then I would be back weeping on Barras's shoulder again because my husband never paid attention to me anymore. "Women," said Barras, "are fickle and never satisfied."

CHAPTER 21

———◄○►———

We were married at midnight on March 9, 1796, at the decaying Hôtel du Mondragon, which had been converted into a town hall. Theresa, Tallien, Barras, and one of Bonaparte's aides acted as witnesses. The hour was so late because Bonaparte had lost all sense of time poring over his maps of Italy and plans for the upcoming campaign. The candles were sputtering and the registrar had already gone off to bed in a huff declaring that when—*if*—the groom ever arrived his subordinate, already dozing at his desk, could marry us.

Theresa and I shivered in our thin white dresses and huddled near the fire. As usual, we had considered our appearances before the weather. To please my husband-to-be, who often told me he found no sight on earth more pleasing than a graceful woman gowned in white, I was wearing white on our wedding night, though it was only a civil ceremony. My arms were bare and the straps of my filmy, flowing Grecian-style gown were held up by bronze cameos of Julius Caesar crowned with laurel leaves, and a third cameo belted the red velvet sash just below my breasts. There were red satin ribbons crisscrossing my limbs from ankles to knees to fasten my golden sandals and I was wearing ruby and sapphire rings on my toes. I was so cold I longed for a full-length ermine coat, but all I had was my red and gold cashmere shawl.

As the clock struck the last stroke of twelve, Bonaparte bounded up the stairs, seized me in his arms, and kissed me on the lips. Declaring me "the most beautiful bride who ever lived," he hung round my neck a great gold medallion with a wreath of laurel leaves encircling the boldly etched words *To Destiny!* It felt cold and heavy between my breasts and I lifted it to examine it as best I could in the light of the dying candles. I had the ominous feeling that it was more than just a pretty ornament but something akin to a dog collar to let the world know who my master was.

But I didn't have time to think; Bonaparte was shaking the clerk awake and urging, "Let's get on with it!" Thus we were married in haste with, I feared, years' worth of leisure yawning before us in which to repent. I just hoped I was doing the right thing. It was *so* hard to be certain! But Barras would ruin me if I didn't go through with it, Bonaparte thought he loved me, and he certainly loved my children. *Be sure to tell them that I love them as if they were my own,* he had once written. *What is yours or mine is so mixed up in my heart that there is no difference there.* He was taking Eugène to Italy with him as his aide-de-camp and he thought Hortense was a darling and doted on each little painted porcelain knickknack she gave him as though it were a great work of art.

"Don't worry," Theresa whispered in my ear. "If it doesn't work out you can always get a divorce!"

But I failed to find much comfort in her words.

I should have taken his lateness as an omen. It would indeed prove to be my destiny—to always wait for Bonaparte, in every way, in all things.

In my bed that night, my dear old pug, Fortune, growled at Bonaparte and refused to budge. I shrugged and told my new husband that he would have to share the bed or sleep elsewhere, as Fortune had the prior claim. When Bonaparte instead tried to shift Fortune, my cantankerous pug lunged and sank his teeth deep into Bonaparte's leg. This time he ruined my coverlet by bleeding all over it.

Two days later when Bonaparte rode off to Italy he was still wearing a bandage. I got up long enough to kiss him good-bye.

"There has never been a love like mine," he said as he embraced me one last time. "It will last as long as my life."

I just wanted to go back to bed, but he insisted that I stand, framed in the window, so he could see me one last time before he rode away.

I was already turning away from the window, yawning, pulling up the sagging straps of my nightgown, and staggering back to bed while he was still blowing kisses and waving good-bye, as excited as a little boy. I was sure I wouldn't miss him at all; as Barras had said, I would have all the pleasures of Paris to console me. And there was work for me to do—as a wedding present, Bonaparte had said I could redecorate the house to render it worthy of a returning hero. "Just make sure to put portraits of yourself everywhere and whatever else you do I shall be pleased," he said.

Before he had even been away a week he had bombarded me with so many letters anyone would have thought that I was the one he was laying siege to. Like cannonballs they came at me, ardent sentiments such as:

> *You are the constant object of my thoughts, my incomparable Josephine, away from you there is no joy—away from you the world is a wilderness in which I am alone.*

> *To live for Josephine, that is the story of my life!*

> *I would be so happy if I could help undress you, and see and kiss your small shoulders, supple, firm white breasts, and pretty little face with your hair tied up in a scarf à la Creole. You know that I always remember the visits to your little black forest. I kiss it a thousand times and wait impatiently for the moment when I will again be in it. To live with Josephine is to live in the Elysian Fields! Kisses on your mouth, your eyelids, your shoulders, your breasts, everywhere, everywhere!*

* * *

It made me tired just to look at them. Just touching them it seemed I could feel the heat coming off his words and the holes the impatient pen had poked through the paper. How the blots must have sizzled as soon as the ink was spilled! He was so ardent, obsessive, and untiring! Many times I would toss them on my little rosewood writing desk, promising I would open and read them later, always later, and write a line or two in answer. But it was *so* difficult; there were so many of them! They just kept piling up day after day until I could no longer see the surface of my desk and they were spilling off onto the floor. Soon their very number, not just their content, was overwhelming me. Such relentless passion is *very* fatiguing!

When I didn't answer his letters he only grew more fervent and frantic, impatient, and possessed of wild notions that I was ill or unfaithful or that I didn't love him. But if I did answer he cursed me for the brevity and blandness of my letters, counting the lines, at most three or five—I really was a poor correspondent and had always hated writing letters—and taking them to heart, as an insult, as the true measure of my love. He said I wrote as coldly as though we had been married fifteen years.

You are the only woman I have ever loved and adored! If you do not love me anymore, there is nothing *left for me! If I have lost your love, I have lost more than life, more than happiness, I have lost* everything! he agonized in words so blotted by tears and ink that it overtaxed my poor eyes just to read them.

One day when he discovered that the glass on the miniature portrait he always carried of me had cracked he became convinced that it was a sign that I was either dying or unfaithful. The whole situation really was too tedious for words! All that hard riding and gunfire, the cannonballs that shook the earth and showered shrapnel, I would have been more surprised if the glass hadn't cracked! But there was no telling Bonaparte that. I was his superstition, his talisman, his good-luck charm, and he considered me one of the rays of his star.

My husband should have been less demanding; after all, I was only doing what he asked me to, renovating our home to make it worthy of him. I threw myself into a frenzy of shopping, consulting with decorators and designers, carpenters, painters, and furniture-makers. I ordered pink roses and swans painted on my bedroom walls and bought a harp and new bronze chairs and tables topped in rose-colored marble and a new, even bigger bed with a tent-like canopy of pink satin. Since I must take even greater care of my appearance now that I had a husband six years my junior to please, I had my dressing room lined entirely, floor to ceiling, with mirrors, and a new marble bath. I had the dining room done over in gold and red and purchased a new mahogany table and chairs.

Since Bonaparte said that he desired to see my portrait everywhere, I took him at his word. I began to pose each afternoon for artists. Many of them were eager to have me pose for them now that I was famous again. So there I was, my painted presence, everywhere in every room, in flowing white dresses and colored shawls glimmering discreetly with gold threads, with cameos and diadems evocative of ancient glories or pink or white roses in my hair, which I had let grow long again. I posed in profile, face forward, or full figure, sitting, standing, or half-reclining on sofas, always with a wistfully sweet, closemouthed smile that lent me a provocative air of melancholy that always made men long to comfort me. Sometimes the paintings showed me standing at windows longing to see my husband return, waiting alone on a garden bench surrounded by roses; they even depicted me reading his letters with a stack of them in my lap and scattered like white rose petals around my feet.

One grand larger-than-life canvas showed me as "Our Lady of Victories," standing with the torn and bullet-riddled flags of conquered nations at my feet and a portrait of my husband on the wall behind me, looking over my shoulder. And there were engravings of me in all the newspapers—Barras saw to that—showing me kneeling in prayer at Notre Dame, praying for my husband and the men who had gone into battle with him, giving alms to wounded and crippled soldiers, or visiting them in hospitals. I felt guilty because these images made me look more selfless than I was. I had never been particularly religious, and the sight of blood, lost limbs, and rotting wounds made me sick and faint. Those pictures were not true portraits of me.

Everyone knew of Bonaparte's great love for me and that he carried my likeness above his heart into battle with him, like a lucky charm he was never without, pressing it to his lips before the first charge and again in thankfulness after. I was his lucky star. As long as he had me, he believed that he could never be defeated, and his ever-increasing string of victories seemed to prove it.

"Vive Madame Bonaparte!" the people would shout every time I appeared in public. Every time my husband scored another victory there was dancing and singing in the street outside our house. I couldn't step outside without being pelted with flowers, poetry, and praise. Everyone adored me and wanted to kiss my hand or hem. I was the subject of songs and sonnets. My likeness was *everywhere,* sold in shops and on street corners, in every newspaper and magazine, even on painted fans, playing cards, and snuffboxes. There were balls and supper parties in my honor; plays and operas were dedicated to me; every time I went to the theater everyone stood up and cheered when I entered my box. No merchant dared deny me credit. All I had to do was walk into any shop in Paris and point and say, "I want that!" and it was mine; it didn't matter if it was diamonds or dancing slippers, an Oriental carpet, a suite of rosewood furniture, or an ancient Etruscan urn.

Every eye appraised me, the women noting every detail of my costume from the top of my head to my toes. I was featured in every fashion magazine; there were engravings and beautiful colored plates of me in all manner of dresses—negligees, afternoon dresses, riding habits, evening dresses, and ball gowns. I was the darling of *Le Journal des Dames et des Modes,* which was widely regarded as the Bible of fashion; even British women smuggled copies across the Channel to see what I was wearing. If I wore roses in my hair or a long gold pin encrusted with diamonds and shaped like an arrow it was news of the most vital importance.

I was famous again; I tried to enjoy it, but my previous experience riding on the comet's tail of Alexandre's fame had tempered my exuberance and taught me how quickly it could all go sour. Adored one day, abhorred the next. Every star that rises must also fall. The end was inevitable; it was only a question of when.

My real happiness came from something that had nothing to do with fame. I was in love again. As cruel Fate would have it, no sooner had I married Bonaparte than I met the man I had been wait-ing my whole life for—Lieutenant Hippolyte Charles. With curly black hair, cornflower-blue eyes, a heart- and knee-melting smile, a wicked sense of humor, and an interest in clothes to match mine, a dandy to the core, he was my soul's *perfect* mate. The first time I saw him in his powder-blue hussar's uniform trimmed with scarlet my heart stood still, and then it melted. I swooned, but he was swift. He caught me in his arms and carried me upstairs, to my room at Theresa's country house. He stayed with me all night and we had champagne and kisses for breakfast and didn't get up until half past two.

I was simply too busy to give much time or thought to corre-spondence. I was being adored by the masses and decorating a house, posing for portraits, and there was *always more* shopping to do, and fittings with my dressmaker, and people would be offended if I didn't accept their invitations, especially when I was the guest of honor, but Bonaparte simply could not understand that. But it wasn't my fault; no woman so preoccupied could have found time to write to her husband! There simply were not enough hours in the day to accomplish everything that was being demanded of me.

Bonaparte decided if I would not write to him, then he must have me with him where he could see and touch me. He began to pester me to come to Italy until I had even less desire than ever to open his letters. I felt sick at my stomach every time a new one ar-rived.

When he found my silence on the subject deafening, he started sending his generals to my door to volunteer their services as my es-cort. I was so *desperate* to stay in Paris that I used all my wiles to win them to my side, to make my excuses to Bonaparte and per-suade him that such arduous travel was not in my best interests. If my body was the fee the generals demanded I paid it gladly; some of them were very handsome and skilled in the amatory arts, so I didn't really mind.

I began dropping coy little hints that I was ill, and Bonaparte leapt to the conclusion that I was pregnant. Since the idea gave him so much pleasure, I let him believe it. From that day forward he wrote obsessively about my "little belly" and how much he longed to see it. *I imagine constantly that I see you with your round little tummy, it will make you look* fascinating!

Of course, he was bound to be disappointed when I revealed that I had been mistaken about my condition, and I knew it was wrong to mislead him, but I just couldn't *bear* to leave Hippolyte. If only I had met him before Bonaparte! As it was, I couldn't even consider divorce. Bonaparte was the hero of France; everyone loved him and celebrated him as their savior. They would *hate* me if I divorced him.

Soon he was bewailing my absence again; his desire to see my round little belly began to outweigh the risks of travel for a woman in my condition.

Without you, I am useless here! he wrote. *I will leave the chase after glory and serving the country to others and come back to Paris to be with you, my incomparable and inconstant Josephine! A thousand daggers are ripping my heart to bits!*

To try to force me to his will, Bonaparte ordered his brother Joseph, the banker of the family, to deprive me of funds. But Hippolyte had the ideal solution—I could join him in a business venture that was bound to reap stupendous profits, thousands and thousands of livres, for everyone involved. Of course I said *yes*.

Since my days as Barras's mistress, I had not been a stranger to the world of black-market dealings, army contracts, profiteering, and speculation. With the aristocracy banished from France, the only men who could afford to support me were engaged in such dubious and shady activities. Now, as General Bonaparte's adored wife, I was able to use my influence to obtain valuable contracts for my lover to provision the French army. It was very exciting, and we now had a legitimate cause to cloak our illicit trysts and explain all the time we spent alone together—we were business partners! Every day we were out and about making deals, buying cheap, and hoping to sell high. Soon the money was pouring in, and I didn't have to worry about Joseph's penny-pinching; I had my own money.

But every time I saw a wounded soldier, a lump rose in my throat and tears filled my eyes—tears the soldiers always mistook for compassion, never guessing that they sprang from guilt. I would always stop and speak to them and empty my purse into their hands. Yet the whole time I was speaking and smiling and dispensing alms, or visiting a hospital as Bonaparte now insisted I actually do, and Barras obligingly arranged, I could not stop thinking about the shoddy, worthless supplies we had sent them: the boots that had their soles sucked off in mud, the sour wine and spoilt milk, rancid meat, moldy grains and putrid eggs, rotten cloth for uniforms that their thumbs poked through when they pulled up their breeches, seams that tore and unraveled, canvas tents that leaked, defective muskets prone to exploding, cracked ramrods, lame horses, and bridles and stirrups that broke under the slightest pressure. I could not help but wonder if I, the one these men venerated and adored as "Our Lady of Victories," the army's good-luck charm, had caused their injuries, cost this man an eye or that one an arm, and another a lifetime as an invalid, and that led to thoughts of the hundreds of others who lay dead upon the fields of battle, never to come home again. Some nights I started awake screaming after a bad dream in which I saw my son, Eugène, die or be hideously maimed when one of the muskets I had supplied exploded in his hands, burning and blinding him, turning his sweet, handsome face into a monstrosity that made even his own mother scream. It made me realize that all those men were some mother's son.

But I just couldn't stop. Life was *Heaven* with Hippolyte, and as long as Joseph held the purse strings, providing myself with an independent income was the only way I could sustain it. Otherwise, I would have to give in and go to Italy. Just the thought of it was enough to make me weep! I wanted to stay with Hippolyte! We went out with our friends and dined and danced every night, then came home and made love until dawn. We slept until half past noon or even one o'clock; sometimes we didn't get out of bed until two or three o'clock. After a leisurely and loving breakfast we bathed and dressed and went out to attend to business, to secure more cheap goods and lucrative contracts. Then it was dinner and dancing and laughter and love all over again before we fell asleep in each other's arms. I couldn't give all that up, I just *couldn't!*

But I had not reckoned on my husband's romantic delirium swaying The Directory in his favor. He was so lovelorn and frantic, so entirely, body and soul, besotted with me, that they feared he really would make good his threats to abandon the campaign for my sake. Barras came to see me, barging into my bedroom before noon while Hippolyte and I were still sound asleep. He yanked me out of bed naked and ordered me to pack. The next morning he was there again to make sure I got in the coach. I can still feel the iron grip of his hand on my soft arm, forcing me in, then slamming the door. Thus I departed for Italy, with six coaches crammed full of luggage and my maid Louise following behind. My only consolation was that Hippolyte was going with me as my escort—Barras had been kind enough to arrange that at least—and I had a new little pug dog Hippolyte had given me after my dear old Fortune died.

CHAPTER 22

———◄○►———

It was a miserable and terrifying journey over high, jagged snow-capped mountains. At times the carriage wheels were so close to the edge I feared we were about to plunge down to certain death. I fainted the one and only time I dared look down. I was dizzy from the heights and sick with a headache half the time. The winds were so cold they cut through me like knives of ice and left my skin red and raw.

The inns that we stopped at were awful, the bedding infected with bugs, and one innkeeper actually dared serve us spinach doused in lamp oil and red asparagus fried in curdled milk for supper. But Hippolyte's room was always next to mine. After we were sure everyone was asleep, he would come to me and we would make love all night. In the morning, we would stagger out and pile into the carriage still half-asleep. We slept through the day as best we could, the sway of the carriage rocking us, and the wheels going over rocks and ruts periodically jarring us awake, sending me into clinging, crying frights. But we had each other, and the night, to dream of.

When we arrived in Milan, Bonaparte was so glad to see me that he cried and covered me with kisses. He swept me up in his arms and carried me tenderly upstairs as though I were some fragile object that might break beneath too firm a touch, though I told him there was no need to exercise such caution. When I took off my veil and voluminous beige traveling coat and he saw that there was no child, he fell to his knees before me, wrapped his arms around my waist, and bathed my belly with his tears. Soon my gown was soaked through. I stroked his hair and murmured something about the mountains, the rutted roads and jarring, jagged rocks. A loud, keening wail rose as though from the very depths of his soul as he realized that our son had been sacrificed to his own selfish desire.

"You mustn't think that! Oh, Bonaparte, please, *never, never* think that!" I cried, feeling suddenly guilty that I had led him to believe he was at fault just to cloak my lies. That really was not my intention. "These things happen, Bonaparte, often without reason. . . . It might not have been the roads after all . . . just . . . nature!"

Within moments his rain of tears had turned to a shower of ardent kisses as hope came surging back. He lifted me in his arms and carried me to the bed, determined to fill me with his love, and his seed. "We shall have a son yet, you shall see! A son who will rule the world!"

I smiled, nodded, and hoped those intense gray eyes would not see through me. Sometimes I thought I didn't have an honest bone left in my body anymore. But what else could I do? The truth would have been ruinous!

Though I still bled every month, I was not certain that children were still possible for me. After I abandoned Rosette in Martinique, I had lost the benefit of her herbal brews and had of necessity switched to a rather caustic douche the midwife recommended. Though it stung and brought tears to my eyes, I had used it religiously after my abortion, for the most part, though there were a few times when I was careless and forgot or, for whatever reason, just didn't bother. During those hellish months when I was a prisoner in Les Carmes, coupling recklessly and desperately with any man who wanted me, I did not have recourse to the douche, or any other preventatives, yet I never conceived, and that at a time when I would have welcomed the chance to plead my belly and stay the descending blade of the guillotine. Afterward, in those hedonistic days when I danced at the Victims' Balls so grateful to be alive, I gave myself just as wantonly; I never said *no* or asked a man to withdraw. Some days when I tumbled out of bed with my head aching from too much champagne the night before I just couldn't bear the thought of that stinging concoction, or only remembered that I had forgotten at an inconvenient moment when it was already likely to be too late to do any good. But I had never had cause to regret my carelessness. And since my marriage to Bonaparte I had never again bothered with the douche. I was happy to be done with it. But no man's seed ever made my womb quicken. Whether it was the abortion, the douche, the prison fever, or something else entirely, I feared my womb was now a sterile and barren place where no seed could ever again take root. But that was something I could never tell Bonaparte; he wanted a child *so* badly, I couldn't bear to disappoint him. Yet every month when he solicitously inquired about the coming and going of my "little red sea," I felt like I was living a lie.

No sooner had I arrived than Bonaparte was bidding me farewell again, making me resent all the more having made the tedious, harrowing journey.

"I will not say good-bye," he said as he embraced me, "for I carry you always with me"—he patted the miniature over his heart—"as my good luck charm."

Even as he rode away he was already writing to me, scribbling madly on his lap desk, the words zigzagging wildly as the carriage bounced: *I thought I loved you, but now that I have seen you again, I love you a thousand times more. Your charms burn my heart and my senses. You must promise me never to cry, for your tears carry away all reason and burn up my blood.*

He left me ensconced in the red granite Serbelloni Palace, surrounded by life-sized bronze statues, servants, and hundreds of pieces of plundered art, paintings and statues that he had stripped from various palaces and the homes of noble families, a ready-made art collection just for me, tribute, Bonaparte said, that he laid at my feet, "though your love is the *greatest* treasure of all, Josephine!" Guests and dignitaries were always streaming in and out, eager to meet the great man's lady, all of whom I must speak graciously to and entertain and accept invitations from in return. I presided over balls, receptions, and dinner parties, scandalizing the locals with my scanty muslin dresses; it was obvious I didn't have a thing on underneath, and when I danced they could see every line of my form.

But it didn't matter how appalled they were, or pretended to be; soon they all were imitating me. Soon every lady passing before me in the receiving line had rose-red rouged nipples glowing through her thin muslin bodice, even the ones old enough that they should have known better than to attempt such revealing fashions, and when they danced, bellies and buttocks jiggled and thighs rippled beneath their transparent skirts.

Everyone adored me and was so anxious to please me and curry favor with my husband. The King and Queen of Naples gave me a parure of perfect pearls, so large, lustrous, and creamy they took my breath away, and the Pope sent me several rare and precious cameos since he had heard that I collected them. But any pleasure I experienced at the moment passed fleetingly. I was superbly bored and dying of boredom. *My husband doesn't love me, he worships me. I think he will go mad. I have seen him only briefly. He is terribly busy,* I dutifully reported back to Barras.

When I could endure the boredom not a moment longer, I let Hippolyte whisk me away for a romantic holiday at a rustic, but decent, country inn with all the necessary and desirable amenities to make our stay a pleasure in every way. But we timed it rather badly. Bonaparte returned unexpectedly, bounding up the stairs, eager to see and embrace me, only to find my bedroom empty. He immediately sat down and poured all his wrath into a letter and sent it flying after me like a flaming arrow:

> *I get to Milan, I fling myself into your room; I have left everything to see you, to hold you in my arms, and you are not there! The unhappiness I feel is incalculable! While I give you all my desires, all my thoughts, every second of my life, Josephine, I willingly submit to the power that your charms, your character, and the whole of your person have over*

*my poor heart, you deny me what I deserve to receive
from you—respect, esteem, and compassion!*

Alarmed by his hot words and temper, I raced back to Milan.
We drove all night, not sparing the horses, even when it rained and
the roads grew muddy and slick. I risked our necks to reach Bonaparte. Then it was *my* turn to race up the stairs and burst into my
bedroom, hoping to find him.

Bonaparte was lying on my bed, haggard and hot with fever, his
clothes soaked through with sweat, leaving a wet outline of his
form on the satin coverlet. His eyes were glazed and he was holding
one of my filmy rose-colored negligees, clutching it to his nose, as
though inhaling my perfume could restore him.

I wept to see him in such a sorry state. I flung myself onto the
bed, mud spattered and weary from driving all night, and burrowed into his arms, weeping and assuring him over and over again
that I was faithful, Hippolyte was just a friend, a diverting dandy
who made me laugh and liked to dance and talk of fashion; he
meant nothing more to me. I had only planned to be away a few
days. I had no way of knowing that my husband would be returning so soon. I needed a change of scene, fresh air, and informality. I
felt so overwhelmed and isolated, yet at the same time suffocated,
in that great big palace, surrounded by servants, with many acquaintances but no real friends, always having to be brave and force a
smile and play the gracious hostess to hundreds of strangers, all the
time terrified that I would fail.

"I fear this role is beyond me," I confessed.

But Bonaparte was quick to reassure me that no, "you were
born to play this part, my Josephine. You are graciousness personi-
fied."

My husband decided to play doctor and prescribe a remedy to
cure my loneliness and unease. He would invite his family to stay
with me. He might as well have dropped me naked with no weapon
to defend myself into a pit teeming with venomous vipers.

The matriarch, Letizia Bonaparte, was like a witch straight out
of a storybook. She never gave me a chance; she *loathed* me at first
glance. She refused to speak directly to me, so that any speech that

passed between us was conducted via a third party, usually with servants or one or more of her dreadful brood acting as intermediary.

They called me "old woman" and "whore," though from what I could tell none of them was a model of morality.

Joseph was always seeking evidence that would convict and condemn me. To see me banished and divorced from his brother's arms and affections was always Joseph's highest ambition.

Pauline at sixteen wore more paint than even the vainest woman does at fifty. She was obsessed with the carnal act and hardly thought of anything else, except her own beauty and ambitions. She gave herself freely, coupling indiscriminately with well-endowed peasants, army officers, servants, and noblemen. If she saw a man she liked she would simply lift her skirts and lie down, exposing her naked female parts, and point between her legs, so language need never pose a barrier to carnal delights. To avoid conception, she followed the advice of an old Corsican witch and inserted a yam inside her. As each yam decayed it led to embarrassing and painful infections, itching, and odors, yet Pauline still stubbornly swore by the technique and resorted to it again as soon as the doctor had scooped out the remains of the last rancid yam.

She resented my popularity; it was her goal to usurp me as "Our Lady of Victories" and the leader of fashion. She openly declared herself my sworn enemy and was always sticking her tongue out at me and calling me insulting names. She was determined to oust me from the pages of *Le Journal des Dames et des Modes*. *La costume est une lutte*—the art of dress is a contest indeed. Every time we appeared in public together she tried to best me, often failing miserably and making a fool of herself, for which she hated me all the more. Once, she appeared at a ball wearing nothing but a tiger skin, golden sandals, and with so many clusters of golden grapes covering her head one could hardly tell the color of her hair, and so much heavy gold jewelry she could hardly move—her necklaces and bracelets were more like a prisoner's shackles that had been dipped in gold than ornaments. I appeared in a gown of delicate pink silk that flowed over my body like liquid overlaid by a layer of pink netting dusted with diamonds, with a chaplet of pink roses in my hair. The fashion magazines were in ecstasy over it, and every woman wanted one just like it. Pauline wanted to scratch my eyes out.

Louis was chronically ill with a disease of Venus, covered with oozing sores and suffering excruciating migraines and pains in his back and legs; just like Robespierre, he imagined that everyone was against him and trusted no one; he imagined enemies hiding in every shadow and behind every bush and statue. If I tried to be polite and offer him a cup of chocolate or coffee he immediately suspected it was poisoned and would call a servant over and order them to test it by taking the first sip.

Jerome, Lucien, Caroline, and Elisa all hated me I think simply because their mother and elder siblings told them to, and perhaps they also felt some personal envy and spite to varying degrees. Heaven knows I tried to charm and win them, to find some common ground that we could meet upon, but I failed dismally.

Perhaps it was more about money than me. The whole obnoxious, greedy, conniving clan saw my notorious free-spending ways as a threat, fearing that I, and my children, would gobble up all the honors and riches that should have gone to them instead.

My in-laws turned what should have been an idyllic Italian summer, divided between the ardent, overpowering attentions of my husband and the sweet, tranquil hours spent in my lover's arms, into hell on earth. I could not wait for it to end.

CHAPTER 23

———◆○◆———

While my husband went on to more and greater victories, taking on Austria after Italy, I returned to Paris. Hippolyte and I took our time, making a leisurely tour of the countryside, enjoying nights filled with romance, sleeping late, and stopping spontaneously for picnics.

But, no matter how hard I tried, no matter how much Rose wanted to dally in a world of daydreams, I could not escape Bonaparte's creation—Josephine. At every stop along the way Madame Bonaparte, "Our Lady of Victories," was feted and celebrated. My carriage passed through triumphal arches and I was showered with flowers and gifts. Choirs of little children and poets sang my praises and mayor after mayor made the same bombastic and overlong speech while his wife and daughters, if he had any, swooned over my dress. And there was *always* a dinner, ball, reception, or play in my honor, where I must put myself on display, looking my best and smiling graciously, when all I wanted was the touch of my lover's hand behind a locked door.

My entry into Paris was like a victory parade; one would have thought that *I* was the conquering hero returned. I was carried through the streets, on a litter like a Roman empress, to smile and wave and accept bouquets from little girls in red, white, and blue dresses. And there were yet more speeches, songs, and sonnets. I thought the day would never end. Then at last, as the sun was setting, they deposited me, so weak and weary I could barely stand on my own two feet, upon our doorstep. In Bonaparte's honor, the name of the street where we lived had been changed from the rue Chantereine to the rue de la Victoire and every window was decked with red, white, and blue bunting and pictures of us—profiles of the savior of Paris, the conqueror of Italy, and his beloved consort, his good-luck charm, "Our Lady of Victories," smiling into each other's faces.

To them ours was a great and inspiring love story, a passion for the ages, for everyone with a beating heart to aspire to; they could not imagine us apart or anyone ever coming between us. With a sinking feeling I realized that I would always have to be with him, forever and ever. I could never leave Bonaparte; I could never spoil this great love story everyone embraced and cherished. Fairy-tale romances never end unhappily; the prince and princess *always* live happily ever after. I would have to spend the rest of my life playing a part, living a lie.

The moment the door closed behind my back, the smile fell from my face. I ran upstairs and fell on my bed, too exhausted to even undress or bathe. I felt like I could sleep for an entire week.

When Bonaparte returned in his own victory parade, I was there, smiling serenely in one of the flowing, graceful white dresses he loved, with Bonaparte's likeness at my breast, a golden arrow in my hair, and a white veil—like a bridal veil—falling modestly over my bare shoulders, perfectly playing the part of loving wife to welcome him home. How the crowd cheered and threw their hats in the air when he took me in his arms and kissed me with great gusto, almost suffocating me with his passion. He wanted everyone to see how much he loved me. He was so proud of his Josephine, his destiny.

"I win battles, but Josephine wins hearts!" he declared.

And when he swept me up in his arms and carried me inside, kicking our front door shut with his boot heel, they cheered all the more.

*   *   *

He loved what I had done with the house; he smiled and praised me and covered me with kisses when I took him by the hand and led him on a tour through every room. But he was livid when he saw the bills. I had spent 300,000 livres decorating a house only worth 40,000. But it wasn't my fault; I had been thinking of the end effect, not expenses. We fought hotly, our first great quarrel, and I wept bitterly, deploying what Bonaparte scornfully called "tears—woman's only weapon!" until finally he forgave me. One way or another, the bills were paid, and the storm quickly passed. By then he had other, more important things on his mind.

Being hailed by all Paris as the conquering hero and savior had gone straight to Bonaparte's head, but it was not enough for him. His triumphs, no matter how great or many, always paled after a time and left him hungry for more and greater glories. He was never satisfied. He truly saw himself as following in the footsteps of Caesar, Hannibal, and Alexander the Great, only Napoleon Bonaparte would be greater than them all. He was consumed by an ambition so great his body could not contain it. He had long taken note of how much the public despised and distrusted The Directory, seeing them all as greedy profiteers with no regard for the common people. "I should overthrow them and be crowned king," Bonaparte often said, "but not yet; now is not the time." He felt no gratitude to his benefactor Barras.

When Bonaparte said such words I trembled. Where would it all end? What glory would be great enough? Truly, I did not think that even a crown could satisfy my husband.

But then he stopped talking of crowns and started planning his next campaign, to conquer Egypt.

"This little Europe is but a pinprick," he said. "I must go to the Orient; all great reputations are won there." And after Egypt he had his eye on India and Turkey; there was seemingly no end to his ambition.

As he had in his childhood, he immersed himself in accounts of Alexander the Great and pored over Constantin de Volney's *Voyage en Egypte,* which chronicled the three years he had spent in his youth roaming that exotic land clad in native dress, getting to know the people and their customs.

"I *must* take Egypt!" Bonaparte insisted. "It has never belonged to a European nation, but I shall take it for France!"

At first The Directory was resistant, but Bonaparte would not take *no* for an answer. He demanded ships and men, and more than arms and soldiers, he must have scholars, historians, linguists, artists, architects, philosophers, and scientists of all kinds, including botanists and zoologists. It was to be a campaign not only to conquer and plunder that ancient and mysterious land but also to enrich our culture and knowledge.

He had me dress up like Cleopatra and preside over balls to promote his cause where I whispered charming and persuasive words in the right ears. Soon the public was fascinated with Egypt, throwing their support full force behind the proposed campaign. Bonaparte had won. He could do no wrong in their eyes. The Directory knew they had been beaten by one man's lust for conquest and a woman's charm.

After much haggling over numbers, away he went with twenty-five thousand men and 180 ships. I cried and clung to him. I wanted to go too! It seemed a grand adventure. The sand and heat and snakes would not bother me after my childhood in Martinique, I assured him. Three hundred women were making the journey as washerwomen, seamstresses, camp followers, cooks, and officers' wives, so why should I alone be left behind? But Bonaparte refused me. "Our Lady of Victories" must stay home and be for the French people a constant and ever present reminder of him, the symbol of his good fortune. "Through you, my Josephine, they shall celebrate and worship me!"

I watched and wept as his flagship, *L'Orient,* sailed away. When not even a speck of it could be seen upon the horizon, I climbed back in my coach and drove to the spa town of La Plombières, where the waters were renowned for restoring fertility. Bonaparte was convinced that it would be good for me. He had studied the statistics; his brother's wife, Julie, was one of them. I must nourish and strengthen my womb in his absence and prepare the fertile ground to receive his seed when he returned. I did not think that even the miraculous waters of La Plombières could help me, but I couldn't tell Bonaparte that. All I could do was agree and pretend I harbored the same hopes as he did.

CHAPTER 24

◄○►

La Plombières was a little village in Lorraine surrounded by pine forests and I thought I might rest quietly there. I was weary of being "Our Lady of Victories," "Madame Bonaparte," and constantly on display, like an actress always onstage. I needed peace and privacy, I needed a rest, to put away Josephine and be Rose again, just for a little while so I didn't forget her too.

But apparently that was too much to ask. Bonaparte had sent heralds riding ahead to announce my arrival, and I was welcomed like a queen, with a band playing, flowers flying, and cheers resounding the moment my carriage rolled into town, passing beneath the triumphal arch that had been erected. Children sang and the Mayor came out to meet me and make a speech and his wife and daughters practically drooled over my dress. It was *so* hard to keep smiling when all I wanted to do was cry.

I found my stay there anything but peaceful. One day when I went out onto the balcony of the house where I was staying it suddenly collapsed, plunging me twenty feet down onto the cobblestone street below. When those who rushed to my aid lifted me I felt like every bone in my body was broken. Every little movement hurt and I screamed and screamed. I was in so much pain I was incapable of a single coherent word.

In truth, I was very fortunate; my spine was not broken as was originally suspected, merely bruised so badly I could not bear to move. But my pelvis had also suffered injuries, a series of delicate fractures, which did not bode well for any future hope of motherhood. There was for a time grave concern about whether I would ever walk again.

An incompetent quack, the so-called "Dr." Martinet was summoned and he promptly ordered a sheep slaughtered and my naked body wrapped in the bloody skin while it was still warm. While I lay there in excruciating pain, swaddled in that horrible sheepskin, reeking of blood, Dr. Martinet bled me from the bottoms of my feet and administered an enema of brandy and camphor followed by a douche of the same mixture for good measure. Afterward, I was plunged into a bath so hot it nearly scalded what life remained out of me, and then I was tucked into bed, lying on my stomach, with a poultice of boiled potatoes on my back. When the potatoes had completely cooled, leeches were put on the blisters they left behind, followed by mustard plasters. This was my life for the next two months.

While I was enduring this barbaric treatment, day after terrible day, in so much pain I wanted to die, and all I could do was cry and worry whether I would be a cripple, Dr. Martinet sat by my bedside and wrote a book, exposing every intimate detail of my injuries and the treatment he prescribed, and arranged to give a series of lectures about how he had saved the life of Bonaparte's wife. The only thing he withheld was the possible repercussions of my pelvic injuries upon my future fertility. With many tears and anguished, heartfelt words, I persuaded him to tell no one of this. I did not want to deprive my husband of all hope of offspring, I said, and it really was for Mother Nature, not medicine, to decide. And, I added craftily, if I *did* have a child, I would give the credit to his treatment, the diligent care he had taken over my shattered pelvis; I would see that he was hailed as a miracle worker. Because he admired Bonaparte so much, Dr. Martinet agreed to honor my request.

Because of me, Dr. Martinet became rich and famous, even people who cared nothing about medicine flocked to buy his book and attend his lectures, and society ladies rushed to La Plombières to be treated by him just so they could say they had the same doctor as Josephine. Privacy, it seemed, had fallen by the wayside. Everyone thought they had the right to know everything about me, even my private, natural functions. *Nothing* was secret or sacred anymore.

I *hated* La Plombières and could not wait to leave. I think the happiest steps I ever took were when I walked out of the house that had become like a prison to me with Dr. Martinet as my jailer and climbed into my carriage. I never looked back. I sincerely hoped I would never see that wretched village, or Dr. Martinet, again.

CHAPTER 25

I arrived in Paris only to discover that my luck had at last run out. Hippolyte was dallying openly with other women. Since my spine and pelvis were injured, dancing and lovemaking were out of the question, and rumor had it I would never walk again, so he had moved on; invalids were not to his taste apparently. My former maid Louise had turned vengeful. I had dismissed her after I caught her stealing, in the act of pilfering my desk with several pieces of my jewelry and a goodly sum of money in her apron pockets, along with some of Bonaparte's letters she hoped to sell to the newspapers. As soon as she left me, she had run straight to Joseph Bonaparte and revealed *everything* she knew about my affair with Hippolyte.

I can only imagine with what voracious glee Joseph had written to inform his brother of my betrayal. The truth almost destroyed my husband; he wept and declared that his life was over and at only twenty-nine he had nothing left to live for. He vowed to divorce me in the most public and sensational way possible, to show the world what manner of woman I *really* was. Letters between the two brothers had fallen into British hands when a French mail ship was captured. Our English enemies took great delight in publishing them in the newspapers for the whole world to read. Now everyone knew—Bonaparte was a cuckold, a laughingstock, and "Our Lady of Victories" was a perfidious harlot.

Things were not going well for Bonaparte in Egypt, even before he received news of my infidelity. Though he aimed to conquer, and conquer he did—Cairo, the Nile, and the pyramids were all his—while he was about it the British fleet, led by their own hero, Admiral Nelson, attacked. They destroyed the French ships, effectively stranding Bonaparte and his men in Egypt and forming a blockade to trap them there and prevent fresh supplies and reinforcements from coming in.

Though he managed to send word back to Paris, writing undauntedly *everything is fine here,* Bonaparte sat and stewed, unable to return to Paris to savor his triumph; all he could do was brood about my betrayal. Then he began paying me back in kind by bedding Egyptian dancing girls. Zenab, the sixteen-year-old daughter of a sheik, fascinated him for a while. After he forgot her, her own people punished her for bedding the infidel foreigner and struck off her head. Next Bonaparte became besotted with one of his officers' wives, the nineteen-year-old Bellilotte Fourès.

A sprightly, fresh-faced blonde with a natural pink rose petal complexion that required no rouge to enhance it, Bellilotte liked to walk around displaying her slim, trim figure in the uniform of her husband's regiment, those tight white breeches I'm told were very eye-catching when encasing her girlish figure. Her long blond braid swayed down her back, the ends tickling her rump, and every man who saw her was *wild* to possess her.

Bonaparte made her intimate acquaintance at a launching of one of the Montgolfier hot-air balloons he had brought with him from Paris. They went up high in the air together, above the Ezbekiya Gardens, and he attempted to ravish her there amongst the clouds. He was apparently successful and when they came down from the skies she was all his.

Soon everyone was referring to her as "Napoleon's Cleopatra" and recounting how he had told the man manning the balloon to turn his back and pulled Bellilotte's breeches down to her ankles and bent her over the basket's rim. I wondered if she had closed her eyes against that dizzying view of the ground far down below where the people looked tiny as ants. Possibly my husband was the very first man to have carnal congress in a hot-air balloon, another conquest for him, well, actually two if one also counts the beautiful Bellilotte. Her inconvenient husband, Lieutenant Fourès, was sent on several fool's errands and high-risk missions to get him out of the way, and maybe even killed, but Lady Luck didn't desert him even when his wife did, and he survived every time.

With his Cleopatra at his side, Bonaparte began playing the Oriental potentate, wearing a turban and rich robes like a sultan, with a jeweled scimitar in his belt. He dressed Bellilotte in Oriental splendor, surrounded himself with giant Mameluke bodyguards, and, fearful of poison, had a food taster sample every dish and drink set before him. He had cause to fear; the army was suffering greatly, and his popularity was declining. Amidst sandstorms and remorseless heat, an epidemic of bubonic plague decimated the French army; those too weak to march were mercilessly left to die baked alive in the sizzling sands. When they seized Jaffa, Bonaparte ordered everyone slaughtered, including women and children. To save ammunition, he ordered his men to use their bayonets. Hundreds were herded into the sea, hacked down when they tried to flee, so they had but two choices—die by the sword or drown.

My husband was mad; he had lost all mercy. I could not help but think that my betrayal was the cruel truth at the heart of it. *I changed Bonaparte, but not for the better.*

Messages from France managed to sneak through the British blockade, alerting him that in his absence foreign armies were encroaching on his territories. Italy was already lost, the Austrians were reviving, and the Russians were massing troops along the Alps and Danube.

British and blockade be damned, Bonaparte was coming back to France! When news reached us, there was dancing in the streets. "He's coming back; all will be well!" was the general belief. "Hail the name we all adore, Bonaparte, the man beloved by France; he will save us evermore!" they sang.

But I was not a part of it. I had come back from La Plombières to find myself persona non grata in Paris. Even Barras scorned me and Theresa and Fortunée were suddenly too busy to see me. Everyone turned their backs on me. No one wanted to know me. There were no invitations to dance or dine, no more gala nights at the theater or opera in my honor.

I was still ill and weak, tormented by aches and pains I feared would never go away entirely, and the idea of public scrutiny frightened me now that everyone had turned against me. I was afraid of being spit at and reviled by the people in the street; I had cuckolded the conqueror and let them all down. The portraits of me sold in shops and on the streets had changed overnight to cruel caricatures of me dancing nude before Barras or dandling an infant-sized Bonaparte on my knee or suckling him at my breast. I even became the subject of a pornographic novel, *The Licentious Life of Madame B.* I needed solace, a sanctuary, a place of peace and safety that was all my own. Somewhere I could lock the doors and let no one in who might hurt me and even the whispers from Paris could not reach me unless I chose to let them in.

I had never forgotten the beautiful château of Malmaison I had glimpsed from my garden in Croissy; when I closed my eyes I could still see it glowing butter gold in the summer sun. It became a beacon of hope for me. I *knew* I would be happy there, so, cost be damned, I bought it. The Molay family, who owned the property, needed money and the house had fallen into disrepair, so they were grateful for my offer. I was too happy to haggle and probably paid them more than it was worth. That first night, sitting by the great fire, listening to the rhythm of the rain on the slate roof, I knew I had done the right thing. I had found my home, my haven; at last, I was at peace.

CHAPTER 26

When I heard that Bonaparte's ship had landed, I put on a flowing white gown and rushed to Lyons, hoping to reach him before his brother Joseph did, so I could fling myself weeping at his feet, and plead my innocence. I needed to persuade him that it was I, not he, who had been betrayed—Joseph *hated* me and had chosen to believe the lies of a disgruntled servant, a thief, whom I had dismissed with just cause; Bonaparte himself would have done the same. But I was too late. He had already departed for Paris by another route.

I was still on the road, screaming at the coachman to go faster, when Bonaparte reached the house on the rue de la Victoire. *Faithless creature, she is off somewhere with her lover,* he assumed. He began emptying drawers and seizing up armfuls of my dresses, hats, gloves, stockings, shawls, shoes, nightgowns, and negligees and hurling them from the windows out into the street. He wanted the house stripped of every sign of me. He wanted me erased from his life.

I arrived in the darkest hours before dawn to find every garment I owned strewn about the streets, but I didn't care. I slipped and tripped my way over them and forced my way through the front door, fighting the servants who attempted to bar it against me and hold me back.

I ran up the stairs, oblivious to the throbbing pain in my spine and hips, and hurled myself against the locked bedroom door, hammering it with my fists, begging Bonaparte to open it, to let me in. He had been misled; Joseph hated me; and Louise, his informant, was a lying thief who had a grudge against me; Hippolyte Charles was just a friend, nothing more; nothing improper had ever passed between us. "I am yours body and soul!" I sobbed, pounding on the door. "Bonaparte, *please* believe me and let me in!"

Hours passed in which he said not a word. When I could no longer bear to stand, I knelt and continued pleading and pounding. Finally, I lay upon the floor, stretched out before the door, weak as a kitten, still pounding and pleading with my bleeding fists leaving behind red trails and smears. Even when my voice grew hoarse and faded to just above a whisper, I never stopped. I *had* to get him to open that door! My whole life depended on it.

The sun rose and when Hortense awoke she found me lying there, in a piteous heap, still pounding feebly on the blood-streaked door, begging Bonaparte to let me in. Hortense—kind, loyal, and understanding Hortense!—ran to me. She worried over my hands and tried to coax me to her room, to rest. When I refused, she stayed and joined her voice with mine, begging the stepfather she both feared and revered to open the door, to not shut me out of his life.

When Eugène arrived he also joined us. My son remained loyal and steadfast, always ready to leap to my defense with good words to say about me, even when I did not deserve it. Even in Egypt with Bonaparte, Eugène had still defended me and urged his stepfather to temper his fury with caution. It might all be malicious rumors designed to discredit me; he himself had never seen me behave with any impropriety in the company of Lieutenant Charles.

Together, united, we became a chorus of three, begging Bonaparte to open the door. And at last he did. He could never resist my children; Eugène was the kind of son every man hoped for, and Hortense was the perfect daughter, demure and sweet. I rushed in before he could think twice and bar the door again. I flung myself into his arms, burrowed against his chest, and tried very hard not to look into his eyes because what I had glimpsed there in that first brief glance frightened me to the core.

There was a new, unfamiliar cruelty there that told me that I, and I alone, had killed every ounce of kindness this man possessed. My husband no longer loved me, and I had no one to blame but myself. He was looking at me with new eyes, eyes that would never again trust me and would always be inclined to doubt me.

The words came out in a frantic rush. I clung and wept. I cried and lied until, at last, my tears—woman's only weapon—conquered the hero.

But it was already too late for us; we were doomed. The damage had been done. I had tarnished his ideal of Josephine; I was no longer a goddess in my husband's eyes. He would never again worship at my shrine. I had fallen from the pedestal he had put me upon and the façade had cracked revealing all my many flaws.

Bonaparte swept me up in his arms and carried me to the bed. He still desired me! And oh, how I clung to him, like never before! I wanted to turn back time, to have again what I had so carelessly, so callously and foolishly, thrown away. In those moments I realized what a precious gift he had given me—no one else would ever love me so much. I suddenly needed that love very badly. I didn't want it to die. It had suffered a mighty blow, but I *had* to find some way to bring it back to life.

Over and over again I told him that I loved him, hoping against hope that would make a difference. But that was a mistake. The cold silver steel glint in Bonaparte's eyes told me that I, like many a foe he had met before in battle, had just walked into a trap. He had me now, Josephine conquered, captured, and subdued, subject entirely to his will. *Your love is the greatest treasure of all,* he had once written me. Now he had it. I had forgotten in my anguish that the prize always ceased to glitter as brightly once it was won and that which lay unconquered over the horizon beckoned more enticingly.

There were tears in both our eyes as we made love. But what were they for? Relief? Gratitude? Grief for the lovely illusion that had died, that I had in fact killed? Or the years of pretense that lay before us?

* * *

The Bonaparte who returned to me was sun browned and bitter. He had grown stouter and cropped his hair. He looked older and harder. Inside, he was tough as leather, not so malleable anymore. He was wary and distrustful, never without his food taster and tall, terrifying Mamelukes.

He had taken me back, but, as proof of my undying gratitude, he expected more from me than ever before.

Rose was faded, dead, dry petals trampled into dust beneath Bonaparte's boots, and in her place he expected his ideal, his immortal Josephine, to flourish and bloom, more radiant than any Rose, and outshine every other woman alive, to be an adoring beacon illuminating his glory and pointing the way to him. *I* was the one who was to worship at *his* altar now, the high priestess of the cult of Bonaparte.

He would show the world that our love was still alive; I was still his incomparable Josephine. The scandal had been a noxious stew stirred up by the British, to tarnish his glory, and my reputation, to deprive the French people of hope and inspiration and muddy the pure white hems of "Our Lady of Victories." But my wholehearted devotion was the price for the starring role in this play. Every ounce of grace and charm and beauty I possessed, every moment, waking and sleeping, was to be dedicated entirely to him. I was to live for him alone, for no other purpose, and to put none above him, not even God and my children. "I win battles; Josephine wins hearts," he was fond of saying, but it was always left unsaid that the hearts I won were all for *him*.

So I made another bargain with another devil and tried my earnest best to keep it. But it cost me even more. I felt the pedestal teeter perilously beneath my feet. The wolves were already at my door. Henceforth, fear would be my constant companion. I would never rest easily. The goddess had sacrificed her immortality; she was mortal now and could be torn to shreds and die. Adieu, security, my greatest desire! The worst part was knowing that I had no one to blame but myself.

CHAPTER 27

———◄○►———

Now that he was back in Paris, Bonaparte's thoughts turned once more to the corrupt Directory.

"There are too many cooks in the kitchen," he said. "France needs *one* man!" He meant, of course, himself.

He was thinking again of that crown, and I was thinking of Euphemia David's long-ago prophecy. It seemed I hadn't thought of it in a very long time; I had outgrown the dream.

"*Please,* Bonaparte," I pleaded, "don't go thinking of making yourself a king!"

"King, no, the memory of Louis XVI is still too fresh," he answered. "I was thinking instead of emperor. I shall revive the splendor of the Holy Roman Emperors. But not right away; the people must be eased into it. . . ."

Emperor. Empress. My blood chilled. I didn't want it now. I had grown up; I was no longer a silly young girl dreaming of becoming a fairy-tale princess. I had had my taste of fame, sweet at first, then sour as vinegar. I had endured the loss of privacy that came hand in hand with popularity and the fickleness of crowds, revering one moment, reviling the next. The false smiles and honeyed words, the whispers behind, and verbal daggers in, my back, and I had had enough of it. I wanted no part of it! I already knew how little it mattered and my happiness was already lost. So what mattered a crown? It would be a heavy yet empty honor.

I sat and watched and smiled and socialized as my husband overthrew The Directory in a thankfully bloodless coup instead of another revolution. Barras and the other Directors were sent into exile. The people were glad to see them go. Before he left, Barras wrote to me; it was only a single line, but a true and pertinent one: *I created both of you!* It was true. We should have been more grateful. Instead, we swept him away, like dust under a rug, out of sight, out of mind. Neither of us wished to remember, but I could never forget.

So as not to alarm the people with the sudden return of royalty, after they had so recently fought a revolution to be rid of it, Bonaparte took the title of First Consul. It was only the first stepping stone on the path to ultimate power. He now ruled France and would conquer the world if he could. What a way to start a new century!

Soon we were living in the Tuileries, the decaying palace that had become Louis XVI and Marie Antoinette's prison. The walls were still stained with the blood of the Swiss Guards who had died valiantly trying to defend the royal family, and the gardens were overrun with prostitutes, vagrants, and lemonade sellers. Upon the front façade was still painted in bloodred letters: ON AUGUST 10, 1792, ROYALTY WAS ABOLISHED IN FRANCE NEVER TO RETURN! Bonaparte ordered it whitewashed and called the decorators and carpenters in to restore all four hundred rooms to their former splendor, the house in the rue de Victoire was no longer good enough for him.

I was given Marie Antoinette's former suite on the ground floor. The bedchamber was all sky-blue satin and gold with Sèvres vases everywhere painted and filled with bouquets of roses, the antechamber was regal purple with mirrors and bronze statues and paintings plundered from Italy, and the reception room, my salon, was done all in yellow and gold. Gold *B*s for *Bonaparte* were everywhere, even on the doorknobs and painted at the bottom of chamber pots, along with regal eagles and swarms of embroidered golden bees, the symbol of resurrection, which my husband had taken as his personal emblem. *His* portraits, larger than life, adorned the walls now, with bronze and marble statues of Caesar, Hannibal, and Alexander the Great standing sentry as though *they* looked up to *him*.

We were waited on hand and foot by servants in liveries embroidered with gold *B*s and bees. Gold, *everywhere* gold! I had ladies-in-waiting, ladies of the bedchamber, ladies of the wardrobe, all overseen by a *dame d'honneur,* footmen, and pages, an almoner, and I was not allowed to set foot outside without an armed escort of cavalry. Bonaparte banished all my former friends and associates, including Theresa and Fortunée, and personally selected all my attendants. No one was allowed to get close to me, to be my friend. We would have no more informality; we had risen above such things. In desperation to have even one familiar face about me, someone I could speak openly and candidly to, I wrote to my mother and begged her to leave Martinique and come to court to be with me, but she wanted no part of my destiny; she had a feeling, she said, that it would all end badly.

Formality, Bonaparte decreed, was the new order of the day, Paris had been lax long enough. It was time for obedience to come marching back; people (women especially) must do as they were told, not as they pleased. He ordered me to do all that I could to charm and coax the old aristocracy back, the émigrés who had fled in terror of their lives and been declared enemies of the Revolution and therefore enemies of France. Bonaparte said we needed the glamour of the ancien regime, people like the Ségurs, the Rochefoucaulds, and the Caulaincourts, who were steeped in elegance and tradition. They had been drilled in court etiquette from the moment they were old enough to walk and would make sure our court ran properly.

I was constantly watched; from every window faces peered in at me. I was always on show, surrounded from rising to retiring. I could not even walk in the garden alone. I never had a moment to myself except in bed on the rare nights when Bonaparte, increasingly desperate for an heir, did not come to me. But even then I wasn't really alone; fear lay right next to me. I would lie awake for hours, exhausted yet sleepless, in the former queen's vast mahogany bed, expecting at any moment to see Marie Antoinette's ghost appear and demand to know what I was doing in her bed.

Just as he changed every facet of my life, Bonaparte also changed my clothes. No more simple white muslin gowns flowing gracefully over my limbs with a colorful shawl thrown with artful carelessness over my shoulders. Limbs and bosoms *must* be covered, no more rouged nipples or peeping areolas. And no more cropped hair *à la Victime* upon the ladies. A woman's hair was her crowning glory, so it must be grown long again, long enough to coil up and crown with bands of jewels and diadems and then let down for her husband's delight when they retired at night. Heavy satins and stultifying velvets stiff with gold and silver embroidery and high stand-up lace collars evocative of the Renaissance were now de rigueur. He was even contemplating the restoration of hoops and panniered skirts; fortunately, I was able to dissuade him. After much argument, he agreed that the silhouette might stay the same, with high waists and skirts falling down in straight lines, but, on all formal occasions the ladies *must* wear heavy trains and no one was to be seen at court in the same gown twice.

I was a living ornament now, designed to decorate my husband's court. I changed my dress three times a day and was expected to look always as perfect as though I were posing for my portrait, never a wrinkle or a loose thread, a tear or a stain, or a hair out of place. Bonaparte demanded perfection, *always, in all* things. It was *exhausting!* Every morning when I rose, put on my lace peignoir, and went to sit at my dressing table, I felt as though I hadn't slept at all.

I spent my days waiting, always waiting, like a bejeweled slave in a sultan's harem, waiting for, both wanting and dreading, the moment when my husband would want me, so I could rush to him. I must *never* keep *him* waiting.

I was exhausted by etiquette. I could understand now why Marie Antoinette had longed to put on shepherdess frocks and escape to the Petit Trianon and her pretend farm.

I *longed* for the weekends when I could escape to Malmaison. I had a whole zoo of animals and hothouses full of tropical plants, a flock of sheep, a working farm, and a vineyard there. I grew pineapples and bananas, palm trees, and orchids in a hothouse to remind me of Martinique. Over fifty varieties of roses bloomed in my garden and I was determined to obtain specimens of flowers and trees from all over the world.

It was only at Malmaison that I found peace. I would put on a simple dress and sit and watch my black swans glide past and walk hand in hand with my orangutan, dressed up in a little girl's frock, and sit at the table with her and feed her turnips with a knife and fork.

I *begged* Bonaparte to let me stay at Malmaison. But he always made me go back to the Tuileries on Monday.

"I was never made for such grandeur," I protested, "I will never be happy there," but he didn't care.

His eyes reminded me that he was the Devil and I had best keep our bargain, or else . . .

He shoved me to my knees before him.

"I expect four things from you," he said. "Worship at my feet; proclaim my excellence to everyone; please me in bed; and give me a son if you can."

An heir was still at the forefront of his mind. In the spring, when he saw the animals with their newly born or hatched young, he turned his bitterness upon me. "It seems that everything here is fertile except *you,* madame!"

To punish me he liked to use my animals as living targets. He shot an emu and a Peruvian llama and mortally wounded a gazelle; the zebra survived, just barely. When he missed my black swans he became so disgusted that he flung his pistol into the lake.

On constant show at the Tuileries, I began my day at eight o'clock with a light breakfast, a bath, and the long, tedious business of dressing, a ceremony I thought designed more to give my attendants something to do than to actually help me put clothes on my back. I spent my days bored nearly to tears, listening to my ladies chatter; sometimes we played cards, interminable games of whist or piquet, or billiards, or they sang or read to me. I received whole bags full of letters now, all of which must be read, and most must be answered, by either my own hand or a secretary's. Bonaparte joined me for lunch, he gobbled his food and was gone in twenty minutes, and then I was left to my ladies again. They helped me change my dress and then the doors of my yellow salon were thrown open wide to receive petitioners and any tradespeople who had goods to show me. For the rest of the afternoon, I had fittings with my dressmakers and milliners and posed for portraits; there were always at least three or four artists painting portraits of me. Sometimes I stole an hour to stroll in the gardens, though never alone; solitude was not allowed.

At any hour of the day Bonaparte might burst in and demand tea and my company or want my opinion about some pressing matter and I must always be immaculately dressed and ready to receive him. There mustn't be a moment's delay; the instant he commanded it my full attention must be entirely his. I must never be tired or out of sorts or betray a lack of interest. Then it was time to change my dress again. Every evening I hosted endless dinners and balls, smiling graciously and listening attentively to upwards of 150 guests, always with a kind and flattering word to say to each.

Most nights I didn't get to bed until two o'clock. And, if Bonaparte deigned to visit me, I might not be able to sleep till three or four. His lovemaking was swift, but his talk was endless. He liked to lay his head in my lap and have me read him ghost stories or massage his brow, and when he had the agonizing stomach pains that were the bane of his existence I was the only one who could soothe him. He needed me—his Josephine. I was the only one he could confide in, and even when he bored me with all his talk of politics and military matters, I had to feign an avid interest. He also liked to stay with me because I was such a light sleeper; if an assassin intruded I was sure to wake and this made him feel more secure.

But things were far from happy between us. Once awakened to all my flaws, Bonaparte wasn't about to overlook or forget them. He told me often that I only looked pretty from afar. When I was at my dressing table sometimes he would station himself behind my chair and stare critically at my face in the mirror as I applied my cosmetics. He would reach out and stay my hand when I started to move the rouge pot away and order, "More!" I had to diet constantly because he loathed fat women. Yet if I was too thin he said

I looked skinny and old. If I appeared in a dress he did not like he threw an inkwell at me, tore it into tatters, or kept the whole court waiting, even an hour or more while I went to change, just so he could have the pleasure of blaming me for the delay. He thought nothing of snatching a shawl that displeased him from my shoulders and tossing it into the fire. Once, when I came before him in a dress he deemed too thin, he grasped it by the hem and tore it up the front all the way to the jeweled belt fastened snugly just below my breasts. "There now!" he cried. "You have what you want— every man in Paris can see your little black forest!" I fled in tears and shame, trying to hold my skirt together to cover me. If my neckline was too low he announced that no one wanted to see "an old woman's sagging teats." If there was an important ball or reception and one of the guests was someone he was very eager to impress, he would often sit for hours in my bedroom making me try on dress after dress until he found one grand enough to suit him. Whenever he saw a pretty woman in a white dress he would comment on how much this pleased him, yet silence reigned when I wore white or else he castigated me because my attire was too plain. If I favored muslin over silk he said the same thing: He *hated* muslin; it was too common to suit his rich tastes. If I *dared* appear in the same gown twice, or in one too similar to another I had already worn, he would loudly remark in full hearing of the court, "That is a very pretty dress, madame, but we have all seen it before! Go and change it at once and do not offend our eyes by letting us see it again!"

I needed to look opulent and outshine everyone else around me, my husband demanded it, so I spent more lavishly than ever before. But whenever Bonaparte saw the bills he berated me. His explosions of rage were truly terrifying. If I spent too little, I was embarrassing him; if I spent too much, I was bankrupting him. I could never find the right balance. Nothing I did seemed to please him and I was left wishing he still saw only his ideal, his perfect dream, of Josephine when he looked at me, not Rose with all her flaws dressed up in Josephine's finery.

He took mistresses openly now—actresses, dancing girls, opera singers, and ladies of the court. Though he professed that they meant nothing to him and only satisfied his lust for conquest, he flaunted them, inviting them to court to perform so I must sit and watch while everyone was watching, and laughing, at me. One of Bonaparte's women, the beautiful contralto Giuseppina Grassini, he actually brought to Malmaison, to sully my paradise, to sing for me on my birthday. He slept with her that night in the bedroom across the hall from me. His family, knowing all that it would take was for one of his mistresses to succeed where I had so far failed and become pregnant, pushed pretty young girls as well as mature women into his path, anyone likely to tempt him. The woman didn't matter to them, only her womb. A pregnancy would prove the fault was mine, not his, and Bonaparte would be done with me at last.

When I wept over his affairs, he slapped and raged at me.

"I am not like other men," he railed. "The ordinary laws of morality do not apply to me!"

Other times he would take me in his arms and assure me, "Those women mean nothing to me. I take them and then forget them."

CHAPTER 28

On New Year's Eve, Haydn's *Creation* was to be performed at the Opéra in Bonaparte's honor. I was halfway down the stairs when I realized my shawl didn't quite suit my gown. Bonaparte was bound to be displeased, he was very particular about such things, so I sent Hortense down to tell him that I would only be a few moments more. In my haste, the heel of my shoe caught in my hem, tearing my gown, and "a few moments more" turned into fifteen and then twenty, then thirty minutes as my ladies swarmed about me, bumping into one another, dropping things, and snapping crossly at one another in their haste, making me want to just swat them all away and dress myself.

At last, in an ivory satin gown overlaid with shimmering gold net and the parure of pearls the King and Queen of Naples had given me, I rushed downstairs, throwing an Indian shawl of deep crimson and burnished gold about my shoulders as I ran, just in time to see Bonaparte's carriage driving away. A footman informed me that the First Consul had gone on ahead. He had only just left and if we hurried we could catch up, so Hortense and I climbed into the carriage that had been brought for us. Bonaparte would be angry if I wasn't there in the royal box for all the people to see us before the performance started.

As we neared the opera house there was a great flash of blinding white light. The carriage felt like it had been swept up on a tremendous wave; it shuddered and rocked as the windows exploded, showering us with shards of broken glass. I heard the horses scream and there was a great crash as the carriage fell over on its side. Then everything went black. The next thing I knew, a man—my husband!—was lifting me from the broken, splintered ruins of the carriage. I was bleeding from a cut on my temple and Bonaparte pressed his handkerchief firmly against it, murmuring something about head wounds always bleeding like the devil. Hortense—alive and safe, thank God!—was standing beside me, staring about her in horrified wonder as she bound her shawl around her arm, to staunch the blood seeping from several small cuts.

"Josephine—you are *still* my good-luck charm!" Bonaparte cried as he enfolded me in his arms and smothered me with kisses. "Had it not been for you, and your infernal shawl, keeping me waiting, my carriage would have been caught in the blast and I would have been blown to bits!"

My ears were ringing; his voice sounded very far away. Though I heard his words, I couldn't comprehend what he was saying. I stepped back from his embrace and stared around me. Someone had tried to kill Bonaparte with a bomb. It had been left in a cart blocking the street where he must pass in order to reach the opera house. All about us, the streets were littered with broken glass, glittering in the moon- and lamplight as far as the eye could see, and the bodies of the dead, and the wounded groaning in agony. I saw men missing limbs and white bones jaggedly protruding from torn and bloody flesh. Slivers of glass stabbed their skin like tiny knives and many had been blinded. At least thirty were dead and twice more had suffered injuries. Hortense and I were fortunate to have escaped with barely a scratch when so many others had suffered much worse. There wasn't a house standing within sight that hadn't lost all its windows, and the roofs of several had caved in, crushing and burying anyone unfortunate enough to be inside.

If we had left the Tuileries on time our carriage would have been almost on top of the bomb when it exploded; it would have meant certain death for all of us. The enormity of it shook me, I felt suddenly very dizzy and weak. Spots danced before my eyes. I staggered and only just had time to reach out to my husband before I fainted again. He caught me and cradled me in his arms, and, for the first time in a *very* long time, I felt safe. How strange that I should feel that way, bleeding and wounded, when we had just come so very close to death.

He loved me again . . . for a little while. I tried to hold on, to make it last. But Bonaparte couldn't give up what I called his "two-minute conquests" and I was sorely afraid that one of them would capture his fascination the way I once had. My jealous tears annoyed him and kept him from my bed. He was restless and ill-tempered and itching to embark on another campaign.

I begged him not to go. I ran after him in my nightgown with my hair flowing down and caught desperately at his arm as he climbed into his coach. But he shook me off.

"My power depends on my glory and my glory depends on my victories," he said. "Conquest alone can maintain me."

"*Please!*" I tried again to push my way into the coach, and into his arms again. "Take me with you!"

But he pushed me away.

"Nature has given me a strong and resolute character, but she has made you out of lace and gauze, just like your nightgown," he said as his fingers plucked disdainfully at the lace.

He closed the door on me. I stood and watched and wept until I could no longer see his carriage.

I was "Our Lady of Victories" once more with the tattered and burnt flags of the fallen being laid at my feet, drinking champagne toasts and hosting grand balls every time Bonaparte's latest victory was announced, consoling the widows and wounded, and being feted and celebrated by all Paris in his absence.

My hero returned victorious, drunk with power, and more obsessed with having a child than ever before. I was thirty-seven now, but it was still possible; his own mother had been deep into her thirties when her last child was born and would have likely continued breeding had her husband not died.

"It is the torment of my life not to have a child," Bonaparte bemoaned his misfortune. "My power will never be firmly established until I have one."

He sent me to La Plombières again, though I pleaded and wept not to go. I knew it would do no good, and it brought back so many unpleasant memories of how much I had suffered there.

"This time it *will* work," Bonaparte confidently asserted. "Believe it will work, and it will. You must set your mind to giving me a son."

As I was climbing into my carriage, about to drive away to the detested place, his brother Lucien sidled up to me and whispered in my ear that I should get a child if I could off another man and palm it off on Bonaparte. I knew it was a trick; my in-laws would like nothing better than to prove me guilty of such duplicity. I was not about to walk into their trap. Besides, if it hadn't worked with Hippolyte, the most passionate affair of my life, then it was doubtful to work with any other man playing the role of stud.

I was desperate and I knew my days were numbered. The waters of La Plombières failed to wake my womb and every time my "little red sea" began to flow Bonaparte brooded and wept with disappointment. Everywhere I turned was the word "divorce" being whispered loud enough to make sure I heard it. I *had* to do *something,* so, to my great and eternal shame, I sacrificed my sweet daughter to try to save myself.

One night in bed, after I had been particularly zealous in pleasuring him, I suggested to Bonaparte that his brother Louis, the mad invalid, might marry Hortense. If they had a child it would be Bonaparte's blood united with mine flowing in its veins, just the same as if it were our very own child, and, provided it was a boy, it could be his heir. My husband thought it was a most ingenious idea and ordered me to start planning the wedding without delay.

Hortense wept when I told her—I let her believe it was all Bonaparte's idea; I couldn't bear to have my daughter hate me—but she stoically accepted her fate.

"My stepfather is a comet of which we are but the tail, and we must follow him everywhere without knowing where it carries us—for our happiness or for our grief," she said bravely.

I tried to atone with gifts—a beautiful white satin wedding dress covered with pearls, a diamond diadem, necklace, and earrings, and ropes of magnificent pearls. But Hortense wasn't me; she merely smiled and, like the dutiful daughter she always was, thanked me for my gifts, but I could tell they meant nothing to her and her heart was breaking. Whenever she looked at Louis, I had a feeling she was seeing prison doors slamming shut in front of her and hearing the clank and rattle of phantom locks.

I lied to myself, even as I lied to Hortense, trying vainly to reassure her that perhaps Louis would be kind. After all, they had *so* much in common—they were both fond of music and liked to read. But I *knew* Louis would make her miserable, he hated me just as much as his siblings and mother did, and he would seek to hurt me through Hortense. He would *never* be kind to her. But I had no choice. I was fighting for my survival; if Hortense and Louis failed to give Bonaparte an heir I was certain to be set aside. The whispers were just too loud to ignore; there *had* to be more than a grain of truth in them. Bonaparte must have said something to someone.

Luck was with me once again. Hortense quickly conceived and gave birth to a healthy son. They named him Napoleon Louis Charles. My husband was elated; now if my womb failed to flourish, there was this child waiting in the wings to assume the mantle of heir. I thought now, whatever happened, I would be safe. My daughter had done what I could not; she had given my husband an heir.

Bonaparte was inching ever closer to a crown. He became more pompous and pretentious every day. He began wearing gold-embroidered red velvet suits and a jeweled sword, more ornament than weapon, and declared his birthday a national holiday. He had coins minted with his profile, wearing a crown of laurel leaves just like Julius Caesar. He decided that the people missed the awe and grandeur of the Catholic Church, so he restored the religion that the Revolution had abolished. On Easter Sunday, for the first time in years, church bells rang in France, summoning the people to Mass. In Notre Dame, I knelt beside my husband, stumbling over the long-forgotten prayers. Afterward, my husband stood and nodded his approval. "Now everything is just like before."

As he gave me his arm and we walked back down the aisle, to wave to the people from the church steps, I could not help but wonder, *Was it all for nothing?* The Revolution and all those thousands of lives lost in Liberty's name, what had it all been for?

I knew better than to try to talk to Bonaparte about it. I knew exactly what he would say if I tried: *Women should stick to knitting and not meddle in politics!* But he would not leave it at that. He would feel the need to punish me for forgetting my place. He had cruelly devised the perfect method: He would summon his latest mistress and order her to be stripped and ready, scrubbed clean of perfume, as it always gave him headaches, and waiting naked in the bedroom across the hall from mine. When he was finished, he would come to me and tell me *all* about it, describing the lady's anatomy and everything they had done together. He spared me *nothing!* As I sat weeping, he would come to me and kiss the top of my head and say, "You are a fool, Josephine; you always weep and are afraid that I will fall in love. Do you not know by now that I am not made for love?" And then he would leave me to sleep alone that night, though I very rarely slept, I was so tormented.

Scoff though he might, I thought my fears justified. Bonaparte had loved me once; it was not inconceivable that he could love again, another, in the same mad, passionate manner. If a woman ever came along who fascinated him as much as I once had, everything would be over for me.

I was fighting harder than ever now to hold on to my husband's affections. I was *desperate* to please him, to keep him interested and satisfied. I was dyeing my hair regularly with dark coffee to keep the encroaching gray at bay, wearing more rouge than ever before, and lining my amber eyes with kohl and shading them with a mixture of elderberries and soot to create a mysterious smoky effect, sometimes enhanced by a shimmer of silver or gold paint.

I appeared in a series of fascinating and exotic gowns that would be endlessly talked about and fill pages in the popular fashion magazines and make Bonaparte proud. One night I was all in gold net in which jeweled and enameled sea creatures were ensnared. Another night my black silk gown was covered in toucan feathers encrusted with pearls. I even had the new gold coins minted with my husband's profile made into a dress; I sparkled and jingled every time I moved, liquid nude silk peeping out between where the coins were joined. I imagined it was almost like wearing a knight's chain mail. Another night I was diamonds and pearls from décolletage to hem and the next I appeared in a sheer black gown encrusted with rubies and sapphires, and after that it was lilac silk overlaid with white netting covered with sparkling amethysts from the palest hue to the deepest regal purple. Hoping to remind my husband of the first night we spent together as lovers, I appeared at our anniversary ball in a sheer, body-hugging blush-pink gown sewn all over with real pink rose petals, a creation so delicate I could not sit down and hardly dared move lest I split a seam or the petals fall away and reveal that I was wearing nothing underneath.

But it was all in vain. I appealed to Bonaparte's vanity, not his heart. He was proud of me—sometimes—but he no longer loved me. The dream had died; Josephine was just a pretense, a role I played, only make-believe on the world's stage. Unfortunately, where my husband was concerned, I now lacked the appeal of other actresses.

All Paris was being titillated by tales of the two actresses currently dueling for his affections—the mature, well-seasoned, and very dignified tragedienne Madame Duchesnois and the fifteen-year-old ingénue Mademoiselle Weimar. While the former delighted Bonaparte with her sensual prowess, the latter coaxed the little boy in him out to play. Whenever Mademoiselle Weimar was visiting him at the Tuileries the corridor outside my rooms would ring with Bonaparte's laughter and her girlish shrieks as they romped in and out of his bedroom and played hide-and-seek amongst the bronze and marble statues. She skipped about quite shamelessly in her shift and bare feet with her long blond hair down in pigtails. He would sit her on his knee and feed her sweets right in front of me; sometimes he even gave her my candied violets.

Bonaparte insisted I accompany him to the theater whenever one of them was appearing in a new play. I had to sit there, smile and applaud, and pretend nothing was wrong and I didn't already know more than I cared to about their more intimate performances. Sometimes Bonaparte made me wait while he visited his actress amours in their dressing rooms backstage. "I'll only be a few minutes," he always said; to him it was a boast that he could "get the job done in three or four minutes." Just because it was true didn't make it any easier to bear. I suppose this humiliation was a just penance for my own infidelities.

CHAPTER 29

In 1804 it finally happened. Bonaparte came in while I was sitting at my dressing table in my lace peignoir with my hair down, layering on the rouge, just the way he liked it. He met the reflection of my eyes in the mirror, bowed, and addressed me as "Your Imperial Majesty."

The wheels had already been set in motion. The frail and elderly Pope Pius VII was coming from Rome to crown him.

Until almost the last moment, I did not know if I would be crowned beside Bonaparte. His family was up in arms, simply livid that "that old Creole whore" might become the Empress of France. They were *insatiable* in their greed and never stopped bickering; even after their brother carved up Europe like a roast and gave them all crowns in their own right or by marriage and overlooked their gross incompetence, it *still* was not enough for them. Mother Letizia said if I was crowned she would not come to the coronation, and my husband's sisters refused to walk in procession behind me and carry my train. "We are better than she is!" they hotly maintained. "She isn't even good enough to walk behind *us* and carry *our* trains!"

Bonaparte had a tabletop model of the interior of Notre Dame Cathedral made and little dolls in costumes evocative of medieval splendor to aid in planning the procession and ceremony. The little dark-haired doll in a long crimson velvet train furred with ermine that was made to represent me was constantly being moved, the center of attention, right beside Bonaparte one day, lost in the crowd the next. She was moved so much the pressure of fingers wore threadbare patches in the velvet. One day I walked in and found the poor little doll outside the model cathedral altogether, lying prone and perilously near the edge of the table, like she was about to fall off the face of the earth.

The whole court took note of this uncertainty. The whispers of divorce were louder than ever now. In fact, they could hardly be called whispers anymore. The word was spoken openly and no one bothered to lower their voice; they didn't care if I heard. My ladies, and the rest of the court, began to snub me, at first in little ways, like pretending not to notice when I entered a room, neglecting to curtsy, arriving late to attend me, ignoring my requests, and finally, the ultimate insult, remaining seated in my presence. Those of aristocratic pedigree, many of whom had been émigrés I had helped return to France and regain their rights and property, began to loudly complain that it was beneath them to have to serve a commoner like *Madame* Bonaparte, who was just "a Creole nobody."

It didn't help that my husband was openly dallying with no fewer than three of my ladies at the time, a trio of blondes ranging from eighteen to thirty, none of whom felt an ounce of gratitude or loyalty toward me.

Elizabeth de Vaudey, one of my ladies of the bedchamber, was ripe and voluptuous, an ash-blond songbird with the cunning of a serpent. She began scorning, deriding, and mocking me, putting on airs as though she had more chance of becoming empress than I did. Bonaparte would drag me out of bed at two or three o'clock in the morning and regale me with the intimate details of their latest tryst. "Madame de Vaudey practically sings an aria when she comes," he gleefully confided.

He was even more smitten with my reader, the lovely honey-blond Anna Roche de La Coste, who affected a studied indifference and refused to give up her own lover even for an emperor. Bonaparte was so wild to win her that he gave her an enormous sapphire ring right in front of the whole court.

His third amour was Adèle Duchâtel, only eighteen with spun

gold hair and dewy blue eyes. She was new to court and married to a man approaching eighty. Bonaparte fell madly in love with her when he chanced upon her eating olives at a buffet supper. "You shouldn't eat olives at night. They're very bad for you! They will give you indigestion!" he scolded as he slapped an olive from her fingers' delicate grasp. Either by cruel intent or accident, my husband forgot that he had asked me to come to him and I walked in on them naked in his bed, interrupting them right at the climactic moment. I fled in the face of Bonaparte's wild rage, but he followed me, naked as he was, and smashed every stick of furniture in my bedchamber, screaming the whole time that he was sick of my spying and he must think of his legacy, which demanded that he take a wife who was capable of bearing children; he owed it to France, he said. He left me weeping on the floor amidst jagged splinters of gilded rosewood, broken mirrors and shattered porcelain, and my own pride.

Despite his valor on the battlefield, Bonaparte was cowardly and timid about broaching the subject of divorce directly with me; he preferred a more roundabout way. He tried to take my children into his confidence, to persuade them to be the bearers of bad tidings, but, to their credit, both Eugène and Hortense refused.

Rather than stoop to begging his stepfather to reconsider, Eugène stood there, straight and stoic, a model man and soldier, and said that if such came to pass then it was his duty to leave the court and accompany his mother wherever she wished to go, even if it was back to Martinique. God bless my sweet boy, I didn't deserve such a son! He was *nothing* like Alexandre de Beauharnais!

The spiteful Bonaparte clan was jubilant; they were certain that I would not be crowned and would soon be sent away. But they overplayed their hand. One spiteful remark too many reached Bonaparte's ears. All of a sudden he seemed to wake up and take note of how everyone was treating me. Before them all one evening, he came to me and took my hand and said loud enough for everyone to hear: "It is only fair that she should be an empress. If I was thrown into prison instead of ascending a throne, she would share my misfortune with me, so she should also share my grandeur." Then he addressed me directly: "The Pope will be here at the end of the month. He will crown us both. Order your gown and start to prepare for the ceremony."

I was so grateful that I flung myself at Bonaparte's feet. I had to stop myself from actually kissing them.

I thought I was safe. He came to my bed that night and he was tender and kind with me. But as I lay with my head on his chest, while he stroked and played with my long hair, he said to me, "I know that I shall never have the strength to oblige you to leave me. I tell you plainly, however, that it is my wish that you will resign yourself and spare me all the difficulties of this painful but necessary separation."

I knew exactly what he was saying: he could not bear to ask me to leave him; he wanted me to do it for him, seemingly of my own free will, to be noble and sacrifice myself, to withdraw voluntarily for the good of emperor and empire alike.

I nodded and swallowed hard, choking back the tears and the egg-sized lump rising in my throat. I would not, I could not, do what he was asking.

"I promise that I shall leave the minute I receive a direct order from you to descend the throne," I said.

Stalemate. Neither of us would make the first move. But I *knew* the end was near. He would have his way; it was only a matter of time.

I had less than four weeks to prepare. Seamstresses and embroiderers slaved day and night over the magnificent white satin gown swathed in gold tulle, embellished with large, milky teardrop pearls, and embroidered breast to hem with swarms of Bonaparte's golden bees. The thirty-foot-long, eighty-pound ermine-bordered crimson velvet train was embroidered with *thousands* of golden bees and bordered by Bs encircled by wreaths of laurel leaves. They were still working, their fingers numb and blue with cold on the icy December night before the coronation when I, grasping like a drowning woman at anything that might keep me afloat, ran to the Pope and begged a private audience with him to ease my troubled soul.

Though he was clearly weary and longed for his bed, Pius welcomed me. We sat together by the fire and I, with tears in my eyes, explained that something was weighing heavily upon my soul—I was afraid my husband and I were not truly married in God's sight, as we had been united in a civil ceremony. I was afraid we might both go to Hell.

In truth, I was not thinking of my soul or Bonaparte's at all. It was a calculated move to fortify my position. I was forty and fighting to hold on to a life I didn't truly want but couldn't bear to lose. I spent every waking hour feeling like I was walking on slippery ice, eggshells, or broken glass, but I feared life without Bonaparte, as his scorned and set-aside wife, would be even worse.

I was hoping that a religious ceremony might carry more weight than a civil one and make it impossible for Bonaparte to divorce me. But Pius did not know this; he thought I was "a true daughter of the church" and that my tears were sincere. Lying to the Pope, this was what I had come to!

Pius agreed that the situation must be remedied at once. He sent for Bonaparte, already in his dressing gown, ready for bed, and told him that we had been living in sin and unless we were married at once, in a proper Catholic ceremony, he would not crown us on the morrow.

Bonaparte had no choice but to submit, so witnesses were hastily summoned, a makeshift altar was erected in my husband's study, and Pope Pius himself spoke the words that would make us one in God's sight. I retired victorious, and alone, to my bed, but I did not sleep. It seemed I had only just lain down before I had to rise again.

December 2, 1804 was a dismal day for a coronation. It was the coldest day of the year. The weather couldn't decide whether it wanted to be snow or rain so had combined the two into an icy slush. Everyone seemed peevish and out of sorts, but still the people gathered, starting at dawn, thronging the streets all the way from the Tuileries to Notre Dame Cathedral. Few of the courtiers had slept well, if they had slept at all, so they greeted the day waspish and abrupt, constantly snapping at one another as they went about their duties. Many of the ladies, fearing to spoil their coiffures, since there were too few hairdressers to attend us all, had had their hair done the evening before and passed the remainder of the night sitting upright in chairs.

This should have been the happiest day of my life, I thought as my attendants dressed me. I had never had so many hands on me at once, except in Barras's orgies. My hairdresser arranged my hair in a pile of shimmering dark ringlets crowned with a diadem of pearls and diamond leaves, and my ladies fussed with the high stand-up lace collar framing my shoulders, fastened a necklace of great sapphires and rubies carved like Egyptian scarabs nested in diamonds around my throat, and earrings dangling with truly enormous pearls that tugged painfully at my ears, while others knelt at my feet to smooth out the glimmering rich folds of my gold-encrusted white satin gown and fasten the sapphire buckles on my satin shoes.

"You have never looked more beautiful, Mother," Hortense said, and squeezed my hand.

"I've never felt more afraid," I whispered as I fought to hold back my tears; it wouldn't do to spoil my rouge or to drip tears infused with lampblack from my lashes down to soil my white satin.

Bonaparte had decreed that his coronation must evoke the splendors of the Renaissance. "What I want above all is grandeur," he said, "and what is grand above all is beautiful," so we were all weighed down with cumbersome velvets and heavy satins and taffetas encrusted with gold embroidery and suffering the scratchy neck ruffs and stand-up collars we had copied from sixteenth-century portraits. The men felt ill at ease in their unaccustomed doublets and puffed breeches, which were far from flattering on those with short and stocky figures like Bonaparte, and wrestled to arrange their stiff robes and embroidered mantles into more flattering, and concealing, folds. My husband's purple velvet mantle and white satin raiments were so stiff with gold embroidery they might have stood alone and sewn with so many diamonds that he looked like a walking mirror. There were even diamonds scattered amongst the gilded laurel leaves wreathing his head. He joked that he was the King of Diamonds. The truth was we looked like we were going to a costume ball that most of us had no desire to attend, in abysmal weather and unflattering costumes we would never have chosen for ourselves.

*   *   *

We rode through the streets of Paris in a glass and gold coach like something out of a fairy tale. The people stood shivering in the rain and stared at us; some waved and cheered, but I thought over-all there was more an air of curiosity than jubilation. When we arrived at Notre Dame, just as Bonaparte was handing me down from the coach, the dark, drizzling clouds suddenly parted and the sun shone down on us, striking our diamonds and gold embroidery so that we glowed like divine beings.

Bonaparte smiled and said it was a good omen. "You're still my good-luck charm, Josephine," he whispered as his lips brushed my cheek.

The people cheered wildly at this sign of affection between us. They still believed in our love story.

I smiled wanly back at Bonaparte and tried valiantly to hold back the tears. *If that is true, how can you even think of giving me up?* I wanted to ask him, right there on the steps of Notre Dame Cathedral before everyone, but I didn't dare.

Then it began, what should have been the crowning achieve-ment of my life. I was walking down the center aisle of Notre Dame, my imperial crown carried on a gold-tasseled crimson cush-ion before me, and my husband's vile and bitter sisters, Pauline, Caroline, and Elisa, seething with ill will as they carried my train behind me. People would afterward say I wore my crown as lightly as a feather, but the truth is my head was heavy and aching the whole time and the weight of my train was almost unbearable. It was like dragging a corpse in chains behind me. My sisters-in-law frequently let it sag to stagger my graceful carriage; they were hop-ing, I think, to make me fall.

Bonaparte had tried to appease his sisters by giving them each a diamond diadem and trainbearers of their own to follow behind them, but nothing could mollify their hate. As I approached the altar, where Bonaparte awaited me, and my foot rose to ascend the first step, they threw my train down in disgust. "Shift for yourself, old woman!" I heard a venomous whisper behind me; I'm certain it was Pauline. I staggered, praying that I would not disgrace myself by falling as my arms flailed and I fought to steady myself as I felt myself being pulled backward by my train's weight. Fortunately,

Bonaparte saw and gave his sisters such a stern, admonishing stare that they paled beneath their rouge and hurried to pick it up again.

Our two crowns sat glittering upon the altar. Pope Pius blessed them as we knelt before him. But when the Holy Father lifted the larger of the two and started to hold it aloft, high above Bonaparte's head, my husband leapt up and took it from him. Turning around boldly to face the crowd, he defiantly set it upon his own head.

"He has crowned himself!" That one astonished whisper rippled throughout the vast cathedral and out into the street, being passed from person to person.

I didn't dare move. I remained as I was, kneeling, hands clasped in a prayerful attitude at my husband's feet. Bonaparte betrayed no sign that he was even aware of the sensation his audacious act had caused and brazenly brushed past the Pope and took the other crown from the altar. He held it high in the air, then lowered it and set it gently upon my head, within the diamond circle of my diadem.

"No one else could ever wear a crown with more grace," he whispered.

But I could take no pleasure in the compliment; there was something about his voice that told me that he was already thinking about the next woman who would wear it after I was gone.

It was done. I was now an empress, exactly as Euphemia David had foretold when I was fourteen years old. *But for how long?* I couldn't escape the silent, frightened whisper ricocheting inside my head like a poor, scared little bird trapped and unable to find its way out. I was so afraid I burst into tears.

Everyone thought I was overjoyed and overwhelmed by the honor my husband had just bestowed upon me. Only I knew the truth; I felt it all slipping through my fingers like water and I was powerless to hold on to it. *Everything is lost!* a little voice in the back of my head whispered as I watched my husband waver, like a dream about to disappear, through the thick veil of my tears.

Put me back up on my pedestal; let me be your goddess again! I stared up at him with beseeching eyes. *I will be worthy of the honor this time!*

I reached out and caught the hem of his white satin robe and raised it to my lips. The gold embroidery was rough and scratched my lips as I whispered, "I love you." For the first time in my life, I actually meant it. But it was too late. Bonaparte didn't even look down at me. He was looking forward to the future . . . a future that I would not be a part of. His love, like everything else, had fallen through my fingers.

CHAPTER 30

Conquered nations, like enemies, seldom lie docile and silent for long. The Austrians had joined Russia in an alliance with Britain against Bonaparte. Of course, he was determined to quash them all.

"Rest easy," he said when he left my bed at four o'clock in the morning, ignoring my tears as I clung to him and begged him to take me with him, "I promise you the shortest and most brilliant of campaigns."

So I was left alone, "Our Lady of Victories" again, visiting hospitals, giving comfort where I could, and letting the people see me kneeling in Notre Dame, praying for my husband and his men, all of whom were some woman's husband, beloved, or brother, and some mother's son. When I grew restless and annoyed Bonaparte with my letters—*I* was now the one who bombarded *him* with too many passionate and beseeching words—he ordered me to La Plombières again to take the waters, to rejuvenate my womb in readiness for his return.

There were great victories, the Austrians were again defeated and the Russians retreated, but there were also great losses. After one battle, twenty thousand Frenchmen lay dead covered in blood, mud, and rain. But my husband was happy: *What after all are 20,000 lost for a great battle?* He was now the most hated and feared man in Europe. When he conquered Vienna, he took up residence in Schönbrunn Palace and toyed with the idea of marrying a Hapsburg archduchess, as they were renowned for their fertility. It didn't bother him at all that they thought him "The Beast of the Apocalypse"; he was more concerned that *the memory of Marie Antoinette is too recent* and marriage to one of her nieces might worry and provoke the French people.

Back in Paris after another fruitless and miserable stay at La Plombières, I was consumed by loneliness and despair. Both my children, my truest allies, were separated from me. When he was carving up Europe, doling out crowns and thrones amongst his family, Bonaparte did not neglect his stepchildren. Unhappy Hortense became the most wretched Queen of Holland and Eugène was married to the pretty young daughter of the Elector of Bavaria; luckily, the match proved a happy one that soon ripened into true love.

You must be brave and remember that you are an Empress, Bonaparte scolded when I bewailed their absence. *You should have more fortitude and confidence, you must be cheerful and amuse yourself.* He was busy with his army and had no time or patience for my tears and fears.

I slept poorly, tormented by strange recurring dreams in which I saw a fair-haired angel holding up a bouquet of flowers. I was terrified of what it might mean, but Bonaparte scoffed at my superstitious fancies and preened, delighted by my jealousy. *The winter nights are long, all alone,* I hinted, but he refused to let me come to him; Paris needed "Our Lady of Victories" more than he did.

Be worthy of me, he commanded, *show more character; I don't like cowards.*

As the Prussians joined forces with the Russians and Bonaparte marched through frozen Poland, determined to crush them, my greatest fear came true at last—my husband found a flesh-and-blood woman who could rival the dream of Josephine.

* * *

The Polish people looked upon Bonaparte as their savior. They turned to him with hope, not fear, in their eyes. Above all else they wanted their freedom from Russia, and Bonaparte had the power to break those shackles. The people sang and danced in the streets of Warsaw to welcome him. Women ran out to minister to the wounded and to offer them food and hospitality.

As he rode through a sea of hopeful faces, hands reaching up reverently to touch his boots and legs, Bonaparte noticed a young woman with long, flowing flaxen hair. In her white dress she looked as beautiful as an angel. Fearlessly she approached my husband and handed him a bouquet of flowers.

"We have been waiting for you to save us," she said matter-of-factly, without a trace of awe or fear in her voice.

When he looked into her blue eyes, Bonaparte fell deep in love, so deep he thought he would drown if he did not possess her.

But this flesh-and-blood angel was a virtuous woman. She acted bored instead of honored when he asked her to dance at a ball that night where she appeared again all in white. It nearly drove my husband mad. He was *wild* to win her. He could not sleep for thinking about her.

I saw no one but you, I admired only you; I want no one but you. He rose from his restless bed to write to her, sending along a ruby and diamond necklace in a red leather case to accompany his letter. Both were promptly returned without a word in answer.

The next night he sent flowers. *Your country will be dearer to me when you take pity on my poor heart,* he declared, adding a warning: *Whenever I have thought a thing impossible to obtain I have desired it all the more.* Nothing *discourages me!*

Devoted to her country, her seventy-two-year-old husband, and their little son, the Countess Maria Walewska possessed a wisdom and gravity far beyond her nineteen years. When her husband and a group of Polish patriots came to her and said the lives and freedom of all her countrymen depended on her surrender, she resigned herself to making the necessary sacrifice, though in private she wept in her husband's arms at the thought of betraying him. But it was for the good of Poland, he reminded her, so she dried her tears, summoned up every ounce of courage she possessed, and in her pure white nightgown and unbound hair she went, like a lamb going to slaughter, to Bonaparte's bed. What she didn't reckon on was falling in love there.

She was ethereally beautiful yet practical as a bourgeois shop-keeper; a young woman with an old soul, who spoke fluent French and was well versed in history and geography; she dressed elegantly, danced and walked gracefully, and was a talented singer and musician; she was the perfect chatelaine of her husband's vast estates, a dutiful and devoted wife and loving mother with an unexpectedly sensual nature that had been slumbering dormant until Bonaparte woke it up. Maria Walewska set my husband's soul on fire. She was everything I wasn't and should have been. She made all my flaws stand out stark naked against the brilliant, blinding light of day and made Bonaparte question how he could ever have fallen in love with me in the first place.

As the long-forgotten Bellilotte Fourès had been "Napoleon's Cleopatra," Maria Walewska became "Napoleon's Polish Wife." He took her everywhere. She tended to his every need like the most devoted wife, equally at home in an army tent as she was in a palace. She listened to his worries, nursed his bellyaches and migraines, delighted him in bed, and evinced a genuine interest in his campaigns. And when she became pregnant she delighted him even more—here, at long last, was clear and certain proof that Bonaparte was not sterile; the barrenness that had afflicted our marriage was no one's fault but mine.

It was disastrous timing. No sooner had Maria Walewska conceived than Hortense lost her son to a virulent attack of measles. Bonaparte was again without an heir, but not without hope. His "Polish Wife" had given him that.

In Paris, Bonaparte's popularity was floundering, army bulletins were greeted with boos instead of hurrahs, and the people were beginning to question and even curse their emperor. Even their reaction to victories was now lukewarm in the face of so many fatalities. When the lists of the fallen were read it was hard to tell which was greater, the outrage or the tears. Men fled the draft in terror, willfully maiming and mutilating themselves or contracting syphilis rather than join La Grande Armée. Families conspired to conceal dodgers and deserters rather than sacrifice their sons to Bonaparte's overweening vanity. Even the court sat around looking tired and downcast.

I was constantly close to tears and fraught with worry; I gnawed my nails and slept poorly. I knew that the end was coming. The court was constantly unkind to me. I hated my life and longed as I never thought possible for the peaceful, easy pace of the life I had shunned and left behind me in Martinique. Not even a new suitor could make me smile.

The brother of the Queen of Prussia, kind, handsome, and so very sweet, Crown Prince Frederick of Mecklenburg-Strelitz was madly in love with me. Though he was a widower and prematurely silver haired, he was fifteen years younger than me. He didn't care, but I did. I had grown timid in my forties and I was too afraid to let love in, and even more afraid of offending Bonaparte and giving him fresh cause to doubt me. He was livid and cursed me to the ends of the earth when he heard that I had been seen at the theater with Prince Frederick. *My only defense,* I wrote sadly to my son, *is to lead a perfectly blameless life. I no longer go out. I have no pleasures. How unhappy do thrones make people, my dear Eugène! I would resign mine tomorrow without a moment's regret! For me the love of the Emperor is everything; I resign myself to Providence and his will.* So I sacrificed what might have been my last chance at happiness, God opening a window after closing a door, and sent Frederick away.

Life in the gilded, stifling splendor of our imperial court now reminded me of the days I had spent in the prison of Les Carmes where everyone sat wary and tense each evening waiting to see if their names would appear on the list for tomorrow's executions. We were all waiting now—waiting to see who would come after me; waiting for Destiny to write the last page of the story; waiting to see how it would all end.

Crafty as ever, Bonaparte decided the time was right to make peace with Russia. He met Tsar Alexander on a raft in the middle of the Niemen River. They discovered that they had one thing in common; they both hated the British, and that was enough for them to swiftly reach an armistice. And there was something else to consider: The Tsar had a pretty and intelligent sister, the Grand Duchess Catherine, and Bonaparte fancied that she would make the perfect royal wife, though he was still mulling over an Austrian archduchess; the Hapsburgs' famous fertility was impossible to ignore—the Empress Maria Theresa had borne sixteen children.

CHAPTER 31

———◀◉▶———

Bonaparte came back to me colder than ever before. He brought his Polish countess with him and installed her in a house conveniently near the Tuileries. He visited her every day and often late at night. Sometimes they went out together disguised as a middle-class married couple and made small talk with shopkeepers. They had been seen several times sitting in the park eating roasted chestnuts or sausages they bought from a street vendor. When the Sultan of Turkey sent lavish gifts, Bonaparte took them to Maria Walewska first and let her take her pick of them. To her credit, she considered this inappropriate and, after selecting one cashmere shawl—the most modest one—for herself to quiet his protests, insisted that the rest be sent to me directly.

It amused Bonaparte that Turkey had a new sultan and sultana, crowned almost at the same time as ourselves, though it was the Sultan's mother, not one of his numerous wives, who ruled alongside him as his empress. The Turkish ambassador presented me with a portrait of her. She looked to be younger than me, with masses of golden hair, hanging down in shimmering waves, scattered with diamonds, reaching almost to her knees. *How curious,* I thought. I had always imagined harem girls as exotic creatures with dusky skin, black hair, and dark, almond-shaped eyes, but this woman's skin was white, it looked as though it had never known the kiss of the sun, and her eyes were blue as the finest sapphires. Her stance was proud and there was a mysterious yet almost mischievous air about her, like she alone knew a secret, and was savoring it, laughing at the rest of the world's ignorance. Her headdress reminded me of the island women's *tignons;* it was a rich blue-green satin crowned with peacock feathers held by a brooch of sapphires and emeralds, and diaphanous veils, layered in shades of blue and green, deep and pale, trailed down her back, to touch the floor. Her gown seemed to be of the same resplendent peacock color, but it was so thickly encrusted with gold embroidery I could barely see the teasing wink of blue-green beneath. The full skirt was slit open to reveal a pair of baggy satin trousers that were gathered in at the ankles, and golden slippers with toes that curled up and in upon themselves. At her waist was a jeweled dagger, its crescent-shaped blade sheathed in a golden scabbard covered with a rainbow of cabochon rubies, sapphires, and emeralds interspersed with tiny, twinkling diamond brilliants. A great yellow diamond, with rays made of smaller white stones, shone like the sun above her bodice. A long necklace of white diamonds, set in the shape of eyes, with irises of various-colored gems, hung around her neck and down past her waist, a talisman I recognized to ward off the evil eye. An immense cabochon sapphire was on the ring finger of her left hand, and her arms, folded across her breasts, were layered in jeweled bracelets all shaped like serpents swallowing their own tails, no end and no beginning. It made me think at once of Euphemia David and her snake; she was said to have had a tattoo of the same motif on the small of her back, though I never saw it. Of course when I thought of Euphemia David I also thought of Aimee and our secret midnight visit to have our fortunes told. But poor Aimee was dead now, bleached white bones at the bottom of the sea, and I, though an empress as Euphemia David foretold, wasn't any happier. I wondered if the Sultana of the Turks beneath all her splendor was truly a happy woman. I doubted it; happiness I was certain never accompanied crowns.

For the time being, Bonaparte's "Polish Wife" was the happy one. But he would betray her too in the end. When there were rumblings about vengeance from Austria, Bonaparte struck a bargain with the Tsar—France would not interfere if Russia invaded Finland or Turkey and the Tsar could do as he pleased with Poland; it was a matter of complete indifference to Bonaparte.

Maria Walewska's sacrifice had been in vain. After the birth of her son, Florian, she went back to her husband. He still loved her. He absolved her of all blame and shouldered the burden himself. He had been amongst the party of patriots who had pushed her into Bonaparte's bed in the hope of liberating Poland; she had not succumbed of her own free will. Count Walewski acknowledged my husband's bastard as his own and gave him his name. He truly was a noble man.

At thirty-eight, my husband was more impatient than ever to lay the foundation for his imperial dynasty. For that he needed a *royal* wife and a *legitimate* heir. Neither my barren self nor his fertile "Polish Wife" would do; we both lacked the necessary pedigree. Though his brother Louis had shown a rare and unexpected kindness to Hortense after they lost their firstborn and she had quickly conceived again, another son, this time Bonaparte was unwilling to consider any heir except one sired by his own loins in a royal womb. He knew that he could do it now; I was the one who had held him back from the happy state of fatherhood. It was all my fault. So I had to go; I had to clear the path to make way for the woman who could make all his dreams come true.

After Mass one Sunday Bonaparte hinted that it was time for me to make "the inevitable sacrifice."

Stubbornly, I shook my head. I played the only card I had left—Bonaparte's steadfast belief in destiny.

I touched the medallion engraved with the words *To Destiny!* that still hung between my breasts like a talisman.

"Our joint destiny has been too extraordinary not to have been decided by Providence," I said. "Only you must decide my fate. I am too afraid of bringing bad luck to both of us if I, of my own accord, should separate my life from yours."

But I knew the end was near. My husband had sent for reinforcements—Hortense and Eugène—to shore me up and soften the blow.

About a week later I was summoned unexpectedly to Bonaparte's bedchamber. I found him lying on the bed, clutching his stomach and groaning, ashen faced and deathly ill. He reached out a trembling hand to me.

"My poor Josephine, I can't possibly leave you!" he sobbed. "The pain is *killing* me! *Please,* remove this heavy burden from my heart!"

He spoke of France, of political necessity, of being cruelly treated by fate, the violence being done to his heart, calling himself the poor put-upon plaything of destiny, but I didn't really hear him, and I certainly didn't believe him. My ears had begun to ring, muffling his anguished cries to mere distant whispers. I felt like I was underwater, sinking fast, drowning. Darkness was encroaching upon my eyes and I couldn't draw my breath. My heart and head hurt in equal measure. The next thing I knew I was lying on the floor and Bonaparte was crouching over me and rubbing my hands.

"Josephine! My dear Josephine! You know how I have loved you! To you alone I owe the only moments of happiness I have ever known, but, Josephine, my destiny is not to be controlled by my will. My heart must yield to the nation! I have only one passion, only one mistress—France! I sleep with her; I live for her; I fight for her. She never lets me down; she pours out her blood and her treasures for me. If I need five hundred thousand men she gives them to me without question! Everything I have ever done has been for her, and everything I will ever do will be for her! You *must* believe me—this isn't for me; it is for *France!*"

"*What a liar you are!*" I whispered so softly I'm not sure Bonaparte even heard me before I lost consciousness again.

When I awakened, I was lying on my bed. My children were beside me, and Bonaparte was standing there with tears pouring from his eyes.

"Nothing will make me go back on it, neither tears nor entreaties," he said as soon as he saw me open my eyes.

Hortense answered him with the coolest, calm dignity, with not a sign of a single tear. "You are the master here, Sire, and no one will oppose you. If your happiness requires it, that is enough. My mother will submit to your will and we will all go away, taking the memory of your kindness with us."

Bonaparte staggered back as though she had struck him. "What!

You are all going to desert me? Don't you love me anymore? If it were my happiness, I would sacrifice it for you, but it is for the good of France, I tell you! You should pity me rather than condemn me for having to sacrifice my heart!"

"Sire, we cannot live near you anymore," Eugène replied. "It is a sacrifice that has to be made and we will make it. We will go away quietly."

When Bonaparte started to again protest, Eugène interrupted, "A son's first loyalty is to his mother, Sire." Bonaparte could not argue with that.

But I could not slink away like a thief in the night. The divorce must be formally announced to the court. It was a gala evening with everyone crowded into the throne room in their finest clothes and jewels. Many wore an air of satisfaction. Bonaparte's siblings were like cats who had drunk their fill of sweet cream. I'm sure they felt their triumph was complete; "the old woman," "that Creole whore," had been ousted.

Now that I belonged to myself again, I disdained Bonaparte's dictates about my wardrobe. I entered the throne room in a simple, flowing white muslin gown, with my hair caught up in a loose coil with a single white rose, and a beautiful pink and gold cashmere shawl draped loosely about my shoulders. I wore only one ornament, the first my husband had given me, the golden medallion inscribed *To Destiny!*

Hortense and Eugène were there on either side of me, their shoulders and loving arms ready to support me, as I approached the dais and took my seat, for the last time, in the more delicate, smaller golden throne beside Bonaparte's.

The Emperor, resplendent in a gold-embroidered red suit, was the first to speak.

"God alone knows what this resolve has cost my heart," he said. "But there is no sacrifice beyond my courage if it is for the good of France. Far from having any complaints, I have only gratitude to express for the tenderness and devotion of my well-beloved wife. She is the jewel that has adorned fifteen years of my life, the memory of which will remain forever engraved upon my heart. I would like her to continue to hold the title of Empress, and, above all, never to doubt my feelings for her; she will always be my best and dearest friend."

I shut my eyes tight against the tears, but they still seeped out. It had all been for nothing. He had conferred upon me the vain and empty title of Empress only to render my fall more remarkable.

Then it was my turn to speak. Every gloating eye was upon me. I felt naked and alone and my knees trembled as I rose from the gilded throne in which I would never again sit. The paper on which my speech was written rattled in my hand. I could not stop shaking.

"With the permission of my dear and august husband," I began, but even my words were trembling, "I declare that, no longer preserving any hope of having children to satisfy the political necessity for an heir, I proudly offer him the greatest proof of my affection and devotion. . . ."

My courage failed me, tears blinded me, I could no longer see to read the words, and the paper they were written on fluttered from my helpless hands like a wounded white bird.

Hortense retrieved it, and as Eugène moved to put his arm around my shoulder she began to read, speaking in my stead, her voice clear and steady.

"'The Emperor will always be my dearest love. I know how much this act, demanded by politics and the wider interests of the nation, has crushed his heart; but both of us nonetheless glory in the sacrifice that we have made for France.'"

Hortense turned and curtsied to her stepfather and presented the paper to him as a memento of this sad occasion; he might as well have it since he was the one who had dictated it.

Quivering with tears, I forced myself to be strong, to stand upright again, alone. My hands shook so badly as I lifted the golden chain from about my neck that I knocked the rose from my hair. I looked down and through the watery haze of my tears I saw its fair, fragile petals scattered about my feet. I cradled the gold medallion in my hands and read one last time the words written there: *To Destiny!* Then I forced myself to just let go; it was no good holding on. Everything had already slipped through my fingers; this was all for show.

I curtsied to Bonaparte and surrendered the medallion that had hung faithfully around my neck since our wedding night. I renounced destiny, the fate that had been written in the stars at the hour of our birth, and embraced free will.

" 'The fault, dear Brutus,' " I whispered tremulously, so softly that Bonaparte alone could hear, " 'is not in our stars, but in ourselves.' "

I had learned to quote Shakespeare—Alexandre would have been *so* proud of me!—but alas, too late, too late!

Bonaparte formally kissed my cheek and handed me down from the dais.

I managed to hold myself together long enough to walk out of the throne room supported by Hortense and Eugène, holding my head up high and ignoring Bonaparte's siblings mocking me as "a feeble old woman," but the moment the door had closed behind us I gasped, "This is the most dreadful moment of my life!" and fell to the floor in a senseless heap. At first they thought I had actually died of grief.

As I lay in my bed, my hair and gown in disarray, my eyes swollen nearly blind from so many hours spent weeping, I heard my door creak open with the last chime of midnight. Bonaparte came to me. I felt the warmth and weight of his body for the last time over mine and the hot, hungry passion of his kisses. From head to toe, he kissed me everywhere. At dawn, he left me.

"Adieu, my dear Josephine; be brave," he whispered, pressing one last tender kiss upon my brow. "I will always be your friend."

CHAPTER 32

In a softly misting rain, as though Heaven was also weeping for me, I left the Tuileries for the last time and drove to Malmaison. I was so weak from weeping I could hardly stand or see and Hortense and Eugène had to help me into the carriage. Though I had left with the dawn—I didn't want to see anyone—the French people lined the roads, standing bareheaded in the rain with their hats over their hearts. "*Vive Josephine!*" . . . "*Vive l'imperatrice!*" they cried.

I didn't deserve their love, but they still loved me. They were on my side. Bonaparte was the one who had shattered the illusion of our great love. They saw me as yet another crushed victim of his accursed ambition.

I was grateful, and I wanted to do something for them in return. So I entrusted Hortense with a special task: to arrange a raffle, to dispose of all my weighty, cumbersome court finery, all the satin, taffeta, and velvet gowns laden down with gilt embroideries and heavy ermine-trimmed trains, since I would no longer have need of them, and give all the money to the poor.

There had always been money to be had from my cast-off gowns. I would wear a dress once, as Bonaparte dictated, then give it to my ladies; usually they sold it. Everyone from governors' wives to German princesses wanted my gowns. I had once attended a quadrille ball where at least half the women were wearing my discarded dresses. I had even seen them on the backs of actresses when I attended the theater. Whenever I reluctantly traveled to La Plombières to take the waters at Bonaparte's command the Governor's wife and daughters usually greeted me wearing my old gowns.

At Malmaison, I kept the lamps turned low; my eyes, weakened by so much weeping, could no longer stand the light. The doctor said my sight was failing, and the terror of going blind made me weep all the more. Like a ghost in my flowing white gowns, I roamed the halls and hothouses and floated aimlessly through the empty rooms, looking for something that could give me solace.

I kept Bonaparte's room exactly as it was when he last left it, with clothes scattered across the floor and the history book he had been reading lying open on the table beside the bed. I wouldn't let the servants touch it, not even to dust it. Sometimes I wrapped myself in an old gray greatcoat he had left behind and curled up in his favorite black Moroccan leather armchair by the fire and wept for hours as my fingers caressed the cuts his penknife had made upon its arms. It was funny to think how I had once deplored this destructive habit of his and wept because he was ruining all my beautiful furniture and now I cherished each mark; I felt each one as a gouge deep upon my heart.

"You mourn the man you wish he was, not the man he truly is, Mother," Hortense tried to console me.

But nothing helped. I was restless and ill. Sometimes I walked for hours in the rain trying to cool my fever. The days dragged by so slow each one seemed to last a lifetime. When Bonaparte sent me a letter gently chastising me because the servants had seen me weeping, I wrote back: *Sometimes it seems as if I am dead and all that remains is a sort of faint sensation of knowing that I no longer exist.*

The golden-haired sultana sent me a present, a bangle of gold shaped like a snake swallowing its own tail. It was engraved, in French, with the words: *In My End Is My Beginning.* I knew it was a heartening message meant to give me hope, telling me that the end of my time as empress, and Bonaparte's wife, was not the end of my life or an occasion for mourning, but a new beginning to be looked forward to, not feared and dreaded. I don't think I ever wore it. I put it in a box with all my other bracelets.

My husband—I could never think of him as anything else—had already moved on, rushing forward, leading the charge, to meet his destiny. He had dallied too long and indecisively over the Tsar's sister, so his second choice "won" by default.

The Archduchess Marie Louise of Austria was eighteen, a tall and sturdy-boned, big-bosomed blonde with a graceless walk, cold and aloof manner, and the unfortunate inbred plump, protruding lower lip known as the Hapsburg Lip that had been disfiguring the countenances of the Austrian imperial dynasty for decades.

While she could speak fluently in French, German, Italian, English, Latin, and Spanish, small talk was beyond her; the niceties of polite conversation completely eluded Marie Louise. Her favorite pastimes were painting landscapes, playing the harp, reading serious books, and eating—fourteen different desserts were routinely offered to her at supper.

She didn't know how to charm and win people like I had. When little girls welcoming her to France curtsied and presented her with posies Marie Louise merely nodded curtly and passed them into the hands of her nearest attendant. Marie Louise greeted the people who lined up to see her like a general reviewing troops.

She saw herself as a virgin being sacrificed to the Minotaur, but she had been brought up to do her duty even if that meant following in the footsteps of her great-aunt, who had been married to the sovereign of France, then dethroned, defiled, and beheaded by its people. But Bonaparte didn't care how she felt or what graces she lacked, or that she regarded him as "The Beast of the Apocalypse"; in his eyes all she was, was a walking womb.

As the court whirled through a series of balls and receptions to welcome her, the public reviled the Austrian archduchess as Marie Antoinette all over again. The common people didn't forget about me; they still loved me and were loyal to my memory. Bonaparte had to order the newspapers to cease writing about me and issue an edict to take my face off snuffboxes and playing cards. Even when the fountains ran red with free wine to celebrate the Archduchess's arrival still the people did not cheer her.

They no longer loved Bonaparte or saw him as their savior. Before he had been a man of the people who had risen up to save them; now he saw himself as a god, above all men. He had made himself an emperor, greater than any king, and conquered half the world, carved it into pieces, and parceled it out for his lazy and inept siblings to rule. He set aside the wife he had called his good-luck charm, and scorned his common blood and sought to ennoble it with children born from a royal womb, to found a dynasty greater even than the Hapsburgs and Bourbons. Sometimes as Bonaparte rode past in his carriage surrounded by guards, a bold voice would cry out from the crowd, "You threw away your luck with Josephine!" He had also thrown away their love, just like I had his. Neither of us realized how much that love mattered until it was too late.

I didn't even know her, but I *hated* Marie Louise. Every time I heard her name it felt like a slap in the face to me. Hortense was ordered to carry her train at the wedding, and my few remaining ladies-in-waiting eventually deserted me; my melancholy was not to their taste, and they preferred to return to court to serve the new empress instead. Who could blame them? They wanted life and light, not to sit in the dark and oppressive sorrow with me. She was young and robust and still had life in her, whereas I was little better than a walking corpse. She waltzed every night in the Emperor's arms; Bonaparte had actually taken lessons so as not to disappoint her. But all I ever did was weep and lay out the tarot cards and squint down at them through my tears and troubled eyes, hoping to find some better fate, or even just a glimmer of hope again.

No one came to visit me, not even old friends from the past like Barras, Theresa, Fortunée, and Hippolyte, and though I was just minutes from Paris, I lived as if I were a thousand leagues from it. Sometimes I wished I had had the courage to cast caution to the wind and marry Prince Frederick when he had asked me to. His love might really have lasted. I might have been happier as a princess than I ever was as an empress.

* * *

Bonaparte chose to embrace the comparisons everyone was making between his bride and Marie Antoinette. When she arrived on French soil, just like the aunt she never knew, he had Marie Louise stripped of every Austrian stitch and dressed anew in all things French; even the pug dog she had brought with her was taken away and replaced with a new fluffy white French bitch. He decided to make their wedding ceremony an exact replica of the one that had united Louis and Marie Antoinette in 1770. He pored over the archives and picked the memories of ancient aristocrats who had attended the lavish ceremony in the royal chapel at Versailles and put seamstresses to work replicating Marie Antoinette's splendid gown of shimmering white satin sparkling with diamonds and edged in ermine.

After the ceremony, an opulent ball was held in the palace of the Austrian Prince Schwarzenberg, one of the guiding hands behind the marriage. So many attended that the ballroom overflowed and the guests spilled out into the gardens to dance amongst the flowers. A slight breeze stirred the long white gauze curtains and they caught upon the candles. The palace was quickly engulfed in flames. Bonaparte and his bride escaped, but dozens died or were crippled or disfigured for the rest of their lives. Bonaparte saw it as a bad omen. It made him wonder if he had indeed divorced luck along with Josephine. But it was too late to change anything; all he could do was go forward wearing a brave face.

Before a year had passed, Marie Louise was pregnant. "I have married a womb!" Bonaparte enthused. He saw her pregnancy as a vindication, proof that the divorce, however unpopular it might have been with the French people, was absolutely the right thing to do. He declared that his son would have the title of King of Rome and ordered a splendid suite made ready at the Tuileries replete with heavy silver furniture and hundreds of liveried attendants to see to his son's every need. Bonaparte was confident that it would be a boy; he didn't even entertain the possibility of a girl.

I was alone at Malmaison, sitting by the fire in Bonaparte's bedroom, with his old gray greatcoat wrapped around my thin white gown, the night of March 20, 1811 when the church bells began to ring, announcing the birth of the imperial child. I sat tense and alert as I counted the cannon fire, my nails breaking as they dug into the marks Bonaparte's penknife had gouged into the arms of his favorite chair. Ancient royal custom decreed the guns would sound twenty-one times for a daughter and one hundred for a son. When I heard the twenty-second shot I knew Bonaparte at long last had a son, an heir born of his fierce ambition and his bride's royal blood.

I knew what was expected of me, so I put on a gown of silver lamé and my diadem of teardrop pearls and diamond leaves and stood on the balcony and watched the red, blue, and gold fireworks exploding in the sky high above Paris. I drank a glass of champagne and toasted the Emperor, the Empress, and the newborn King of Rome. Then I went to my desk.

I wish you joy, I wrote to Bonaparte, but I must have wept a thousand tears over those four little words. *I will always love you!* my heart cried out but my hand didn't dare write. I had no pride, but I had to pretend I did. He always wanted me to be brave, to be worthy of him. He had what he wanted; he would never repent of his mistake and take me back now. The divorce and his marriage to Marie Louise were set in stone, cemented by the birth of this royal child.

"You are now only a memory to him, no longer a dream!" I sobbed. "Adieu, Josephine!"

PART 4

---◆---

NAKSHIDIL

CHAPTER 33

In the morning I awoke, nested in silken sheets, with Abdul Hamid
leaning over my pillow, smiling down at me, with love in his eyes
as he stroked my golden hair, fanning it out over the pillows as he
whispered my new name—*Nakshidil*. "When Lâle comes for you in
a little while, you are to say this word to him . . ." he said, and he
told me another new Turkish word.

It was too much trouble to struggle back into my French finery,
so Abdul Hamid gallantly gave me his silken robe, the one he had
worn the night before. I marveled at how even up close it was almost impossible to glimpse the color of the silk beneath the dazzling embroidery. He said it was mine to keep, to have it made into
whatever garment I wished, and if the amount proved insufficient I
had only to let him know and I would have more of it. "It will
please me very much to see you wear it," he said. He then pressed a
sparkling yellow diamond, the pure color of morning sunshine,
into my hand. It was so big it completely filled my palm. He said he
wanted me to have it because it reminded him of the sun in my hair,
and he gave me a little velvet pouch filled with smaller white diamonds of various sizes, courtiers that I might have set around this
sun king of gems.

When Lâle came for me, I was standing there in the Sultan's

gold and silver robe with my hair flowing down like liquid gold about my hips, holding the yellow diamond in one hand and the velvet pouch in the other.

I did as the Sultan told me and spoke the whispered word aloud: "*Ikbal.*"

Lâle's jaw dropped so low I thought it would slip its joints. He glanced past me at Abdul Hamid.

"*Ikbal.*" The Sultan nodded and smiled.

This time, as I trod the Golden Path, I held my head up high and smiled in triumph.

It was unprecedented. After only *one* night I had gone from being barely an odalisque, one of five hundred concubines all living in constant hope of catching the Sultan's eye and most never succeeding, or a *gōzde* (in the eye), noticed but not yet bedded, to the rank of royal favorite—*ikbal*.

How did I do it? Everyone wanted to know. I knew *nothing*! I was an infidel, a *Giaour*. I knew *nothing* of Turkish customs and etiquette; my vocabulary didn't even consist of a handful of words. I was a virgin, entirely ignorant and untutored in the arts of love; before that night I hadn't the faintest idea how to please a man. Though a Sultan might enjoy many virgins in his lifetime, they were *never* sent to him without some degree of schooling in the erotic arts. Yet not only had I been given a jewel, a *yellow* diamond, of such startling rarity and quality; I had also been given the Sultan's robe of special silk.

Back in the dormitory when Lâle tried to gently take it from me and I told him what the Sultan had said, his knees completely failed him and he sank like a stone down onto my divan. The women clustered around us were equally dumbfounded when Lâle told them what I had just said.

I didn't understand. What was all the fuss about? I thought it very kind, and generous, of the Sultan to give me a robe of such costly and beautiful silk.

"This kind of silk is called *seraser,*" Lâle explained. "There is none finer in all the world; it is encrusted with embroidery of real gold and silver threads so thickly that even when you hold it to your eye it is hard to glimpse the color of the silk beneath. The very best of its kind, such as this, is *has ulhas,* the purest of the pure. No one but the Sultan is allowed to wear it unless he says so, and Abdul Hamid has given you that right. Women have served him for years and even borne his children and never attained that honor. Do you have *any* idea how special you are?"

"You are saying I could have a future as rich and bright as these silver and gold threads"—I glided my hand over the glimmering material—"if I embrace it," I hugged Abdul Hamid's robe close about me.

"We understand each other perfectly." Lâle smiled. "Lady Nakshidil."

My education then began in earnest; I seemed to go straight from the Sultan's bed into the schoolroom. That very morning the women started almost at once upon my vocabulary. As I was dressed for the day they taught me the names of the various garments, pointing to either the ones I was putting on or those they were themselves wearing: *gömlek* (chemise), *salvar* (trousers), *entari* (the décolleté bosom-baring gown with its full skirt slit open in front to reveal the trousers beneath), *kaftani* (caftan), *mintan* (short embroidered jacket), *yelek* (vest), *kusak* (sash), *yasmak* (face veil), *hotoz* (a tall round felt hat with a flattened top), *takke* (cap), *tulbend* (turban), *sorguç* (turban ornament), *feridje* (cloak), *sipşip* (slippers), and *kub kob,* the high-soled wooden shoes I had worn to protect my feet that first night in the bath. Though I already knew a few of the words from when I had helped Abdul Hamid disrobe, I didn't let the women know that.

They then began to point to one another, telling me their names: Zehra, Safiye, Besame, Aysha, Kösem, Esmee, Seza, Zeyneb, Nefi-zar, Zernigar, Güfem, Zibifer, Tabisafa, Kashilmar, Mihrimah, and Simandi.

There was so much to learn and I was determined to sop it all up like a sponge. I was a firm believer in the old adage knowledge is power.

The harem was a world full of rules, not unlike the convent had been, only here we were encouraged to glorify, *not* mortify, the flesh. Nakedness held no shame here, lovemaking was openly and frankly discussed, odalisques attended the School of Love and were instructed in all the erotic nuances, and women routinely practiced upon each other in the hopes of refining their skills; to be ready in case they were summoned to the Sultan's bed was the excuse that was invariably given. No woman would openly admit that she preferred another woman's caresses since the sole purpose of the harem was to please a man, one man—the Sultan. Such a bold admission might lead to dismissal or even death for any woman who was not to all appearances dedicating every aspect of her life to the Sultan's pleasure, whether he ever noticed her or not.

Just like a convent, the harem was a world of closed walls and veils. No lady of the harem was allowed to show her face unveiled to any man except the Sultan, not even the princes. The black eunuchs, the "Keepers of the Roses," the "Guardians of Delight," did not count, as castration had deprived them of the vital male part in early childhood long before they had ever known the pleasures a woman's body had to offer. The burning sands they were buried in from the waist down immediately after the operation were said to burn all semblance of desire out of them. But this was not true; many were bitter, melancholy beings tormented by pangs of phantom desires they could not act upon, much as a man who loses an arm still sometimes feels a maddening itch where his elbow used to be. The harem women knew this and some took a fiendish delight in tormenting their protectors with kisses and caresses, flaunted displays of naked flesh, self-pleasure, and overt Sapphic dalliances.

On the rare occasions when women were allowed outside the harem walls for picnics or boating excursions, they must always be veiled and attended by several strong and vigilant black eunuchs, enough to thwart any attempt at escape as well as offer protection against any threats or temptations a beautiful woman given a rare taste of freedom might encounter in the open air.

Some women in the past had been known to cunningly make use of the "bundle women," as the Jewish peddler women who were sometimes allowed inside the harem to sell cheap, gaudy fabrics, baubles, bangles, and trinkets were called, bribing them with jewels, or playing upon their sympathies, to smuggle out messages and arrange assignations. On rare occasion a woman had even been known to smuggle a lover into the harem disguised as a bundle woman. There was a story about a sultan who had caught his favorite in a closet with a man she had snuck inside in this manner. Without opening the door, he had simply thrust in his saber, again and again. He didn't stop until their screams died and their blood, mingled like their bodies had been, flowed out in a river of red from beneath the door.

There were daily lessons in the Turkish language for all newly acquired odalisques. Since it violated their religion to enslave a fellow Muslim there were no native Turkish girls in the Sultan's harem. All were foreign infidels, mostly mountain and peasant girls from Russia, Croatia, Armenia, Romania, Circassia, Nubia, Egypt, Georgia, Syria, and Greece, and the occasional Spaniard or Italian. They were either abducted by bands of marauders or pirates as I had been—such men always had a shrewd eye open for pretty girls ripe for a rich man's harem, cherry-picking the best for the Sultan—or sold by parents who would rather see their daughters the concubines of a rich man than the wives of poor ones. Some orphans and others with a mind of either a practical or lazy bent, desiring the best for themselves, came willingly to the Sultan's harem, some of them starry-eyed with dreams of becoming his favorite, others merely desiring a life of luxury and ease, more comfortable than milking cows or slaving over a cookstove. Each girl was given a new, Turkish, name and ordered to forget the past and think only of the future, to reinvent herself anew.

Once the rudiments of the Turkish tongue had been acquired there were daily lessons in music, dancing, embroidery, calligraphy, singing and the recitation of poetry, eating gracefully with the right hand, never allowing food to touch the left, and utilizing only three fingertips, the complex coffee ritual, the all-important arts of love, and religious instruction, since all were expected to forget their past beliefs and become Muslims themselves. Though many, like me, secretly remained true to their own faith and only went through the motions of converting. But even if it was only playacting, as long as we did it gracefully and respectfully it was enough. Appearances in the harem were everything; few rarely looked beyond the surface for depth and meaning.

For those who wished to learn a useful trade, especially plainer girls with little hope of ever captivating a sultan, there were lessons in music and making confectionary, perfumes, cosmetics, calligraphy, jewelry, cooking, and practical as well as ornamental sewing, and many became highly skilled at the most ornately detailed embroidery and carpet and tapestry weaving. Some even studied sciences such as astronomy, horticulture, mathematics, and medicine. A plain face didn't necessarily bar the door to a prominent position in the harem. If they displayed intelligence and ability, such women might still rise to be Mistress of the Robes, Keeper of the Baths, Mistress of the Sherbets, Keeper of the Jewels, Mistress of the Kitchens, Keeper of the Storerooms, or Reader of the Koran. And, like the moon-faced lady in blue I had met my first night in the harem, one fortunate female might become the Kahya Kadin, the Mistress of the Harem, if she passed her thirtieth year and displayed great resourcefulness, strength of character, and a talent for administration.

There was a strict hierarchy in the harem. Odalisques were the lowest-ranking concubines, those who lived in daily, desperate hope that the Sultan would someday drop his handkerchief for them. Since there were generally about five hundred, most were doomed to lifelong disappointment. Many he never noticed at all; others he bedded and then forgot. *Ikbals* were the favorites, and those who bore him a son were called *kadins*.

Sultana Valide was the position every woman aspired to. A man might have as many women as he pleased, but he would only ever have one mother, and she occupied a cherished position in his heart and home, whether it be a hovel or a palace. The Sultan's mother ruled with absolute power alongside her son. She was the most powerful and influential woman in Turkey, her rank equivalent to that of an empress. She was the only person her son truly trusted. Her rooms adjoined his; she was his confidante and counselor in all things. As the Veiled Crown and Queen of the Veiled Heads, she ruled the harem and every concubine who entered it must have her approval. Her apartments were the heart of the harem, its four hundred rooms were situated around the Valide's courtyard, and she knew everything that happened. The Kizlar Aga was her second in command, and the Kahya Kadin third, and they kept her well informed. Everyone from the lowliest to the highest hungered for the Valide's friendship. She was showered every day with gifts, flattery, praise, secrets, and useful information: *anything* to win her favor, and, through her, the Sultan's.

Since Abdul Hamid's mother was long dead, there was currently no Sultana Valide; the Kizlar Aga ruled the harem in her stead, aided by the Kahya Kadin.

All the women who had borne the Sultan a son were deadly rivals. There was no friendship between the *kadins,* only malice and mistrust. Murders and poisonings, of infants and mothers alike, were far from uncommon within the harem walls, or even outside. A story was often told of how many years ago one jealous and ambitious *kadin,* spying a rival sitting on a stone overlooking the sea with her infant son on her lap, simply walked up behind her and shoved them both down to drown, thus getting rid of both of them and bringing her own son one step closer to the throne.

Often, unless a woman was highly favored and the Sultan decided to grant her the honor of motherhood, any odalisque or *ikbal* who fell pregnant was forced to submit to an abortion. Limiting the number of legitimate heirs reduced the killings and scheming somewhat but never eliminated it entirely. As long as there were women in the harem, there was always the possibility of preferment and pregnancy. Abdul Hamid, though he had twenty daughters, only had two living sons, thirteen-year-old Mustafa and an infant boy called Mahmoud; all the others had died in infancy or childhood, either innocently or through treachery.

To keep the heir to the throne safe, for centuries it had been the custom to incarcerate him in a gilded prison of sorts called the Kefess, the Golden Cage. To safeguard the heir from assassins, sent by ambitious *kadins* desirous of moving their sons up in the line of succession, these princes would enter the Kefess at the age of seven and abide there in splendid isolation, seen and spoken to only by their physician and tutors, and, sometimes, the Sultan. To ease their boredom, they were pleasured by specially selected and sterilized concubines, who, like the white eunuchs who served them, were mute with slit tongues and perforated eardrums, to render them impervious to bribes, corruption, and gossip. These princes only came out of their cage to be buried or to ascend the throne, and by then the silence had driven some of them mad. Abdul Hamid was

forty-five years old when he came out of the Kefess; he hated it so
much he promptly abolished the custom, thus sparing his nephew
Selim "this living tomb of loneliness and silence."

The *kadins* who bore daughters were safer; these girls were valuable marriage pawns in the game of allegiances and alliances, but
not deemed important enough to kill for. Many married outside the
palace walls while others remained in the harem all their lives like
pampered, overfed cats, the more industrious ones rising to an ad-
ministrative position or cultivating a particular skill. Some of the
more sensually inclined sultanas, as these princesses were called,
behaved almost like sultans, acquiring little harems of their own
comprised of favorite women. They even parodied the handkerchief ceremony to announce whom they had chosen to share their
bed and had golden tiles laid in the corridors leading to their doors
to make their own Golden Paths.

The most powerful and feared *kadin* of all was Mustafa's mother,
the dark and dangerous Senieperver; she was determined to be Sultana Valide whatever the cost. She despised the shy, gentle dreamer
Selim, who stood in the path between Mustafa and the throne, and
any woman Abdul Hamid favored instantly earned Senieperver's
enmity. "I am *nothing* if I am not *first* here!" she would fume, pac-
ing the floors like a furious, caged tigress, whenever the Sultan
availed himself of his harem. Sometimes she was so angry that she
slashed at hangings with a dagger or threw anything within reach at
her maidservants, pets, dwarves, and the eunuchs. She would even
beat and bite them if she was mad enough and could not get at the
rival who had provoked her rage. She had once, in a blind rage
when a certain odalisque was summoned three nights in a row to
Abdul Hamid's bed, thrown her pet monkey in the fireplace and
her favorite dwarf out a window.

Sooner or later the women Abdul Hamid favored over Senieperver always sickened and died, young, healthy, and beautiful,
in their prime, shining bright one moment, snuffed out like candles
the next. Senieperver was fascinated by botany, particularly plants
with poisonous qualities. She was rumored to have poisoned Selim
at least once, but she covered her tracks so well that not even the
Prince's Greek physician could say with certainty that Selim's illness
had not been a natural one. But every time Selim had a stomach

upset or a fever all eyes turned warily to Senieperver, all wondering if she was responsible and if she would succeed this time.

Mustafa, though only thirteen, was a thoroughly spoiled, lethargic, and fat, greedy piglet entirely in his sow's power. When his tutors tried to teach him, he threw tantrums, as well as books and inkwells at them. Sometimes he even bit them. He would never make a politician, only a puppet, wholly content to let others rule the empire in his name. To him, being sultan meant wealth, greatness, and power, the right to put himself first and please himself always in all things, but he would keep it all within his hands, his bounty showered only on a loyal precious few, never used for the greater good, to help the Turkish people. On the contrary, he would bleed them dry with taxes to pay for his excesses, and if they didn't pay the Janissaries would make sure they bled out in agony. Through Mustafa, Senieperver would have absolute power, and the very thought was enough to make the whole harem tremble, for she was a woman with a long memory who formed grudges readily and never forgot or forgave.

The smiles and honeyed words and caresses Senieperver began to shower upon me almost daily radiated insincerity. I smiled back at her and received her attentions and gifts gracefully with the careful appearance of gratitude, but I knew she was as deadly as a fer-de-lance and only a fool would trust her. I always found some excuse not to partake of the food she brought me and the drinks I, so woefully clumsy, invariably spilled, often upon her gowns. Nor did I wear the garments she gave me; I had heard there were ways of infusing gloves and other garments with poisons. This woman was my enemy and I knew that she would always be there waiting for the *one* weak moment when I let down my guard and then she would strike at me.

Lâle was worried and sought to warn me.

"Teeth are not hearts," I hastened to reassure him. "A smile does not always mean a good heart. I know better than to trust Senieperver."

CHAPTER 34

As an *ikbal,* I no longer had to sleep in a dormitory; I was given my own room, a diamond-encrusted gold coffee service all my own, great carven chests and cabinets to hold my growing collection of jewels and finery, and a maid to serve only me.

I chose a girl named Naime because her name reminded me of the one I had been born with—Aimee. Her parents had sent her to the harem, hoping to provide their daughter with a better future, but an unfortunate scar on her cheek that she always tried to hide with a forward drawn wave of her blue-black hair and veils had led Lâle to reject her. She was about to be sent to the auction block and sold again, on to another, less exacting, man's harem or to be a household slave, when I asked to have her for my maid.

Abdul Hamid sent for me almost every night. Each night was better than the last. Now when I walked the Golden Path my feet skimmed quick and light across the golden stone and Lâle panted to keep up with me. I waited impatiently all day to be with my royal lover, filling the hours in between with sleep and as much knowledge and diversion as I could cram into them. We had settled into an easy familiarity that was very comforting and dear. He would talk to me of his woes: the stagnant splendor of Turkey; the greedy Russians encroaching upon its borders; the voluptuous Tsarina Catherine as insatiable for Turkish territories as she was for young male bodies; and the corruption eroding his own elite guard, the Janissaries.

Once they had been the proud guardians of the Sultan's throne, the loyalest of the loyal; now the Janissaries were prone to making Sultans topple from their thrones. The Janissaries resented any opposition or attempts at discipline. They liked the old ways best and considered change their worst enemy; they accepted bribes and sold favors and roamed the city looting and plundering the bazaars and terrorizing the people. Though the Janissaries were supposed to lead austere lives and remain celibate, they would rape any woman they chose and strike off men's heads at random, gouge out eyes, or nail anyone who offended them to walls by their ears. Sometimes the Janissaries would leave a victim to bleed to death blind and deaf with every limb severed and their tongue cut out. Whenever the Janissaries were displeased they would overturn the great kettles in which they received their weekly rations of rice from the palace kitchens and beat on them with the long-handled spoons they wore in their tall felt hats. There was no sound more likely to strike terror in a sultan's heart than that of the Janissaries beating on their kettledrums.

Abdul Hamid would heave a heavy sigh and draw me onto his knee and beg me please to help him forget, to amuse him and make him laugh.

I would tell him what I had learned that day, such as to devour feta cheese with my fingertips with the utmost grace or to eat halvah without getting sesame seeds stuck in my teeth, and, in bed, I would show him what I had learned in the School of Love. I happily did anything and everything I could to chase his cares away.

But whenever I was not with him, loneliness encroached on me, even though I was never truly alone.

While I was impervious to Senieperver's feigned benevolence, it saddened me far more that many of the other women who had shown me small kindnesses began to turn spiteful and cold. There were petty acts of meanness, such as leaving pins in my clothes, pulling or knotting my hair while braiding it, or stabbing me when "helping" me to put on a brooch, spitting in my coffee or sherbet when my back was turned, or concealing medicines that would have a laxative or soporific effect in my food to keep me from going to Abdul Hamid. One woman in the baths "accidentally" dipped the end of my braid in the caustic hair-eating paste so a good five inches had to be cut away. Women bearing bowls of indigo or henna also had the "misfortune" to trip over me so that the bath attendants had to labor long and hard before I was presentable and could go to Abdul Hamid again.

When I showed the Sultan the blue and white glass beads fashioned like eyes that Lâle had given me to guard me against the evil eye, he went him one better and had the court jeweler make for me a long diamond necklace of more than one hundred eyes, each one set with an iris of a different gem, including emeralds, sapphires, topazes, and amethysts, with black spinel pupils. Of course this extravagant and loving gesture only made me more envied. But I didn't care. It became my favorite necklace; along with the pearl cross my parents had given me and the snake charm from Euphemia David it formed a trio of treasured talismans, and I was never seen without it. I also began to have a henna tattoo of a serpent swallowing its own tail drawn regularly upon the small of my back, just like Euphemia David had been rumored to have. Those words—*in my end is my beginning*—a prophecy fulfilled, and the truth in them, meant so much to me, I wanted this symbol always upon me, inked into my very skin or symbolized in sparkling gold, gems, and diamonds.

Each month when I bled and could not go to the Sultan's bed as I was considered unclean, there was much jubilation and preening in the harem. All the women took extra care over their appearance, striving to appear the most beautiful and best dressed in the hope that they would be the one to supplant me. How disappointed they always were when Abdul Hamid chose to spend those nights alone and no one was called to walk the Golden Path. They were crestfallen to see the Chief White Eunuch, the Kapi Aga, who acted as the Sultan's valet, hurrying to my door every morning and night that I was unwell to ask on behalf of his master how I fared, if I had slept well, if I was in pain, or if I desired or required anything. His kindness only made them hate me more, but I treasured it above all the jewels and gifts Abdul Hamid ever gave me.

One day while I was at my lessons someone left several cucumbers, eggplants, and long yellow squashes concealed in my bed. I returned to find the Kahya Kadin and several black eunuchs staring down at this hoard of vegetables. When I asked what was amiss they all frowned and regarded me with the gravest expressions.

"Those are not mine!" I cried, bewildered. I didn't understand why anyone would do such a thing. And why all the grim faces? What was all the fuss about? Was I being accused of gluttony or stealing?

The eunuchs were ready to beat me with the soles of their red slippers; fortunately, they could do nothing to me without Lâle's sanction and he could see that I was genuinely bewildered. Such vegetables, he explained, were never allowed intact inside the harem, only sliced. Possessing them whole was a serious offense, as some women had been known to make use of them as a substitute for a man's member. This was strictly forbidden. The women of the harem might kiss and "play at" sex as much as they pleased, such things were never taken seriously, but only the Sultan's phallus was allowed to penetrate their bodies.

Some women were even more devious; they would feign friendship just to get close to me, to try to discover the secret of my allure, and then turn against me, betraying confidences or opening me up to ridicule. As a result, I began to grow more guarded whenever anyone approached me with a smile and friendly overtures. Though I might respond in kind, I was always on guard, always reminding myself not to do or say anything I would not be comfortable having the whole harem see or know.

Even with all the lessons that occupied my days, and the nights I spent with the Sultan, there were still many empty hours to fill. Driven by curiosity and boredom, I sometimes engaged in Sapphic diversions like the other women. I was learning so much in the School of Love and I discovered that it was fun to play in the baths and practice my newly acquired skills. I felt so sophisticated, decadent, and daring, now that I understood what the nuns had feared and what all that hands above the bedclothes and bathing in robes and darkness nonsense was about. I was beautiful, golden, and different, and even though the other women might envy and resent me, or even hate me, many nonetheless desired me. But without genuine affection for each other, I found these amours left me feeling curiously hollow and empty inside. They fulfilled my body, but not my soul. I tried to take pleasure, and give it, solely for pleasure's sake, but I just couldn't do it; even though it felt very good, something was always missing at the heart of it.

The closest to true friendship I ever came was with Besame, the woman who had given me my first taste of sherbet. She was twenty-eight years old; her parents, hoping to provide their only daughter with a better life, had sold her into the Sultan's harem when she was fourteen. Abdul Hamid had bedded her twice, first when she was fifteen, then again at seventeen, but he had not noticed her since. That suited Besame just fine; she was content with her comfortable life and the company of women. She had a wonderfully bawdy sense of humor and delighted in making pastries with erotic names and shapes to amuse the harem. They were the most decadent pastries imaginable, always abundantly rich, sugary, and buttery, stuffed with so much honey or cream they overflowed at the first bite, "the better to tempt another's tongue to licking and lips to kissing," Besame would slyly say, and it was quite true.

She would often come to my room bearing a plate of freshly baked Lady's Lips, Nipples, Navels, or Fingers and sit on my bed with me. She would always take the first bite and then feed me the next with her own fingers. It was her silent way of showing me that Death was not hiding in the sweet things she brought me. Then I would choose the next, hold it to her lips first, and then to my own. And there was always much licking and kissing and giggling in between bites as the pastries spilled their sweet stuffing over our lips and chins before we moved on to more intimate diversions.

I was lonely and would dearly have loved a confidante, a companion whom I could trust entirely. But that was not to be; something always held me back from giving my trust completely. Too many times friendship had proven feigned and false, and even sweet, bawdy Besame could not win over my wariness. One of the saddest days I have ever known was when I finally admitted to myself that I no longer believed in anyone's sincerity; it seemed like a part of my heart died that day. But by then I had already learned that trust could be deadly.

One day I found seven *mendils,* colored handkerchiefs, on my bed. Each one contained a different flavor of Turkish delight (*rahat lokum*). This was a custom amongst harem women, I had learned, for a secret admirer or would-be lover to give such gifts. Each color conveyed a meaning: There was red for passion, pink for true love, green for carnal intentions with no deeper connection, orange for heartache, black for despair, purple for suffering through love, and blue for hope. To give me all seven, someone must be either very confused or suffering desperately for want of me. As I sat down on my bed and unwrapped the sweets and began to eat them I wondered who it could be and if she would soon reveal herself to me. Maybe we would have fun together.

After the second piece, I began to feel a terrible fire burning in my throat that not even water or sherbet would quench. When I stood up, the room began to sway and spin. I felt the heat rising, filling my throat. It was as though an invisible noose was being tugged tight about my neck, making it increasingly hard for me to breathe. I only just managed to call for help before I collapsed and lost consciousness.

I awakened in Abdul Hamid's bed with his Greek physician standing over me. I heard a girl sobbing. Lâle had found the guilty one and brought her to the Sultan for judgment. My secret admirer, a girl named Gulbahar, had murder, not love, on her mind. She was made to kneel before the Sultan, the closest she had ever been to him before. She wept and clung and kissed the hem of his robe and the jeweled slippers on his feet. Abdul Hamid stared down at her in pure disgust and motioned for the black eunuchs to take her from him. She was made to kneel before a small gilded table and the colorful handkerchiefs and Turkish delight were set before her.

"She only had two," Abdul Hamid said, pointing to me. "Pray that the remaining five are enough to kill you; poisoned sweets will be a far more pleasant way to die than the death that I will devise for you if I have to."

She perished in the utmost agony, writhing and screaming as though her insides were on fire, on the Sultan's red and gold carpet while he stood motionless and merciless above her.

Within a few days I had completely recovered, but I never forgot how close I had come to death that day; trust in what I thought was a sweet, romantic gesture had brought me to the brink. It was a very sobering thought.

My introduction to opium almost took me back to that same

frightening precipice. I couldn't believe I made the same mistake twice, and in so brief a time.

One lazy afternoon, Simandi, a woman I mistakenly believed to be a friend, presented me with some dark chocolate pastilles. They reminded me of the cocoa that grew at La Trinité. I lay on my bed thinking of my parents and the home I would never see again. Tears seeped from my eyes as I let each morsel of rich dark chocolate melt lingeringly upon my tongue. There was a strange bitterness at the heart of them. Simandi stroked my hair and kissed me and told me it was nothing, just the way they were prepared here, with special herbs and spices. I would soon grow accustomed to the taste, she promised, and even come to crave it as most of the women in the harem did. A strange lethargy began to steal over me as Simandi began to undress me, murmuring that she hadn't meant to make me feel sad, but she knew a way to make me feel better. My eyes and limbs grew very heavy and my tongue felt like an acrid lead weight in my mouth. I felt the weight of Simandi's dark hair on my thighs as she kissed her way down my body. I was too weary to respond to her lovemaking, yet I lacked the strength to ask her to stop. I couldn't keep my eyes open or even lift one finger.

When I opened my eyes again seven whole days had passed. Lâle and the Sultan's physician were standing over me, and Abdul Hamid was there holding my hand tight, willing me back to life. Opium, distilled from the more potent white poppy, mixed with hashish, musk, and ambergris, had been at the dark heart of the chocolates Simandi had given me. Unaccustomed to opium and unaware of its presence within the sweets, I had eaten too many, and my heart had almost stopped. Its beats had grown so slow, sluggish, and faint that more than once the doctor had given me up for dead. A shroud had even been prepared for me. No one believed I would ever wake up; that I did was hailed as a miracle. "Allah be praised!" Abdul Hamid must have cried a thousand times as he covered me with tears and kisses.

Abdul Hamid, concerned by one too many "accidents" befalling me, sent Lâle to the slave market to find a woman of sufficient strength to safeguard me. He bought a giantess named Kuvveti, which means "Powerful." She was a rugged Georgian mountain girl, nearly six feet tall, of a race rumored to be descended from the fabled Amazon women. She could break a man's neck with a single blow, run like a gazelle, and easily sweep me up in her strong arms and carry me away at the least sign of danger. I was the only one amongst the five hundred harem women to have a bodyguard and this made me feel even more isolated.

Kuvvetti took her duties very seriously. She was fiercely loyal to me. She never let me out of her sight except when I was with the Sultan. Even then she slept stretched out across the threshold, just like she did in my own bedchamber, so that no one could get to me without first stepping over her and in between the two fierce guards that stood flanking the Sultan's door. But no one ever dared attempt that; my giantess could break ankles with her bare hands. Even when I welcomed another woman into my bed, Kuvvetti remained watchful and alert, though I said that she might sleep or seek some pleasure for herself. But Kuvetti would not leave me. One never knew when a foe might unexpectedly emerge from hiding inside a friend like a wolf in sheep's clothing.

My miraculous recovery was celebrated with a great open-air picnic on the banks of the Bosphorus. It was the first time I had been outside the harem walls since I arrived and also my first proper view of Topkapi Palace from the outside. Perched on a promontory between Europe and Asia, lapped by the waters of the Golden Horn and the Bosphorus, it was truly vast and breathtaking to behold. Both magnificent and maleficent, it was at once a palace and a fortress; a city within itself, its stone walls encompassed palaces within palaces, mazes within mazes, whole miles of twisting and turning corridors and staircases, the harem, baths, servant and guest quarters, the apartments of important courtiers and members of the royal family, the grandest of all belonging to the Sultan, the Sultana Valide, the Kizlar Aga, and the heir to the throne. There were libraries, throne rooms, presence chambers, reception halls, the Council Chamber, special dormitories just for the palace's dwarves, mutes, and fools and separate ones for the white and black eunuchs. There were great halls for entertainments, barracks for the royal guard, the reviled and dreaded Janissaries, mosques, prayer rooms, hospitals, apothecaries, the quarters of the harem midwife and court abortionist, several schools, uncountable kitchens, laundries, and storerooms, stables, guardhouses, granaries, menageries, aviaries, including a special one just for housing nightingales, pleasure gardens, hothouses, orchards, courtyards, pools, kiosks, pavilions, prisons, torture chambers, and treasure vaults. There was even a great ice pit where ice, carried down by mules from Mount Olympus, was stored wrapped in flannel for the making of sherbets and other cold delicacies, and the Hall of the Sacred Mantle where the relics of the Prophet, Mohammed, were housed and where sultans went to pray and be crowned. The palace was large enough to harbor thirty-five thousand souls; it reminded me of the world's largest anthill. And within its walls and underneath its floors was a whole warren of secret passageways and chambers. One could spend their whole life in Topkapi Palace and never see all of it.

Great black iron cauldrons were brought out to boil ears of corn and whole lambs were roasted on spits, gilded pitchers inlaid with precious gems filled with every flavor of sherbet imaginable were passed around, and there were music, singers and dancers, jugglers, acrobats, magicians, fortune-tellers, and puppet shows to entertain us.

Abdul Hamid presented me with a gilded barge of my very own, another honor unknown in the harem, with a dozen oarsmen to row it. There was a gilded canopy for me to sit beneath, with curtains of fine pale pink gauze and a second set of gold-embroidered rose velvet that might be drawn to veil me from the world, or to protect me if I felt a sudden chill, and piles of pink and gold brocade cushions for me to rest upon, and trailing in the water behind, attached to the stern by golden chains, was a school of bejeweled golden fish called *hirame*. Any afternoon I wished it when the weather was fine, as long as I was veiled and properly attended by black eunuchs chosen by Lâle, I might go out and enjoy a pleasure cruise upon the Bosphorus. I was even given my own musicians to accompany and play for me while I enjoyed the fresh air and freedom of the sea.

I wore a new gown made of the Sultan's silk encrusted with gold and silver threads embellished with tiny twinkling diamonds and pearls, with trousers of pale golden champagne satin and golden curly-toed slippers underneath the full, open skirt. The Sultan's yellow diamond, shining like the sun, radiating white diamond rays, filled my décolletage, the necklace to guard me against the evil eye was about my throat, and a wealth of diamonds and pearls were scattered in my golden hair, cleverly suspended from slim golden chains attached to my little round flat-topped hat. Though my veil, fringed with gold and pearls, hid all of my face but my eyes, I was smiling all the time. I sat on a cushion at Abdul Hamid's feet and ate *five* ears of corn and gorged myself on roast lamb, *börek,* plump little pastries stuffed with meat and cheese, and the flaky layered, honey-drenched, nut-laden pastry called baklava. I was famished after my long, slumbering fast.

I smiled up at Abdul Hamid when he reached for my hand and slipped onto my finger an enormous cabochon sapphire with a star captured inside.

Despite all the dangers that surrounded me, I had never felt so safe, cherished, and loved before. When this man looked at me and held my hand I never wanted him to let go.

CHAPTER 35

I was taken by surprise one day when the heir to the throne, Prince Selim, shyly approached me, stammering his request as he fumbled with his spectacles. He would put them on for a moment, just long enough to get a clear look at me, then take them off again, and conceal them in the full embroidered sleeves of his caftan only to take them back out and put them right back on again.

Speaking in such strangely accented French I barely recognized my own language, he asked me if I would read some of his French books aloud to him. He knew his accent was atrocious, and he was anxious to improve it. He had learned the language from his Italian tutor, Lorenzo, and that, along with Selim's native Turkish, accounted for his uniquely awful accent.

Selim confided that he greatly admired the French and he had even written a letter of friendship to King Louis XVI, though he had been disappointed in the short, stilted, formal reply he had received several months later.

I told Selim I would be happy to help him with his French; my Turkish might profit by the experience as well, and it would be a pleasure to read some French books again. I urged him not to be downhearted about King Louis's stiff phrasing. The King of France

was a very shy man, I explained, a man more at ease in his own
company, with his beloved books, and the clocks and locks he liked
to make, than with other people, especially strangers. Everyone
said he was like a fish out of water amidst all the court pageantry
and he was often, unjustly I thought, judged cold and aloof.

Selim had amassed a marvelous library of over three hundred
French books; there were works of history, fairy tales, philosophy,
novels, plays, poetry, science, medicine, military tactics, and even a
full set of the encyclopedia. Each one was beautifully bound. It was
customary in Turkey that each prince of the blood must learn an
honest trade, and bookbinding was not only Selim's chosen profes-
sion but also his passion. "Beautiful books deserve beautiful bindings," he said, and often set those texts he considered jewels of
wisdom, verse and prose, into bindings rich with gold, silver, pearls,
and precious gems.

I began to read with him for an hour or two each afternoon. At
first I read to him; then we began to take turns, passing the book
back and forth between us, so that I might correct his pronuncia-
tion. Often we would linger sipping coffee and discussing what we
had just read. He delighted in asking me many questions about
France, the customs, people, and government, and I in turn learned
much from him about Turkey.

Through Selim I learned that France was in a terrible state of
upheaval, a full-blown revolution was sweeping the land, much
blood had been shed, most of it aristocratic, and the King and
Queen were now prisoners of their own people. Things had gone
rapidly from bad to worse since I had left. I wondered about Rose
and prayed that she and her children were safe. Perhaps she had finally had her fill of Paris and gone home to Martinique?

I enjoyed talking with Selim; he was a gentle, soft-spoken, beautiful dreamer. Beneath his jeweled turban, his head was filled with
noble ideals and dreams of dragging his country out of the mire of
ancient traditions that he believed only held Turkey back and made
people think it a primitive and barbaric land. He wanted to modernize the law, education, and the whole system of government, using
France as his inspiration. He wanted a printing press, a newspaper,
French books translated into Turkish, and to encourage friendly

diplomatic relations between his country and mine. Most of all, he despised the Janissaries, the enemies of progress, and the terror and peril of sultans, and dreamed of replacing them with a new, modern army. He hoped, one day, when he was sultan, to ask the French to help him accomplish this by sending officers to advise him and help equip and train his new army. Everything—infantry, artillery, cavalry, navy—was to be modern and new, modeled precisely on French lines. And he wanted new ships, not heavy, antiquated relics, and to build a cannon foundry and new walls and forts.

Selim's eyes shone like stars when he spoke of it, and I could not help but be drawn in. He made me want to share his dream, to see it all come true someday. But there was a certain vulnerability about Selim that also made me fear for him. There was a disturbing delicacy about his face, a weakness of the chin, a feminine cast about his eyes, that made me fear he would crumple in the face of cruel reality. He was so happy ensconced in his little private world of books and dreams, musing about philosophy, or sitting on the rim of a white marble fountain, playing his lute, or reciting poetry, in his brocade robes and turban amongst the tulips in the garden where his pet white peacocks roamed, that I could not even imagine him occupying a throne of absolute power, commanding all that he surveyed. He was a lovely, gentle man who would have made a far better, and I think far happier, scholar than a sultan; there was no ruthlessness or meanness in him at all. To be a great ruler and change the world a man must have not only the will but also confidence in himself and his convictions. Yet whenever I saw Selim sitting on the dais beside Abdul Hamid for some court entertainment or ceremony he seemed woefully out of place, wretchedly uncomfortable in his stiff-backed and bejeweled throne. He was like a bat caught in the sudden blinding brightness of full day wanting to fly back to the safe dark haven of its sheltering cave.

I felt a special tenderness in my heart for Selim, something akin I think to what I would have felt if I had had a brother or a male cousin near my age whose friendship I cherished, but not *carnal* love, *never* passion. Selim was simply not a man to stir a woman in that manner; he might arouse a woman's maternal feelings, the urge to nurture and protect, but not her baser natural instincts. My heart belonged to Abdul Hamid and I dreaded the day when Death would close his eyes and take him away from me. I didn't even want to think about that day.

The time I spent with his sweet nephew began to fuel jealous feelings and fancies in Abdul Hamid's heart and head. One night when I went to him, he told me a story, an old Turkish fable, that also concealed a veiled warning.

"Once upon a time, a nightingale loved a rose," he began as he drew me down to sit upon his knee, "and the rose, aroused by its song, awoke trembling upon her stem. It was a white rose"—he caressed the pale skin of my bare arms beneath the slit gold-latticed coral satin of my trailing, floor-length sleeves—"like all the roses in the world at that time—pure, white, innocent, and virginal. As the rose listened to the nightingale's song, something in her heart was stirred. Then the nightingale came ever so near and whispered into the quivering heart of the white rose: 'I love you.' At those words, the little heart of the rose blushed, and in that moment, pink roses were born. The nightingale, encouraged, came closer and closer, and though Allah, when He created the world, intended that the rose alone should never know earthly, carnal love, the rose opened her now pink petals wide"—Abdul Hamid's hand drifted down, between my legs, and caressed me through my coral satin trousers, causing me to grow moist and tremble with desire—"and the nightingale stole her virginity. In the morning, the rose, in her shame, turned red; thus the red rose was born. And although, ever since, the nightingale has come every night since to ask for her divine love, the rose has refused him. For Allah never meant roses and birds to mate. And though the rose trembled at the voice of the nightingale, her petals remained forevermore closed to him."

We sat in silence for a moment, and then he asked me what I thought.

"I think that I am neither a rose, nor is Selim a nightingale, nor have you, Allah's Shadow on Earth, any cause for the least concern that his voice might make me tremble and open my pink petals," I said frankly.

I stood and gave Abdul Hamid my hand.

"I also think that that which you do not attempt to chain you keep more freely *and* firmly bound."

"Ah, Nakshidil!" he sighed as he enfolded me in his arms, his fingers weaving through the golden waves of my hair. "Why could I not have been a young man like Selim when you came into my life? It is the curse of old age to always believe that youth wants youth."

"But age has given you wisdom and taught you patience and kindness," I answered, "and I would not trade that, I would not trade you, for anything, or anyone. Just think—if I had come to you in your youth, hasty lust might have blinded you and prevented you from seeing me, and loving me, as you do now. Once you were sated you might have been done with me, my novelty would have quickly paled and you would have been on to your next conquest, and I would have spent the rest of my life languishing like a fat, pampered cat on a velvet cushion instead of coming to you like this." I looked deep into his dark eyes and caressed his bearded cheek. "I would not sacrifice a single year of your life, or even a single wrinkle or the gray hair you hide under that terrible black dye, for a young man's body, whether it was your soul within it or another's. It is you, as you are, that I love," I said, with my heart and the whole truth in every word, and then I kissed him.

In the morning I awoke so ill I thought I had been poisoned again. I struggled and stumbled across the room, bile burning my throat and tears blurring my eyes. I could not contain the sickness and grasped the nearest vase and vomited into it. Before I was finished, I fell, the great green and gold vase, almost as high as my breasts, falling with me and shattering beneath my weight.

Abdul Hamid woke at the sound and found me groaning and gasping, naked and miserable upon the floor, shivering, pale, and weak in a pool of broken porcelain and vomit. He tenderly stroked back my hair, heedless of the mess that soiled it, and gathered me up in his arms and carried me back to the bed. He sent for his physician and brought a gold basin filled with water and tenderly cleaned me as best he could while we waited.

The Greek physician came and examined me and, after asking a few significant questions, solemnly delivered great instead of grave news. I was pregnant.

I had the most arduous and unpleasant pregnancy I think any woman ever endured. The sickness never left me. I lost flesh even as my belly swelled. My hair lost its luster and my skin took on a sickly yellowy ashen hue and there was a constant, panging ache in my pelvis and lower back. The mere mention of food made me ill. The smell or sight of it made me retch. I lay abed all day, so listless and weary no matter how many hours I slept that I could barely bear to lift my head up. It took every ounce of will I possessed to rise, bathe and dress, and go to Abdul Hamid, carried in the gilded litter he now sent every night to carry me along the Golden Path, and to smile for him and assure him that I was well.

Even when it was deemed no longer safe to take pleasure from me, he still sent for me every night. He liked to talk over the business of the day with me and hold me in his arms, my back resting against his chest and his hands enfolding my belly, to feel the child move within. He gave me an even larger apartment with sumptuous hangings of *has ulhas* silk twinkling with diamonds and pearls, and the ebony wood bed and the cradle beside it, to await our child's arrival, were both encrusted with bloodred rubies.

My rivals reveled in my sickness and the loss of my looks and spent even more time than ever over their own beauty rituals and practicing the arts of love, confident that the day would surely come, and soon, when Abdul Hamid would tire of me and desire another livelier and healthier woman.

At any given hour the baths were crowded with women, all desperate to be more beautiful than ever before. The dressmakers and embroiderers feared for their sight, they were at their labors day and night, and the bath attendants' arms ached to the point where they would almost have welcomed amputation they were in such demand for massages, but the harem of Sultan Abdul Hamid had never looked more alluring. The women's hair shone like black satin and their dark eyes sparkled like starry nights. They plied their pumice stones more diligently than ever before, lined their eyes with black kohl or even ink, reddened their lips and cheeks with cochineal, whitened their skin with a paste of jasmine and almonds, used masks of egg whites to tighten their skin, and experimented with a hundred and one perfumes, and rubbed their skin with a cream made of pulverized pearls to lend it luster. They washed their long hair with egg yolks or even butter to make it shine and some even resorted to henna and indigo to lend its darkness enticing, come hither red and blue flashes. They painted intricate lace-like designs and whole gardens of flowers on their skin with henna; some even dared draw delicate but erotic pictures on their denuded pubic mounds and even perfumed their interiors by crouching over bowls filled with fragrant embers of frankincense, sandalwood, and myrrh, using their robes like a tent to prevent the sweet fumes from escaping. The singers had never sung better, the dancers had never possessed such sinuous sensuality, and those who recited poetry had never put such passion into the words before; even the shadow puppet shows exuded eroticism. Every woman was wishing, *willing* Abdul Hamid's handkerchief to drop for her, but it never did. From the night I met Abdul Hamid no other woman's foot ever trod the Golden Path.

The women gossiped, and some even gloated, about how grim and solemn the harem midwife and the Sultan's physician looked whenever they left my room after examining me. Some even came in feigned solicitousness just for the pleasure of standing over me, to see with their own eyes just how low and wretchedly ill I was. Bets were being placed all over the palace about not whether but *when* I would die, would I succumb before the child was born or after, and if it would die too, or, if by Allah's grace I survived, I would retain the Sultan's favor.

As the hour of birthing grew nearer, a great gilded kiosk with one immense open-air chamber was prepared for me in the palace gardens amidst a sea of red and yellow tulips. It was scrupulously scrubbed from floor to ceiling and the walls were painted red. The bed was laid with red silk sheets and a quilt of the same material, and a diaphanous red curtain was hung across the center of the room like an immense veil. A birthing chair, like a throne of gold ornamented with rubies, and pitchers, and basins, and even birthing utensils made of gold were brought in and laid out in readiness. Even the linen towels the midwife would use were embroidered with golden threads.

In the harem the birth of a sultan's child was viewed as a celebration. Instead of giving the expectant mother privacy, alone with the midwife and a trusted few she wished to have near in her travail, the doors were thrown open wide in welcome and any woman or eunuch who wished to might enter. Everyone came in their finest array bearing gifts, including the wives of important men eager to gain or retain the Sultan's favor.

Endlessly replenished refreshments were served on gilded plates with drinks poured from golden pitchers into golden cups. The smell of strong coffee was constantly in the air. One hundred strong and sturdy mules had been sent on the seventy-mile trek to the great ice pits on Mount Olympus to bring pure, fresh snow to make sherbets especially for this occasion. Every manner of fruit juice available was put to use to flavor them, and there were even some special ones made of violets and roses or coffee flavored with cloves. My favorite, cinnamon, was there in abundance, but I was too sick to even think of taking a sip.

Musicians, dancers, singers, the palace dwarves, jugglers, acrobats, magicians, and puppeteers all came to perform for the lady laboring in agony upon her glittering gold birthing chair with only a sheer red curtain not quite modestly veiled between them and her open legs. The midwife had only to move away for them to see everything.

Everyone believed I was going to die and they had all come to see it. The triumphant reign of the golden-haired *kadin* was about to end. Her pearl-white skin would be even whiter when all the blood had drained out of her, they whispered.

There was so much red in the room it seemed awash in blood. I was unbearably hot; the maids assigned to fan me only annoyed rather than cooled me with their cruel eyes and malicious chatter. One of them kept "accidentally" resting her hand on the back of the birthing chair, just where my hair fell, and pulling it. If I hadn't been in so much pain I would have gotten up and slapped her; I was just mad enough to do it. Even Naime's tears falling on my face as she stood over me, wiping away my sweat with a perfumed hand-kerchief, failed to cool me. My eyes kept fading out of focus, I was light-headed and nauseous, and twice I vomited.

The noise was simply *unbearable!* Why couldn't I have peace and quiet? I caught hold of Lâle's hand and begged him to make them all leave. He looked down at me with sad eyes and said he was sorry, but that was not permitted, this was a centuries-old tradition. I didn't want all these people dancing, juggling, singing, telling jokes, and performing puppet shows, acrobatics, and magic tricks all at the same time through a hazy red curtain, all trying to distract me from my pain, ingratiating wives kneeling beside my chair to show me the gifts they had brought me and my unborn child, servants of-fering me sherbet, candied fruits, Turkish delight, feta cheese, and cool melon slices to help keep up my strength, dwarves making funny faces capering in circles around my chair making me feel even dizzier, and the harem women all watching me with hard, nar-rowed eyes, waiting to see the life leave me. My head began to spin and I had to close my eyes. There was a high-pitched ringing in my ears drowning out the noise on the other side of the curtain. The pain was like a red fist pummeling my stomach and then reaching up, between my legs, deep inside of me to savagely grab and twist. My nails raked furrows in the gilt arms of my chair and blood streamed from my lips when I bit them to keep the screams from flying out.

Untold hours passed; sometimes I was encouraged to rise and walk about, or to lie upon the bed and rest, but nothing eased the pain and I always ended up back in the chair again with the mid-wife kneeling between my legs. She massaged my stomach and some-times had me kneel on all fours upon the bed while she crouched behind me, attempting to shift the child within. She said it seemed to be turning cartwheels inside of me.

The Sultan's physician was summoned and the midwife stepped away, into a corner, to consult with him. The midwife gestured frantically, adamantly, and the doctor frowned and shook his head. His expression was very grave and she seemed close to tears. And then my enemy Senieperver, head to toe in black encrusted with rubies, with ropes of those big bold red sparkling stones entwined in her turban and hair, layering her throat and wrists, and bloodred brilliants spotting her veils, swept in like a queen and went to speak with them.

Lâle, alert at my side, started toward them, but at his approach their intense little cluster broke apart, and Senieperver sailed grandly past him as though she didn't even see him. Yes, she even dared snub the Kizlar Aga. She came to stand before me, towering over me, and this time I saw pure evil in her soulless black eyes.

"They are going to try to save your child by cutting it out of you with a knife," she said coolly, "but you will not live to see it. The harem is full of beautiful women; one more or less will not matter to Abdul Hamid. Do not bother to beg for it; your life is worth *nothing*."

Silence, I suddenly noticed, had fallen all around us. There was a rustle of heavy silk behind Senieperver and all fell to their knees as Abdul Hamid approached and laid a jewel-heavy hand upon her shoulder.

"You do not speak for me, Senieperver," he said, his soft tone more ominous than any words shouted in anger. He thrust her aside, ignoring her when she threw herself down upon her knees and began kissing the hem of his robe.

"You!" He pointed to the doctor and the midwife. "Attend her!" He indicated me as I groaned and writhed and grasped the arms of my chair, determined to hold on to my life and the one laboring to be born inside me. "Look at me and listen well," the Sultan said as they knelt before me, peering between my legs and shaking their heads and frowning helplessly. "If there is a choice to be made you will save her. You will do everything possible to save the Lady Nakshidil, and if that fails, then you will do the *impossible* and save her, or else her labor will be as *nothing,* smooth as silk, compared to the pain that *you* shall suffer before you die."

He then turned to regard the harem women, performers, palace servants, and dignitaries' wives all staring at us in amazement. Such a scene had never transpired in the history of the harem. The Sultan had never entered a birthing chamber before. What Senieperver said was generally held true—a woman's life counted for nothing, her sole purpose was to please the Sultan, and if she died in childbirth she died gladly sacrificing herself for the gift she was giving him.

Abdul Hamid's stare seemed to take them all in one by one. But this time the women trembled with terror at having the Sultan's eyes linger upon their faces.

"She is worth more to me than all of you," he said.

Senieperver was still groveling and kissing the hem of his robe and he kicked her away like a man annoyed by a dog trying to mate with his leg.

He came to me and knelt at my side, unclasped my quaking hand from the arm of the chair, kissed it, then held it tight, entwining his fingers with mine.

"Come, Nakshidil," he said gently, "hold on to me, and we shall do this together. . . ."

And that is what we did. I don't know how, but God, or Allah, gave us another miracle. With a last wrenching, tearing pain my son slipped from my body in a gush of blood, still and blue as my eyes.

"He is dead," the midwife said, laying his body in the golden basin on the floor between my open legs. She said it as though it were nothing at all, in the same voice as she might have said, *It is going to rain*.

"*Give him to me!*" I cried, and when she hesitated I slapped her. I had never struck anyone in my life before, but, weak as I was, I slapped her so hard I left the print of my hand on her face and my rings cut into her cheek, bringing bright rivulets of ruby-red blood. I snatched up my son and gave him my own breath. I massaged his little heart through his tiny blue chest and begged him *please* to "*Live! Live!*" In desperation, I pounded his small back. "*Breathe!*" I begged. And he did. God, or Allah, *someone,* answered my prayers. My son coughed and spluttered and the blue began to fade from his skin, replaced by a healthy pink. And then he cried, hearty and loud, protesting the indignity of being struck on his first day of life.

"We have a son," I said as I cradled his little body against my breast.

"Allah be praised!" Abdul Hamid said as he enveloped both of us in his arms. "We have a son! A son with hair of gold just like yours, Nakshidil! This is a good omen." He touched a tiny gilt curl, glimmering through the blood of my body. "His name shall be Altin—Golden! And when he is sultan, with you as his mother to guide him, he shall usher in a golden age; in Turkey everything shall be golden! If only I could live to see it!"

I had never seen Abdul Hamid so happy before.

"You will!" I promised him with tears streaming from my eyes. "Come what may, you shall live forever in my heart, and in our son's—I shall see to it!" I swore.

"Nakshidil"—he leaned his brow against mine—"for me, everything already is golden; it has been since the day you came into my life."

CHAPTER 36

In Martinique we have a saying: When you have bad luck, a grain of rice will break your head, a butter leaf will cut your foot open, a snake will bite you with the tip of his tail.

We were too happy. Some might say the loas, the djinns and *ifrits,* whatever name one wishes to give evil spirits, saw us and envied our happiness, so they had to take it from us.

I was in my room one day, lying on my bed cooing over little Altin, when one of the black eunuchs rushed in. I must come at once, he said; Abdul Hamid had been taken ill and was asking for me with what might be his dying breath. I didn't think; I leapt up, leaving Altin in the care of his nurse, Esimee, and raced from the room with Kuvvetti dashing after me, our feet flying over the Golden Path.

I found the Sultan sitting on his divan with his jeweled hookah, perfectly well and surprised to see me. The eunuch who had summoned me had seemingly melted into the walls. I thought he was right behind us, but I hadn't given him another thought after he had delivered his message.

My heart stood still and then started racing right along with my feet as Kuvetti and I ran back to my room. But we were too late. Esimee lay atop the splintered remains of my son's ruby-encrusted ebony cradle, the precious stones scattered upon the carpet like drops of blood mingling with her own. When I turned her over blood burbled from the deep gash in her throat as she struggled to speak. "I tried . . ." Her eyes drifted toward the window as her life took flight.

"Do not look!" Kuvetti cried. She swept me up in her arms and carried me, fighting futilely, from the room. Over her shoulder I saw my son silhouetted against the setting sun glowing like orange embers through the gold-latticed windows. He was dangling from a silken noose tied to the curtain rod.

The eunuch who had lured me away was found with his throat cut, floating facedown in the Bosphorus. Not a soul in the harem claimed to know or to have seen anything. No one had seen me rush out of my room nor anyone enter in my absence. No one had heard Esimee's dying screams or the wood of the cradle smashing. If Altin had cried before he died no one heard that either.

Abdul Hamid swore vengeance, he promised me he would discover who had done this terrible thing and kill them in the most merciless manner possible, but I didn't care; more deaths would not bring Altin back to life. And I *knew* who had done this; even if no evidence pointed to Senieperver the truth did.

But Senieperver was also the mother of Abdul Hamid's son, the former favorite I had supplanted, and he could not bring himself to condemn her without proof. Anger and instinct were not enough. Of course, she swore both ignorance and innocence. She deluged me with condolences and sympathy so sickeningly sweet that just the sight of her, or the sound of her voice, made my stomach churn.

I sank into a deep depression. All I did was sleep and weep. I pushed all food away. I neglected my person and Abdul Hamid. I no longer went to him and didn't care if any of the other women did. I didn't care about anything anymore. No one could even offer me the consolation that I might someday have another child; birthing Altin had wrecked my womb.

One night I awakened to see Abdul Hamid standing over my bed.

"I have something for you," he said.

He stepped aside and an ebony-skinned woman approached carrying a small boy in her arms. His skin was the golden rich color of caramel and his eyes dark and almond shaped beneath a fringe of straight black hair. He clung to his nurse and stared down at me with a grave dignity combining wariness and curiosity. He seemed so solemn and still for such a little boy.

"This is my son Mahmoud," Abdul Hamid said. "He is two years old. His mother died giving life to him. I give him to you now."

The Sultan motioned to the nurse, she bent, and, of their own accord, my arms rose up to accept Mahmoud. The moment his arms closed around my neck and our eyes met I *knew* this was meant to be. I felt the grief drain from me and life, and love, come surging back up to fill me again. In that instant I found, I *knew,* beyond a shadow of a doubt, my purpose in life.

"Take him and make him the sultan our son would have been, the sultan that I should have been," Abdul Hamid said.

He laid a gentle hand on his son's dark head in blessing. "May he be gentle with his women, ferocious and victorious on the field of battle, humble in the mosque, and superb on the throne."

"He will," I said with absolute conviction.

I think I truly discovered what love means when Abdul Hamid gave Mahmoud to me. It was the only way he could give me a part of himself to be with me after he was gone, and another child, to cherish and call my own, since my damaged womb could never bring forth another, and to give Turkey the golden future he had promised on the day our own son was born.

There is so much weight already on these little shoulders, I used to think whenever I looked at my adopted son, *but I will help you bear the burden.*

We astonished the court, long accustomed to regarding women as possessions and ornaments, by becoming a happy, contented little family. Not only did I defy the odds and survive childbirth and keep the Sultan's favor, but Mahmoud salved my grief and saved me; as his mother I found purpose and meaning. I flourished and regained my health and beauty, and Abdul Hamid loved me more than ever before. At every court ceremony and entertainment, I was there at Abdul Hamid's side, often seated on a cushion at his feet with my head resting against his knee, and Mahmoud was always right there with me. I would not make the same mistake again and leave him alone and vulnerable the way I had Altin. Now whenever Senieperver's gaze lighted upon me and Mahmoud my eyes flashed back a warning, telling her that I would fight like a tigress for this little one. Lâle had told me once that there were no second chances in the harem, but I had been given one, and I would *never* take that precious gift for granted.

Even as he was learning his native tongue, I began to teach Mahmoud French and we studied the Koran and the Bible together and compared and contrasted their tales and teachings. As he grew, every day without fail I told him stories—fables and fairy tales, of heroes like Alexander the Great, the Emperor Charlemagne, and more ambiguous ones like Robin Hood, the thief who stole from the rich to give to the poor, the titillating but altruistic tale of Lady Godiva's naked ride, and of every other heroine, saint, king, queen, hero, and villain I could remember, meet, or rediscover in Selim's books. I told Mahmoud of my own life, the magical isle of Martinique with its voodoo queen, my family, Mama and Papa, little Marthe and wild cousin Rose, my voyage across the sea to France, the tedious years I had spent in the convent matching my will against Mother Angélique's, and everything I knew of history, law, humanity, and religion, the good and the bad and the in-between, acts of courage and cowardice, justice and injustice, even the terror and turmoil of revolution sweeping through France, destroying all its beauty and grace. I told my son anything and everything I could think of that might prove useful and valuable in molding Mahmoud into a man of wisdom, refinement, and enlightenment, a man who would embrace progress, not shy away from it, a sultan who would preserve the best of his country's customs and cast away the worst, and use his power for the greater good. I even told him the proverbs, the memorable, dearly familiar sayings unique to Martinique.

The serpent doesn't hate the man who kills him; he hates the man who said: "Beware! A serpent!"

The monkey never finds her child ugly. (I applied this one to Senieperver and Mustafa.)

Women love scandal more than bees love honey.

Words in the mouth are not heavy; talk is light.

You must sleep on the riverbank to understand the language of the fish.

If you would eat the ox's head you must not fear the eyes.

A dog has four legs, but he cannot take four roads.

A good foot saves a cowardly body.

Every firefly gives light for his own self first.

The monkey knows which tree to climb; he will not attempt to climb a thorn tree.

The thief does not like to see his partner carry the sack.

Teeth are not the heart. A smile does not always mean a good heart.

My son would *not* be the lazy, pampered, selfish creature Senieperver had whelped if I could help it, and I would move heaven and earth if I had to, to keep my promise to Abdul Hamid. I borrowed books from Selim and read whenever I could to further my own knowledge and when Mahmoud was given a tutor I sat veiled behind a latticed screen and learned along with him.

Abdul Hamid gave me a walled garden all my own where roses, jasmine, honeysuckle, and the bloodred amarantus flowers called "love lies bleeding" grew around a gilded kiosk. There was a pond filled with gold and silver fish and water lilies beside a gray granite bench and black cypress tree at the heart of it, and here I would sit every day and talk with Mahmoud. Sometimes Selim joined us in our conversations, though I was always careful not to appear overly familiar with him lest Abdul Hamid's heart and head be troubled by jealous stirrings again.

In the winter of my twenty-second year, Abdul Hamid developed a bad cough. He simmered with a persistent fever yet shook always with a chill. No fire or furs, not even my love, could keep him warm enough. The doctors dosed him and leeched him and purged him, but really they could do nothing, my beloved's fate was in the hands of God, or Allah.

I hardly ever left his side. Abdul Hamid wanted it that way. Even when he tended to matters of state, conferring with the Kizlar Aga and the Grand Vizier, foreign ambassadors, and the Chorbaji-Bashi, the chief of the Janissaries, I was always there, silent and shrouded in my veils, watching secretly from a latticed gallery above the Council Chamber. It comforted him to know I was there. When he was too weary, I made the decisions. When he grew forgetful, I was his memory. He said my common sense was good for Turkey and I was the best tonic of all for its ailing sultan.

He waved aside my worries and promised me that he would be well by spring. "The most wonderful thing in the world will happen to me then . . . with your consent." He smiled and kissed my hand.

In April, at the annual tulip fête, he confided, it was his dearest wish to emulate an earlier sultan, Süleyman the Magnificent, who had astonished the world, and rocked Turkey to its foundations, when he disbanded his harem and took his favorite *kadin*, Roxalena, the Russian slave girl with the blazing red hair and matching fiery spirit, as his official wife and consort, bestowing upon her the rank of Empress that was usually accorded to the sultan's mother. It was the greatest tribute and testament to his love that Süleyman could bestow upon his beloved and Abdul Hamid wanted to do the same for me.

"My happiness is complete," I said as I lay within the circle of his arms.

But it was not to be. When the dawn came softly stealing through the latticed windowpanes Death stole his life away. I awakened in his arms and knew at once something was wrong. Abdul Hamid was cold and blue beneath the ermine quilt. His arms were stiff and cold about me, like a rigid cage made of skin and bones, and a length of my hair was twined around one of his hands like a golden bandage. When Lâle came, as he always did, to escort me back to the harem, I required his help to free myself from my lover's last embrace.

Before I left the Sultan's bed, for what I knew would be the last time, I used Abdul Hamid's jeweled dagger to cut off my hair where it was wound around his hand. He was holding it so tight, I liked to think it was a last message to me, telling me that he would never let go. I kept the dagger, as a remembrance, and let him take my golden locks to the grave with him.

"There will never be a day when I do not think of you," I said, and kissed his brow and closed his sightless eyes.

I felt my heart break and scatter like bits of red stone to make a mosaic that might be pieced and glued together in the semblance of a heart's shape but would never be whole again. But this time I couldn't surrender to the darkness and sink deep into the black mire of depression as I had when I lost Altin; I had to hold on and stay strong for Mahmoud. Senieperver would be watching me closer than ever before, her sharp eyes seeking out the chink in my armor.

Now that Selim was sultan, Mustafa was one step closer to the throne, the heir apparent, and his half brother, Mahmoud, was next in line, all three of them cousins and brothers cast as pawns in this most dangerous game of dynastic chess, so deadly the Devil himself might have devised it.

Selim was seen as weak, an idealistic dreamer who lacked the will to make his dreams real. But those dreams were nonetheless dangerous to all enemies of progress. Mustafa was a lazy, self-centered sybarite willing to leave all the business of ruling the empire in the hands of his power-mad mother and the corrupt and brutal Janissaries. Not a one of them had a single care for Turkey and its people, only their own selfish interests. Then there was Mahmoud, too young yet to be seen by anyone but Senieperver as a serious threat, but as he grew from boy to man that was certain to change. If Selim failed and Mustafa seized power, Mahmoud would be the great golden hope of every downtrodden, wronged, and abused soul in Turkey, and with Mustafa on the throne there would be *thousands* of them. Senieperver would not suffer such a formidable rival to live. I would have to be the wall standing between my son and death.

Abdul Hamid had left me with a strong purpose to shore up my grief. "Take him and make him the sultan our son would have been, the sultan that I should have been," he said when he gave Mahmoud to me. I would dedicate my life, to my last breath, to my last drop of blood, to keeping that promise.

CHAPTER 37

———◦———

I stood upon the crenellated walls and watched the white-shrouded body of my lover, my friend, my would-have-been husband, Sultan Abdul Hamid I, being borne out of Topkapi Palace upon a plain wooden bier, to be entombed with his ancestors in the imperial mausoleum. There was no coffin, for the Muslims believed that the body must be returned directly to the earth with the head pointing toward Mecca. His nephew, the newly proclaimed Sultan Selim III, led the funeral procession. The only women allowed to walk behind him were the professional mourners Lâle had hired. Not one of the five hundred women who had belonged to the Sultan, known, desired, aspired to his favor, bedded, or even truly loved him were allowed to see him to his grave. The hired mourners shrieked and tore at their black hair and fell to the ground and groveled and rolled in the dirt and threw dust on their veiled heads, making sure the Kizlar Aga got his money's worth. It was quite a spectacle.

My heart was a fountain of endlessly flowing tears. I wore white, the color of mourning, spangled head to toe with diamond brilliants weeping teardrop pearls. I had been brought up to believe that it was bad luck for a bride to wear diamonds and pearls upon her wedding day or else in the years to come she would have cause to shed many tears. Though most women put luxury over superstition and wore these impressive adornments anyway, it seemed somehow most fitting that I should wear these emblems of sorrow now as I mourned the husband of my heart.

Mahmoud stood solemnly beside me and held my hand.

"You really loved him," he said.

"With all my heart," I answered, "and always will. I didn't really begin to live until I met him, and the funny thing is everyone who ever knew me thought I was dead, but I had never been more alive. And he gave me the greatest gift of all—you!" I knelt and embraced my son.

"No." Mahmoud smiled and shook his head as he wrapped his arms around my neck. "He gave *me* the greatest gift of all—*you!*"

I smiled through my tears and stroked his thin little face. "You are the reason my heart still beats."

"Don't cry, Maman." Mahmoud reached beneath my pearl-fringed veil to dry my tears with his own silk handkerchief. It was blue, the color of hope. "You will be with him again someday. The Koran says: *The fortunate fair who has given pleasure to her lord will have the privilege of appearing before him in Paradise. Like the crescent moon, she will preserve all her youth and beauty and her husband will never look older or younger than thirty-one years.*"

"Abdul Hamid will like that." I smiled and even laughed a little through my tears. "He always lamented the years that lay between us, but in Paradise he won't have to worry about that anymore. He will be both the man I love and the man that he wanted to be."

I strained my eyes for one last sight of my beloved as the doors of the royal mausoleum swung open wide and swallowed him. As the top of his white-shrouded head disappeared inside I reached out my hand as though my love could bridge the distance and caress him one last time. Then he was gone. I didn't wait to see the rest of the procession pass; none of that mattered. As tears blurred my eyes, I let Mahmoud take my hand and lead me back inside.

It was the custom that when a sultan died his harem was banished to the Old Palace, the Eski Saray, the Palace of Tears, the House of the Unwanted Ones, to live out their remaining years celibate and bitter. Situated down by the sea at Seraglio Point, it was mocked as an almshouse for old ladies, though its residents could be as young as twelve and most were in the prime of life and beauty. Its nearness to the sea was a constant reminder to those that dwelled within that their survival was truly an act of charity. Men who had dived off the point often came back with tales of hundreds of bodies, women sewn into weighted sacks, standing upright, bowing and swaying, with the current. That could very easily have been the fate of the dead sultan's harem, but the new sultan chose to be merciful and grant them a living death instead of a watery grave.

Entombed alive within the Eski Saray's grim gray walls, waited upon by sad-eyed and arthritic eunuchs too old and feeble to serve in Topkapi Palace, these discarded women spent their days weeping to the tune of melancholy music or else seeking consolation in food now that there was no sultan's eye to catch, and no one to care if they got fat, or finding solace in Sapphic affairs. Some of them could not bear to live without the sun of the sultan's favor and committed suicide. Those he had never noticed and bedded believed their lives had been for naught and lamented that they would live and die without ever knowing a man's touch. Some of them decided the eunuchs were better than nothing and did what they could with them; a man's hands and mouth after all are still capable of giving pleasure even when he lacks the vital member. The moment the sultan died time was said to stop for the women in his harem, only it didn't really, it yawned on and on for years and years and years and years. . . .

Far better, I thought, to be a sultan's sister or daughter. The sultanas were also sent away from the splendors of Topkapi Palace, but they went to begin new lives as the wives of provincial governors or other men of wealth and eminence.

As the reigning favorite, the First Kadin, I had no choice but to go with the others to the Palace of Tears. My heart broke yet again when Lâle told me that this meant I must also leave Mahmoud. It would be up to the new sultan, Mahmoud's cousin Selim, and Mahmoud's tutor to ensure my son's safety now. Entombed in the Palace of Tears there was nothing I could do to protect him; I would be powerless.

* * *

As I embraced Mahmoud one last time and climbed into my litter, to join the long, mournful procession of women and baggage heading down to Seraglio Point, my life changed again in a way I never expected.

Selim appeared, resplendent in red and white, his new authority resting lightly as a silk cloak upon his shoulders. Saddened by his uncle's death, Selim was yet euphoric in anticipation of all the wonderful things he planned, and he wanted me there to see them.

Boldly, he advanced, put his arms around my waist, and lifted me down from my litter.

"Your place is here," he said, "with Mahmoud, and with me."

CHAPTER 38

It was unprecedented; no *kadin* belonging to a dead sultan had ever been allowed to remain in Topkapi Palace after her Lord and Master died. The whole palace was in an uproar. Malicious tongues began to wag about Selim and me. Senieperver threw a magnificent tantrum. She descended from her litter and refused to budge and ordered her servants to take her things back inside. If I was staying with Mahmoud, she must be allowed to stay with her son too. Mustafa needed her, she said, as much as Mahmoud needed me. Selim, cowed by her fury, and in the spirit of fairness, allowed it; he could think of no justifiable reason to refuse. And it didn't really matter where she was. Senieperver would never stop plotting against him; it would be easier to watch her under the same roof.

Selim immediately set to work changing our world. He began with books. The full French *Encyclopédie* must be translated into Turkish so the people could reap the benefits of its knowledge. This was followed by volumes on mathematics and military tactics, scientific treatises, poetry, plays, philosophy, and novels. And there should be new schools and the system of taxation must be improved; the people's backs were breaking under the strain of the sums they must suffer to pay, and the tortures the Janissaries doled out when they couldn't pay. Turkey's fortifications must be strengthened, the navy was a travesty, the ships lumbering and antiquated, and something really must be done about the pirates; the Barbary Corsairs were a terror and menace to every soul who sailed upon the sea.

The turmoil in France had begun to subside, the Revolution was over, Louis XVI and Marie Antoinette were amongst the thousands who had died, their heads stricken off by a killing machine known as the guillotine, royalty had been abolished, and a body of government called The Directory ruled the Republic of France now. Selim sent the Directors letters, proclaiming admiration and friendship and requesting that a capable and clever officer be sent to evaluate and help retool the Turkish army; everything must be made new and modern.

While he waited for an answer, Selim began to pay awkward court to me. Though he had a brand-new harem, he had yet to make use of it.

He *despised* the ceremonial visits to the harem, but they were a tradition, a ritual, as old as his bloodline. So reluctantly Selim would go forth, with the Kizlar Aga walking ahead of him, ringing a golden bell to alert the women to his presence and announcing: "Behold our Sovereign, Emperor of the True Believers, Shadow of Allah upon Earth, The Prophet's Successor, The Master of Masters, Chosen amongst the Chosen, our Padishah, the Sultan, Selim III! Long live our sultan! Let us admire him who is the glory of the house of Osman!"

The women would be thrown into a frenzy of preparation. Though they sat around all day, devoting themselves to looking their best in case the Sultan came, there was always some last little thing to be done, another touch of cochineal, an adjustment to the hair, a pair of slippers or a vest changed for another, as no odalisque ever appeared before her Lord and Master in the same costume twice. They would assemble in two long rows and the Sultan would walk between them, like a general reviewing his troops. As he passed, every woman hoped he would pause before her and drop his handkerchief. After this inspection, he would be invited to sit upon a divan and plied with sweetmeats and sherbets, a savory snack, or coffee or tea if such was his pleasure, and the newest or most promising women, handpicked by the Sultana Valide, if there was one, or the Kizlar Aga if there was none, would be brought before him for a closer look. When he saw the one who pleased him best, if he had not already done so he was supposed to drop his handkerchief. But Selim never did. Every time he took out his handkerchief the women's hopes rose, only to crash when he only made use of it to blot his brow or blow his nose. He never even put on his spectacles during these visits, so all the odalisques, their beauties and charms, and the toil they had taken over their toilettes, passed by him in a blur. Selim could not see clearly more than three inches past the end of his nose. He would sit and nibble comfits uncomfortably and then he would stand up and leave.

The women were puzzled and miffed. There they were, three hundred beauties all brought in fresh for his pleasure; how could he not want even *one* of them? Two rumors were current: One said that Selim preferred boys; where women were concerned he was still a virgin.

Such a thing was not unknown or uncommon. The white eunuchs who served as the Sultan's body servants, dressing and bathing him and serving his meals, were always lovely young creatures with slim, pale, smooth bodies smothered in attar of roses. Christians like me, taken by pirates or as the spoils of war while they were still in early childhood, they were often gilt or red haired. It was not at all unusual for them to stir a man's lust; their beauty rivaled most women's. It was only when—if—they grew older, faded and flabby, bitter, bored, that they lost their allure and were sent to serve elsewhere in the palace while new fresh and beautiful ones were brought in to replace them, in and out of the sultan's bed. The white eunuchs' lives were likened to the brief span allotted a butterfly; they did not tolerate the operation that deprived them of their manhood as well as the black eunuchs did and many remained frail creatures and died young. A white eunuch who attained the age of twenty was considered old. Only one retained lifelong power, for however long he lived and was fit to serve, the Chief White Eunuch, the Kapi Aga. As the Kizlar Aga ruled the harem, he ruled the Selâmlik, the men's domain.

The other rumor pointed the finger of blame directly at me. Everyone had seen Selim pluck me from my litter and countermand centuries of tradition by commanding my continued presence in Topkapi Palace. Many ears had heard him say "Your place is here, with Mahmoud, and with me."

We were both young and attractive; it was hard not to believe that attraction, not altruism, was the reason he had insisted upon my staying. Whenever I went to Selim's library, to read and talk with him, everyone suspected the worst of us: that conversation was just a cloak to conceal lovemaking. Lâle, conveniently forgetting the damage done to my womb, worried endlessly that I would conceive a son by Selim. My protestations that we were not lovers fell on deaf ears. No one believed me. Maybe that was because Selim wanted us to be and it showed in his eyes every time he looked at me.

Time passed and the gossip continued, Selim still ignored his harem, and no new heirs were born to the Osman dynasty. He was busy with his reforms, and I occupied myself with my son's education and took my pleasures where I found them. It was a quiet life, and a peaceful one, I was content. Selim and I remained friends and I did my earnest best to ignore the yearning in his eyes that told me that he wanted more.

One night he sent Lâle to me with my old trunk. Out came the pink taffeta ball gown, and all its accessories. I was amazed to see it; I had thought it long gone, if I had even thought of it at all. I suppose it must have been sitting in a storeroom somewhere. Selim wanted me to put it on. Lâle clearly disapproved, but he was the Sultan's servant; he couldn't very well advise me to refuse.

It was funny how foreign the petticoats, stays, silk stockings, and high-heeled shoes, fancier versions of the clothing I used to wear every day, now seemed. I had become so accustomed to Turkish clothes I felt like I was looking at a stranger when I stood before my mirror in protruding panniers and pink taffeta flounces with my hair caught up in mounds of curls garnished with silk roses, gold tassels, and pink plumes. My figure had grown fuller in the years since I had come to Topkapi Palace and the stays bit much tighter, the laces straining to hold me inside this lavish pink confection. I wanted nothing more than to take it right back off so I could breathe freely again.

"Shall we?" Disapprovingly Lâle held out his hand to me. My white fingertips and his black ones barely touched across my jutting panniers as he accompanied me, for the first time since Abdul Hamid had died, down the Golden Path we used to walk together almost every night and again the morning after.

Kuvetti, as always, followed silently several steps behind me.

Selim's eyes lit up at the sight of me. His hands reached out to touch me, then hesitated and fell down at his sides.

"This is the first time I have seen your face unveiled since the night you first wore this." His fingers shyly caressed a pink taffeta flounce.

"I have changed much since then," I said.

"You are even more beautiful now!" he breathed, and then he lowered his eyes and blushed.

He said that he had a gift for me. He led me back out into the corridor and down another where I had never been before.

"This is for you, all for you," he said as he stopped before a certain door and handed a gilded key to me.

Opening that door and crossing that threshold was like entering another world—a vanished world that no longer existed for me as anything but a memory and, sometimes, a dream. With walls papered in apple green and white stripes painted with delicate pink rosebuds, a carpet abloom with pink roses, sofas and armchairs and footstools upholstered in pink-and-white-striped silk, their gilded woodwork carved with elaborate bouquets of roses held by cherubs, rosewood cabinets and tables, gilt-framed mirrors crowned with cupids, a great golden harp in one corner, and a white harpsichord painted with pink roses and golden flourishes in another, this might have been Marie Antoinette's very own sitting room. Vases of Sèvres porcelain, painted and filled with pink roses, sat on the rose marble mantel, flanked by porcelain shepherdesses. There was even a porcelain clock painted with delicate pink rosebuds. A sideboard was filled with silver and crystal; I hadn't eaten with a spoon or a fork or clasped the delicate stem of a wineglass between my fingers since I sailed away from Paris. Paintings by Fragonard adorned the walls. A lady in peach, swung high in a swing, exuberantly kicked off one shoe, exposing her plump thighs above her white stocking tops, and lovers met in leafy bowers, secluded vestibules, or the privacy of bedrooms with rumpled white sheets thrown wide and inviting, like the sheets of the pink four-poster bed I glimpsed through another door.

I stood dazed in the center of it all with Selim at my side, smiling expectantly at me, tentatively holding, and shyly caressing, my hand. Tears pooled in my eyes. He had done all this for me, and I didn't want to seem ungrateful, and he was clearly expecting joy and gratitude. . . . Though I would always love and cherish the memory of France, this wasn't me anymore; it wasn't who I wanted to be. Aimee Dubucq de Rivery was dead and Nakshidil stood in her stead, inhabiting her skin, doing things that long-lost convent schoolgirl would have blushed at, and maybe even fainted, if she had ever even dared to imagine them.

At last Selim broke the silence. "I can't let you go back to France, but I can bring France to you, Aimee," he said.

"Don't call me that!" I cried.

"Why not?" He frowned. "It is your name."

I shook my head. "Not anymore."

He didn't, he couldn't, understand. I wanted to help bring Turkey out of the darkness into the light, to bring the best of France to my adopted land, but I didn't want to go backward, only forward. My future was here, with Mahmoud, in Turkey, and I wouldn't have it any other way.

"Thank you . . . for all this, for going to such trouble for me," was all I could really say. I hoped it was enough.

His hand was at my waist, tentative and shy. His lips timidly moved in quest of mine.

"Selim . . . no . . . ." I pulled away.

"But Aimee, I love you!" he cried. Now the tears were in his eyes.

"Nakshidil," I corrected firmly. "I no longer answer to any other name; Aimee died a long time ago, and where she ended, Nakshidil began."

"As you will." Selim reached for me again.

"No!" I stepped back from him. "Your harem is full of beautiful women—"

"But they are not *you!* I don't want any of them! *Only you!*" Selim clasped my waist, this time making a manly show of strength, determined to draw me close against his chest, and for his mouth to smother mine with kisses.

I turned my face away, denying him my mouth, as I struggled free.

"You mustn't say such things again to me; if you do, I will have no choice but to go to the Old Palace and join the others who belonged to Abdul Hamid."

As I spun around, hurrying toward the door, one of my panniers knocked over a vase, scattering pink roses and porcelain all over the carpet. As I ran out the door I stumbled and almost fell over Kuvetti.

"Come!" I cried as I righted myself, brushed the tears from my eyes, and started off at a clumsy trot. The dress was so heavy, and I was afraid I would end by turning my ankle; my heels felt like they were walking on stilts, making an embarrassingly loud tap-tapping as my pink shoes carried me swiftly back down the Golden Path, all the way back to the harem.

I asked Lâle to help me. Together, we got me out of that clumsy, confining dress and took all the feathers and roses out of my hair. I snatched up the pair of silk trousers nearest to hand and stepped into them, pulled a caftan over my head, and fastened on a veil.

Hugging huge, bulging pink armfuls, Lâle and I went out into the courtyard and lit a bonfire of French vanity.

I felt a sense of relief, contentment and peace, as I watched it all burn. Through the rising smoke, I happened to glance up, and I saw Selim watching from a window. His hands were pressed flat against the gold-latticed glass. There was such a look of pain upon his face that I had to turn away. Maybe I only imagined or felt them, but I was certain I saw tears pouring from his eyes, dripping down from beneath the gold frames of his spectacles.

When there was nothing left but odds and ends of whalebone and steel sitting in piles of ashes, I went to the baths. It was late and there were none about but a few bath attendants. I sat naked on a blue marble slab and took the opium pastille I had begged from

Lâle. Since that first terrible experience I usually shied away from opium and hashish as well, but tonight I felt the need of it. I sat and soaked in the dreamy, steamy atmosphere, letting Hatice, an attendant I favored, work her soothing fingers through my hair and ladle perfumed water over me. When she took me to the couch to massage me, I encouraged her to do much more and make love to me. It was just one more way of running away from Selim and the naked desire and need I saw all too often in his eyes.

CHAPTER 39

——◦——

While the Turkish people rallied around their enthusiastic, eager young sultan and his bright, bold dreams, their eyes shining with hope every time they caught sight of him riding by in his gold-curtained litter or astride his black horse with its bejeweled saddle, the Janissaries despised him more every year. In black of night they tore down what he built, defiled his new schools, and gathered great piles of his newly translated books and set them afire. They ran amok in the Great Bazaar, and overturned booths and baskets and smashed jars in the spice market, and killed wantonly and randomly. A merchant who pleaded with them to spare his wares had his eyes gouged out so he would not have to witness his property's destruction. A boy who meant only to be helpful by picking up pomegranates that spilled from a stall the Janissaries had smashed had his hand cut off for stealing. And outside the palace kitchens they beat their kettles, relentlessly sounding their discontent, and a warning, to Selim. It reminded me of the voodoo drums that used to shatter the quiet of the peaceful island nights. And every morning, without fail, we were certain to find another loyal supporter of our wonderful modern dream slain, his body dangling from a tree or his severed head set where we would be sure to stumble over it.

At the same time, the Russians were menacing our borders. The

Janissaries with their fierce waist-length black moustachios and sabers were no match against the might and majesty, and modern guns, of the Russian army. They quite easily wrested the Crimea away from us.

While the Janissaries retired to their barracks to lick their wounds and bang their kettledrums, Selim sat on the floor, like a little boy playing with toy soldiers, thoughtfully maneuvering his little model men and rearranging their lines to win phantom victories. He was dreaming of the day when the Nizam-Djedid, his New Army, would march forth, a wholly modern army, cavalry, infantry, and artillery, each man loyal to the backbone, incorrupt and ready to die if need be for Turkey and the Sultan.

The Directory in France had fallen; an ambitious little Corsican general, Napoleon Bonaparte, a real man risen from the ranks of the people, an unparalleled military genius who dreamed of conquering the world, and had already carved great slices out of Italy and Austria, ruled now as the First Consul. After a lengthy silence, he at last responded to Selim's request for assistance by sending us General Sebastiani and a corps of French engineers and naval officers.

I had a feeling that this Bonaparte was not a man to be trusted. I sensed that he, a ruthless conqueror, had set his sights on Turkey. Sending Sebastiani was a veiled gesture, to outward appearances a response to a request for foreign aid, a maneuver calculated to forge friendly ties between Turkey and France, but actually a reconnaissance mission. If Bonaparte made our army, he would know it inside out, including, when the time came, where the weak links were and how to break them.

Sebastiani was in Constantinople as Napoleon's eyes and ears, friend now, foe when the time was ripe. But, since he was here, we might as well make use of him, I reasoned. We had a need and he could fulfill it. He could make Selim's dream Nizam-Djedid march into reality. We would deal with Bonaparte later.

Selim said I had grown harsh and cold. I was suspicious and wary of my own countrymen who had most generously come to help us. He thought me too mistrustful while I thought him too trusting.

"I am by birth a Creole, not a Corsican," I said, "but I have been reborn a Turk."

*   *   *

For my thirtieth birthday, Selim, recalling my tales of the Mont-golfier brothers and their marvelous hot-air balloons, arranged a special treat for me. A green-and-white-striped balloon was waiting for us in the verdant fields of Dolma Bagtché. Selim lifted me into the straw basket and up we went, soaring high above the golden domes of the city. Beneath us, the people craned their necks, waved, and cheered as they ran along, following our progress as best they could; some even took to the sea in little boats to get a better view of us.

It was wondrous to behold from so high above—the French of-ficers drilling and putting the Nizam-Djedid through its paces, the new cannon foundry, the shipyards bustling with men the size of ants swarming over our new ships, the engineers and workmen re-inforcing our fortifications and directing the placement of guns.

High above the golden spires, Selim took me in his arms again. His fingers lowered my veil, baring my face fully to his, as his lips found mine. This time I didn't resist; I let him kiss me. I didn't want to spoil it for him. And I knew things were less likely to go too far in a balloon flying high above the city, crowded into the straw basket with the balloon's pilot pretending not to see or hear us, than if Selim and I were alone together in a private room in the palace.

For me, that kiss was a conciliatory gesture.

For Selim, it was another dream come true.

"Aimee, I love you!" he whispered as he shuddered in breath-less urgency against the curve of my neck.

His brown eyes were like a wounded puppy's when I didn't tell him that I loved him back. But I couldn't say what my heart didn't feel.

When we returned to solid ground, at sunset every mosque in Constantinople was crowded with men giving thanks for Sultan Selim's safe descent from the heavens.

Back in the harem, I tried to find every excuse not to be alone with Selim. The forlorn look in his eyes whenever we met in the company of others told me that he knew.

Why won't you love me? his eyes beseeched me every time.

But I couldn't answer.

* * *

Sebastiani worked wonders. Already the Nizam-Djedid was something to be proud of. Selim delighted in every parade, mock battle, and inspection and dreamed of the day when they would vanquish the Janissaries. But others were watching too, and with much less enthusiasm.

Senieperver and the Janissaries concocted a bold scheme to ally themselves with the British, bartering favorable terms for when Mustafa became sultan. By the time we learned of their plans, the British fleet, resentful of our alliance with their archenemy Bonaparte, was already sailing in our direction. We had to act fast. Sooner than we thought, the mettle of the new Turkish army was about to be tested.

Selim's strength wavered in the face of grim reality; we were outnumbered, we should surrender now, he said, while we could still do it peacefully, before the smoke and heat and bloodshed of battle, and get the best terms possible from the British. But Sebastiani and I held firm. A show of strength can make a difference even when you are weak and outnumbered. The Nizam-Djedid would stand; Constantinople would not fall. We would not consider any other possibility.

Sebastiani rode out amongst the people and stirred them up into such a patriotic fervor that they rose up to defend their city. Nobles and commoners alike wheeled cannons through the streets and ranged themselves along the walls. People collected stones that we could use in lieu of cannonballs if we ran out, and anyone who had anything they could use as a weapon came out, ready to fight and, if need be, die with us.

I stood cloaked and veiled between Selim and Sebastiani atop the Galata Tower and watched the English ships round Prinkipo Island. Time seemed to drag unbearably. We waited tensely for the first shot to be fired. Then, a miracle happened—God had given me so many!—a mighty wind rose up. The British ships were battered and scattered and left so shaken and disorganized that General Duckworth made the decision to turn back and sail for home. We had won without a single shot being fired or a single life lost.

* * *

In the French sitting room Selim had made for me, we cele-brated with General Sebastiani and his wife, Fanny, a sweet dark-haired young woman with lively brown eyes, who was swollen great in expectation of their first child. She didn't have to say anything. I could tell she was very excited about becoming a mother.

Sebastiani brought a bottle of champagne, and though Selim as a devout Muslim shunned it, he was happy to see the rest of us toasting our victory. I even let Mahmoud beg a sip from my glass and he fell instantly in love with the bubbly golden wine.

It was an interesting experience to meet a Frenchwoman again. Fanny and I were fascinated by each other's clothes. The fashions in France had changed dramatically. Gone were the days of hoop skirts and panniers, and powdered towers of outlandishly deco-rated hair. Dresses now harkened back to ancient Rome and Greece, flowing down naturally over the body in straight, simple lines with just a hint of a train trailing behind, but eschewing a woman's nat-ural waist to clasp just beneath her breasts with a jeweled belt or simple sash. Right after the Revolution there had been a craze for short shorn hair, the coiffure *à la Victime,* but now women were growing their hair long again, twisting it up in loose buns with little kiss curls or wisps framing their faces, or, for more formal occa-sions, intricate arrangements of braids ornamented with ropes of pearls, jeweled bands, or diadems.

We laughingly decided that one day, after Fanny's baby was born and she had regained her figure, we would trade. I would put on her clothes and she would put on mine. She had never worn trousers and thought my short embroidered vest and blouse with gauzy puffed sleeves, jeweled pillbox hat trailing veils, and curly-toed slippers would be a novel experience. She even talked of hav-ing her portrait painted in such attire so she could show all her friends back in France.

She was curious to see more of the harem and our customs and I agreed, when she was recovered from her confinement, to take her on a tour. The mischief-maker in me remembered my first reac-tion to the baths, with all the naked, lolling odalisques, and the rit-uals I had taken for personal assaults upon my modesty, and wondered what Fanny would make of it all.

"I promise you many interesting stories to tell your friends," I assured her.

Sebastiani also interested me. Though he had helped us greatly and was being hailed by the people as the Hero of Constantinople, I knew his first loyalty was to Napoleon, so I could never quite trust him, yet I found myself nonetheless attracted. He had charm, strength, and brilliance, and those fine qualities combined with his lean but muscular physique encased in tight breeches and a coat smothered in gold soutache, a full head of gold cupid curls, and gilt-flecked amber eyes . . . well, it really was no wonder that he was known to cause women back in France to erupt in drawing room riots. He was both soulful and sensual, an almost irresistible combination in either a woman or a man. Fidelity was not a fixture in most French marriages, but he seemed genuinely devoted to his darling Fanny.

To please Selim, I tried to occasionally spend a little time in the French sitting room, so he would not think I was unappreciative of his gift. I was always careful to choose a time when I knew he would be elsewhere and unlikely to seek me out, hoping to be alone with me. I would sit alone and read, embroider, or else just think, though I found the sofa and chairs terribly uncomfortable now that my body had become accustomed to the Turkish habit of lolling on soft cushions and divans.

I was sitting there one afternoon when General Sebastiani came in to leave a book he had promised to Selim. They had become such good friends that Selim had generously given him the run of the palace; he was welcome anytime, to converse, dine, enjoy the baths, and make use of Selim's extensive library of French books. They even rode horseback and practiced archery together, so it was not exactly a surprise to see Sebastiani walk into the sitting room, appearing completely relaxed as though he were entering a room in his own home. I had been told that they often sat and talked together in this room; that would explain why Sebastiani was bringing the book here.

I was quite alone and had taken my veil off; I had no reason to think that anyone who shouldn't would see my face. I instinctively reached for the veil, but Sebastiani stopped me. There was a look in his eyes that should have made me run, but it didn't.

What is hidden behind the veil fascinates every male and Sebastiani was no exception. He liked what he saw and he wanted to see the rest of me. It started with a caress of my face, followed by his fingers in my hair, a kiss, light at first, but then more urgent, mouths opening, devouring, tongues mingling and probing, as his hands found my breasts. We lay back on the striped sofa, but that was neither comfortable nor practical, and we ended up naked on the rose-covered carpet.

It felt good to know a man's body again, one I desired and had chosen of my own free will. The right to choose, to take and give freely, was almost as pleasurable as the act itself.

I lay back afterward very aware that if I had still belonged to a sultan what I had just done was enough to send me sinking in a weighted sack into the Bosphorus. But I didn't belong to a sultan, though Selim wanted me to. I belonged to no one. I occupied a unique position in the harem no other woman had ever attained. I had been spared the living tomb of the Palace of Tears, I remained at Topkapi Palace for my son, but I was no longer sure what rights I had and didn't have. What if I wanted to leave or marry? Was that allowed? Could I? Was what I had just done still a crime punishable by death? I had betrayed no one. Abdul Hamid was dead and I was not an odalisque in Selim's harem. I couldn't be; women were not passed down like possessions. Where did I stand exactly?

Sebastiani propped himself up on one elbow and stared down at me.

"What are you thinking?" he asked.

"Everything and nothing," I sighed. "It is better not to ask."

"Who are you?" He leaned over me. "I am very curious to know— How did you come to be here? What is your name? Your *real* name?"

I shook my head and rose and began to put on my clothes.

"Why won't you tell me?" he persisted, sitting up naked, cross-legged on the carpet.

"It's a name I will never answer to again," I said, "so it is best forgotten."

I had no idea if my parents still lived or what had become of my sister, Marthe. If anyone knew my real name, they might make inquiries, inquiries that might cause pain. I preferred to keep my silence, and my secrets.

"Why must you be so maddeningly mysterious?" he sighed. "I would just like to have a name to call you that is really your own."

"The one I have *is* mine, someone I loved very much gave it to me, and I would have no other even if I could. You had better get dressed; we shouldn't linger here like this," I said, and handed him his clothes. A snuffbox fell from his coat pocket and I picked it up. There was a portrait of a beautiful dark-haired woman's face on the lid ringed in diamonds. I recognized her instantly.

"Who is she?" I asked. I was not about to lay my cards on the table and reveal what I already knew.

"You won't tell me your name, but you ask me hers?" Sebastiani said as he stepped into his breeches.

I shrugged my shoulders and continued dressing in silence.

"She must be someone very special for you to carry her likeness in your pocket," I observed. "You seem at first glance very devoted to your wife, yet after what we have just done—" I shrugged—"I would not be at all surprised if you had another mistress, or even several."

"Oh, not her! *Never* her!" Sebastiani laughed. "She is Bonaparte's wife; he calls her Josephine, but her name is really Rose. She was the wife of Alexandre de Beauharnais, but they separated. He went to the guillotine and she almost did too."

I *knew* it! It *was* Rose! She had survived the Revolution; she was alive and married to the man who now controlled the destiny of France.

"If she is General Bonaparte's wife, why do you carry her picture then?" I asked.

"Many of the men do. The General considers her his good-luck charm, he is madly in love with her and always carries her likeness with him into battle, so we do the same, just in case there is some truth in it," Sebastiani explained.

"Ah"—I nodded—"well, we all have our superstitions." I turned around and showed him the serpent swallowing its tail tattooed on the small of my back.

Sebastiani stepped up close behind me, lifted the heavy golden weight of my hair over my shoulders, and nuzzled my neck and ear. "I do love my wife," he whispered, "I love her very much, but that doesn't mean I can't love anyone else. And it's my business where I choose to put my prick." He nuzzled and kissed the back of my neck again. "Tell me your name. . . ."

To stop his questions, I turned around and stopped them myself with my own mouth. But every time we met he asked me the same question—*What is your name?* It rapidly evolved into a battle of wills.

I was right, he was very charming, attractive, and intelligent, soulful, sensual, a very skillful lover, and a brilliant tactician, but he was also not to be trusted. We met several times more in the French sitting room. I let him make love to me because I enjoyed it, but I never told him the name I was born to. That was my secret to keep; I would never share it.

CHAPTER 40

Fanny Sebastiani died giving birth to a little girl. When he held his newborn daughter in his arms for the first time, over the bloodstained sheets covering his wife's cool and still, lifeless form, the wild dogs named Guilt and Grief tore General Horace Francois Bastien Sebastiani apart. Nothing would satisfy him but to retreat at once, back to France, with the baby girl who looked so much like his dead wife that he had to name her Fanny. No other name would do.

We never met again.

He informed Selim of his intentions via letter. After he finished reading, Selim looked up at me and asked, "Are you going with him?"

I knew in that moment that Selim knew—Sebastiani had been my lover.

"No," I answered, and put my arm around Mahmoud's shoulder, "my place is here, with Mahmoud, and you."

Selim gave me a timid smile across the top of the letter. "I am glad you are staying."

"So am I," I said. I never told him that Sebastiani had never asked me to go. If he had, my answer would have been *no*.

* * *

Senieperver and the Janissaries saw the moment of weakness they had been seeking and seized it. Selim had come to depend on the military genius and friendship of Sebastiani, the Savior of Constantinople. He felt lost and powerless without Sebastiani to advise him. Months and many letters passed between them, but Sebastiani could not be persuaded to come back, and eventually he stopped answering Selim's letters. He blamed himself for bringing Fanny to Constantinople; he convinced himself that if she had remained in France she would never have died. To him, Turkey would forever remain a cursed place, one where he wished he had never set foot. There was nothing Selim could do to sway him. Nor would Napoleon send another man. This only confirmed my suspicions that he had his eye on Turkey. The weaker and more desperate and vulnerable we were, the easier we would be to conquer. But other things were more important to him at the moment. Bonaparte saw Turkey as a woman he could take any time he wanted. There was no hurry: she would keep until he had time for her.

Mustafa's faction chose their moment well. They struck in the dead of night without warning.

Startled awake at sword point, sitting up in his bed, still befuddled by sleep, Selim readily surrendered the throne to Mustafa.

He told me so himself when the three of us—Selim, Mahmoud, and me—were herded into the Golden Cage, the Kefess, as prisoners, to await death. It might be minutes, it might be hours, days, months, or even weeks, but it was coming, and on swift wings. At sixteen, my son was a man now, the one every downtrodden soul in Turkey would look to when Mustafa's reign of tyranny began. The sands in the hourglass were already running out for him.

I sat in silence, my arm around Mahmoud's shoulder, both of us staring at the carpet. None of us dared say a word; I think we were all afraid of the hurt they would do.

When he could stand the silence no longer, Selim confronted me. "Look at me," he said. His hand reached out to roughly wrench up my chin, to make me meet his eyes. "You think I did wrong, that I should not have abdicated."

I said nothing. His fingertips bit hard into the flesh of my jaw.

"Answer me! Tell me the truth!" he demanded angrily. I had never seen him like this before.

"Do you really want me to tell you the truth?" I asked tiredly.

We were interrupted by servants who brought us food and clothes. Apparently we would be here in the Cage, waiting for death, long enough to require nourishment and a change of clothes.

Selim snatched up a gilded pitcher and poured sherbet into a cup. He drank it down greedily.

"Selim! No!"

"You shouldn't do that!"

"It might be poisoned!"

Mahmoud and I protested, our voices mingling in fear and concern for Selim.

"Good! I hope I have drunk death!" Selim said. Suddenly he rounded on me and flung the half-empty gilt cup of sherbet at the wall. "You didn't answer my question!"

I was angry now. *Very* angry. I stood up and squared my shoulders and stared Selim right in the face.

"All right, I will answer you; I will tell you the *exact* same words I spoke to Abdul Hamid the first night I went to him: *I would rather die on my feet than live on my knees!* And there you have my answer!" I sat down again and folded my arms across my breasts.

With my words, all the life, all the spirit, seemed to go out of Selim. He sank down wearily onto the divan opposite us.

"You're right," he said. "I shouldn't have done it."

Time passed. The sun rose and then set again. Two more prisoners were brought to join us—the Kizlar Aga, Lâle, and my giantess, Kuvetti. The sun rose and set again and then again before the night when there were footsteps and the rattle of sabers outside the golden door of the Kefess as we sat huddled around a brazier of coals, trying desperately to get warm. It was raining outside and the night was very cold.

We stood as one, looking anxiously toward the door. We all knew Death was coming.

Selim caught me in his arms and kissed me hard.

"Love requires sacrifice, always remember that, and how much I love you," he said just before he moved toward the door.

Mahmoud and Lâle tried to stop him, but he shook off their arms.

"Be the sultan I tried, and failed, to be, only better," he said as he swiftly embraced his cousin.

When the Janissaries threw open the door Selim practically flung himself upon their swords. A punch to his face shattered his spectacles and I saw red blossoms of blood where his eyes had been as he staggered blindly toward them once again, bleeding from a hundred wounds, arms out as though he meant to embrace Death.

Sabers at the ready, they were already turning toward Mahmoud. I instinctively stepped in front of my son, though he tried to move around me, to stand between me and death. Abdul Hamid's dagger was at my waist, as always, but I knew it wouldn't be enough.

It was then that Kuvetti acted; with a mighty roar of pain as it seared away the skin from her palms, she snatched up the brazier and flung the red-hot coals inside right into the Janissaries' faces.

I didn't wait to be told. I grabbed Mahmoud's hand and began to run. My loyal Kuvetti had bought us time, but minutes only.

We flew through the Djinn's Gate into the harem proper, the part of the palace I knew best. They weren't far behind us. I had to think fast. The Sultana Valide's chambers were empty; they would not have had time to make them ready for Senieperver yet.

"This way!" I said and hurried Mahmoud into the Valide's vast private bath.

"They will be looking everywhere for us down here; we have to go up!" I said, and pushed him toward the great empty fireplace and up the iron ladder the chimney sweeps used.

Up and up we climbed onto the rain-slick blue-gray tiles of the palace roof. It was almost like walking on ice. I slipped as the roof pitched down and Mahmoud grabbed hold of me and pulled me back up. We sat for a moment and clung to each other in the pouring rain and, then, slowly but surely, we began making our way carefully across the vast slippery rooftops of Topkapi Palace, doing the best we could to stay out of sight and away from windows, taking shelter and rest when we could behind cupolas, domes, and chimneys. For my plan to work, we must wait until daylight. Mustafa needed to sleep. Now he would still be alert, receiving reports, while the Janissaries searched the palace for us, but eventually he would sleep. He might even take a gilded pill of opium as I had heard he often did. That was what I was waiting for—for morning and that first waking befuddlement.

There were times, for which we were most thankful, when the roof we must traverse lay flat, but others when it slanted sharply and all we could do was hold on to each other tight and pray that God would make us, when we needed it, as sure-footed as mountain goats and save us from falling. The moon was both our friend and foe that night; while it lit our way, it could also reveal us.

The hours passed and the black sky grew gradually lighter, shifting to a deep charcoal gray and then to the color of a silver pearl, but still the rain didn't stop. When the sky was the pale, pure yellow of fresh butter the rain at last began to subside. Our fingers were blue with cold and we could scarcely feel them or our feet. Such coldness brings clumsiness. I began to rub my hands with all my might, to make the blood move and my fingers strong, steady, and sure enough to do what they must do. I clenched my hands into fists and then uncurled then and continued to rub them. Everything now depended on my two hands.

We were above the Sultan's rooms now. I moved carefully along, seeking a window where I could see Mustafa, in his bed, sleeping soundly.

I took a deep breath and braced myself.

"Stay here," I said to Mahmoud. "Do not come down until I tell you to."

I began to hammer on the glass, using the metal bands of my rings to produce an annoying tapping when my fist alone failed to rouse Mustafa. At last he sat up and rubbed his eyes and turned, with a frown of annoyance in my direction.

Before he could think to alert the guards, I clasped my hands together in a prayerful attitude. "*Please!*" I said. "*Please!*"

Mustafa sat up and thrust his feet into fur-lined golden slippers and threw on a robe as he stumbled and fumbled toward the window. He yawned as he opened the latch.

Soaked to the skin, my clothes and hair weighed down by rainwater, I presented a most pitiful sight as I clambered in. I quickly fell to my knees and kissed the hem of Mustafa's robe.

"We fled onto the rooftops last night because we were frightened," I said. "We saw Selim die before our eyes, so horribly, his chest bleeding from a hundred wounds, his eyes put out when the glass of his spectacles shattered." As I spoke, tears ran from my eyes. "It is a mother's first instinct to protect her son, as you well know; your own has been especially vigilant. You are the Sultan, Mustafa IV, long may you reign, and we surrender ourselves to you now and pray you will deal mercifully with us. If we must die, let it be swiftly with as little pain as possible. I know, were your positions reversed, my son would show you, his brother, the same mercy."

"Where is he?" Mustafa asked, stifling another yawn.

"He is just outside the window there. His ankle, I fear, is broken. Mahmoud!" I called. "Come, but be careful of your ankle! Would you help him, please?" I turned pleading eyes upon Mustafa.

He yawned again and stepped past me and the brothers each extended a hand to the other. I didn't hesitate. I took Abdul Hamid's dagger from my gown and plunged it over Mustafa's shoulder while his back was turned, straight into his heart.

I would stain my soul with blood and endure eternal damnation to save my son.

"Love requires sacrifice," I said, echoing Selim. No truer words had ever been spoken.

Mustafa barely had time to scream. Guards poured in as Mustafa's dying blood bathed my feet and Mahmoud leapt into the room and wrapped his arms protectively about me.

The guards stopped and stared. Mustafa lay dead at my feet. The floor was slick with blood. I still held his father's dagger clutched tight in my trembling hand.

"You are the Sultan," I said to Mahmoud, and started to kneel.

Mahmoud's hands stayed me and instead he knelt and raised my dripping wet hem to his lips and kissed it. "I would be nothing without you, Sultana Valide Nakshidil."

EPILOGUE

---◆◯◆---

Sitting in the Tuileries eating decadent desserts with his plump Austrian wife and watching their son play with his gilded scepter-shaped rattles, Bonaparte grew fat and complaisant. His unwieldy empire proved an impractical dream, impossible to efficiently govern, and the French people resented having to starve and struggle to pay taxes to support the lavish lifestyle of their self-proclaimed Emperor and his court. The price of bread kept soaring and the draft gobbled up so many able-bodied men from sixteen to sixty that it was not uncommon to find villages inhabited only by women.

When Tsar Alexander violated the terms of their peace treaty and began trading openly with England, Bonaparte set off with six hundred thousand men, boasting that he would conquer Russia in twenty days.

What Napoleon didn't know was that Sultan Mahmoud, curiously stricken deaf and mute when called upon to repay past favors and aid the French, who had helped modernize Turkey's army during his cousin Selim's reign, had signed a secret treaty of peace, ending the centuries-old enmity between Turkey and Russia. Mahmoud was known to be a man of his word. Thus freed from worry about the Turks, the Tsar need no longer defend his borders against them; he could withdraw the troops stationed there to deal exclusively with Napoleon.

There was something else Napoleon didn't know. Mahmoud was not only a man of his word but also a man of honor with a keen sense of justice, loyalty, and family. Josephine, though he had never met her, was, to Mahmoud's mind, family. He had grown up hearing stories about the island wild child Rose who had been reborn, reinvented, as Napoleon's incomparable Josephine, his lucky charm, Our Lady of Victories. Mahmoud's mother, Nakshidil, the erstwhile Aimee Dubucq de Rivery, had loved her and always remembered her fondly; that was enough for Mahmoud. When the perfidious Napoleon set Josephine aside so callously to take a fertile Austrian broodmare for a wife, Mahmoud, recalling the tales of knights and chivalry his mother used to tell him, decided that he would be Josephine's champion. He would bide his time, doing nothing overt, as in war one never warns one's enemy; when the time was right to strike Mahmoud would know it.

"We are not strong enough to triumph over Russia, nor are we humble enough to accept defeat at their hands; therefore, peace, not war, is the answer," the Sultana Valide counseled her son as they sat beside the fishpond beneath the cypress tree in her garden.

They would encompass Napoleon's destruction by doing nothing. The peace treaty had nothing to do with France: it was between Turkey and Russia. Sometimes revenge really is sweet.

It turned out the Tsar barely had to lift a finger. La Grande Armée was no match against the brutal fire and ice of the Russian landscape. Men died of heat, exhaustion, and disease, and, when the winter set in, cold and hunger devastated them, frost bit away their fingers and toes and noses, some even resorted to cannibalism to try to stay alive. In their weakened state, the Frenchmen were easy pickings for the Russian soldiers. Patriotic-minded peasants also did their part. The Frenchmen unfortunate enough to fall into their hands were beaten to death with hammers, while others were thrown alive into cauldrons of boiling water or impaled upon stakes through their anuses. Only ninety-three thousand crept and crawled back to France, most of them maimed and all of them more dead than alive. The balls to celebrate their "victorious" return were known as "wooden leg balls" because so many of the men were missing limbs.

Many noted that Napoleon's first campaign since divorcing Josephine was a disaster. Marie Louise could not fill the shoes of "Our Lady of Victories." La Grande Armée no longer existed.

When Napoleon learned the astounding truth about the sudden and surprising peace between Turkey and its mortal enemy Russia, he acknowledged the brilliance of the veiled strategist behind it. "The sword is beaten by the mind," he said with grudging respect.

Tsar Alexander wasn't finished with Napoleon; the back of the beast might be broken, but it wasn't dead yet. He formed an alliance with Prussia and marched on Paris, determined to conquer. And conquer he did. Bonaparte was taken prisoner, forced to abdicate, and exiled to the island of Elba. Louis XVI's brother, the Comte de Provence, now styled Louis XVIII, returned from exile and the monarchy was restored.

When Tsar Alexander called on Josephine at Malmaison he was completely captivated by her grace and charm. He visited her every day, often partaking of the château's famous ice cream, *glacé Malmaison,* made with the bananas and pineapples Josephine grew in her hothouses to remind her of her island home, and garnished with raisins and rum from the West Indies. Some whispered that the Tsar and the former empress had fallen in love, but there was no truth to the rumors.

Everyone suddenly remembered Josephine fondly; old friends as well as the courtiers who had snubbed her at the end of her marriage all made their way to her door. The people of France still loved her. In their minds, Bonaparte's misdeeds never touched Josephine; she was another suffering soul who had been cruelly wronged by him. Soon crowds were flocking to Malmaison to visit the zoo, walk in the gardens, watch the black swans gliding on the lake, smell the roses and view her vast art collection, and see the gracious lady herself.

Josephine turned no one away. She was society's brightest star again. Besides the Tsar, the King of Prussia, Prince Maximilian of Bavaria, the Grand Duke of Baden, Prince Leopold of Austria, Grand Duke Constantine, and Prince Tchernicheff were amongst her most frequent visitors. The new King of France sent kind and frequent messages to reassure her that she was safe in the wake of Bonaparte's fall and he looked forward to meeting her and that she would be most welcome at his court. Even a chance of love, in the person of Prince Frederick of Mecklenburg-Strelitz, came back.

One night, after dancing together at a ball, Josephine and the Tsar were strolling in the moonlit gardens of Malmaison when she was suddenly taken ill. At first everyone thought it was just a cold, even the doctors didn't take it seriously, but within days Josephine was deathly ill with a high fever. A red rash covered her body, and her throat was swollen nearly shut so she could scarcely breathe or speak.

She drifted in and out of consciousness, in her delirium calling often for Bonaparte. When the doctors told her there was no hope and she must make her peace with God, she summoned up all the strength she had left and ordered her attendants to dress her in a pink silk peignoir and rubies and help her into a chair. She said a tender farewell to her children and received the last rites. She died at noon on May 29, 1814, a month shy of her fifty-first birthday.

When she lay in state in her black-draped mahogany coffin, more than twenty thousand people filed past to pay their respects. Prince Frederick followed her coffin to its final rest, carrying her heart encased in a silver vessel. He was the last of the sad procession to depart, lingering long weeping over her white marble tomb. Even as they celebrated their liberation from "that devil Bonaparte" all of Paris mourned the incomparable Josephine.

Exiled in Elba, Napoleon learned of Josephine's death from a newspaper. He shut himself up in a darkened room and refused all food for several days. A year later, when he escaped, the first thing he did upon landing on French soil was rush to Malmaison and implore anyone who had been there at the time to tell him of Josephine's final hours. "Did she leave any word for me?" he asked over and over again, unable to accept that the answer was *no*.

Bonaparte and the ragtag remains of his army, his last loyal followers, were crushingly defeated at the little Belgian village of Waterloo. For the first time the cry of *"Sauve qui peut!"*—"Save yourselves!"—was heard as what remained of Bonaparte's great dream, La Grande Armée, fled before the eight-foot spears of the Prussian lancers.

Exiled to an even more isolated island, St. Helena, Napoleon spent the last lonely years of his life tormented by headaches and stomach pains, surrounded by images of Josephine, eating off plates with her picture painted upon them, and playing lonely games of solitaire with cards bearing her likeness. "She had her failings," he was often heard to say, "but at least she would never have abandoned me."

One April day when he was confined to his bed, he started up screaming that he had just seen his beloved Josephine. He clutched at his valet's lapels and wept. "She would not embrace me. She disappeared at the moment I was about to take her in my arms. She is not changed. She is still the same, full of devotion to me. She told me that we were about to see each other again, never more to part."

Ten days later, on May 5, 1821 at the age of fifty-one, Napoleon died. His last words were *France, La Grande Armée,* and *Josephine.*

Marie Louise had returned to her family in Austria and forgotten all about Napoleon. In August 1814 while taking the waters at the spa of Aix-les-Bains she fell in love with her escort, Count Albrecht von Neipperg. She had no idea that the notorious seducer had been heard to boast "in six weeks I will be her best friend, in six months her lover." It didn't even take a month for Marie Louise to fall into his arms. She bore him three children out of wedlock, as she remained officially Napoleon's wife until his death. The couple eventually married, and when Neipperg succumbed to heart failure in 1829 Marie Louise took a third husband, a Frenchman, the Comte de Bombelles. She died of pleurisy in December 1847.

The child known as the King of Rome, Bonaparte's long-desired heir, never left a mark on history. He died of tuberculosis in Vienna at the age of twenty-one.

One stormy November night in 1817 twelve oarsmen braved the wild waves, winds, and lashing rain and rowed a golden barge carrying two of the Sultan's guards across the Golden Horn to the Monastery of Saint Antoine. As the winds howled and the shutters rattled they entered the chapel where the priest, Father Chrysostome, knelt in prayer. They bound and blindfolded him and carried him out to the barge, to make the same desperate journey back to Topkapi Palace. Time was of the essence; it must not be squandered on anything, not even explanations.

"The black camel of death has knelt outside the harem," was all they would say in answer to Father Chrysostome's fearful and anxious questions.

An ancient stoop-backed Negro in rich robes and a towering yellow turban reminiscent of a tulip had the dubious honor of escorting the first Catholic priest to ever enter the harem to the Sultana Valide's bedchamber.

The Sultan known and loved as Mahmoud the Great, clad in his curious mix of modern French and traditional Turkish dress, knelt in anguished tears beside the bed.

Sultana Valide Nakshidil was dying. That long-ago night spent out on the rooftops of Topkapi Palace in the pouring rain had fatally weakened her constitution; she had ever since been prey to coughs and fevers. A fatal consumption of the lungs was about to claim her life.

The Sultan rose and, with great dignity despite the intensity of his sorrow, welcomed the priest and led him to the bed.

"My mother, you wished to die in the Catholic religion; let that wish now be fulfilled," the Sultan said as he bent over the bed, stroked back the still golden hair and kissed her burning brow.

Father Chrysostome, the first man in many a year, besides the Sultan, to see Nakshidil's still beautiful face unveiled, heard her confession, granted her absolution, and administered last rites. He remained with her, praying until the end, stunned by the truth that had been revealed at last. Aimee Dubucq de Rivery had not died at the hands of pirates; she had lived. Josephine was not the only empress from Martinique; there had been two of them.

As the Sultan knelt beside the bed, clasping Nakshidil's hand tight against his heart, tears raining from his eyes, she reached out her other hand and touched his face. "Euphemia David was right," she said with a last, lingering look of love. "It *was* worth it. Because of what I leave behind—you, my son!" And with those words, she died.

She was laid to rest in a splendid tomb on the summit of the fourth hill of Constantinople. Sultan Mahmoud himself, a scribe renowned for the great beauty of his calligraphy, inscribed her epitaph:

MAY HER BEAUTY NEVER BE FORGOTTEN.
MAY HER FAME AND GLORY FOREVER BE UNVEILED.
NAKSHIDIL, EMBROIDERED UPON THE HEART, HER NAME.
SULTANA VALIDE SHE WAS WHEN THIS CROWN OF EARTH
WAS PLACED UPON HER HEAD.
THROUGH THESE WORDS I INSCRIBE
AGAIN I LIVE THROUGH THE AGONY
AND SORROW OF HER DEATH
IN COUNTLESS TEARS THE BLOOD OF MY HEART
FLOWS FROM MY EYES.

By the time of his death in 1839 Mahmoud had entirely reformed the system of government, taxation, and education, established a national newspaper and free worship, and abolished the slave trade in Turkey. No more young boys were castrated to serve as eunuchs and no more women were abducted or sold into the Sultan's harem; they entered only of their own free will, though during his reign the imperial harem was largely neglected. Mahmoud fell in love with a sweet and humble Armenian girl, who served as a bath attendant, and fathered six children with her.

For the first time the harem women were granted greater freedoms, including more frequent picnics, pleasure trips, and shopping excursions outside the palace walls and lessons from a real French dancing master, and they were no longer required to sever all ties with friends and family. Mahmoud never stood in the way of those who wished to leave and marry; he gave them gifts and wished them lasting love and lifelong joy. His lone act of violence against women was to have Senieperver, Mustafa's scheming mother, sewn into a weighted sack and thrown in the Bosphorus the same day her son died. It was the only certain way to stop her from seeking vengeance for Mustafa's murder.

Mahmoud honored his cousin Selim's memory by maintaining the Nizam-Djedid, a fully modern army for Turkey, and took a serious interest in scientific advances. He instituted a system of quarantine that saved hundreds of lives whenever plague swept through the city and established a medical school where dissection was allowed in the interests of serving mankind through science, despite the Koran's proscription on opening dead bodies even if the deceased was a thief who had stolen and swallowed the most precious pearl.

He also popularized eating with silverware instead of the fingertips, introduced the waltz to Constantinople, and built a modern theater and opera house. He preferred to wear a fez instead of a turban and in his own wardrobe combined modern Western with traditional Turkish dress. Instead of kneeling on the floor, men were encouraged to remain standing and bow at the waist before the Sultan; Mahmoud thought it more dignified.

He was hailed by all as just and fair, a man who led by example. When a judge sentenced a malefactor, guilty of some petty crime, to suffer five hundred lashes and the man died before the hundredth one had been delivered, Mahmoud invited the judge to dine with him at Topkapi Palace. A banquet of five hundred sweet cakes was laid before the judge and Mahmoud ordered him to eat every single one. When the judge became horribly ill after only fifty cakes, Mahmoud observed, "If a mere fifty cakes, a thing much pleasanter than the lash of a whip, cannot be endured, how can anyone be expected to survive five hundred?"

He made it a point to always live his life by the words of wisdom his mother had taught him from early childhood: *Think of what you ought to do so that you need never reproach yourself for what you ought to have done.*

His reign also saw the destruction of the Janissaries. When he stood upon the steps of the Mosque of Sultan Achmet, with a modern pistol on one side of his belt and the jeweled dagger of his father on the other, and raised the sacred green banner of the Prophet and called upon his people to ride with him against the Janissaries they were with him every step of the way. The Janissaries were slaughtered out of existence, never to rise again.

Mahmoud truly was a sultan who was gentle with his women, ferocious and victorious in battle, humble in the mosque, and superb on the throne. Every promise was fulfilled.

TWO EMPRESSES

Brandy Purdy

About This Guide

The suggested questions are included
to enhance your group's
reading of Brandy Purdy's
Two Empresses.

DISCUSSION QUESTIONS

1. Discuss the personalities of Rose/Josephine and Aimee/ Nakshidil. How are they alike? How are they different? What are their greatest assets and greatest flaws? Which do you like better and why? Which woman do you think had the happier life and why?

2. How do you explain Euphemia David's uncanny prediction that both girls would grow up to be empresses? Did she possess genuine psychic powers or was she merely a clever charlatan who made a lucky guess? Napoleon and Josephine are both big believers in destiny; Aimee is more skeptical. What do you believe? Is one's fate preordained or can our actions alter it?

3. Rose marries twice and has many lovers. Discuss the various men in her life. Which ones made her happiest and why? Were any of the relationships founded on true love or were they all just casual dalliances and symbiotic or parasitic relationships with each person using the other for their own reasons? Aimee was the beloved of three sultans—Abdul Hamid, Selim, and her adopted son, Mahmoud. Discuss each of these relationships. Who do you think was her greatest love? Do you think she was a woman of passion or practicality or did she manage to successfully combine both qualities?

4. Everything seems to slip through Rose's fingers; she can't hold on to anything or anyone for long. She is impulsive, addicted to shopping, and never puts anything by for the future despite her worries about losing her looks and the onset of old age. She readily admits this is a serious problem but never does anything to change it. What advice would you have given her?

5. Rose never goes to visit Aimee in the convent; she always makes excuses. Do you believe her reasons for not going were justified? Would the life of either woman have been any different if they had rekindled their childhood friendship?

6. Aimee's fate is regarded as worse than death. Do you agree? Do you think she was right to maintain her silence and never try to contact her family? Do you think it would have only caused her parents greater pain to know she was alive in the Sultan's harem?

7. Discuss the role fame plays in the story. Does it ever bring any of the characters true and lasting happiness? How is the reality of fame different from the dream of fame? Is fame a good or a bad thing or does it depend on how a person uses their fame?

8. Both women have their names changed by the men in their lives. Rose becomes Josephine and Aimee becomes Nak-shidil. How does each woman's life and character change when she is given a new name? Did Rose truly lose herself in Josephine? Does Aimee's life truly begin when she is presumed dead by the world? Is her new life as Nakshidil a better or worse one than Aimee's would have been if it had followed the traditional path?

9. Did Napoleon really love Rose or only his ideal of Josephine? Theirs is regarded by many as one of history's great love stories. What do you think of the truth about the two personalities behind the romantic façade? How were they good for each other? How were they bad? Were they right to marry? Why or why not? Josephine never reveals to Napoleon her doubts about her fertility; was she right to have kept this a secret from him? What would you have done in her position?

10. Discuss the lives of the women in the Sultan's harem, the rituals, rivalries, affairs, ambitions, and acts of treachery. Do you think it was a good or happy life for these women or a velvet-cushioned prison with gilded bars where the inmates wore silk and jewels?

11. Discuss the roles modesty and exhibitionism play in this novel. In the convent girls are taught to keep their bodies covered and to never touch them sensually or out of curiosity; the girls are told to mortify rather than glorify the flesh.

On her wedding night Rose is embarrassed when her aunt dresses her in a lace negligee, yet a few years later Rose is wearing transparent gowns and even parading about nude for Barras's pleasure. In the harem women embrace their sensuality and glorify their bodies; they spend long hours lounging about nude in the baths and even attend a special school to study the erotic arts. Discuss how Rose's and Aimee's attitudes about modesty and sensuality change over time and why.

12. Discuss Aimee's rise to prominence in the harem. Do you think it was due solely to her unique appearance—blond hair, blue eyes, and white skin? Do you think her story would have been different if she had been a brunette? Discuss the manner in which she is presented to Abdul Hamid, in her pink Parisian ball gown as part of a zoo on wheels. She is given a choice, to submit to the Sultan or die; what would you have done in her position?

13. As she rises to favor and suffers several "accidents" and betrayals, Aimee grows increasingly mistrustful. She longs for a confidante, a real friend, but cannot let her guard down enough to let anyone in. Do you think she was right to be so wary? Should she have been more receptive to overtures of friendship?

14. Why can't Aimee return Selim's love? Why does she repeatedly turn away from his declarations of love? When he asks her to put on her French ball gown and come to him and presents her with a French style sitting room, why does she reject him and her past? Why does she burn the dress?

15. Selim and later Aimee both say "Love requires sacrifice." Do you think this is true? What sacrifices do they make for love and why? Were they right to? Aimee kills Mustafa to save Mahmoud and make him sultan. Do you think she was right to do this? Would you have done this for your own child?

Connect with Us

Visit us online at
KensingtonBooks.com
to read more from your favorite authors, see books
by series, view reading group guides, and more.

Join us on social media

for sneak peeks, chances to win books and prize packs,
and to share your thoughts with other readers.

facebook.com/kensingtonpublishing
twitter.com/kensingtonbooks

Tell us what you think!

To share your thoughts, submit a review,
or sign up for our eNewsletters, please visit:
KensingtonBooks.com/TellUs.